ALSO BY CHRISTIAN JACQ

The Ramses Series
Volume 1: The Son of the Light
Volume 2: The Temple of a Million Years
Volume 3: The Battle of Kadesh
Volume 4: The Lady of Abu Simbel
Volume 5: Under the Western Acacia

The Stone of Light Series
Volume 1: Nefer the Silent
Volume 2: The Wise Woman
Volume 3: Paneb the Ardent
Volume 4: The Place of Truth

The Queen of Freedom Trilogy
Volume 1: The Empire of Darkness
Volume 2: The War of the Crowns
Volume 3: The Flaming Sword

The Judge of Egypt Trilogy
Volume 1: Beneath the Pyramid
Volume 2: Secrets of the Desert
Volume 3: Shadow of the Sphinx

The Mysteries of Osiris Series
Volume 1: The Tree of Life
Volume 2: The Conspiracy of Evil
Volume 3: The Way of Fire
Volume 4: The Great Secret

The Vengeance of the Gods Series
Volume 1: Manhunt
Volume 2: The Divine Worshipper

Tutankhamun: The Last Secret
The Black Pharaoh
The Tutankhamun Affair
For the Love of Philae
Champollion the Egyptian
Master Hiram & King Solomon
The Living Wisdom of Ancient Egypt

About the Translator

Sue Dyson is a prolific author of both fiction and non-fiction, including over thirty novels both contemporary and historical. She has also translated a wide variety of French fiction.

The Judgement
of the Mummy

CHRISTIAN JACQ

Translated by Sue Dyson

**POCKET
BOOKS**

London · New York · Sydney · Toronto

A CBS COMPANY

First published in France by XO Editions under the title
Le Proces de la Momie, 2008
First published in Great Britain by Simon & Schuster UK Ltd, 2009
This edition first published by Pocket Books, 2010
An imprint of Simon & Schuster UK Ltd
A CBS COMPANY

1 3 5 7 9 10 8 6 4 2

Simon & Schuster UK Ltd
1st Floor
222 Gray's Inn Road
London WC1X 8HB

www.simonandschuster.co.uk

Simon & Schuster Australia
Sydney

A CIP catalogue record for this book is available from the British Library

ISBN 978–1–84739–785–0

Black and white drawings
© Sylvie Pistono, from F. Janot, *Les Instruments d'embaumements
de l'Egypte ancienne*, Le Caire, 2000, (p. 521 and p. 532); © Sylvie Pistono,
from W. R. Dawson, *JEA* 13, 1927, (p. 523); © Sylvie Pistono, from Mariette,
Dendera (p. 526, p. 527, p. 528, p. 530, p. 531); © Sylvie Pistono, from
Mariette, *Philae* (p. 525); © Ian Bott from Christine El Mahdy, *Mummies,
Myth and Magic*, Thames & Hudson Ltd., London (p. 522).

Typeset by Ellipsis Books Limited, Glasgow
Printed and bound in Great Britain by
CPI Cox & Wyman, Reading, Berkshire RG1 8EX

In an enlightened age such as ours,
one of the greatest mysteries of all is set out before us.

BELZONI

1

London, 30 April 1821

The giant recoiled in fright.

Greenish light was radiating from the sarcophagus, glowing eerily in the darkness.

Giovanni Battista Belzoni mopped his brow and waited for his heart to stop pounding. He, the renowned Italian Titan who had discovered so many wonderful Egyptian antiquities, was not going to be afraid of a mummy, a mere corpse which had lain inert for thousands of years! This was simply the result of tiredness, a desire to see his great exhibition triumph, and a slight hallucination . . . After facing up to so many genuine dangers, the archaeologist was not going to let himself be enslaved by the superstitious belief that certain mummies had the power to come back to life.

Belzoni raised the candlestick so that its light fell over the acacia-wood sarcophagus, inside which lay a mummy carefully wrapped in linen bands and in a perfect state of preservation. It came from a tomb on the west bank of Thebes, the kingdom of the dead.

Tonight, the cream of the capital of the British Empire would be present as the archaeologist unwrapped this unique specimen, and the press would continue to sing his praises. He had returned to London in March 1820, after ten years' absence, during which time he had made many extraordinary discoveries in the land of the pharaohs, a gigantic storehouse of treasures. Reporting the event, *The Times* had predicted that Belzoni was soon to publish a book and open an exhibition. The masses adored ancient Egypt, and enthusiasts were expecting a great deal of Belzoni. They would not be content with accounts of his travels; they wanted to see marvels imbued with mystery.

The adventurer's career had been extremely difficult, yet he had been welcomed as a hero. High-society salons competed fiercely for his attention, there were countless invitations to dine with the great and the good and in-numerable ladies of all ages had attempted to seduce him.

A hand touched his shoulder, and he started.

'You are nervous, darling!'

'Sarah! I thought I saw ...'

'Do tell me.'

'No, it's stupid.'

It was Sarah, the tall and beautiful Irishwoman, the faithful wife who had accompanied him on all his travels without a word of complaint, the first European woman to cross the Nile's first cataract and to discover the second. Sarah, whom no ordeal had ever daunted. She and Giovanni made an impressive couple, and they had become the toast of high society.

'What happened?' she persisted.

'For a moment it seemed as if this mummy was . . . alive!'

Sarah embraced the giant.

'Fear is a good counsellor, is it not? Let's cancel the unwrapping and leave this old Egyptian undisturbed.'

'Impossible, darling! So many important people are impatient to see this relic, and several journalists have promised to write articles, on which the success of my exhibition will depend. This dead man is nothing but a dried-out body, far from his native land. Has science not overcome false curses? We forced our way into a pyramid, a forgotten temple and an immense tomb in the Valley of the Kings, and we are still alive, famous and will soon be rich! Egypt does not bring us misfortune; quite the reverse. This mummy will charm the audience, and my reputation will be assured.'

Sarah approached the sarcophagus.

Her husband was right: it was impossible to cancel this long-awaited evening, or they would risk being discredited and losing the fruits of many years of uninterrupted effort. And why would dark forces attack someone who loved antiquities and who was willing to risk his life to bring the past back to life?

A wooden box containing a mummy, entirely devoid

of life: that was all it was. Giovanni was a tireless worker and had excelled himself. It was understandable that he might display signs of weakness on the eve of the opening of an exhibition that would establish him as a peerless archaeologist.

All was calm and silent.

'Let's go and have a drink and prepare ourselves,' suggested Sarah. 'You'll outshine all your guests.'

Belzoni took his wife in his arms. 'I want you.'

She gave him a coquettish smile. 'I would like that too, but I think it's more important for you to try on your new frock coat.'

The pair blew out the candles and left the vast room where the mummy lay.

As he had turned his back on it, Belzoni did not see the strange, greenish light emerge from the head of the sarcophagus and bathe the body that had been taken from its house of eternity. It was accompanied by a smell of incense, the substance that rendered mortal flesh divine.

The arrival of the mummy, imprisoned in this frozen, sunless place, did not mark the end of its journey through time and space.

2

As his wife lay on the bed in their large bedroom, Belzoni sat in a high-backed green-leather armchair, leafing through his book. It was entitled *An account of the works and recent discoveries in the pyramids, temples, tombs and digs in Egypt and Nubia, and of a voyage along the Red Sea coast, in search of the ancient city of Berenice, and of another journey to the oasis of Jupiter Amon.*[*]

The English publisher, John Murray, who specialized in accounts by explorers such as David Livingstone, was delighted with the success of the first edition, despite criticisms from Lord Byron, who considered the author's English bad.

But what a triumph it was for the Italian giant born in Padua in 1778, the son of a barber who had hoped to see

---

[*]A number of quotations have been taken from this work, published in England in 1820 and again in 1979, under the title *Voyages in Egypt and Nubia* (Pygmalion), and have been put into Belzoni's mouth.

him become a priest! While he was half-heartedly studying mechanical engineering in Rome, the troops of the future Napoleon I had invaded Italy. In 1803, fearing that he would be forcibly enlisted by these butchers, Belzoni had taken refuge in England, the land of freedom.

London was a merry, bustling city with a love of theatre and entertainment. There were jugglers and acrobats everywhere, and the young giant's size did not go unnoticed. Engaged as a strongman, in the summer of 1803 he took to the stage of the popular Sadler's Wells Theatre, thanks to a helping hand from an Italian whistler, who was delighted to be able to assist a fellow countryman. Billed as the 'Patagonian Samson', Belzoni became a star who could – without apparent effort – lift up a dozen men standing around the edge of the iron ring that encircled his exotic costume! Then he performed at St Bartholomew's fair, a popular place for entertainments, where the Titan from Padua asked for volunteers to form a human pyramid.

'Do you remember those days?' murmured Sarah.

'I can still see that fat fellow, fed on triple steaks and spice-bread. He thought he could defeat me! But he became part of the pyramid, nonetheless.'

'A foretaste of Egypt . . . You were a sort of pyramid builder, weren't you?'

They burst out laughing.

But Belzoni wanted to forget that period of his life, despite the flattering judgement of the *Gentleman's Magazine*, which praised the strength of the fairground strongman who could 'carry on his colossal carcass twenty-two people at least, moving across the stage as majestically as an elephant transporting Persian soldiers'.

'Eight years, Sarah. Eight years of exhibiting myself all over England!'

'Such a past does not accord well with your new status as a famous archaeologist, I agree. So we'll forget the Patagonian Samson and celebrate only the great Belzoni.'

He adored his wife's humour and level-headedness, and he kissed her tenderly.

'Before the audience arrives, I would appreciate a glass of gin.'

Sarah stood up, opened a concealed cabinct and poured her husband a drink.

The giant mustered all his courage.

'This evening,' his wife reminded him, 'you will have to confront old ladies with excessively powdered faces: real horrors compared with mummies. I wish I could take you far away from here and go back to travelling.'

Belzoni laid his enormous hand on his book.

'This is the start of our new life, my darling. The account of my explorations and excavations has met with astonishing success. Do you realize? It's even being translated into French and German! I don't give a damn for wet blankets like Byron, and I'm proud of having written the book myself, without help from anyone. It may not be elegant, but it's a faithful account. The reader feels as though he's taking part in my adventures and entering those fabulous monuments along with me.'

7

Feverishly, he showed her the thirty-page article in the *Quarterly Review*.

'"Belzoni must be regarded as an energetic and effective pioneer in the field of searching for antiquities," the editor writes. "He makes it possible for anyone who wishes to follow that path." Isn't that a magnificent compliment?'

'And very well deserved!' retorted Sarah, gazing admiringly at her tall, muscular husband.

Belzoni had a fine head of hair, a high forehead and refined features, and wore a magnificent moustache and sideburns, which were kept carefully trimmed. His powerful neck expressed his firm character, but she alone knew how tender and delicate he could be.

Someone knocked at their bedroom door. Sarah opened it.

Outside stood James Curtain, their loyal Irish servant, a discreet and dedicated man with a lean physique. He had long since given up all attempts at a private life in order to devote himself to the Belzonis' well-being.

'You look . . . you look splendid!' he exclaimed. 'Such elegance! This evening will be a great success, I'm sure of it. The first carriage has just arrived, bringing the owner of a paper mill: a small, excitable woman who is demanding at the top of her voice to see you.'

'Make her wait,' ordered Belzoni, 'and light just one candlestick in the mummy chamber. We must put our audience into the right mood. Our basement is just like a crypt!'

The giant applied some cologne, checked that his moustache was in perfect order and congratulated himself on the elegance of his outfit, which was the height of London fashion. He looked almost like an august university professor, ready to offer a little of his knowledge to a group of awed laymen.

'It's not just old ladies,' observed Sarah. 'Some are young and pretty, and I shall be keeping a close eye on you. Didn't Hercules transform himself into Apollo?'

'You have nothing to fear, my love! What other woman would be mad enough to share my appalling existence?'

Sarah nodded.

'Remarkably perceptive of you, Giovanni. Nevertheless, I shall be vigilant. I hope that the mummy will attract these ladies' attentions and divert them away from admiring you.'

Carriages arrived outside the house one after another, disgorging well-known personalities who were eager for sensation. Watching a real Egyptian mummy being unwrapped was no ordinary spectacle, and the limited number of places available had led to intense, even treacherous battles between applicants. Although assailed by requests for complimentary passes, Belzoni had maintained his dignity, insisting that tickets would be distributed according to the order in which replies to the official invitation were received.

Greedy for novelties of all kinds, the London of King George IV prized the East and Egypt in particular. Was the old land of the pharaohs not the cradle of wisdom, the shrine of initiations and mysteries, and the guardian of the secret of eternity? Despite the Arab invasion, pillage and destruction, priceless treasures still remained buried there. Belzoni's discoveries had excited people's imaginations, and thousands of curiosity seekers were waiting impatiently for his exhibition to open its doors in Piccadilly. In the meantime, a privileged few would have the good fortune to witness the 'rebirth' of a mummy which, rumour had it, was quite exceptional. And the great Belzoni was not in the habit of disappointing his admirers!

The hall was filling up fast. Aristocrats, bankers, merchants and scientists were preparing for an unforgettable experience.

James Curtain reappeared in the doorway to the bedroom, his eyes wide with terror.

'Sir . . . It's incredible!'

'Explain yourself, my boy.'

'The sarcophagus . . . It moved!'

'Have no fear: it's merely an illusion.'

'No, no, it moved!'

'Have you drunk too much gin?'

'A little more than usual, it's true, but I swear to you . . .'

'Don't worry, James. I know about sarcophagi. And this one will bring us a fortune. Is the lighting satisfactory?'

'As sinister as you could wish!'

'Perfect! The moment has come to greet our guests. If the mistress of the house would kindly lead on . . .'

The majestic Irishwoman walked slowly down the staircase leading to the lobby. Behind her came Giovanni Battista Belzoni, who filled the space all on his own.

Conversations halted instantly. Even those who were accustomed to the finest society receptions were dazzled by the charisma of this unusual couple.

'Is the mummy ready?' asked an old aristocrat in a croaky voice.

'It seems in excellent form to me,' answered the giant. 'The London air suits it.'

Everyone laughed.

When Sarah opened the door to the spacious basement where the sarcophagus had been placed, a heavy silence fell over the assembled throng.

For they were about to disturb a dead man's repose.

3

'This is an archaeological and scientific experiment,' declared Belzoni. 'Mummies are objects which belong to a distant past, not the bearers of malevolent forces. I've been involved with hundreds, and I'm in perfect health!'

The giant's confidence reassured those who were anxious.

'Please enter,' Sarah invited them.

The basement of the private residence was a former vaulted cellar, remarkably large and with walls covered in saltpetre.

With the aid of his walking stick the old aristocrat trotted in, followed by a hungry mob. People jostled each other as they formed a circle around the dimly lit sarcophagus, the more impolite guests using their elbows so as not to miss anything.

Solemnly, Belzoni ordered the other two candelabra to be lit.

Instead of reassuring the audience, this additional light

made them anxious. Would darkness not have been preferable?

With a confident gesture, Belzoni removed the lid of the sarcophagus. To him, it weighed no more than a feather.

'In an enlightened age such as ours,' he declared, 'one of the world's greatest mysteries is set out before us. Ladies and gentlemen, this is one of the old Egyptians who thought they could defeat death with the aid of mummification. A vain hope, but a magnificent kind of madness! Will modern science lead us to immortality? It's up to our researchers to conquer it and to declare the triumph of progress. This evening, you will witness a moving testament to the past, to which we should pay respect.'

The mummy was remarkably well wrapped.

'This is the finest-quality linen,' declared Belzoni. 'It was produced in the royal workshops.'

'Is this the body of a prince?' asked a dandy.

'Very likely,' ventured the giant. 'Dr Bolson, would you be kind enough to assist me?'

The pathologist stepped stiffly forward. Clad all in black, he was a very pale man with deep-set brown eyes.

'I will, Mr Belzoni.'

The archaeologist and the doctor lifted the body out of the sarcophagus and laid it on a marble table.

One eighty-year-old lady fainted; two dedicated manservants carried her out. At the sight of the mummy, which was of an impressive size, several of the spectators felt ill at ease.

'Shall we continue?' asked the pathologist.

'We must stop insulting the Almighty!' thundered an Anglican clergyman, brandishing the Bible. 'The impious are trampling on our faith and trying to impose the law of the devil embodied in that horrible thing. May fire destroy it and deliver us from our sins!'

Belzoni seized the clergyman by the wrist. 'Don't exaggerate, reverend. We are here to witness an archaeological event which would not insult the Lord.'

'Don't deceive yourself, unwary man! This accursed creature is sullied with black magic, and liberating it will lead to calamities. We must burn this mummy immediately!'

'Calm yourself,' ordered Belzoni, pushing the clergyman to the back of the room, 'or I'll break you in two.'

The threat was effective. Given the size of Belzoni, the vicar would have to confine himself to fulminating silently.

'Well said,' sniggered the old nobleman. 'I cannot bear religious claptrap. Now then, show us this Egyptian!'

The mummy had one curious characteristic: it was wrapped in a piece of linen which stopped at the top of the skull. Delicately, Belzoni removed the shroud.

'I shall help you fold it,' declared Kristin Sadly, the plump, excitable owner of a paper mill.

'Be careful,' advised Paul Tasquinio, a prosperous trader dressed in the latest shade of purple. 'Apparently, that kind of fabric brings bad luck.'

The plump woman shrugged her shoulders and carried out her task, albeit nervously.

'I'll pay for it and take it away,' she whispered in Belzoni's ear.

The giant nodded. Despite his fame, he was always short of money.

There was a second surprise: another linen wrapper, held in place with cord at the ankles and the chest.

Belzoni used scissors to free it, then rolled up the almost-transparent shroud.

'Just a moment,' cut in the austere Francis Carmick, a famous politician. 'I should like to buy that fabric.'

The man's syrupy voice contrasted with his rugged, imperious appearance, dressed as he was in an extremely expensive frock coat.

Business is booming, thought Belzoni, surprised to discover that the bandages were in a perfect state of preservation. Anyone would have sworn they had just come out of the weavers' workshop, protected by the 'two sisters', Isis and Nephtys, whose task was to prepare for the resurrection of their brother, Osiris.

Belzoni scratched his chin, while Dr Bolson remained imperturbable. Together, they attacked the bandages that covered the face.

'Mine!' exclaimed the famous actor Peter Bergeray, who specialized in Shakespeare.

He hitched his red cloak on to his shoulder, revealing a glimpse of his Hamlet costume, complete with sword, and took the magnificent and substantial wrappings from the archaeologist.

'To be or not to be, that's no longer the question with mummies,' sniggered the old aristocrat.

The mummy's face was revealed.

The audience let out a gasp.

It was a relatively young man, with a solemn, serene face and open eyes. His black hair was intact.

The embalmers had never before created such a masterpiece.

'He's alive!' exclaimed Paul Tasquinio.

Two ladies swooned, and several spectators left the room.

'Have no fear!' shouted Belzoni, and his authority calmed the audience. 'This mummy is exceptional, I agree, but it's nothing but a desiccated corpse. No one has anything to fear. We shall continue.'

The first row had significantly thinned out. Without a trace of fear, Tasquinio bought an immense chest bandage.

Along the left flank, where one would expect to see the incision used by the embalmer to remove the entrails, lay a tightly sealed, oblong vase.

'That belongs to me,' decided landowner Andrew Young, an extremely ugly sixty-year-old with a gravelly voice.

'It's a very rare, perhaps unique piece,' objected Belzoni.

'Name your price. I didn't come here for nothing, you know.'

The archaeologist bowed, and the tall, rather flaccid-looking fellow seized the vase. He knew this type of object very well, and this time he hoped to win the jackpot.

The unwrapping continued. The deceased was a robust man, with a slender, harmonious body.

Belzoni held up an amulet in the form of an eye, a small marvel made from carnelian.

'That intrigues me,' declared Sir Richard Beaulieu, an Oxford don and specialist in the history of religions. 'I have an interest in the study of ancient superstitions.'

The demands of such a learned man could not be denied. Condescendingly, he pocketed the amulet.

To his left stood a young woman, whom Belzoni had not previously noticed. Dark hair, green eyes and satin skin gave the woman a rare elegance and an Eastern charm. The archaeologist avoided looking at her, for fear of incurring Sarah's wrath, and went on removing the wrappings from the mummy.

The feet had been embalmed with extreme care and seemed ready to walk. There was one final surprise: the linen band which had preserved them was covered in hieroglyphs.

A form of writing which was unfortunately indecipherable! According to recent reports, the Englishman Thomas Young and the Frenchman Jean-François Champollion were locked in a fierce battle to solve this mystery at last and open up the great book of ancient Egypt, which had been closed since the Arab conquest of the seventh century AD.

Henry Cranmer stepped forward. The supremely wealthy owner of spinning and weaving workshops in Spitalfields, he had a moon-shaped face, sausage-shaped fingers and a plump belly.

'This piece interests me. It will fit well into my collection of ancient fabrics. Can we discuss a price?'

Belzoni nodded. This evening was turning out to be extremely profitable.

'What a handsome young man!' sniggered the old aristocrat, pointing his walking stick at the mummy, which had now been completely unwrapped. 'Such attributes must have satisfied a good many females in heat. Ah, if only I were ten years younger, I . . .'

His housekeeper seized him firmly by the shoulders and drew him to one side.

'Strange,' commented the pathologist. 'Ordinarily, the brain and viscera were removed. But this corpse appears intact! The muscles seem to be in good condition, and one would swear that this Egyptian were about to sit up. What do you plan to do with him, Mr Belzoni?'

'The usual custom is to get rid of it.'

'What a shame to throw this mummy out with the rubbish! Allow me to purchase it so that I may dissect it and discover the embalmers' secrets.'

'As you wish, doctor.'

'Meat for my dogs, that's how this corpse will end up!' yapped the old aristocrat, brandishing his cane.

The Italian giant addressed his audience.

'That is the end of the session! You have had an opportunity to gaze on one of the products of the ancient Egyptians' ingenuity. A mere appetizer, for tomorrow you will be open-mouthed in admiration when you see the splendours exhibited in the Egyptian Hall in Piccadilly.

Dear honoured guests, I invite you to an inaugural visit, before the rush of the common crowd!'

A salvo of applause greeted Belzoni's generosity.

'Congratulations, maestro!' exclaimed a journalist from *The Times*. 'I wasn't disappointed and I can promise you an article full of praise. Mummies of that calibre could almost reconcile one to death! And now, the exhibition . . . Not a single person in London will miss it!'

Pushing his way through the ranks of onlookers, the Anglican clergyman rushed towards the mummy, knife in hand.

'Die, horrible pagan!'

Belzoni caught the vicar's arm just as he was about to plunge the knife into the mummy's heart.

'Get out of here,' he ordered.

'The Almighty will punish the impious! You have no right to exhibit this ghost.'

The giant pushed the clergyman out of the room, as he continued to vituperate.

'People like that hold back the progress of science,' remarked Sir Richard Beaulieu. 'I approve of your determination, Mr Belzoni.'

'As do I,' added the industrialist Henry Cranmer. 'If the Church wishes to survive, it must evolve.'

The spectators congratulated Belzoni warmly. The enigmatic young woman with the green eyes had disappeared.

Tenderly, Sarah took her husband's arm.

'A triumph,' she declared in delight.

4

Piccadilly was full of shops attempting to entice in customers. But on 1 May 1821 people forgot their desire to shop and gathered around the entrance to the Egyptian Hall designed by the architect Peter Robinson. Robinson had taken his inspiration from the drawings of the Frenchman Vivant Denon, one of the members of the famous expedition to Egypt ordered by Napoleon. Hence, right in the heart of London stood an imitation of the front of the temple at Dendera, in Upper Egypt, dedicated to Hathor, goddess of love and joy. Londoners loved the building, which dated from 1812.

At the end of the first day's admissions, Sarah reckoned up the takings: one thousand nine hundred admissions, at a half-crown each! People were enchanted, the press was enthusiastic and the future looked rosy. Without a doubt, the doors of the exhibition would remain open for many months.

Giovanni Battista Belzoni savoured his success as he

walked, alone, through the wondrous world he had created. As visitors stepped across the threshold of this building, which was the only one of its kind, they abruptly stepped back in time, into the world of the pharaohs, facing gods like falcon-headed Horus or Anubis, the disturbing jackal. Osiris, king of those deceased who were judged to be 'of righteous voice', and therefore worthy of eternal life, reigned over the exhibition and captured everyone's imagination. Wrapped in a white shroud, he proclaimed the defeat of death and the victory of resurrection.

Belzoni had reproduced, life-size, two of the chambers from the immense, magnificent tomb of Seti I, father of Ramses II. In so doing, he enabled visitors to step through the doors of the subterranean world as revealed by the Valley of the Kings. The pillared antechamber and a chamber covered in symbols emphasized the presence of the invisible world and transported the soul beyond mere appearance.

Other drawings conjured up the fabulous Nubian temple of Abu Simbel, the work of Ramses II, and the pyramid of Khephren, whose entrance Belzoni had discovered. Between antique-style columns stood disturbing lion-headed statues, representing Sekhmet, the mistress of power, whose emissaries provoked sicknesses and disasters. Papyri and various small items from the Italian's excavations added to the fascinated visitors' enjoyment.

His wife joined him.

'We could not have hoped for so much, Giovanni. Why do you look so concerned?'

'The mummy brought us a fine sum, but perhaps I ought not to have offered it up as a spectacle. That man was incredibly beautiful and . . .'

'Not a man,' objected Sarah, 'a relic which is now in the hands of Dr Bolson. Forget it.'

'Wise advice, my darling.'

'We've been invited to lunch tomorrow with a duke. And in the evening, Professor Beaulieu will introduce you to his colleagues from Oxford. I'm proud of you, so very proud!'

Sir John Soane's home, at no. 13 Lincoln's Inn Fields, was made up of three houses knocked into one, on three floors. Born in 1753, the illustrious owner of the dwelling was a fashionable architect. He had been awarded the Royal Academy of Arts gold medal at the age of twenty-three and had had the good fortune to marry the daughter of a wealthy entrepreneur. She had unfortunately died very young, and Soane had thus come into sufficient money to sustain a comfortable life. Commissions from the state joined those from the aristocracy, and Soane displayed his talent by building or renovating Parliament, St James's Palace, the Royal Hospital at Chelsea and the Bank of England. He became a magistrate and rose to become one of the most important figures in British high society.

But his real passion was collecting works of art, notably antiques. That is why he had transformed his house into a museum, bringing together statues, funerary urns, mouldings from Roman temples, bronzes, engravings and paintings by Hogarth, Watteau, Canaletto and other famous artists.

Sir John Soane was quite tall, with dark hair, a long face and a jutting chin. He often appeared detached from the realities of this world and lost in his reveries. A rather sad smile recalled his past ordeals.

A friend of Sir Richard Beaulieu, he had gladly agreed to receive the Oxford professors and show them his treasures. The arrival of a surprising couple, made up of a giant and a statuesque woman, did not pass unnoticed.

'Ah, Belzoni!' exclaimed Professor Beaulieu. 'Come, dear friend. Allow me to introduce Sir John Soane, an architect of genius and the leading expert in the works of art of the British Empire.'

Sarah curtsied, while Giovanni bowed.

'I have heard a great deal about you and your exhibition,' said Soane with a critical look.

'Will you grant me the honour of visiting it?'

'I detest crowds and, according to the newspapers, they fill the place every day.'

'I shall open the Egyptian Hall for you at a time to suit you,' promised Belzoni, 'and you shall savour the marvels brought back from Egypt on your own.'

'Most kind of you, Belzoni. I have been told that there is an enormous alabaster sarcophagus decorated with strange figures.'

'I removed it from the largest, most beautiful tomb in

the Valley of the Kings, and it was quite an undertaking to bring it all the way to London!'

'A remarkable feat, indeed. I shall be most interested to examine the monument. Forgive me, I must say good day to a Minister.'

Stuffy Professor Beaulieu seemed almost joyful. 'Your sarcophagus interests him, Belzoni!'

'I've promised it to the British Museum. A masterpiece of such importance . . .'

'Business is business! You must decide. Now, my colleagues would like to make your acquaintance.'

The social niceties began. The first-floor drawing room of the vast dwelling had lemon-yellow walls and drapes, a pale yellow sofa, a fireplace and a large mirror. The bookshelves were filled with works devoted to art and archaeology. Every guest wanted to see the central part of the house, the Dome, which was lit by a rotunda with red, blue and yellow panes of glass, casting enchanting light effects.

With the aid of a lorgnette, the landowner Andrew Young was examining a Roman bas-relief carving depicting a bare-breasted goddess.

'Tell me, Belzoni,' he said in his hoarse voice, 'do you have any other Egyptian vases in stock?'

'A few.'

'Sealed?'

'I don't think so.'

'But I must have them sealed! The rest hold no interest.'

'That's not my opinion, and . . .'

'I don't care one jot for your opinion. Get me this type of artefact and we shall negotiate.'

As the giant moved away from this boorish fellow, he bumped into Francis Carmick, the politician with the syrupy voice. 'Congratulations, Belzoni. Your exhibition is a complete success. It will last for many months and charm an immense number of people. Escaping into the past is sometimes most agreeable.'

'Bringing those treasures back to London wasn't easy!'

'I'm quite sure it was not, dear friend! I fully appreciate your efforts and cannot encourage you too strongly to continue your task. I assume you have some exciting projects planned?'

'You can be certain of that, Mr Carmick.'

'Wouldn't you like to reveal them? I like you, and discretion is a good counsellor. There are so many jealous people and evildoers! I would like to have your opinion on a precise point: is mummification really serious?'

The question astonished Belzoni. 'I don't understand.'

'Yes, yes, you do . . . We'll talk about it again soon, and you'll give me as much specific information as possible.'

A fierce glint entered the politician's eyes.

'I demand answers, Belzoni. No equivocation, or you'll suffer for it. Now do you understand me?'

The giant had a desire to pick Francis Carmick up and hurl him out of a window. Seeing how irritated her husband was, Sarah led him away.

They bumped into the old nobleman, who was leaning

25

on his walking stick. 'You're seen everywhere, Belzoni! Old Egypt is a wonderful source of business. How can its repugnant art so dazzle honest folk? Your silver tongue enables you to do extremely well out of it. Continue, and you'll make your fortune. And that unwrapping of the mummy . . . What a spectacle! To whom have you entrusted that handsome young man?'

'To Dr Bolson. He wishes to study the process of mummification.'

'Rubbish! That charlatan will sell the mummy to the highest bidder. A bad move, my boy! Now, I shall obtain pieces of that mummy and give them to my pack of hounds before the next hunt. My dogs and I will have a wonderful time.'

Sniggering, the old man walked away, striking the wooden floor with his cane.

'Ten seconds more, and I would have smashed his skull,' admitted the giant. 'That old man is nothing but a bag of hatred! These salons are full of useless objects, and that one crowns them all.'

'Keep calm,' urged Sarah. 'You still have important people to meet.'

The beautiful green-eyed woman was standing between two funerary urns, looking dazzling. She was deep in discussion with a specialist in Greek mythology and a professor of Latin.

Sir Richard Beaulieu came to fetch the Belzonis and led them into a circle of distinguished and decorated philosophers.

'Do you know the identity of the mummy you unwrapped?' asked a corpulent man with a beard, who had written a treatise on the feet of amphorae at the time of Pericles.

'That's impossible,' replied the giant. 'There was a linen band covered in hieroglyphs, but those signs remain indecipherable.'

'A competition has been set in motion, has it not?'

'The great Thomas Young has a considerable start,' agreed Belzoni. 'I'm convinced that he'll soon be able to read this mysterious writing. The secrets of the old Egyptians will not resist science.'

'Glory to England!' proclaimed Sir Richard Beaulieu.

The scholars applauded their colleague.

Out of the corner of his eye, the Italian noticed the young, green-eyed beauty leaving Sir John Soane's house. Light as air, she disappeared.

The professor had also turned to look at this fascinating silhouette.

'Do you know that woman, Sir Richard?'

'That is Lady Suzanna ... a veritable goddess of antiquity! She has often attended my lectures on the history of religions. She has a large fortune and the whole of London is at her feet.'

'Is she married?'

'Single, to the great displeasure of her innumerable suitors!'

'The moment has come for us to withdraw,' said Sarah.

'Your presence has enchanted this gathering, dear lady,' purred the scholar.

'I should like to make a request of you in private, Sir Richard,' ventured Belzoni.

'We shall meet again at my home, where I shall gladly listen to whatever you have to say.'

5

The old nobleman's servants could no longer bear their employer. Aggressive and capricious, he made their lives impossible, waking them ten times a night with the sole intention of preventing them from sleeping. And he talked constantly about his latest obsession: obtaining pieces of mummy after the autopsy and throwing them for his dogs to eat!

Although suffering with his hip, the old miser continued to do harm and destroy careers thanks to his numerous connections. And now there was a new enemy for him to destroy: the Titan from Padua; that man Belzoni who had been spreading the superstitions of Egypt in the heart of London. The aristocrat detested antiquity in general and Egypt in particular. He believed only in the Industrial Revolution, the rule of the banks and reducing weak people to slaves. Sensitive to his arguments, King George IV was conducting a policy of progress and brushing aside those who resisted.

The housekeeper awoke at seven o'clock, surprised that she had been allowed to sleep in peace. She went down to the scullery, where the nobleman's valet, cook and washerwoman were eating their breakfast.

'Didn't the old man disturb you?'

'A quiet night at last!' exclaimed the valet. 'He's been getting his strength up to go and see Dr Bolson and fetch some pieces of mummy.'

'How horrible!' declared the washerwoman, pushing away her porridge. 'Almighty God will punish that monster.'

'In the meantime,' commented the cook, 'you'd better take up his coffee, scrambled eggs, toast and Oxford marmalade – it's the only kind His Lordship will tolerate.'

'I'll do it,' decided the housekeeper.

Carrying the heavy silver tray, she slowly climbed the massive oak staircase and reached the first landing, decorated with realistic paintings of fox and stag hunting scenes. In them, the elderly lord himself was shown slitting the animal's throat as its eyes pleaded for mercy.

The housekeeper set down the tray on a low table and knocked at the door.

No reply.

The old man was getting deaf.

She knocked louder. Ordinarily, he shouted 'Enter' in an irritated voice.

Intrigued, the housekeeper pushed open the door and noticed the open window. A pale sun lit up the four-poster bed.

At first she didn't understand what she was seeing.

A body, ripped apart, in a lake of blood . . . Impossible – this must be a nightmare!

Stiff with fear, she approached.

Her screams made the walls of the house tremble.

The clergyman was convinced that the devil had possessed the mummy that Belzoni had unwrapped. So he had written him a letter, promising him damnation if he did not immediately close the doors of his exhibition, a satanic lair devoted to pagan deities. Did the Bible not call Egypt the kingdom of evil? By opening a breach in the very heart of London, by exhibiting that immodest mummy to the gazes of believers, and by propagating the taste for an evil religion, this man Belzoni was guilty of insulting Our Lord.

Heaven's fire would soon punish this impious man, and his ambitions would be reduced to nothing. But the immediate danger was the mummy! By studying it, Dr Bolson was practising a dangerous art. Did he not run the risk of discovering the secrets of the embalmers and sullying Christian morality?

The clergyman did not like the pathologist, whose faith was shaky, who did not attend the house of God assiduously, and who lived in sin with young mistresses. Consequently it was futile to ask him to give up dissecting the Egyptian mummy and throw it into the rubbish.

There was only one solution: to kill the mummy once and for all, by stabbing it through the heart.

The clergyman knew where Dr Bolson worked, and he sharpened the blade of his knife. This time, Belzoni would not stop him! The priest, who followed a religion which respected its principles, had long wanted to do something in the Lord's honour. That mummy had come back from the darkness, and it had given him a chance to carry out his ambition.

He knelt and recited a psalm, exalting divine power.

The creak of the chapel door interrupted his worship. Slowly, he turned his head. 'Who's there?'

The half-light masked the intruder's face.

'Kindly leave! I am meditating and do not wish to be disturbed.'

The unexpected visitor advanced.

'Oh . . . it's you! Please come back tomorrow. Today, I don't have a second to spare you. Do you understand?'

The answer was a heavy silence.

'Do you understand?' repeated the clergyman. 'Outside! But . . . What are you doing? No, no, I beg of you! Don't . . .'

The fatal blow was delivered with force and precision. As he died, the priest had the horrible impression that he saw the eyes of the mummy.

The new operating theatre at St Thomas' Hospital had been in use all day. The décor of this ice-cold place consisted of a rough wooden table for the patient, vats of sawdust to catch the blood, ewers, iron pans and a disturbing collection of saws, pincers and knives, which were used by the surgeons. On the wall was written in large letters *Miseratione Non Mercede* – 'Act out of compassion and not from a thirst for profit'.

Tonight belonged to Dr John Bolson, a night during which he would perform an autopsy on Belzoni's admirable mummy. He lit the gas lamps and gazed for a long time at this uncommon subject. Anyone would have sworn it was a sleeping man, enjoying a peaceful repose.

The doctor felt uneasy: did this relic harbour some form of life? It was a stupid question, unworthy of a man of science! And yet it obsessed him. And there were bizarre elements which disturbed him. The embalmers seemed neither to have extracted the brain nor performed any abdominal incision. As for the state of preservation of the tissues, it was unimaginably good! To cut into this thousand-year-old flesh, destroy this masterpiece which had conquered time, to offend the magic of the ancient Egyptians . . . The pathologist continued to hesitate.

Deciding not to carry out a systematic exploration of the mummy would be a sort of cowardice. Since chance had entrusted him with this treasure, he must exploit it. Did the immortality of the body lead to that of the soul? A modest, unknown doctor, Bolson would become a celebrity and, beyond notoriety, would perhaps possess the ultimate secret of those initiated into the mysteries of Osiris. That is why there were no witnesses to this massacre.

The pathologist put on a grey coat. Despite repeated washings, it still bore traces of blood. From a pocket he withdrew a notebook in which he would note down the details of his autopsy.

Armed with a saw, Bolson was about to attack the skull when a door banged.

Who dared disturb him? Probably a cleaner who did not know he was there. Irritated, he determined to expel the intruder without further ado.

Suddenly, most of the gas lamps went out.

He saw a silhouette in the half-light.

'Get out!' ordered the pathologist. 'I have reserved this room until dawn.'

The silhouette advanced.

John Bolson strained to see.

'Oh, it's you . . . I'm sorry, but no one is allowed in. An autopsy is not like a sideshow.'

The unexpected guest was holding a long iron rod with a curved end.

'A mummy hook! A brilliant initiative, but I don't have need of your services. Kindly withdraw and leave me to work in peace.'

The last lamp went out. All that remained was a greenish halo surrounding the mummy.

Caught unawares, the pathologist had no time to defend himself. And not a sound emerged from his throat as it was pierced.

6

Former Inspector Higgins was enjoying the first day of his expected retirement and gazing at the garden of his house. He lived in a charming small village in Gloucestershire, in the middle of the countryside, far from the noise and bustle of London, where he had spent many long years serving law and order.

His retirement had been expected because Higgins – who was regarded as an exceptional investigator achieving remarkable results – had raged against the state of decay in the police force, which was ineffective and corrupt, and he had proposed the creation of a new institution, which he wished to call Scotland Yard.[*] Faced with a refusal by the conservatives who made up the government, he had worked hard to produce caustic reports. But in vain.

Crime would continue to prosper, and the capital would

[*] It was created a few years later.

become less and less safe. But that was no longer his problem, and he could enjoy the tranquillity of his vast white stone house, surrounded by centuries-old oaks. Windows with leaded lights punctuated two storeys built according to divine proportion and crowned by tall chimneys.

At last he had a chance to re-read Shakespeare's *The Tempest* and explore the exciting narrative by Belzoni, that famous seeker of Egyptian treasures! Higgins was excited by the competition between several scholars, all of whom wanted to decipher hieroglyphs. Belzoni was in favour of the Englishman Thomas Young, but the former inspector had not discounted a curious Frenchman, Jean-François Champollion, who was despised by his colleagues and suspected of sympathy for the bloodthirsty tyrant, Napoleon.

In the company of two faithful friends, his cat Trafalgar and his dog Geb, Higgins was planning long woodland walks and peaceful evenings by the fireside, not forgetting the meticulous upkeep of his rose garden. There was just one shadow on the horizon: the unbending personality of his housekeeper, Mary, who imposed strict mealtimes and ruled her entire domain with a rod of iron. But her gifts as a cook, particularly with sauces and fresh cream, were sufficient to endear her to guests.

The tinkle of the bell on the front gate reached the ears of the former inspector, who was busy sorting out paperwork. Mary was already trotting along the gravel path, ready to shoo away the unwelcome visitor.

From the window of his office, Higgins heard an animated conversation. He went downstairs, accompanied by his long-legged black dog, a cross between a pointer and a Labrador.

'Some weasel-faced fellow wants to see you,' Mary informed him. 'He claims he's from the government. Shall I send him away?'

'Let me talk to him first.'

'But they forced you to retire!'

'Perhaps it's a courtesy visit.'

The housekeeper shrugged. 'Well, tell him to wipe his feet properly and not dirty your office. I have a rabbit to prepare and I don't want to spend all my time sweeping up after him.'

Mary went back to the kitchen, her preferred domain, and Higgins went to greet his guest, a man in his forties who had the look of a banker. His small, inquisitive eyes and stiff bearing gave him a rather off-putting appearance.

'Allow me to introduce myself: Peter Soulina. His Majesty's government asked me to come to see you.'

'I'm no longer employed.'

'Don't deceive yourself, Inspector Higgins; we need your skills.'

'Is that a request or an order?'

'An order. You've been reappointed to your former position.'

The emissary's tone of voice brooked no refusal.

'Please come in.'

Higgins led the visitor to the large drawing room. Deep leather armchairs, a low sandalwood table from India, Persian carpets and Egyptian statuettes created a warm and magical atmosphere.

'Take a seat, Mr Soulina, and please set out the reasons for your visit.'

'You have solved some very difficult cases in the past, inspector, and my superiors appreciate your sense of discretion.'

We've scarcely begun, and already I'm on slippery ground, thought Higgins. 'Must I remind you that my suggestions for reorganizing a deficient police force were rejected en masse?' he said.

The official stiffened. 'We shall talk of that later. The current emergency outweighs all other problems.'

Higgins was intrigued. 'Is it really so serious?'

'Indeed. A veritable catastrophe is threatening the kingdom.'

The unfortunate individual did not appear to be joking.

'I fear I may not live up to your hopes,' lamented Higgins.

'We're convinced of the contrary and will grant you whatever resources are necessary. In London you will have an office and a team entirely devoted to the investigation.'

'An investigation . . . into what?'

Peter Soulina cracked his knuckles. 'Could I have a glass of water?'

'May I suggest a glass of Scotch?'

'Given the situation, that's not a bad idea.'

At first sight the government envoy did not seem at all sensitive. But he looked defeated and clearly appreciated the comforting strength of the amber liquid.

'It's a bad business, Higgins, a terribly bad business. We have three corpses on our hands, and not just anybody's. The first victim was a fantastically wealthy old aristocrat, the second an Anglican priest and the third a pathologist. The unfortunates were all slaughtered. The killer removed their brains and viscera with some sort of hook.'

Higgins was astonished. 'Are you talking about the technique used . . . by an Egyptian embalmer?'

'We mustn't get carried away! It's a macabre scenario, linked to the success of Belzoni's exhibition. I need not tell you, inspector, that one must learn to be wary of appearances. Let's forget the sordid details and deal with the heart of the matter: the political nature of the victims.'

Higgins smoothed down his pepper-and-salt moustache. The situation was proving remarkably murky.

'Our king, George IV, is a man of progress,' continued Peter Soulina. 'His courageous policy needs moral and financial supporters. Virulent enemies are attempting to undermine the country's foundations, and there are some who would not hesitate to kill. That is the explanation for these crimes.'

'I should like to know in what way the three victims are linked to the government.'

The emissary frowned. 'We are moving into deep water, inspector.'

'Conducting investigations blindfold will not lead anywhere. If you want me to arrest the guilty party or parties, provide me with as much information as possible.'

'The government is hoping for complete success, there's no doubt of that! So I've been authorized to reveal facts relating to state secrets.'

The future was darkening and retirement seemed ever further away. Words like these promised some anxious days to come.

'The elderly nobleman was financing our party. Secret funds, of course, which do not feature in any budget. His contribution was far from negligible, and his death has dealt us a rather harsh blow. The clergyman's task was to convert influential clerics to our vision of the future world. Preachers mould simple souls and the content of their sermons is still important. His death has deprived us of a secret ally. As for the good Dr Bolson, he infiltrated scientific milieux to our advantage, promising posts to our declared supporters. The opinion of intellectual circles matters a great deal in the eyes of the government. And above all, no lessons in morality, inspector! Politics has its rules, and our leaders are thinking only of the nation's greatness. The end necessarily justifies the means, and naivety would lead to failure.'

Higgins said nothing. He wanted to hear the final revelations.

'Only one enemy knew the real roles of the aristocrat,

the clergyman and the pathologist: a formidable enemy who, at the start of the year, set a fatal trap for several members of the House of Commons and of His Majesty's private cabinet. We have arrested a number of conspirators and killers, but not their leader, Littlewood. It's up to you to find him, inspector. Otherwise he will continue to kill and threaten the regime. It is a difficult and dangerous mission, I admit.'

'Is there proof of his guilt?'

The senior official did not hide his irritation. 'The government is in no doubt about it; therefore neither should you be.'

Higgins looked Soulina straight in the eye. 'I shall conduct this investigation as I see fit. Either you give me carte blanche or you will have to find another inspector.'

Peter Soulina poured himself another whisky.

'People told me that you were a stubborn man,' he admitted, 'and I was expecting this kind of demand. Understood, Higgins.'

'I shall search for this man Littlewood, but that does not mean that I may not also investigate all other available leads. When I've arrested the killer or killers, you may conduct the trial as you see fit.'

'Higgins! How dare you . . . ?'

'No play-acting, Mr Soulina. Putting criminals under lock and key is my modest contribution to the fight against evil. After I have done so, experts serving the government apply the law, not justice.'

The government emissary rose to his feet. 'We must

not waste time philosophizing. Are you willing to return to London first thing tomorrow?'

Higgins nodded.

'His Majesty and England are counting on your efficiency, inspector. Littlewood is a destroyer, a wild beast thirsty for blood. He must be prevented from doing harm.'

As he accompanied his guest to the front door, the inspector noted that his dog Geb, although an extremely sociable animal, did not show any sign of affection towards Soulina. Higgins could tell from the look of contempt in Soulina's eyes that he detested animals.

After the intruder had left, Mary emerged from the kitchen to survey the state of the floor.

'There's cleaning up to be done,' she announced. 'And your retirement didn't last long.'

7

The letter from the landowner Andrew Young was so insistent that Belzoni and Sarah had decided to accept his invitation. But their carriage, drawn by two horses, was making slow progress along a muddy road in the driving rain.

The Italian missed the heat of Italy, even though it could be stifling. But at the moment he must make his mark in England and add wealth to fame. A good network of buyers of antiquities would provide him with a solid financial base, and he could then set off again to find new treasures, raising his prices in the process.

Young was a commoner who had amassed a fine fortune by carefully applying the judicious advice he received from his banker friends in the City. A merciless moneylender and elusive crook, he had legally stripped a senile aristocrat of his estate, dismissed some of the staff and reduced the pay of those who remained in his service. His ugly, sour-tempered wife spent her days making inedible cakes and mistreating her servants.

This upstart had a curious passion for ancient Egypt. Through his reading, he had become convinced that the pharaohs' scholars had made prodigious discoveries, which had little by little been forgotten. His visit to Belzoni's exhibition had strengthened this opinion. In this era of countless inventions and technical progress, he was convinced that the exploration of ancient knowledge would lead him to major finds, which might prove lucrative.

'I don't like the man,' said Sarah. 'When he looked at the mummy, it was as if he wanted to devour it like a famished carnivore! He won't bring us anything good.'

'I'm convinced that the opposite is true. He possesses many contacts in the world of finance and could obtain clients for us.'

'Clients and funds . . . which would enable you to return to Egypt?'

'Not before I've become a member of the London *establishment*! The success of my book and the exhibition are excellent first steps, but they are still not enough. I must win the trust of important people, who are determined to recognize my merits. We shall live in a fine house and host receptions for the cream of society. Don't worry: an army of servants will free you from all domestic cares!'

Sarah kissed her husband lovingly. He had always been a dreamer and would continue to be. It was both his strength and his weakness, and this madness had given him the energy needed to accomplish insane tasks.

Immense fields of cereal crops surrounded Andrew Young's stately home. Even if England was turning resolutely towards industry, it was necessary to feed a rapidly increasing population of twenty-one million inhabitants. Because of the Corn Laws, the price of bread was maintained at a high level, to the despair of the poor. The major landowners, on the other hand, profited from the situation.

A pretentious house overlooked farm outbuildings. A Gothic-style turret gave it a warlike aspect, and visitors almost expected to see archers appear on the battlements. The Belzonis' carriage halted before an ivy-clad porch.

A liveried servant opened the door and helped Sarah to step down.

'I shall take you to Mr Young.'

All along the corridors hung the heads of stags and wild boar. The master of the house was in the middle of a vast armoury, examining an antique pistol with a loupe.

'Ah, Belzoni! Delighted to see you again. My respects, dear lady. You look delightful.'

Sarah did not smile. This tall, indolent-looking man with yellowed rabbit-teeth made her feel uneasy.

'I take it you're admiring my collection? Years of research! Human ingenuity fascinates me. Dreaming up these engines of destruction required genius, and we shall continue to make progress. Nevertheless, we should pay homage to the past and not forget the first arquebus! An eminent archaeologist such as yourself, Belzoni, must understand me.'

'Indeed.'

'Personally, I drink only apple juice. Perhaps you would prefer something alcoholic from my distillery?'

'Gladly,' replied Sarah. 'We need something to warm us up.'

The Belzonis sat down on a tired-looking sofa, while Andrew occupied a straight-backed rustic chair. Above his head hung a pair of blunderbusses.

The servant brought a bottle and two glasses, which he filled with a dark brown liquid. Sarah was chilled to the bone, and drank a large gulp.

'That's not just apple juice,' she commented.

'It's a blend,' agreed Young. 'I keep it for my most honoured guests. You are famous now, Belzoni! I shall never forget that fabulous mummy and its incredible state of preservation. By the way, what has become of it?'

'I entrusted it to Dr Bolson, who wished to examine it. Certain details worried us, and I should like to know more.'

'What were the results?'

'I've had no news from the good doctor, but I shall contact him without delay.'

Young got to his feet and paced the room. His indolent air would have sent even a hysterical person to sleep.

'Have you brought me an intact vase, Belzoni?'

The giant removed an alabaster phial from the pocket of his voluminous coat. The landowner's eyes fixed on the stopper, which was made of dried grass and straw.

'Can you guarantee me its authenticity?'

'I removed it from a well filled with mummy debris.'

'Mummies,' repeated Young. 'Perfect, perfect!'

He stretched out his hand, but Belzoni tightened his grip on the phial.

'Let us first proceed to a gentleman's agreement. This marvel is beyond price.'

'I shall open it, look inside and pay if the contents interest me.'

The giant burst out laughing. 'You cannot be serious, Mr Young! All archaeological adventures carry a risk. At the worst, you will have a unique piece which will be easy to resell.'

A glimmer of hatred filled the landowner's dull gaze. Even Sarah was frightened by it.

'That's not my custom, Belzoni, but I accept your conditions. Wait for a moment, and I shall go and fetch the necessary.'

'Accept what he offers you,' Sarah whispered into her husband's ear. 'That fellow is unsavoury and dangerous.'

The giant was not enjoying the stifling atmosphere of the armoury. He too could not wait to leave.

The sound of Young's footsteps rang out. He reappeared, carrying a purse.

Sarah stood up. 'I deal with the accounts.'

'Will this sum suit you, dear lady?'

She untied the strings and examined the contents. 'Perfect.'

'I'm happy to have concluded this first business deal!

This is the start of a fruitful collaboration,' announced the landowner.

'We must return quickly to London,' said the young woman.

'I would have liked to show you round my estate. Next time, no doubt.'

'No doubt.'

'Whatever you do, don't forget: if you have any more closed and intact vessels, offer them to me. To me and no one else. Otherwise I shall be extremely disappointed. Extremely.'

The word was heavy with menace.

'Good day,' said the Titan of Padua in a firm voice.

Once the Belzonis had gone, Young rushed back to his laboratory, where he spent most of his time. On the verge of a discovery that would make him a fortune, he dared not use the treasure he had bought from Belzoni during the unwrapping of the mummy. Before doing so, he preferred to use a similar substance and check his theory.

He removed the stopper from the little vase he had purchased for a prohibitive price and examined the contents with a loupe.

He was extremely disappointed.

It contained nothing but the remains of unguents, stuck to the inside.

In rage, Young shattered the vase with a hammer.

Belzoni would not get away with this deception. Nobody mocked Andrew Young with impunity! But he needed the Italian to obtain the materials necessary to continue his research.

So the landowner decided that he would manipulate the pretentious giant and his unbearable wife, obtain what he wanted from them and then destroy them.

A sudden feeling of anxiety tightened his throat. What if that witch had tricked him? He ran to the small cabinet decorated with laughing devils and opened it with the key he always carried on him.

The precious oblong vase had not disappeared.

8

Inspector Higgins returned to London with a heavy heart. He would have preferred to enjoy a happy retirement in the country, and not have to confront the worst aspects of a capital city which was developing in ways he deplored. Admittedly, after twenty-five years of war, England was at last experiencing peace. In 1814 the United States of America and the British Empire had ceased hostilities and become allies. And the death of Napoleon on St Helena, on 5 May 1821, had been a cause for rejoicing in many European countries. This time, the bloodthirsty tyrant was beyond doing harm to anyone. Would the new king of Great Britain and Ireland, George IV, be able to take best advantage of this happy time?

Born in 1762, the new sovereign had become Regent in 1811 and had duly succeeded his father, George III, who had succumbed to madness. George IV's behaviour as a rake, and a gambler who was constantly in debt, did nothing to reassure the politicians; and the scandalous lawsuit he took out against his wife, Queen Caroline of Brunswick, in order to obtain a divorce, in addition to his string of mistresses, made the monarch unpopular with the public. Fortunately, George IV did not govern and delegated power to his Ministers in the Tory Party, which was deeply conservative and protective of royal authority.

The Tories had an abiding obsession: averting a revolution comparable to the one that had broken out in France in 1789, bringing horror, death and destruction. Everything possible must be done to prevent such a disaster. Consequently, public meetings were forbidden. But would silencing the voice of opposition be sufficient to save the reign from serious disturbances? Parliament was composed solely of aristocrats, and the large industrial towns, which were at the forefront of economic development, were not represented. The head of the government, however, was willing to listen to Catholics and dissidents from the Church of England, who were anxious for reform.

The Industrial Revolution was turning His Gracious Majesty's kingdom into the foremost world power. Intensive exploitation of coal mines, mechanization of the mills, a more extensive canal network, the improvement of roads using McAdam's invention and the first goods railways were all creating a new landscape, much to the dislike of country folk. As for steamships, real sailors who knew their wood and their sails regarded them as hideous monsters.

The capital was constantly growing, and the wealthy

and middle classes were growing richer, while the working class suffered harsh living conditions. Difficult work, a long working week, low salaries and high food prices risked unleashing social disturbances which might place the regime in danger. The government was determined to nip them in the bud.

Crime was experiencing a formidable rise, with bands of thieves robbing honest folk. The government's response was to set up new courts and new prisons, without bothering to train an adequate number of competent police officers.

Inspector Higgins's cab halted outside a new building, close to the Fleet Prison, an establishment reserved for wealthy detainees. They had the benefit of a vast courtyard, where they could play skittles and tennis and sit on benches reading or discussing their future.

A police officer in plain clothes rushed out of the porch and busied himself with Higgins's luggage.

'Welcome, inspector. Your private rooms are on the second floor, and the meeting room is on the first. Will you require dinner?'

'Later. Please summon all my colleagues. Give me time to settle in, and then we shall discuss the situation.'

The government's emissary, Peter Soulina, had provided Higgins with comfortable surroundings: a cosy drawing room, an office, dining room, bedroom and a bathroom with all the latest fittings. The inspector freshened himself with eau de toilette Chèvrefeuille Tradition, which had been very popular in the sixteenth century at the court of

Elizabeth I, smoothed his greying moustache, changed his shirt and frock coat, then checked his reflection in a large mirror with a gilded frame.

When Higgins stepped into the meeting room, ten police officers leaped to their feet and gazed at their new leader, who had a well-established reputation. The inspector was a man of average height, dark-haired with greying temples, kindly looking but with a mischievous glint in his eye. He had a reputation for being one of the finest detectives in the kingdom. Incorruptible, extremely difficult to manipulate and indifferent to honours, Higgins was hardly impressive at first sight. Yet he had a gift for extracting confessions, and people soon saw that he had a gift for taking control of situations.

'Thank you for your welcome, gentlemen.'

A soldier stood up. 'I am Colonel Borrington, appointed by the government to head this special unit, whose task is to fight the troublemakers who wish to attack the institution of the monarchy. Our role is to protect England and King George IV. Long live His Majesty!'

Higgins nodded. 'Please be seated.'

Colonel Borrington was around sixty years old, with a square head and shoulders to match. His face wore a permanent scowl.

'I should like to understand,' Higgins said calmly. 'Is this brigade under your command, colonel, or mine?'

Borrington tugged at the hem of his uniform jacket. He scratched his throat, avoided the inspector's gaze and bravely confronted adversity. 'The government has entrusted us with a vital mission, and I shall respect its instructions to the letter. I and my men are therefore at your disposal.'

'Would you be kind enough to hand me the files relating to the murders of the clergyman, the nobleman and the pathologist?'

'It was not necessary to pile up paperwork,' stated the colonel. 'The facts are clear and the conclusions of our investigation leave no room for doubt. These were three political and symbolic crimes. The insurgents struck at religion, the aristocracy and science, displaying their devilish determination to undermine the bases of our society.'

'Have you identified the guilty party?'

'These abominable killings point to Littlewood, the ringleader of the conspirators who are seeking to over-throw George IV and bring about chaos. That monster is devoid of all morality and commits the worst atrocities. That is why we must arrest him with all speed.'

'Do you have any proof?' Higgins asked.

'I've just given it to you. Only Littlewood could have slaughtered those three unfortunates.'

'Did you find any . . . material clues?'

'Don't look for pointless details, inspector. Concern yourself with a single goal: the arrest of Littlewood.'

'Have you drawn up a battle plan?'

The colonel's hostility abated somewhat. 'Of course. My men know what to do, and one of our informants is bound to set us on the right track.'

'Remarkable,' commented Higgins. 'So all I have to do is wait for detailed reports.'

'Exactly!' exclaimed the colonel in delight. 'Your reputation is well deserved, inspector, and we shall work together extremely well. Don't overtax yourself; enjoy our fine capital city and rely on me to supply you with the results of our investigations. That man Littlewood will not escape us.'

'Forgive my meticulousness, but I would like to read the police report setting out the facts.'

The colonel handed the inspector a file comprising three pages.

'I penned these lines myself,' explained Borrington, 'and I'm planning to hand them to the authorities tomorrow.'

Each sheet of paper was devoted to one of the victims and gave a brief description of the crime. Given the similarities, the colonel had concluded that there was a single murderer, the conspirator Littlewood.

'Excellent,' commented Higgins. 'I don't need to sign. After that journey, I would benefit from a little rest.'

'A servant will bring you your meals, inspector. Ask for whatever you want and don't hesitate to inform me if you require anything.'

As he climbed the stairs, Higgins wondered why the government, represented by Peter Soulina, the king of hypocrites, was attempting to implicate him in this masquerade.

A policeman's caution, his approval of an investigation conducted correctly . . . Higgins's reassuring words still carried a great deal of weight, and the appearance of legality would allow the colonel's unit to have a free hand and suppress those opponents to the regime who had gathered together under the banner of Littlewood.

The authorities were forgetting one important point: when Higgins was given a job to do, he saw it through to the end. He would identify the murderer or murderers of the clergyman, the aristocrat and the pathologist, and he would do so by conducting real investigations.

Consulting the colonel's ridiculous file had given him the information he needed: the victims' addresses. With the aid of a well-sharpened pencil, he noted them down in a black leather-bound notebook.

When the doorman of the building saw him leaving, he was astonished. 'Inspector! Aren't you going to . . . sleep?'

'I need some air.'

9

Fog was gathering in the capital. Because of factories and countless workshops, it was full of pollutants, making the air almost unbreathable. And fumes from chemical works, with the smells of paint and varnish, created a dirty atmosphere and filled the citizens' lungs.

The man the authorities called Littlewood adapted wonderfully well to this protective fog.* He let it envelop his existence and hide his true identity, the better to prepare for revolution. The French had made a good start, before failing lamentably by allowing Napoleon to seize power. They should have continued with the Terror, eliminating every last resister and imposing the will of the people everywhere.

Littlewood had dedicated himself to this immense task. He knew how to defend the cause of the miserable and the oppressed, and would spearhead a giant wave that

* The term 'smog' was not yet in use.

would sweep away outdated institutions. Eliminating leading citizens would not suffice; he must attack the summit of state and kill King George IV, the corrupt libertine. At the announcement of his death, crowds would rise up and proclaim Littlewood their saviour.

Given his position, nobody would suspect him! The police were led by incompetents and would never succeed in identifying him. They did not know that their informants were in Littlewood's service and provided them with numerous false leads!

And the leader of the conspirators had an unexpected ally: Belzoni's mummy. Present at the unwrapping, he thought he was hallucinating as he gazed at that intact body, which had vanquished decay and death. He planned to seize hold of that magic and use it against his adversaries.

The director of St Thomas' Hospital was deeply distressed.

'I've never seen anything so horrible, inspector! My respectable colleague, Dr Bolson, was slaughtered. What devilish creature could have committed such an abomination? Just imagine: they pierced the back of his neck, then extracted the cerebral matter through the nostrils!'

'The work of an embalmer,' observed Higgins.

The director stared, open-mouthed. 'Are you serious, inspector?'

'Did you find the murder weapon?'

'Here it is.'

The director handed Higgins a bronze hook, a little over a foot long.

'Is this one of your surgical instruments?'

'Not that I am aware of. Have no fear, I washed it carefully. My unfortunate colleague's body was buried the day after the murder, and the official cause of death was a heart attack. The authorities insisted that no one must hear about this tragedy.'

Higgins wrapped the hook in a linen handkerchief.

'What was Dr Bolson working on?'

The director looked uncomfortable. 'You won't believe me! He . . . he was carrying out an autopsy on a mummy, which Belzoni, the organizer of a very fashionable exhibition, brought back from Egypt. A mummy so admirably preserved that it appeared alive. I gave him permission to use our operating room during the night.'

'Could I see this mummy?'

The director looked down. 'Unfortunately not . . . It's disappeared. When I gazed on the horrible sight, the mummy had gone. Bolson was stretched out on the operating table, with the hook beside his skull.'

'So it was you who discovered the crime?'

'Not entirely, inspector. The maid who sweeps the room before the surgeons arrive was the first to suffer that atrocity.'

'I would like to speak to her.'

'Pointless, I can assure you! That honest employee will have nothing to tell you.'

'Allow me to insist.'

'As you wish, but you are wasting your time.'

'Where does she live?'

'In a small attic room at the hospital. I shall take you there.'

He found a minuscule room, a skylight, a sagging bed, a rickety chest of drawers and a frozen old woman, wrapped in a large shawl.

'This gentleman is a police officer,' said the director. 'He wishes to ask you some questions. Don't be afraid. It won't take long.'

'Please be kind enough to leave us alone,' said Higgins in an amiable manner.

Although unhappy, the director did so. The inspector closed the door, reached into the pocket of his frock coat and took out a metal flask containing brandy, the only remedy against the fog.

'Would you care for a small pick-me-up?'

Warily, the old woman sniffed the flask. Satisfied, she took a large mouthful.

'Good stuff!' she exclaimed. 'At least you don't mistreat poor people. Happy to have met you. Now I'm going to sleep.'

'What did you see when you entered the operating room?'

'Listen, good sir, the director ordered me to keep my mouth shut. Otherwise I'll be kicked out into the street without a penny. So I'm saying nothing.'

'That's an understandable attitude,' agreed Higgins. 'Nevertheless, your employer's position is not as secure as it seems. As I have full powers, I can arrest him for threatening a witness and concealing evidence.'

The old woman sat up. 'Are you joking?'

'I want to cast light on this affair,' stated the inspector quietly, 'and I have no intention of using kid gloves on anyone. Telling me the truth won't get you into trouble.'

The old woman drew back and regarded the inspector attentively. 'Despite my experience, I'm almost tempted to trust you. I want to keep this room and my job as a cleaner. I sleep well here. And rubbing shoulders with sawbones doesn't bother me. Will you really protect me?'

'Absolutely. Whatever you tell me will remain secret.'

'Is there any of that brandy left?'

The old woman emptied the flask.

'I started work at five o'clock in the morning,' she said, 'and I was washing the floor of the operating theatre. It's a terrifying place, but you can get used to anything ... Anyway, I thought so! My candlestick lit up the strangest sight: a man in a black frock coat, stretched out on the wooden table, with his eyes put out and blood all over his head. I don't believe in anything, but I crossed myself! I was in a panic, and I ran off to wake up the director.'

'Did you see the mummy?' Higgins asked.

'What's one of those?'

'Was the victim alone in the operating theatre?'

'Er . . . yes.'

'Did you handle the murder weapon?'

'You're mad, inspector!'

'But you did pick something up.'

The old woman cowered again. 'That's not true.'

'Why lie to me? I'll buy the item from you.'

'Ah . . . And you won't say that I sold it to you?'

'I discovered it myself, didn't I?'

'I was planning on getting a good price for it!'

'Would this suffice?'

When she saw the banknotes, the old woman's eyes nearly popped out. It was a small, unhoped-for fortune which would enable her to eat better food.

She knelt down and reached under the bed, pulling out a book spattered with blood.

'It was laid on the dead man's head. With binding of this quality, it would have been a shame to leave it there.'

The work was a collection of psalms. It included an ex-libris label with the name of a clergyman whose passionate sermons incited simple souls to drive unbelievers and prostitutes out of London.

The man of God had signed his name. There was just one unfortunate detail: he too had been murdered, since he was one of the three victims specified by Peter Soulina, the government envoy.

10

The mummy lay in a crypt, safe from profane eyes and murderers, saved at the last minute from destruction. But the unwrapping had deprived it of its magical defences and its ability to travel through time. Little by little, its vital force would weaken and its soul-bird, the *ba*, would no longer have the strength to fly up to the sun where it derived its energy.

Its saviour had only one year in which to give it back its original integrity and re-establish the incorruptible nature of the Osiran body, which was not merely human remains but the realization of the alchemical Great Work, 'the perfect accomplishment of gold', the flesh of the gods. All the elements scattered during the horrible spectacle staged by Belzoni must be brought together and put back in their rightful place. It was the only way in which to ensure the survival of this exceptional mummy, a masterpiece of the Egyptian embalmers' art.

Each day, the saviour would speak the ancient ritual

incantations that would put off the evil day. The magic of the Word was vital but would not be sufficient to prevent a disaster. If the mummy died, the forces of destruction would avenge it; forces whose violence was such that no technical progress could counter it. The modern world had neglected the world of the soul, becoming infantile and careering towards its own destruction, caring only for what was visible – a minuscule appendix to the invisible world.

Bolson the pathologist would not massacre any more mummies, the fanatical clergyman who loathed Egypt had been silenced for ever, and the elderly nobleman, who wanted to dismember Osiris once again and throw the pieces of his body to his dogs, had provided a choice morsel for the Soul-Eater. This monster sat beneath the scales used to judge souls, and its task was to destroy evil individuals, thus condemning them to a final death.

The rescuer raised both hands above the mummy's head. Wavy lines emerged from them, the expressions of a benevolent energy. It nourished the *ka* of the sleeping man with the smiling face, the creative power which linked him to that of the gods. This vessel, symbol of eternity and vehicle for the soul, must be preserved.

Civilized people of the nineteenth century knew nothing about death and very little about life. Followers of progress, they had reduced a portion of humanity to slavery. By destroying mummies instead of preserving them, they were cutting links to the afterlife and limiting themselves to the condition of mortal insects.

The task promised to be difficult, even impossible. During the unwrapping, the rescuer had not expected to see a beloved person, someone who had emerged from the depths of the past.

Mummies were neither objects nor archaeological remains. And this one had benefited from a special kind of treatment, enabling it to dwell on the narrow border separating life from death. It was up to the rescuer to bring it to the right side by eliminating the obstacles, one by one.

Higgins's careful search of the operating theatre at St Thomas' Hospital had not unearthed any new clues. He decided to continue his investigation by visiting the residences of the three victims who, by some fortunate coincidence, all lived in the same area of the West End.

Higgins was an excellent walker, and he strode along the recently flagged pavements in the light cast by gas lamps. The London of George IV was constantly expanding, in particular to the west, where fine districts were developing, encompassing Westminster Abbey, Parliament, the Ministries, theatres, clubs, parks and the fine residences of aristocrats and the wealthy. Thanks to the architect John Nash, the capital's urban development was experiencing a sort of golden age, reserved for the West End, containing imposing dwellings with porches flanked by columns. Georgian houses were formed into terraces, testifying to their owners' opulence. Nash had reduced the use of wood in house frontages, favouring the monumental style and heavy doors.

A factor in residents' comfort was the square, an enclosed green space reserved for their use. They alone possessed a key, and no one else could enter. Plane trees provided welcome shade, and these private gardens gave the nobles, bankers, businessmen and doctors the impression that they could breathe more easily in the swiftly growing city.

It was eleven o'clock at night, and Higgins needed to find somewhere to stay. One of his friends, a member of the inner circle of experts at the Bank of England, lived nearby. In accordance with their code of honour, they helped each other whenever necessary.

The financier welcomed him with open arms, and went straight down to his cellar to fetch a bottle of Scotch.

Early the next morning, Higgins went to Dr Bolson's residence. His older sister, an elderly woman in poor health, took a long time to open the door and was openly hostile. The inspector eventually succeeded in charming her, and she gave him permission to explore the austere interior of the house where she had lived with her brother.

There was no trace of any mummy.

On the other hand, the entire library was devoted to works written by doctors in antiquity. The pathologist had assembled hundreds of files on mummies, often written by travellers with a shaky pen. Notes, in the dead man's hand, summarized his analyses and his plans, foremost among them the autopsy on Belzoni's mummy.

*   *   *

The clergyman's residence was most attractive, with a well-kept lawn at the front. His housekeeper, a red-haired Welshwoman, was shaking out bolsters when Higgins arrived.

'The police ... What are you looking for?'

'A mummy.'

'This house is in mourning, inspector, and this is no time for jokes.'

'Will you allow me to come inside?'

'Absolutely not!'

'Then go and pack yourself a small suitcase.'

The Welshwoman dropped the bolsters. 'What does that mean?'

'It means I'm taking you to prison.'

'To prison? Me? But I've done nothing wrong!'

'We shall see about that. I'm charging you with obstructing my enquiries and concealing evidence, until I find something worse.'

'Come in, inspector – and search wherever you like!'

The comfortable, two-storey house comprised ten rooms. Two of these had been converted into an oratory and a chapel. Pious pictures covered the walls, even in the kitchen and bathroom. There was a surprise in store in the clergyman's bedroom: a life-size drawing of Belzoni's mummy! Numerous needles had been driven into the head, heart, hands and feet of the Egyptian with the peaceful face.

The housekeeper snivelled, nervously twisting a handkerchief.

'Who discovered your employer's body?' asked Higgins.

'I did, very early in the morning, exactly a fortnight ago. It was a Sunday. He was a punctual man, who always took breakfast at precisely seven o'clock. I was astonished when he didn't appear, and I dared push open the door of his bedroom. And there, there . . . I saw him.'

She started sobbing.

Higgins helped her to sit down and gave her time to calm herself.

'The clergyman was lying on his bed, with blood all over his head. There was a metal object sticking out of his nostrils. I think . . . I think someone had removed his brain!'

'An object like this?' enquired the inspector, showing her the bronze hook.

'Exactly the same!'

'What became of it?'

'The undertaker threw it away. The church ordered that he was to be buried the very next day, and it was announced that the clergyman had succumbed to congestion of the lungs. How sad! Ever since he visited that exhibition, he'd been obsessed with that mummy, so much so that he cursed anyone who had a fondness for ancient Egypt. It was bound to end badly. Why hasn't the murderer been arrested?'

'Do you know who it is?' Higgins demanded in astonishment.

'Of course, but the police ordered me to keep my mouth shut! Otherwise they would throw me in prison.'

'You can talk to me.'

The Welshwoman frowned. 'What if this is a trap? You're a police officer!'

'I have only one aim: to put the guilty party under lock and key.'

His solemn tone impressed the housekeeper.

'I may be wrong, but I'll trust you. The murderer is a pathologist, Dr Bolson.'

'Do you have any proof?'

'Two days before the murder, I served them a dinner which ended in a fist fight! The clergyman had invited the doctor to dinner in order to forbid him to carry out an autopsy on the mummy. According to my master, there was a danger that it would liberate fearsome energies. The only solution was to burn it. Dr Bolson laughed in his face, called him an obscurantist and a madman. As the clergyman cursed him by reciting a psalm of vengeance, the pathologist promised him that he would kill him rather than let him touch the mummy. I can still remember his words: "I will strangle you and empty your brain from the back!" And it was no empty promise . . .'

Higgins took notes in his black notebook.

'You're the first person I've told everything I know, inspector. It won't get me into trouble, will it?'

'Have no fear.'

The inspector searched the house from the attics down to the cellars, but there was no trace of the missing mummy.

'The clergyman didn't have time to post this letter,'

said the housekeeper, handing Higgins a sealed envelope. 'I think you should have it.'

The missive was addressed to Belzoni.

Higgins broke the wax seal and read the last lines written by the clergyman:

As I have already told you, celestial punishment will strike you down if you do not immediately burn the mummy which you have brought forth from hell. Only Jesus Christ has the right to bring the dead back to life, not the magicians of ancient Egypt. The mummy threatens the true faith. Do as I say, or I shall take radical measures.

11

The front of the elderly aristocrat's London residence was adorned with two monumental statues, one depicting a bare-breasted Diana the huntress, and the other Hercules strangling the lion of Nemea. As it was four o'clock in the afternoon, the code of aristocratic etiquette permitted Higgins to call. But he had to be sure to knock on the door in the correct manner. One knock, and no servant would open it to the yokel who behaved in such a way. Two swift, nervous knocks signified that it was the postman. A series of elegant, rhythmic knocks indicated the arrival of a gentleman, wearing a fashionable hat and gloves and carrying a cane.

Higgins observed the code, and a footman opened the door.

'Can I help you, sir?'

'I am Inspector Higgins.'

'Do you have an appointment?'

'It seems that your employer is no longer in any position to make them.'

The servant flinched. 'Isn't that tragedy now closed?'

'I wish to search the premises.'

'I don't have the authority to allow you to.'

'Then take me to someone who can.'

The servant took the police officer to the servants' hall, where the butler was handing out the final wages to members of staff who would have to go and try their luck elsewhere.

'It's shameful!' protested a plump maid. 'That old skinflint paid us a pittance, and now we're being dismissed without a word of explanation!'

'Our employer had no heir,' explained the butler. 'This house is going to become a hunters' club, and our services aren't required.'

Higgins stepped forward. 'Who discovered the body?'

All eyes turned to look at him.

'This gentleman is a police officer,' revealed the footman awkwardly.

The butler shrugged.

'Permit me to be surprised by this incongruous visit. Our master has been buried, and the terrible accident he suffered was a severe ordeal for us. It's now time for calm remembrance.'

'Is the word "accident" quite correct?' Higgins asked in astonishment.

'Indeed it is,' cut in the irritated butler.

'Liars!' protested the maid. 'I was the first one to see the body, and it didn't look like an accident to me!'

'Kindly remember your place,' her superior demanded, shocked.

'What place? I'm no longer one of that old miser's slaves, and I'll say what I like!'

'Would you show me round?'

'Out of the question!' raged the butler.

The inspector looked at him coldly. 'I'm investigating a murder, and I would not advise you to hinder my progress. Such behaviour would incline me to regard you as guilty.'

'Inspector, you cannot think such a thing! I'm innocent, I . . .'

'In that case, be discreet.'

'The old man's rooms are on the first floor,' said the maid. 'I'll take you there.'

A massive staircase led up to the first floor. The walls were lined with hunting trophies.

'The old man was a sadist,' revealed the servant. 'He took pleasure in slaughtering does, stags and wild boar. He even cut the throats of sick dogs that couldn't keep up the pace. It was hell here. We were forbidden to speak while we worked, forbidden to make a sound, forbidden to talk to visitors, forbidden to go into the garden, forbidden to eat outside mealtimes and forbidden to laugh! We had to get up at six, light the fires, empty the chamber pots, take up the tyrant's breakfast – and he was never satisfied – change the sheets and all the rest . . . Never has a corpse made me so happy! And yet it wasn't pleasant to look at.'

The vast bedroom resembled a little Egyptian museum, with statuettes, pottery, fragments of stelae, pieces of papyrus and some mummy bindings.

'The old man was besotted with these antiquities,' said the maid. 'The mummy, the mummy . . . It's all he ever talked about! The moment he woke up, he started raving fit to scare you. The old man wanted to buy it, cut it into pieces and throw it to his dogs. He was a complete madman, I tell you! And he was the one who was cut up like a common piece of meat. Someone handy with a scalpel took out his brain and his guts. Thanks be to that person! He's rid us of a vile fellow.'

'Did you find the scalpel?'

'It was more like a sort of hook, with the end bent back. Someone had thrown it away, cleaned up the old lord and washed the bedroom. So as to avoid scandal and terrifying people, his remains were collected and buried on his estate in Sussex. The cause of death was said to be a horse riding accident. And we servants weren't even given a bonus to keep our mouths shut! In any case, nobody believed me, and the others were too afraid to contradict the authorities. The old skinflint's forgotten! His hatred of mummies didn't bring him happiness.'

Higgins examined each item in this macabre museum. He was intrigued by a mother-of-pearl box, for there was nothing ancient Egyptian about its lock.

With the aid of a multi-bladed tool, a gift from a burglar who had reformed, he managed to open it.

The box contained around a dozen letters from the

fanatical clergyman, promising the old nobleman a terrible death if he continued to take an interest in mummies.

'Just before the murder,' Higgins asked the maid, 'did your employer receive . . . strange visits?'

'At least one, from a pathologist who was in a great hurry to see him.'

'Do you know his name?'

'Bolson. I was the one who took his walking stick and gloves. That fellow really scared me! So I listened at the door of the drawing room where the old man received him. It was a strange business, I can tell you! The pathologist ordered him to leave him in peace and not to covet the mummy he was planning to dissect. Otherwise he promised that he would cut him into pieces. And he didn't sound as if he was joking! The old beast tried to hit the doctor on the head with a vase of flowers, but he pushed him away. And the pathologist repeated his threats. In my opinion, you don't need to look any further for my unworthy employer's murderer!'

After taking notes, Higgins carried out a search of the house. Perhaps the nobleman had stolen and hidden the mummy? But that slender hope was disappointed.

Night was falling as Higgins walked along slowly, thinking about what he had discovered. Indifferent to the hurly-burly of London and the bustle of cabs and carriages, he felt that he was caught in the trap of a formidable affair, which might involve state secrets. If so, he would not get out of it alive unless he ran away.

But the inspector's personality precluded that kind of behaviour, which was unworthy of his ancestors' tried-and-tested courage. In the Higgins family, the search for truth was the most important thing, whatever the circumstances or the difficulties.

Peter Soulina, the government envoy, was a practised liar. Clearly, he had been chosen because of this second-rate talent. By implicating Higgins in this famous hunt for a conspirator, which had been entirely made up, the senior official gave his machinations a respectable appearance.

Higgins's first observation was that there was an incredibly strong bond uniting the three victims: Belzoni's mummy.

A cab slowed down and approached the inspector.

A man armed with a pistol leaned out and fired. Amid the din of countless wheels turning on the bustling street, the sound went unnoticed.

Sure that he had hit his target, the marksman ordered the cab driver to speed away.

A shoeshine boy saw Higgins collapse and rushed towards him. 'Sir, sir! Are you ill?'

The inspector got to his feet. The bullet had torn the left shoulder of his thick overcoat and inflicted a small flesh wound.

'Thank you, my boy, I'm quite well . . . Except for my boots. I feel that your services are essential.'

The shoeshine boy quickly made the gentleman's shoes look respectable again, and received double the usual amount for his trouble.

Among the qualities demanded of an investigator was a good memory for faces. Higgins never forgot a face, even if he had spotted it for only a moment. And the marksman's face was not unknown to him. He was one of the members of Colonel Borrington's unit.

One of the soldiers who had been put at his disposal in order to find the conspirator Littlewood had been ordered to kill him. In other words, the inspector was following a lead which displeased His Majesty's government in the extreme.

12

'How do I look?' Giovanni Battista Belzoni asked his wife. 'The barber tortured me, and I hope the result is worth it.'

Sarah walked round her husband with a smile on her lips.

'I shouldn't admit it, but you look magnificent. All the women will fall in love with you.'

'Don't worry. I'm only visiting an Oxford professor who is as dull as ditchwater.'

'You swear?'

'I swear.'

The giant took Sarah gently in his arms.

'You are and always will be my only love, Giovanni.'

'We are one for always, my darling. Together, we have experienced the worst and the best. And now I shall provide you only with the best! It's up to me to persuade Sir Richard Beaulieu to grant me the post that is rightfully mine.'

'Be patient and don't get to the point too quickly. The English set great store by etiquette, and that pretentious scholar likes the sound of his own voice.'

'You know my talent for diplomacy.'

Sarah said nothing. The Titan of Padua's diplomacy rested on two principles: charging forward and destroying the obstacle. She loved him that way and had no wish to see him change. In Egypt they had shared exciting times, and whenever he yielded to discouragement Sarah had seized the torch and encouraged him to go on. He was an adventurer, and he would stay that way.

A downpour had been succeeded by a shower, and the unmade roads were becoming muddy, making it difficult for traffic to circulate. Pedestrians were spattered with mud, and elegant ladies were afraid of soiling the hems of their luxurious gowns. As Belzoni was travelling in an expensive carriage driven by his Irish servant, he would have the privilege of keeping his brand-new clothes immaculate.

A legion of roadmen were cleaning the main roads and collecting up the dung from the thousands of horses that criss-crossed the streets of the capital. A flock of sheep destined for an abattoir blocked the progress of Belzoni's carriage, and he worried that he might arrive late for his meeting. Pigs and bullocks also used the road, heading for Smithfield, and it was not rare to hear the protests of alarmed citizens, drowning in this animal lake.

Professor Beaulieu lived in an old house on Tottenham

Court Road. The road was blocked off by a tollgate, the proceeds from which served to finance the frequent repairs to this very busy main road. At six o'clock precisely, Belzoni knocked at the solid-oak door.

A footman opened the door, took his hat, cane and gloves and led him to the large drawing room on the ground floor, which stood between the dining room and the library.

'Please sit down. Sir Richard will be here presently.'

Belzoni chose to remain standing.

The scholar was fond of sixteenth-century furniture and the heavy wooden chests of the Middle Ages. The accumulation of these items made the atmosphere oppressive, particularly as the windows were obscured by velvet curtains.

The austere professor, whose expression seemed devoid of all joy, appeared. 'Welcome to my home, Belzoni. Have you become accustomed to our climate?'

'London is the capital of the world, and one must bow to its rules.'

'An excellent remark, dear colleague. Would you care for a glass of port?'

'Thank you.'

'We shall leave gin to those who frequent public houses, and savour this nectar.'

The professor – a man full of his own importance – sat down, and the Italian did likewise. The manservant brought two half-filled glasses and then left.

'Rumour has it,' ventured Sir Richard, 'that your

exhibition is an undeniable success. Thanks to you,
England is discovering the curiosities of ancient Egypt.
The common folk marvel, and we scholars will soon
uncover the secrets of that vain civilization.'

'Vain?' Belzoni was astonished.

'Vain and contemptible,' confirmed the professor.
'Those enormous pyramids, those gigantic temples, those
outsized tombs . . . What follies, built at the cost of thousands of slaves' lives! The pharaohs thought they were
gods and ruled as tyrants.'

'I'm not certain . . .'

'Your book amused me greatly, Belzoni, as an account
by a seasoned explorer, filled with entertaining anecdotes. But I'm talking to you about science. When Thomas
Young, our illustrious scholar, has deciphered hieroglyphs,
that infantile form of writing, we shall fill in the historical gaps and show once and for all that Greece and Rome
were superior to Egypt.'

'The beauty of the tomb paintings in the exhibition . . .'

'Don't exaggerate, Belzoni. We are in the presence
of an exotic style which exceeds the limits of good taste.
Gods with animal heads on human bodies! My God,
only a sick brain could have conceived such monstrosi-
ties. The public will tire of these stupidities, believe
me.'

'Did the Greeks not praise the wisdom of the Egyptians
and attribute great importance to the mysteries of Osiris?'

'Don't listen to such nonsense, dear friend! Repeating
it would discredit you. The Egyptians were primitives,

prisoners of magic, incapable of rational thought. Which reminds me . . . Why did you wish to see me?'

Controlling his rising anger, Belzoni emptied his glass of port and looked straight at the scholar.

'Thousands of visitors have been admiring the superb alabaster sarcophagus in the exhibition,' declared the Titan of Padua. 'It was quite a feat to bring it to London. It's one of the major masterpieces of pharaonic art, and it deserves to be exhibited at the British Museum . . . on condition that I'm offered a suitable price. Given your connections with the curators, could you begin negotiations? Of course, I will not prove ungrateful.'

The professor's face became openly hostile.

'According to our sovereign George IV, a gentleman is recognized by the fact that he has a good deal of leisure. Now, leisure activities demand a certain degree of material prosperity. Nevertheless, in all circumstances, a true gentleman manifests his contempt for money. So, Mr Belzoni, your proposition shocks me profoundly. Consequently, I didn't hear it. Is there anything else?'

The giant kept his composure. 'You did me the honour of reading my book, which has been a great popular success.'

'Popular,' repeated the professor with a disgusted air. 'That's the problem, Belzoni! The common people don't have the capacity to appreciate real scientific works, and vulgarization is a mortal sin. Putting knowledge within the grasp of just anyone seems to me to be an unpardonable fault.'

'My writings are the reports of a field archaeologist, not a bookworm!' thundered the Italian. 'They make fundamental contributions to science, and I hope for official recognition.'

'I beg your pardon?'

'Have I shocked you a second time, Sir Richard?'

'Not shocked, stunned! "Official recognition" . . . So what is it you wish for, Belzoni?'

'My book is the first serious study of Egyptian antiquities. I opened the pyramid of Khephren, the temple at Abu Simbel and the largest tomb in the Valley of the Kings. I transported the colossal bust of the young Memnon* and discovered numerous remains of inestimable worth. Clearly, a new branch of science has been created, and I feel that I'm capable of passing on my knowledge to students.'

Professor Beaulieu scratched his ear. 'Are you seeking to obtain . . . a post as a teacher?'

'Exactly, Sir Richard. Your position at Oxford enables you to give it to me.'

Hands on knees, the scholar burst out laughing. 'I've never heard such rubbish! You, a university don . . . Have you lost your mind?'

'The study of ancient Egypt deserves to become a science, and I'm the person best placed to defend that cause.'

'Belzoni, Belzoni! You are raving, my poor friend!

* Ramses II.

You cannot imagine for a moment the seriousness of the university courses taken by our students at Oxford and Cambridge. It takes long, hard years of work to train highly qualified specialists. You, dear fellow, are nothing but an amateur and an adventurer, good for entertaining the crowds. As for Egypt, that land of barbarians, it's nothing but a museum of eccentric objects, prized nowadays by naive collectors. The fashion will pass.'

White-faced, the giant rose to his feet. 'Do you refuse to help me?'

'The very fact that you ask such a question proves your stupidity, my poor Belzoni! Harvest the fruits of your exhibition, sell your finds and return to Egypt to replenish your stock. There's no place for you in London.'

13

When he caught sight of Higgins, the orderly could not decide whether to be relieved or angry. 'Inspector! Colonel Borrington is furious. He was planning to send the police out to look for you.'

'Good day, my friend.'

Higgins went up to the colonel's office and opened the door without knocking.

The expressionless soldier started. 'Where did you get to?'

'Summon your men immediately.'

'By what right . . .'

'I must remind you that you are theoretically under my command. It's time to put the government's instructions into practice.'

Despite Higgins's calm demeanour, the colonel decided not to protest. And everyone gathered in the large meeting room.

'One person is still missing,' commented the inspector.

'Correct,' agreed Borrington.

'I wish to see that man with all speed.'

'Impossible.'

'For what reason?'

'That is a military secret.'

'Kindly summon Peter Soulina, colonel. Otherwise your career and that of your little unit will end in a shameful manner.'

'Inspector, I . . .'

'Be quick about it.'

Peter Soulina's small, inquisitive eyes expressed discontent and anxiety.

'Have you encountered unexpected difficulties?' he asked Higgins and Borrington.

'I demand the removal of military secrecy.'

'Inspector! That's not the role of the police.'

'One of Colonel Borrington's subordinates attempted to kill me by shooting me from a hansom cab. I collapsed, letting him believe that he had succeeded. And this attacker has now disappeared: a man who was a member of the unit which was placed at my disposal.'

Silently standing to attention, the colonel threw the government emissary a look of desperation.

'Very well,' said Peter Soulina, 'that is indeed a small problem. We must succeed in resolving it among gentlemen.'

'You could tell me the truth,' suggested Higgins.

The senior official paced up and down, hands folded behind his back.

'The reality is not very cheering, inspector. The conspirator Littlewood is a formidable adversary and he uses disconcerting methods.'

'For example, bribing a soldier and instructing him to spy on Colonel Borrington and obtain first-hand information relating to any action undertaken against him. When he saw me arrive on the scene, Littlewood took fright and decided to kill me. His right-hand man knew me, and was therefore the individual best placed to act promptly.'

Borrington gaped. 'How . . . how do you know?'

'It is my job, colonel.'

'You are unfortunately right, inspector,' confirmed the government emissary. 'Following the disappearance of this officer, a rapid investigation proved that he had been corrupted.'

'That man Littlewood really is very strong,' remarked Higgins. 'Successfully infiltrating one of his henchmen into the secret service is quite an achievement!'

'You will now understand more clearly why the authorities are so worried.'

'I understand above all that Colonel Borrington's current unit has been corrupted and that the next one will suffer the same fate. It's impossible to continue like this. Either I'm allowed to conduct investigations in my own way or I return home.'

In desperation, the soldier sought out his superior's gaze. Irritably, Peter Soulina nodded, signifying the end of Borrington's mission. Crestfallen, the colonel left the office.

'The incident is closed,' decreed the senior official. 'First thing tomorrow, a new squad of police officers chosen by lots will be ready to assist you.'

'Pointless.'

'Surely you're not planning to confront Littlewood alone!'

'Our police force is suffering from a serious malaise,' stated Higgins. 'The reports I submitted emphasized its state of decay and the rule of corruption, but the authorities chose to close their eyes. The only chance of success is for me to use my own networks, which are unknown to Littlewood. If Littlewood exists . . .'

Peter Soulina flinched. 'Do you dare doubt it?'

'I do.'

'Inspector! Are you accusing the government of some kind of machination?'

'It wouldn't be the first time, or the last.'

'Be serious, I beg you! Littlewood has already killed, and he's determined to foment a revolution in order to overthrow the throne. Are the murders of the clergyman, the nobleman and the doctor not enough for you?'

'No, Mr Soulina.'

The senior official stopped pacing and sat down in the colonel's armchair.

'I would like an explanation, inspector!'

'My preliminary investigations didn't establish Littlewood's guilt. Judging from the clues I gathered, the three victims killed each other. Moreover, they're all linked to a mummy which has now disappeared.'

'Most unlikely!'

'Yes and no,' replied Higgins, consulting his black note-book. 'The facts are stubborn, the illusions countless. We must free ourselves from preconceived notions, accumulate material evidence and not obstruct the path to the truth. Dr Bolson killed the old aristocrat and the pastor, and the pastor killed the doctor. Material clues and witness reports corroborate this version of the affair.'

Peter Soulina frowned. 'The old nobleman was the first victim, was he not?'

'Probably. The culprit was the clergyman.'

'And then it was his turn?'

'The doctor killed him.'

'And last on the list was Dr Bolson!'

'Murdered by the clergyman, according to material evidence.'

'But that's impossible, inspector, since the clergyman was already dead!'

'That detail had not escaped me.'

'Someone planted false clues to throw you off the scent, and that person is none other than Littlewood, as I told you! He attacked the symbols and allies of power, and he's attempting to make you go round in circles.'

'Let's assume that is true,' conceded Higgins. 'There's still the mummy.'

The senior official thought for a while. 'Reassure me, inspector . . . Surely you don't believe that it's come back to life and murdered three people?'

'Egypt is a mysterious land, and no one should contest the power of its magicians.'

'We are in the nineteenth century,' Peter Soulina reminded him. 'Ampère has just discovered electrodynamics, science is making giant leaps forward and superstitions are collapsing. And you're theorizing about a murderous mummy?'

'The clergyman, the nobleman and the pathologist wanted to destroy it. In its place, how would you have reacted?'

'Let's stop this charade, Higgins, and find Littlewood!'

The inspector produced the bronze hook.

'This is the object used to kill Dr Bolson. Two similar weapons, which were unfortunately thrown into the rubbish, were used to extract the brains and viscera from the old nobleman and the clergyman.'

'Ugh, how horrible! Only a maniac like Littlewood could have committed such atrocities.'

'Does he have a good knowledge of the traditions of ancient Egypt?'

'Why do you ask?'

'Because this object is an embalmer's hook, used while preparing the body prior to embalming.'

'See sense, inspector!' begged the government emissary. 'Forget this business of mummies and concentrate on a single goal: the arrest of Littlewood. Where can I contact you?'

'I'll contact you.'

'You . . . don't trust me?'

'Somebody tried to kill me, Mr Soulina, and official buildings are full of indiscreet ears. Give me a confidential address.'

The senior official scribbled it on a piece of paper. 'I shall be there every Sunday,' he promised.

14

The duchess was eighty years old. Ten of these she had spent growing up, and the other seventy being unpleasant to people. She was consistently malevolent, and took a great delight in slandering, humiliating and destroying others. In spite of her reputation as a she-devil, she remained a celebrity, and anyone who wished to make a name in London must visit her drawing room and take tea with her.

So Sarah Belzoni, who much preferred the Nubian desert, had felt obliged to accept an invitation which all ladies dreamed of receiving. She had been obliged to buy a dress in the latest fashion, a confection of red silk and embroidered lace.

'You look magnificent,' declared the seamstress.

Sarah thought of Giovanni. He was hoping for so much from his meeting with Professor Beaulieu! If it went well, he would obtain a post as an archaeologist at Oxford and would be free from financial worries. With the duchess's aid, Sarah could open the doors of high society to her husband. Together, they would take possession of this new territory and be able to defend themselves against predators who were more dangerous than wild beasts.

The duchess had ten guests, all refined society ladies with the exception of Sarah, a curious creature from an unknown world. The duchess's friends reproached her for inviting Sarah, but they felt an unexpected frisson of excitement at the prospect of eating this naive girl alive, ill-prepared as she was for such an ordeal.

When the Titan of Padua's wife appeared, everyone was struck dumb. She was so tall and elegant, and seemed far from overawed.

Sarah instantly detested the drawing room, with its faded draperies and tired chairs. There were too many paintings of hunting scenes, and the overall effect was stifling.

'I'm delighted to welcome you, my dear,' said the duchess in her nasal voice. 'Take a seat to the right of me.'

The place of honour, thought a stuck-up creature with odd-looking features.

Two servants brought in a silver teapot, porcelain cups and a tray of biscuits and salmon canapés.

'I drink only white tea from China, which is rare and expensive,' declared the duchess. 'And as you can see, I tolerate only the purest spring water. Each stage in preparing this delicious beverage is strictly controlled, though I do permit the addition of a drop of milk.'

Two silly little geese chuckled with pleasure. They had heard the duchess's words a thousand times, but they were still delighted by them.

'How did you survive in the middle of nowhere, my dear Sarah?'

'In Cairo and Luxor, apart from the ancient monuments, traces of civilization still exist. On the other hand, the desolate lands of the Great South made life difficult.'

'In London, the summer heat is unbearable enough,' observed a silly goose. 'Down there, it must be horrible! Sweat, thirst, soaked clothing, odours ... I daren't even think about it!'

'A wise precaution,' observed Sarah.

Stifled laughter greeted the stranger's remark.

'This year,' the duchess went on, 'the season* promises to be dazzling. There will be remarkable art exhibitions and concerts, handsome athletes will enliven the Thames regattas and there will be exciting cricket matches. We have come a long way from Egyptian barbarity!'

To the satisfaction of her guests, the lady of the house was regaining the upper hand.

'Did you spend time with the natives?' asked a worried Austrian baroness, peering through a solid-gold lorgnette.

'Without them, my husband would not have succeeded in bringing so many superb items back to England.'

'My poor dear, how you must have suffered!'

---

* The season lasted from May to August. Festivities, cultural events and society gatherings took place throughout London society.

'We met many people of quality,' declared Sarah.

Indignant whispers ran round the little court.

'Sample the marvels created by my pastry chef,' ordered the duchess.

The large drawing room was transformed into a poultry coop, as the ladies chattered and stuffed themselves with pastries. Sarah contented herself with a cup of tea.

'You detest these imbeciles,' whispered the duchess, 'and you're right. Given your character and your appearance, dear friend, I'm expecting a great deal of you. You'll enjoy stirring up this mud, unleashing the tempest and subduing these empty minds. There is one condition, however.'

Sarah pricked up her ears.

'An ill-assorted couple is destined for disaster, my child. I've heard talk of your Italian brute, and I spotted him at the exhibition. He is unworthy of you and will be unable to integrate himself into good society. Leave him, and marry a wealthy aristocrat. I shall introduce you to some excellent candidates and you can make your choice. Follow my advice; you'll not regret it. Experience makes a person see things clearly.'

The proud Irishwoman got to her feet and emptied the contents of her cup on to an extremely valuable Persian carpet.

Exclamations of outrage rang out.

'I shall be delighted never to set eyes on you again, duchess,' declared Sarah Belzoni as she walked out of the drawing room.

*   *   *

It was almost midnight. Giovanni had not returned, and Sarah was beginning to worry. Her nerves on edge, she had downed several glasses of gin, the alcohol of the poor, and had divested herself of her showy gown. James Curtain, the servant, had long since gone to bed.

At last, the front door banged shut, and she heard the Titan's footsteps on the stairs.

Sarah threw herself into his arms. She could see from his crestfallen expression that he had failed.

'Get me a drink, please. When I left that accursed professor's house, I walked blindly for hours to calm my anger. I should have strangled him and shattered him into a thousand pieces!'

'That would not have been very constructive,' commented the Irishwoman.

Belzoni seized the gin bottle and sat down on the edge of the bed.

'Total failure!' he confessed. 'Sir Richard Beaulieu treated me like a yokel, an adventurer and an amateur. He refuses to speak to the British Museum in order to facilitate the purchase of the alabaster sarcophagus because, in his opinion, Egyptian exoticism will soon go out of fashion. Exoticism . . . the poor fellow! He has no sensitivity.'

'We'll manage without him,' ventured Sarah. 'That sarcophagus is such a marvel that we're sure to obtain an enormous sum for it. Sir Richard will kick himself. And what about your university post?'

'He laughed in my face! I, a field archaeologist,

obtaining a university chair ... Unthinkable! I must be content with amusing the public and entertaining simple souls. Such contempt wounded me deeply, Sarah.'

She caressed his face.

'The words of imbeciles and conceited people are worthless,' declared Sarah. 'Can you imagine your Oxford professor climbing the hill at Abu Simbel or organizing the transportation of a colossal statue? That smug, self-centred fellow is nothing but a malevolent shadow. The wind will carry him away. But you are Giovanni Battista Belzoni, as solid as the cliffs in the Valley of the Kings, and your fame will never be erased. You must persevere in your attempt to sell the sarcophagus and to obtain an official post.'

'When I think about confronting this London jungle, with its predators and its traps ... Sometimes I lose heart.'

'I'm beside you, Giovanni. Together, we are indestructible.'

'How did you fare in your tea party with the duchess?'

'In the worst possible way,' revealed Sarah. 'In the eyes of those high-society ladies, I was a curious beast, a spectacle not to be missed! That poultry coop stuffed with geese made me laugh, up to the point when the duchess suggested that I should leave you and marry a real gentleman.'

The giant seized his wife's hands. 'That old hag dared to ...'

'Have no fear. I won't be invited again. She didn't like the way I drank my tea.'

Belzoni threw himself down on the bed.

'I'm tired, Sarah. As I walked along, I thought about that magnificent mummy that Dr Bolson is studying. Why hasn't he given me the results of his research? We could organize a lecture together.'

'Tomorrow is another day, my darling, and I've seen enough mummies today. Are you really so tired?'

When she unhooked her bodice, the Italian felt a new vigour course through him.

15

Thick fog covered the London docks. After half a day of sunshine, an ill wind had blown it back. Sometimes dark green, sometimes a brownish orange, there was nothing attractive about the colour of the Thames. The river was becoming a sewer, into which poured the by-products of abattoirs, tanneries, breweries . . . Corpses floated in it. Hardened to this sad sight, the conspirator Littlewood thought of the terrible conditions in which East End workers lived. Each day, obtaining water was a serious problem. In many places a single tap served several houses, and people had to battle to obtain a good place in the queue, early in the morning. They filled as many buckets and bowls as they could, and often had to ration themselves. The rich, on the other hand, took baths and washed their vegetables whenever they wished.

When Littlewood came to power, he would force the aristocracy to serve the poor. Dressed in rags, duchesses would wash floors with dirty water and lords would spend hours carrying heavy vessels. Watching them collapse from exhaustion would be a magnificent sight.

One image fascinated the conspirator: that of the heads of the French nobility, cut off and displayed on the ends of stakes. Those pallid faces and dead eyes no longer expressed arrogance. Only a bloody revolution could really change people's minds.

Littlewood gripped the handle of his knife. Someone was approaching.

The corrupt police officer from Colonel Borrington's unit emerged from the mist. Corrupting him was a great coup, successfully achieved thanks to a prostitute whose services the officer often used. Either Littlewood would denounce him and his superiors would put an end to his career, or the unwary fellow would bend to his demands, in exchange for a fitting remuneration.

The police officer had not hesitated for a moment. At regular intervals, he informed the revolutionary about the plans of Colonel Borrington, who failed lamentably whenever he attempted an arrest.

The intrusion of a government emissary, charged with a special mission, had intrigued Littlewood. When he learned that Inspector Higgins, a first-rate investigator, had been appointed to head some kind of secret service, the conspirator realized the danger. This time, the government was playing its trump card.

But the government reaction had come too late, for Littlewood's networks were already firmly in place. A good proportion of East End workers would welcome a revolution, and the weakness of the forces of order, which were fragmented and lacked a real leader, would be a decisive advantage. George IV was an empty-headed womanizer, incapable of leadership, and he had abandoned power to the reactionaries of the Tory Party, whom the revolution's leader would exterminate with his own hands.

The officer was dressed in serge trousers and a much-mended jacket, and he looked like one of the countless down-and-outs searching for work on the docks.

'Is it done?' demanded Littlewood.

'It's done. Inspector Higgins suspected nothing; my cab approached carefully. I fired, and he fell down. The cab driver didn't understand what was happening at first, and I had time to run away. You're rid of that impediment, once and for all.'

'Good work, my lad.'

'Colonel Borrington is an imbecile, but eventually he will realize my role in this. Now, as you promised, you must hide me and pay me.'

'I always keep my promises,' declared Littlewood, 'and I'm going to provide you with a completely secure hiding place. Before you left your post, did you learn anything new regarding me?'

The two men walked slowly, side by side, in the direction of a warehouse.

'You can sleep soundly! The colonel will be transferred to a provincial town and his team dissolved. Higgins's death will sap the government's morale, and they will return to the good old policing methods, whose ineffectiveness has been demonstrated a thousand times over.'

'One awkward detail remains, my friend.'

'What's that?'

'You know my face and my real name.'

'The secret will be well kept, believe me!'

'It's difficult to trust a traitor, particularly one who is a police officer. A thought worries me: are you, in reality, in the service of the government and attempting to double-cross me?'

'I've killed an inspector and abandoned my post!'

'But was that just a smokescreen?'

'I swear that it was not!'

'Ah, false oaths! I've heard so many, even from the mouths of my own best friends. One cannot be too suspicious, especially when one is fighting the current regime.'

Three stocky men sprang out of the fog and surrounded the police officer. The size of their clubs froze him to the spot in terror.

'These honest dockers will deal with you.'

The condemned man attempted to flee.

A simple kick knocked him to the ground. And the clubs went to work.

Indifferent to the fate of this second-rate individual who had become fleetingly useful, Littlewood walked away. The sound of the corpse plunging into the dirty waters of the Thames brought a half-smile to his face.

His official duties rendered him above suspicion and

enabled him to obtain the funds needed for his crusade. As he progressed, he would be forced to eliminate other detritus. The final victory depended on it.

The magnificently whiskered chief physician at St Thomas' Hospital observed the Titan of Padua as if he was about to deliver a diagnosis.

'You seem in excellent health to me, Mr Belzoni. What ails you?'

'I haven't come for a consultation; I've come to ask you for news of Dr Bolson.'

The chief physician scratched his mutton-chop whiskers.

'Bolson, Bolson . . . And he is a pathologist?'

'Indeed.'

'He's not a member of the hospital staff.'

'But this is where he was planning to carry out an autopsy on a mummy.'

'A mummy . . . Are you certain about that?'

'I brought it back from Egypt myself and entrusted it to Dr Bolson.'

'How bizarre . . . I haven't heard anything about that kind of experiment, and I don't know this honourable colleague myself. If I were you, I would go to his house in search of enlightenment. Try to keep yourself fit, Belzoni.'

The giant returned to his carriage and asked his servant to drive faster. James Curtain was beginning to get the hang of the ever-wilder London traffic. The fine districts of the West End were no exception to the rule, and cab drivers had to show audacity and dexterity.

The rain grew heavier, and the unpaved streets became slippery. James Curtain just managed to avoid a speeding barouche and reached his destination as night was falling.

Belzoni rushed up to the pathologist's front door and knocked loudly, several times.

A curtain moved aside.

'Who's there?' asked a feeble voice from inside.

'Belzoni, a friend of Dr Bolson. I would like to talk to him.'

The door opened slowly.

A wizened old woman appeared, looking fragile enough to shatter.

'Haven't you heard? My brother has passed away.'

'My condolences,' stammered the giant, shocked. 'How did it happen?'

'I don't know.'

'Was it an illness, an accident?'

'I don't know.'

'That's impossible, madam! You must have been informed about the cause of death.'

'I have nothing to say to you.'

'Did your brother say anything to you about a mummy?'

'Certainly not.'

The old woman slammed the door in his face.

In his dejection, Belzoni did not feel the rain soaking through his clothes. The doctor and the mummy had both gone . . . What was the meaning of this imbroglio?

16

Higgins's banker friend had given him the keys to a comfortable, discreet apartment in the City, situated on the top floor of an office block with two entrances. Following the assassination attempt, which had almost cost him his life, the inspector knew that he must take as many precautions as possible and find himself secure accommodation whose existence was not known either to the government emissary or to police chiefs of dubious integrity.

The City's Square Mile was the heart of finance and business, ensuring that the kingdom prospered and had international influence. Since the year AD 45, merchants and corporations had settled there and, despite the great fire of 1666, the district had been reborn from the ashes and retained its original vocation. The Stock Exchange boasted of being the seat of tolerance, since no nation was a stranger to it and it never excommunicated anybody; the only heretics were dishonest people and bankrupts.

Founded in 1694, the 'old lady' of Threadneedle Street, otherwise known as the Bank of England, had been dreamed up by a Scotsman, William Paterson. Originally a private institution designed to provide money in order to win the war against the French, it became the state bank in 1766. In 1788, despite the small amount of space at his disposal, the architect and collector John Soane created a new building, taking care to leave a blind wall facing the street in case of riots.

At night, the City was empty and police patrols easily spotted any suspicious individuals. Moreover, two of the inspector's subordinates would take turns watching the building where he was staying. At first sceptical about the very existence of Littlewood, Higgins now believed it likely that there was a conspiracy aimed at destroying the monarchy. The French Revolution had demonstrated that the worst was always possible. Up to now, social disturbances had had a limited impact, since they lacked a coordinator. If Littlewood succeeded in fulfilling that role, England might falter, or even succumb. And since Higgins's task was to arrest the leader, he represented a major obstacle which must be eliminated as a matter of urgency.

State and criminal matters were intermingled. This sombre prospect should have persuaded the inspector to go back to the country and enjoy his well-deserved retirement.

But there was that mummy – the vanished mummy, which he wanted to find because his intuition told him that it was the key to an extraordinary enigma. As he pursued his enquiries, attempting to save his country from disaster, would he touch the boundary separating life from death?

From a young age, Higgins had been interested in antiquity in general and the Egypt of the pharaohs in particular. Several journeys had enabled him to explore the pyramids, temples and tombs, and he had spent long hours in contemplation before these mysterious masterpieces. The hieroglyphic texts preserved a wisdom that was as yet indecipherable but whose full extent would eventually become apparent. Who would be the first man to raise the veil concealing the message of the ancient Egyptians: Thomas Young or the Frenchman Champollion?

The central part played by this missing mummy had nothing to do with chance. The word derived from the Arabic *moûmîya*, meaning 'wax, tar', referring to the substance used during embalming, which gave some mummies a blackish appearance. It resembled pissalphate, which Muslim doctors used to treat both fractures and nausea, as well as many other conditions. As the flesh of mummies was an extremely abundant material, it was freely prescribed. According to the prestigious scholar Avicenna, eating mummy cured palsy, palpitations, stomach disorders, abscesses, liver problems and epilepsy. So the remains of the ancients were attacked, and thousands of Osiran bodies were cut up, reduced to powder, made into a paste and delivered to the apothecaries of

Alexandria and Cairo. Entire mummies were sold to Europeans, who were greedy for this remarkable remedy, and Arab peasants constantly profaned tombs to extract their precious occupants. A text of 1424 stated that the looters boiled up the mummies, then collected the flesh, which detached from the bones, and the oil that floated to the surface of the boiling liquid. Germans, English and French sought out as many mummies as possible, complete or in pieces, and sent them back to their respective countries. At eight shillings a pound, in the eighteenth century, business was booming!

In addition to medical backing, important individuals approved of this sinister trade. François I regularly consumed ancient Egyptian flesh, convinced that it improved his digestion. A leather bag always hung from his horse's saddle, containing a fragment of mummy.

How many men, women and children, all ritually embalmed, had disappeared, becoming the victims of stupidity and greed?

In 1582 the surgeon Ambroise Paré raised the first voice against consuming these bodies, to which the Egyptians had accorded so much importance and respect. His *Discourse on Mummies* stated that they should not serve 'as food and drink for the living; this wicked drug is of no benefit to the sick, but causes them great pain in the stomach, with a stinking mouth and severe vomiting, which is rather the cause of disturbances in the blood, and causes bleeding rather than stopping it'.

This warning was not enough to interrupt the traffic

in mummies, and the Egyptian government eventually prohibited the export of these ancient corpses, taxing offenders heavily. Good intentions slowed down the trade a little, but the prices went up and the rarity of the product attracted more enthusiasts.

Repeated incidents aroused anxiety. A number of boats transporting mummies fell victim to storms or even shipwrecks, and these misfortunes were attributed to their special cargo. After being patient for a very long time, were the remains of the ancient Egyptians beginning to rebel and punish the profaners?

The followers of black magic entered the game. Procuring an authentic mummy could increase their powers tenfold. Charged with a power that they could misappropriate to their own advantage, these relics offered them a decisive weapon in their fight to impose the rule of evil.

Higgins took this threat seriously. Assuming that Littlewood was behind the murders of the clergyman, the old aristocrat and the pathologist, he had linked his actions to a mummy, which had now vanished, and had used an embalmer's hook as a murder weapon.

Since it was devoid of importance in his eyes, Littlewood could have abandoned the hook in the operating theatre at St Thomas' Hospital, alongside the pathologist's body. He had, however, taken it away, with an obvious intention: to use it again – but how?

Higgins was faced with a sort of demon, capable of manipulating occult forces in order to realize its ambitions. And his path was strewn with murders.

At first a hostage and a victim, had the mummy been transformed into a fearsome ally? If he presented such a theory to the government and the police, Higgins was liable to be committed to a madhouse. So he must keep silent and continue the investigation, following his own intuition. Finding the mummy might perhaps deprive the conspirator of his lethal weapon.

How was he to find the right lead? He must question the foremost expert on Egyptian archaeology, the field archaeologist who had made spectacular discoveries and was the 'owner' of the missing mummy. It was time to meet Giovanni Battista Belzoni and find out if he was entirely innocent.

17

Belzoni broke the seal on a large envelope and withdrew a superb invitation card. As he read it, a smile came to his face.

'It's an invitation to lunch at the Travellers' Club! Do you realize, Sarah? It's one of the most exclusive places in the capital! Are my talents at last being recognized?'

The tall Irishwoman did not bother to don a dressing gown before reading the words on the thick card.

'I'm proud of you, Giovanni'.

'Unfortunately, I can't take you with me. The clubs are reserved for men.'

'Even the land of freedom has its imperfections. Let's forget that detail and concentrate on making you look elegant. I shall choose your outfit, and the barber will make you look like an emperor.'

The giant's expression darkened.

'Are you afraid of British high society?' asked his wife anxiously.

'No. I'm thinking about the death of Bolson and the disappearance of *my* mummy. What has become of it?'

'It will have been dismembered and thrown out with the rubbish, like so many others.'

'What a sad fate! Sometimes I wonder if we're wrong to manhandle those remains and . . .'

Sarah kissed her husband. 'You're the guest of the Travellers' Club of London and probably one of its future members. How far you have come, Giovanni! When we arrived in Alexandria, on 9 June 1815, I knew that I had been lucky enough to meet a great man, capable of working miracles. Egypt has given you her treasures, and now you are about to conquer the capital of the world.'

Pall Mall* was the first London thoroughfare to be lit by finely wrought gas lamps, in 1807. It boasted a host of wealthy clubs, among them the Travellers', founded in 1815. This was a 'meeting place for men who travel abroad, where they receive as honoured guests the principal members of foreign missions and travellers of note'. Only remarkable men who had travelled at least a thousand miles from London could hope to be admitted to the club, whose small number of members were forbidden to talk about business and savoured the joys of distinguished conversation.

Belzoni was impressed by the club's façade, which was Italian in style. Clearly it marked a frontier between

---

* The name is derived from 'Paille Maille', a game resembling croquet.

the ordinary and the exceptional. The moment he stepped across the threshold, he was approached by a chamberlain who knew each of the members.

'May I help you, sir?'

'My name is Belzoni and I've been invited to lunch.'

The chamberlain examined the invitation. 'Indeed so, Mr Belzoni. Welcome to the club. I shall take you to the library.'

Coloured carpets, leather armchairs, a marble fireplace, Roman columns surmounted by a stucco frieze inspired by the bas-reliefs of antique Greece, and row upon row of travel books gave the place a highly cultural air.

Feeling ill at ease, the Titan of Padua sat down in a corner of the vast room. He was served a glass of champagne and small pieces of toast topped with caviar.

A man of average height, discreetly elegant and with an open, friendly face, came towards him.

'Pleased to meet you, Mr Belzoni. My name is Higgins. Allow me to congratulate you on your discoveries in Egypt.'

The giant got to his feet.

'Is the champagne to your taste?'

'It's wonderful, but . . .'

'You're wondering why I invited you here? The first reason is obvious: you are an illustrious traveller, and this club should pay homage to you.'

'And . . . the second?'

'I need your archaeological knowledge. I have reserved a room where we can eat in complete privacy.'

The menu was not without its charms: fillets of turbot in a cream sauce, lobster vol-au-vent, roast black grouse and a peach compote, all washed down with a solid Pomerol which emphasized the delicate flavours of the food.

'Five years of uninterrupted excavations!' recalled Higgins. 'You worked unstintingly, Mr Belzoni, and the old land of Egypt has rewarded you. Your exhibition is a complete success, and your discoveries have earned you fame. Are you planning to recommence your explorations?'

'Not immediately.'

'Have you encountered any difficulties?'

'I must admit that my enemies are many! I'm a man who likes to work in the field, and I can face up to adversity. When we arrived in Egypt, my wife Sarah, my servants and myself, no one made our task easy: quite the reverse! Because of hidden scheming, Mehemet Ali Pasha, the absolute master of Egypt, rejected my hydraulic machine, even though it would have improved irrigation and relieved the unfortunate peasants. I'm a trained engineer, but he humiliated me! Fascinated by the richness of the antiquities, I decided to set off on an expedition to bring forgotten treasures back to light. Everything I undertake excites me, and I become deeply committed. I lived among the Arabs, learned their language, slept in tombs, searched the desert and followed tracks leading to the Red Sea and the Bahariyah oasis. Unfortunately, Mr Higgins, this world is full of jealous and twisted peoplc! They have criticized my spirit of initiative, my methods for transporting the antiquities and my over-direct method of exploring ancient monuments, and now they want to sully my name by denying my merits!'

'Doubtless you are talking about the attitude of Henry Salt,* the English consul-general in Alexandria?'

Belzoni's fork halted in mid-air. 'You know him?'

'He is considered a perfect gentleman.'

'Salt, a gentleman? He is a schemer of the first order, and an upstart who is incapable of recognizing other people's worth!'

'So in your eyes,' ventured Higgins, 'he would rival the French consul-general, Bernardino Drovetti† in medi-ocrity?'

Belzoni grew sombre. 'That man is my worst enemy! He's the leader of a veritable gang of thieves who loot antiquities, and I came into conflict with those bandits several times. Drovetti has just returned to the official post from which the Bourbons ousted him, and now he fulfils the offices of consul, looter and friend of Mehemet Ali! In Luxor his henchmen attempted to kill me by accusing me of stealing antiquities. My servant was brutally disarmed, and a double-barrelled rifle was pointed at my chest. Arabs armed with sticks beat me all over, and Drovetti's accursed band promised me the worst

---

* Born in Lichfield on 14 June 1780, died in Alexandria on 30 October 1827.
† Born in Livorno, Italy, in 1775.

punishments. Given the number of assailants, I thought I was done for. And I was accused of having killed a man who drowned during a crossing from Thebes to Cairo!'

'How did you escape from this ambush?' asked Higgins.

'Just as I was about to try to force my way through the blockade, Drovetti himself appeared! His bodyguards were armed with pistols and ready to fire. That brigand of a consul ordered me to dismount from my horse, and a shot rang out behind me. Forced to obey, I stepped down. Then Drovetti's tone softened. Humiliating me and proving that he was stronger was enough for him. As long as he was there, he dared say, I wasn't in any danger! And now that accursed diplomat is all-powerful.'

'You're big enough to bring him down, are you not?'

'I'm just one man, Mr Higgins! The tyrant who governs Egypt doesn't like me and listens only to Drovetti, the general of an army of pirates. As Salt refuses me his support and is playing his own game, my room for manoeuvre is very narrow.'

'Surely the glory you have acquired through your exhibition and your book has rendered you immune from attacks?'

The giant emptied his wine glass, which was instantly replenished.

'I wish it were so! In order to get past Drovetti and Salt, I need an order for an official mission and that game is not yet won. Speaking of which, dear sir, are you a great traveller?'

'It's just an instructive hobby,' Higgins admitted.

'May I know what office you hold, and the reason for your invitation?'

Higgins looked directly at the Italian. 'I owe it to you to give you specific details.'

The Italian froze. 'Are they . . . embarrassing?'

'I'm an inspector of police, Mr Belzoni, and I'm conducting a particularly delicate investigation.'

'The police . . . A crime . . . How does that concern me?'

'Did you entrust a mummy to a pathologist called Dr Bolson?'

'I did, and I've learned of his death, but I can't find out if the mummy has been destroyed!'

'This was no ordinary death, Mr Belzoni, and your mummy is linked to three murders.'

18

This statement left Belzoni stunned. 'That's difficult to believe, inspector!'

'Indeed it is, and moreover you're the only person who may consider this hypothesis plausible. For you, the magic of ancient Egypt isn't merely a word.'

'I wouldn't go so far as to assume that a mummy is capable of coming back to life and committing crimes!'

'Even with this?'

Higgins placed the bronze hook on the table.

'It's a fine object . . . if a little disturbing! It was used to extract the brain from the corpse before embalming.'

'I found it beside the body of Dr Bolson, who was preparing to study your mummy,' revealed the inspector. 'Someone didn't approve of what he was doing and killed him. Two similar hooks were used to kill an elderly nobleman and a clergyman who was determined to destroy the mummy. The clergyman was planning to send you a letter reminding you of his previous warnings. If you didn't burn that embalmed corpse, which was the enemy of true faith, heaven would punish you.'

'That madman shouted curses at the unwrapping,' recalled Belzoni.

'Was the elderly aristocrat also at the spectacle?'

'Indeed he was. I can still see him with his cane and his air of superiority! He was an odious man, imbued with his own privileges, who hated the ancient Egyptians.'

'That was definitely the man. According to a witness, he was obsessed with your mummy. And its disappearance worries me.'

'It was of an exceptional quality, inspector. To tell the truth, I've never seen its equal. It looked more like a person asleep than a dried-out corpse. Perhaps I ought to have halted that extraordinary funeral ceremony! But the guests had paid handsomely, and I have great need of money. Because the relic was so perfect, I entrusted Dr Bolson with the task of examining it. Did it harbour secrets?'

Cognac was served, and the Italian did it honour. The warmth of the alcohol made him want to speak in confidence.

'I've searched many tombs, inspector, and gazed on hundreds of mummies. Exploring those caverns is not an enjoyable experience. There's a shortage of air, your lungs burn and there's a risk of fainting. Often, you cannot find a foothold, and you have to crawl across flints and limestone debris which skin your hands and your face. A passageway, another, then another, and low-roofed chambers. Anxiety grips you, and you wonder if you are descending into hell. You're suffocating, you need to rest and you sit down . . . on a mummy, which you flatten like a hatbox! Gripped with terror, I rolled down amid a noisy jumble of broken bones, bandages and fragments of rotten sarcophagi. For a quarter of an hour I was as motionless as stone, hoping that silence would return. If I moved, the din began again! Walk on, and I crushed another mummy! And you cannot imagine the number of caves filled with these remains, sometimes lying down, sometimes standing and leaning against the walls. You breathe in the dust that arises from the decomposition of the embalmed corpses, and you are exhausted when you re-emerge from their sepulchres, where death is continually at your shoulder.*

'A formidable experience,' commented Higgins.

'And one which I repeated several times! When I didn't return to Luxor, I set up camp at the entrance to a tomb along with some Arab troglodytes and spent hours questioning them. They knew the hiding places of antiquities and sold their information at such ridiculous prices that I had to drive a hard bargain and not show the slightest sign of impatience. Their spades were no longer used to dig the earth but to excavate the floors of tombs and can also be used to hit curious people over the head! A lamp, lit by rancid oil, lit up the bas-reliefs and our interminable

---

* We have respected Belzoni's terminology and mode of expression, so that his emotions are clear.

discussions. We drank milk, ate bread and poultry roasted in an oven heated with . . . the debris of sarcophagi and bones! The Arabs feel no respect towards the ancient skulls from which they profit in order to improve their daily lives. By spending time with them, I became as indifferent as they were, I must confess. When sleep came, I dozed off at the bottom of a well of mummies.'

The inspector turned a keen-eyed gaze on him. 'It takes courage to undergo such ordeals. What was your true goal, Mr Belzoni?'

This strange Englishman had destabilized the Titan of Padua. Despite the fact that he was a police officer, he felt inclined to trust him. 'The Arab looters aren't imbeciles. "If the foreigners attach a price to antiquities," they told me, "it's because they are worth ten times more than what they are offering to pay." Myself, I was interested not only in mummies but also in what they concealed: amulets, jewellery and papyri. And that made the transactions arduous, for the Arabs had amassed real treasures and would not have sold them cut-price!'

'Given your determination,' observed Higgins, 'you managed to negotiate.'

The giant's chest swelled. 'I'm proud of having done so, inspector. One must get to know these people and not despise them. By living with them, speaking their language and respecting their customs, I tamed them. People who are pretentious or impatient fail.'

'But you succeeded.'

Belzoni poured himself some more brandy.

'In return for a suitable fee, they took me to the right places, and I collected marvels. Shouldn't science show me some gratitude?'

'You're beginning to harvest the fruits of your labour, and this is only a start.'

'Thank you for that encouragement, inspector.'

'The problem of the mummy remains. Do you think that the Egyptians managed to overcome death?'

'Certainly not!'

'Aren't you troubled by the legend of Osiris, who was murdered and brought back to life, according to the mysteries related by the initiate Plutarch?'

'A legend is still a legend,' declared Belzoni, 'and one's imagination easily takes flight on contact with the ancient Egyptians. Nevertheless . . .'

'Nevertheless?'

'In certain circumstances, it's true, I felt troubled. Don't get the wrong idea! We're in the age of science, I'm passionate about technical progress and we Westerners know the value of reason. Soon, superstitions will have disappeared.'

'But not mummies,' objected Higgins. 'And what if our science were incapable of understanding their mysteries?'

'Dr Bolson was to have enlightened us! That horrible death . . .'

'Do you suspect anyone, Mr Belzoni?'

The question stunned the giant. 'Absolutely not, inspector!'

'Not even if you think about it?'

'Murdering three people and stealing a mummy . . . It doesn't make sense!'

'Dare I ask a favour?'

'Please do, inspector.'

'Would you be so kind as to show me round your exhibition and comment on the masterpieces you've brought together?'

'It would be an honour. Which day would you prefer?'

'As soon as possible.'

'Why not this evening, after the exhibition is closed to the public?'

'Perfect, Mr Belzoni.'

One last sip of cognac, and the two men left the Travellers' Club, where illustrious travellers smoked their pipes and cigars as they read explorers' accounts of their adventures.

Slightly tipsy and troubled by this conversation, the Titan of Padua bumped into an elegant lady. She dropped her parasol and would have collided with a gas lamp if Higgins had not managed to hold her back at the last moment.

'Forgive me,' begged the Italian, red with confusion. 'You're not hurt, I hope?'

'The pain is far from unbearable,' replied the pretty brunette with the green eyes, whose gown was worth a fortune.

'You . . . Weren't you present when I unwrapped my mummy?'

123

'I had that privilege, Mr Belzoni. Allow me to introduce myself: I am Lady Suzanna. Despite this rather sudden encounter, I'm delighted to see you again and congratulate you on revealing so many splendours to us.'

'Can you forgive my clumsiness?'

The young woman gave him an impish look. 'On one condition: grant me a private visit. Once you've explained these mysterious works to me, they'll begin to speak. Shall we say . . . this evening?'

'I would have been happy to grant your request, but I've just reserved this evening for one of the members of the Travellers' Club: this gentleman, Mr Higgins.'

'I shall step down in favour of Lady Suzanna,' cut in the inspector.

'Your courtesy is that of a gentleman,' declared the charming aristocrat. 'Let me suggest a solution: is our archaeologist willing to accept two special guests?'

'I'm at your disposal,' agreed Belzoni.

'And what about you, Mr Higgins? Can you tolerate a woman who is curious about the mysteries of antiquity?'

'Your unexpected presence is a gift from the Egyptian gods, Lady Suzanna.'

The young woman smiled. 'Until this evening: nine o'clock, at the Egyptian Hall.'

A hansom cab stopped, she stepped nimbly into it and the vehicle pulled away.

'She seems unhurt,' commented Belzoni, relieved.

'You forgot to return her parasol,' remarked Higgins.

The giant held the fragile object firmly.

'It completely slipped my mind! She's extremely charming, don't you think? Chance offers us many surprises.'

'Many of them far less pleasant,' agreed Higgins.

19

Belzoni's enthusiasm mounted as he showed Higgins and Lady Suzanna round his exhibition.

'As they couldn't find any models to imitate, the Egyptians were obliged to be creative. Nature had endowed them with such fortunate faculties that their genius could still, today, supply us with new ideas after all the ones we've borrowed from them. The Greeks derived everything from Egyptian architecture. What makes ancient Egyptian sculptures so admirable is the bold way in which they were executed. Imagine the calculations necessary to create colossal statues without missing out the smallest detail! However, the proportions of the head had to be adjusted, as it was designed to be seen from a distance. Otherwise the finished statue would have lacked effect. And what patience was required to carve the hieroglyphs and paint those countless figures which decorate the temples and tombs!'

As he looked at drawings depicting the fabulous scenes

from Pharaoh Seti I's house of eternity, Belzoni recalled the month of October 1817, during which he had discovered the largest and most beautiful tomb in the Valley of the Kings. Some people accused him of having used a battering ram to smash through the door, but he remembered above all his feeling of wonder. The incredible extent of that monument, which burrowed deep into the rock, the phenomenal number of decorated chambers, the journey leading from the visible world to the chamber of resurrection . . . He shared each and every step with his two guests, who were immersed in a world populated with divinities.

'Were there any treasures left?' asked Lady Suzanna.

'The looters had carried off the countless masterpieces which had filled the tomb,' lamented Belzoni. 'All I retrieved were a few terracotta figurines, varnished and painted blue.* There were also some wooden statues designed to contain papyri and fragments of other sculptures. But in the centre of the Bull Chamber† I was greeted by a sarcophagus whose equal does not exist in the whole world!'

Belzoni, Lady Suzanna and Higgins gazed at this unique alabaster monument, the highlight of the exhibition.

'Look,' said the Italian, holding up a lamp, 'it becomes

---

* The *ushebtis*, whose task was to carry out certain kinds of work in the other world, instead of the person who had been reborn.
† As he was unable to decipher the king's name, Belzoni called Seti I's house of eternity the 'tomb of the Apis', because of the discovery of a mummified bull.

transparent when you place a light behind one of its panels! You can then make out its carved decoration, made up of hundreds of little figures, each no more than two inches high. Never has Europe received an ancient Egyptian piece of such quality!'

Lady Suzanna and Higgins shared the archaeologist's fascination.

'In your opinion,' said the young woman, 'what is the significance of these scenes?'

'I think they show some sort of funeral procession and protective images of the king lying in his sarcophagus.'*

'I assume his mummy had gone?'

'Unfortunately so, as had the lid. We found a few fragments of it here and there, but it was impossible to put them back together. After taking imprints of the bas-reliefs, and finishing the models and drawings of this royal tomb, I set to work removing this alabaster sarcophagus. It was a very delicate undertaking, for the slightest jolt could have shattered it. By being constantly vigilant, I managed to avoid any accidents. As soon as it was out in the open air, my men brought me a strong chest and we slid the marvel inside. Then there was a long and difficult journey to the Nile. The ground was uneven, there were sand and pebbles everywhere, and the sun was burning hot . . . You cannot imagine how hard that journey was. Like the ancient

---

* They are, in reality, scenes taken from the 'Royal Funerary Books'. They retrace the underground journey of the sun, into which the pharaoh's soul is assimilated, and its rebirth.

Egyptians, we used rollers and wet the ground. And the sarcophagus reached the boat which was headed for Cairo. Then Alexandria . . . and London! And I don't regret having rescued this pinnacle of ancient Egyptian art: shortly after my exploration, and in spite of the channel I ordered to be dug to divert rainwater, the tomb was flooded. As my instructions hadn't been followed, a torrent filled the galleries, and several bas-reliefs were spoiled, notably at the corners of the door pillars. Entire figures fell, and I did my utmost to repair the damage. The sight of such harm caused me immense pain.'

Moved, Belzoni caressed *his* sarcophagus. In selling it to the British Museum, he would provide the illustrious institution with a unique piece and lay the foundations of his own fortune.

Higgins walked round the monument. He dreamed of the moment when the hieroglyphs would become readable and begin to speak again. This stone vessel, bearing symbols, must surely be an entire book, whose magical content preserved the pharaoh's soul.

A shadow of pain darkened the Italian's expression.

'Is something wrong?' Lady Suzanna asked anxiously.

'When I opened the door of that sublime tomb,' declared Belzoni sombrely, 'I thought my merits would be recognized. Instead of that, the newspapers from Europe fomented a veritable conspiracy against me. There were attempts to discredit me, the importance of my work was ignored and my discoveries were greeted with silence or even attributed to other people! I wrote numerous letters re-establishing the truth, but the rumours and the lies didn't stop. Venomous tongues claimed that Arabs had already visited my tomb and that I'd paid them to show me the entrance! I begged Consul Drovetti to set the facts straight and undertook to pay five hundred piastres to anyone who could prove he had entered that sepulchre before me! And, of course, nobody came forward.'

'Is there some kind of ringleader, capable of organizing this conspiracy aimed at destroying you?' asked Higgins.

'I don't know,' admitted the giant.

'Was identifying him the main reason for your return to England?'

'I had to leave Egypt to prove my competence by publishing a book and organizing this exhibition.'

'A total success, Mr Belzoni.'

'I'm not so sure! I still have a long way to go, and my enemies won't allow me any room to manoeuvre.'

'Are you so sure of that?' asked Lady Suzanna in surprise.

'I'm afraid of them!'

'I sense that you're more than equal to confronting them, especially with the protection of the Egyptian gods.'

'Do you accord such importance to this very ancient religion?' asked Higgins.

'I don't believe in our absolute superiority, and I deplore the lack of respect towards the ancients,' confessed the young woman. 'As we gaze at these drawings and this sarcophagus, we are lost in admiration and realize how ignorant we are. Are there not vital secrets hidden behind these enigmatic figures?'

'They may not remain enigmatic for much longer,' prophesied Belzoni. 'A learned Englishman, Thomas Young, is on the point of deciphering them.'

'Don't you believe Champollion has a chance?' asked the inspector in surprise.

'Not for a moment! He's too far behind.'

Lady Suzanna examined a modest chest containing pieces of fabric.

'They were used by the embalmers,' explained the Italian.

'Were all Egyptians mummified?'

'Not the poor: their corpses dried in the sun before being wrapped in coarse cloth and piled up in a cave. There, they were mixed up with the mummies of cows, sheep, foxes, fish, birds and even crocodiles! These caves are of little interest to looters. They contain neither jewels nor papyri, only these poor remains. Wealthy people paid for a sycamore-wood sarcophagus decorated with scenes relating moments from their lives, and a roll of papyrus was placed inside. The mummies of priests benefited from special treatment: arms, legs, toes and fingers were wrapped separately, with numerous interlaced strips of linen, and they wore bracelets and leather sandals. And the tombs of kings and nobles contained a multitude of riches, gold objects, statues, stone vases, and jars for the viscera, as if the dead wanted to surround themselves with everything used to maintain life.'

'Your admirable mummy, with its radiant face, is so different from the idea we have of death. He must have been a great person,' ventured Lady Suzanna.

'A king would not have been better treated,' agreed Belzoni.

'Where did it come from?'

'Thebes.'

'From a specific tomb?'

'I don't know. The sarcophagus had been removed from its hiding place, and the Arabs didn't give me precise details. The name and history of this noble feature in the writing on the wrappings, and one day we shall know his name.'

'What has become of this mummy?'

The giant felt uneasy. 'It's been submitted for study by scientists and—'

'It's disappeared,' cut in Higgins, 'and I'm searching for it.'

Lady Suzanna appeared dumbfounded. 'Searching for a mummy . . . Are you an archaeologist?'

'No, an inspector of police.'

The aristocrat's admirable green eyes filled with astonishment. 'Why are the police interested in the remains of an ancient Egyptian?'

'Because they're implicated in a murder case.'

The pretty brunette turned to Belzoni. 'Did you know this?'

'Inspector Higgins informed me.'

'A killer mummy? That's insane!'

'It hasn't yet been charged,' Higgins corrected her.

The young woman smiled. 'A fine cause to defend! If you take it to court, I shall defend it.'

'Are you . . . a barrister?'

'That is a profession closed to women, or so it appears, but I've overcome all the obstacles. And I'm proud of my early successes. Only difficult cases interest me.'

'We're a long way from any trial, Lady Suzanna.'

'Nevertheless, you're thinking in terms of a murderous mummy, capable of coming back to life, moving, even transforming itself by taking on the appearance of a gentleman!'

'We mustn't get carried away. At this stage of the investigation, it's merely an important clue, a sort of treasure attracting covetousness.'

'Who is the victim?'

'I'm sorry, but I cannot answer that.'

'And what about you, Belzoni? Will you speak?' asked the young woman.

'The inspector would not approve of any indiscretion, it seems to me.'

Higgins nodded.

'The law of silence! I'm accustomed to it. This story excites me, gentlemen, and I'm determined to know more. One of my foremost faults is obstinacy. So we shall meet again. Thank you for this guided tour, Mr Belzoni. It was a real privilege. Good day, inspector.'

The Titan of Padua gazed after her, open-mouthed, as the magnificent, ethereal creature left the Egyptian Hall.

'What a temperament! I wish you good luck, inspector.'

'I still have two or three questions to ask you, Mr Belzoni.'

'I'm happy to answer them straight away.'

'Given the lateness of the hour, your memory might fail you. Will you come to lunch again at the Travellers' Club? I'm planning to sponsor your application for membership, and the food is quite agreeable. Shall I see you tomorrow?'

'Tomorrow.'

20

After telling his wife everything, Belzoni sank into a
leather armchair and smoked his pipe. Sarah was dealing
with invoices. The couple's financial situation was still
precarious.

'You seem troubled, Giovanni.'

'That Inspector Higgins is a strange fellow, a kind of
father confessor. Without violence or aggression, he gets
you to talk to him and entrust him with your little secrets.
He's a sort of formidable hunter, at once warm and ruthless!'

'Since you've done nothing wrong, what do you fear?'

'Nothing, absolutely nothing!'

'A second invitation to the Travellers' Club – what an
honour! We're making progress.'

'I didn't dare tell you . . .'

Sarah looked worried.

'Higgins has suggested putting my name forward for
membership.'

'You, a member of the Travellers' Club . . . That would indeed be justice! Excellent news, my darling. You'll meet important people who will help you to bring your plans to fruition.'

'We mustn't forget the fly in the ointment: Higgins is a police inspector and he's questioning me because of the missing mummy!'

'It can't have gone far,' said Sarah with a smile.

'Aren't you forgetting the three murders?'

'They don't concern you, Giovanni. Get into the inspector's good graces, become a member of the club and continue to forge your path.'

The giant did not tell his wife about Lady Suzanna. In certain circumstances it was better to remain silent. He emptied his pipe and got dressed.

As Sarah was submitting to a final inspection, the servant James Curtain came in. 'A gentleman is asking to speak to the great Belzoni urgently.'

'A gentleman? You are sure?' asked the Irishwoman.

'To judge from his clothes, he's wealthy.'

'And he really said "the great Belzoni"?'

'I was merely summing up his many and varied praises.'

'This fellow is liable to make me late,' said the Titan of Padua.

'It's not raining, and James can drive the carriage swiftly. Let's see if this stranger is the bearer of any interesting propositions.'

The Judgement of the Mummy

Sarah herself showed the gentleman into the drawing room, adorned with drawings and paintings devoted to the landscapes of the East.

'Allow me to introduce myself,' said the thin, edgy visitor. 'I am Dr Thomas Pettigrew. I specialize in surgery and anatomy. Allow me to congratulate Mr Belzoni on his fabulous exhibition.'

The giant merely nodded.

'A man like you is a benefactor to humanity and science. We still have so much to discover, especially with regard to mummies! Unfortunately I didn't have the good fortune to be present at the unwrapping of what – rumour has it – was an exceptional specimen. Would you grant me the immense privilege of looking at it?'

'It's no longer in my possession,' confessed Belzoni.

'Ah . . . Has it been destroyed?'

'Probably.'

'What a pity . . . I have the firm intention of undertaking a detailed study of mummies and discovering the secrets of the ancient Egyptians. Do you have one you could sell me, by any chance?'

The Italian hesitated. 'Possibly. These are rare pieces, Dr Pettigrew, and . . .'

'Money is no object. Name your price.'

'I have to attend a meeting. Shall we meet at the Egyptian Hall tomorrow night at eight o'clock?'

'Perfect, Mr Belzoni!'

Thomas Pettigrew bade farewell to his hosts and left.

'He's rather strange,' commented Sarah, 'but passionate.

And the death of Dr Bolson has deprived us of a specialist. We could try this one.'

Littlewood called a meeting of his principal collaborators and told them some excellent news. George IV's police force was ineffective and corrupt, and was incapable of detecting them or hindering their actions. Only one man, Inspector Higgins, had represented a relative danger. His elimination had left the field open for the conspirators, and Colonel Borrington, who was a complete imbecile, was certainly not going to succeed in arresting them. That pontificating soldier had no idea that Littlewood had just bought one of his assistants, who had been won over to the revolutionary cause. So he would know the colonel's intentions even before he had distributed his instructions to the forces of law and order!

At his clandestine meetings, Littlewood always wore a mask. His former companions had been executed, and the new ones, who came from working-class areas, placed their trust in this apostle of the poor and exploited. Some believed he was a great lord, others a wealthy industrialist, some a scientist; but all that mattered were his undisputed authority and determination to overthrow the regime and give power to the people.

Littlewood distributed money to the poor and improved their living conditions. Was that not sufficient proof of his dedication? Thanks to him, the labouring masses would finally know happiness, and the wealthy would be sent to work in the fields and factories. They would abolish the aristocracy's privileges and tear up elegant ladies' gowns! Soon, a tide of humanity would invade the fine districts of the West End and pillage the superb properties. Even the Bank of England would fall into the hands of the insurgents.

When Littlewood spoke like this, with passion, his listeners were in the palm of his hand and believed that the dream could come true. As in France, the oppressed must realize their strength and fear neither the authorities nor repression. Was the victory of the poor not within their grasp? True, the tyrant Napoleon had succeeded the revolutionaries and brought terror and desolation throughout Europe. But Littlewood would not imitate him; he would place power in the hands of people's committees.

After his speech, it was time for decisions to be made.

'My friends,' Littlewood declared, his voice filled with emotion, 'we're going to strike a great blow and destroy the symbol of this oppressive state.'

The conspirators' faces tensed.

'You don't mean . . . the king?' asked a boilermaker anxiously.

'Yes, George IV himself,' confirmed Littlewood. 'Once he's gone, the government will collapse and the revolution will triumph.'

'Killing politicians, yes, but the king . . .'

'That fear is reprehensible, my friend, for it nourishes the enemy! This monarch is nothing but a puppet, everyone knows that. Nevertheless, he embodies our misfortune.

139

By killing him, we shall demonstrate our power and make the masses rise up. When the head of Louis XVI was cut off, France obtained liberty, equality and fraternity! The death of George IV will bring us even more.'

'How will we do it?' asked an unemployed man.

'The operation promises to be particularly difficult,' conceded Littlewood. 'That's why, before undertaking it, I need your agreement. If you follow me, raise your hand.'

Fourteen of the fifteen members did so. The boilermaker abstained.

'As the majority is overwhelming,' decreed Littlewood, 'I can therefore set out my plan to you. I'm going to buy servants and coachmen who will inform me as to the king's movements. Knowing his timetable is vital. We shall find a moment when he's without protection, and we shall strike. Patience and rigorous organization are the keys to our success.'

'Death to the tyrant!' shouted a docker, and the other conspirators joined in, with the exception of the boilermaker.

Once again, Littlewood had unleashed his supporters' enthusiasm. Led by him, the people of London would change the world.

'Given the scope of our plans,' declared the leader, 'absolute secrecy is essential.'

He approached the boilermaker and placed a hand on his shoulder.

'There's just one danger: that someone who is determined to inform the police might infiltrate our ranks. He would have no chance of success, for I would know about him.'

Littlewood seized the artisan by the hair, pulled back his head and, with his right hand, slit his throat swiftly and precisely.

Bleeding copiously, the unfortunate man took two steps forward. The docker tripped him up, and several conspirators trampled on the dying man. His corpse would join the others floating in the river.

The last victim was not a traitor, but he had made a fatal mistake by refusing to follow the leader of the revolution, who would not tolerate any opposition.

21

'Allow me to recommend the eels stewed in wine sauce and the rack of beef with vegetables,' said Higgins to Belzoni. 'The wine waiter has chosen an old Burgundy, which is close to perfection.'

The private salon of the Travellers' Club was hung with gold drapes and paintings depicting explorers confronting wild beasts or menacing natives.

'I've contacted several eminent members, who will not oppose your candidacy,' revealed the inspector. 'Final success will take time, and I must ask you to be patient. If you had to relate your most spectacular exploit, which would you choose?'

'The conquest of the Nubian temple of Abu Simbel,' the giant replied without hesitation. 'You cannot imagine the difficulties I had to confront. Nubia is a poor and dangerous land. Its savage beauty makes one forget the ordeals, but the greed and rivalries of the tribal chiefs put me constantly in danger. Fortunately, I had succeeded in training a small band of reliable people, and we set off to attack the enormous mass of sand which was obstructing the façade of the great temple and preventing access to the interior. Rumour had it that it was stuffed with treasures! It was July 1817, inspector, and the baking heat ought to have halted all work. But I succeeded in persuading my team that this insane labour was worth the trouble. We dug a sort of channel into the heart of the dune and, on 1 August, a passage opened up into emptiness. It was a fortunate discovery, for it led to the temple, which hadn't been invaded by sand. You can imagine my excitement! There was just one worry: could I breathe? To my great surprise, despite the terrible heat and thanks to fissures in the rock, we felt better than we had outside. And what marvels we found there: paintings, sculptures, colossal figures, beautiful hieroglyphs, battle scenes and a curious shrine housing four figures of gods.* There were also several oblong chambers equipped with stone benches, where precious objects had probably been stored. We had difficulty in drawing, for our sweat soaked into the paper.'

'And the treasures?' asked Higgins.

'Two figures of lions with the heads of sparrow-hawks, and a seated figurine.† It was scant booty and I was extremely disappointed, I confess. But the site is extraordinary! Four colossi representing the pharaoh adorn the front of the

---

* The *ka* of Ramses II, Amon-Ra, Ra-Horakhty and Ptah.
† The kneeling statue of Paser, governor of Nubia under Ramses II.

temple, the largest statues ever created. They must be excavated so that the splendour of the whole temple can be restored. And the entire edifice was carved out of the rock, standing a hundred feet above the Nile. Anyone who reaches that temple will have an unforgettable sight.'

'An exciting adventure, Mr Belzoni. When my investigation is at an end, I shall urge the Travellers' Club to organize an expedition to gaze on Abu Simbel. Are the eels in wine to your taste?'

'Absolutely delicious.'

'I still have a few small questions to put to you.'

'Do they concern . . . the mummy?'

'I should like precise details regarding the evening when the unwrapping took place. You and Dr Bolson were the only two people who took part?'

'Indeed.'

'That type of spectacle attracts wealthy amateurs, eager to acquire souvenirs. If you would be so kind as to give me the buyers' names . . .'

There was nothing menacing about Higgins's calm tone of voice. And yet the giant felt as if this request was an order. Behind the friendly face of this attentive host hid an obstinate investigator.

'These were legal transactions, inspector, and my wife Sarah has drawn up receipts for the fortunate collectors. The first linen wrapping went to Kristin Sadly, a plump, excitable woman who was anxious for complete discretion.'

'For what reason?'

'I don't know, inspector. I had never met her before, and I don't think I shall see her again. But one of the other enthusiasts didn't pass unnoticed, for it was the famous actor Peter Bergeray, the prince of dandies! He wanted the bandages covering the mummy's eyes and fixed a very high price himself. Unfortunately, I'm still waiting for payment, and Sarah will soon be sending him a reminder. There was another surprising purchaser, Francis Carmick, a politician. He acquired the second linen shroud, which was tied at the mummy's ankles and chest. And he wasn't only interested in that magnificent specimen! Rather unpleasantly, he demanded specific details from me regarding mummification, and aimed thinly veiled threats at me should I not give him satisfaction.'

'Did you do so?' asked Higgins.

'Indeed not! No one dictates how Belzoni behaves.'

'Carmick is an influential individual, who's predicted to become a Minister. He's entirely dishonest and immoral, and has already trampled on numerous hard-headed adversaries. I would advise caution.'

'When one has confronted a tyrant like Mehemet Ali and highway bandits like those of Consul Drovetti, one doesn't run away at the sight of a politician!'

The delicious rack of beef with vegetables calmed the Titan of Padua. And the warmth of an exceptional Burgundy helped to jog his memory.

'A strange fellow dressed in purple, Paul Tasquinio, acquired the immense chest band, which was a good thirty metres long. The transaction was swift; he didn't haggle over the price. The following customer was of the same ilk! The landowner Andrew Young bought a rarity from me, a small oblong vase which was tightly sealed and laid along the mummy's left flank. In my opinion, he's a skinflint! Given the size of his estate, he's hardly without funds.'

'Did he invite you to visit him?' Higgins asked in astonishment.

'Sarah and I were invited to his country house, which stands amid his many acres of land. Young is a collector of old weapons and of sealed vases from Egypt. He demanded that I provide him with others, with an insistence which particularly annoyed my wife. She detests that unpleasant character, whose ugliness makes her uneasy. We were happy to return to London, I must confess.'

'Did you nonetheless procure the items which he desired?'

Belzoni sighed. 'Business is business, inspector. Young knows the rules of the game, and he'll pay the price, but we'll never become friends. In general, collectors live only for their passion and forget humanity. The man who bought the linen foot wrappings, Henry Cranmer, probably belongs to that category. And that piece of linen will be one of his most important pieces, because of its inscriptions. They may perhaps include the name of the man who was mummified.'

'And who has now disappeared,' Higgins reminded

him. 'Do you think the mummy was stolen by a collector?'

'That's not impossible.'

'Have we been through all your purchasers, Mr Belzoni?'

The giant hesitated. 'There's one more.'

'Do you find it hard to speak of him?'

'Sir Richard Beaulieu, an Oxford professor, is a high-flying academic. I hadn't imagined he would purchase a pretty amulet in the shape of an eye. From his point of view, it's a mere bauble fashioned by superstitious and mentally retarded people.'

'Do you find such a judgement shocking?'

'It's complete stupidity! Professor or not, that man is full of nonsense. From his high, authoritarian horse, he spouts all kinds of rubbish. And that priggish pedant has opposed my desire to receive official recognition by setting the university authorities against me.'

'In other words,' remarked Higgins, 'you're not on good terms.'

'I hope to win his esteem. A scholar of that stature cannot be a complete idiot, and eventually he'll appreciate the importance of my discoveries. And then we'll be reconciled.'

Higgins had been taking notes throughout, in his black leather-bound notebook.

The dessert, a flavoursome plum tart, delighted the diners.

'This time, Mr Belzoni, have you listed all the buyers?'

'I haven't omitted anyone.'

147

'Was Lady Suzanna not present?'

'She was, but she was content to observe the spectacle.'

'So you didn't sell her anything?'

'Nothing, inspector.'

The head waiter served a vintage brandy. Dry-mouthed, the Italian attempted to slake his thirst.

'I received a curious visit, inspector, from a Dr Pettigrew, who is interested in mummies and who wishes to purchase one. He hopes to study them and learn the secrets of the ancient Egyptians. A strange coincidence, don't you think?'

'That's a word which doesn't feature in my vocabulary,' replied Higgins.

'Pettigrew appears to be a serious customer, and he has told me that he's no financial problems.'

'Do you have a mummy to sell him?'

'A specimen which is second rate compared with the one that has disappeared, but it's worth trading!'

'Where do you keep it?'

'In a storeroom at the Egyptian Hall.'

'If you proceed with this transaction, Mr Belzoni, please grant me a privilege: to be there when it happens.'

22

Dr Pettigrew arrived looking extremely excited and carrying an enormous suitcase. He followed Belzoni to the storeroom in the Egyptian Hall, eager to see the mummy the Italian had agreed to sell him. The doctor had paid the price without haggling, and was in a hurry to take possession of his new acquisition.

Dr Pettigrew arrived looking extremely excited and carrying an enormous suitcase. He followed Belzoni to the storeroom in the Egyptian Hall, eager to see the mummy the Italian had agreed to sell him. The doctor had paid the price without haggling, and was in a hurry to take possession of his new acquisition.

Outside the door, he found an elegant man of average height, with a perfectly groomed, greying moustache.

'Is this your assistant?' asked Pettigrew.

'I'm Inspector Higgins.'

'The police? We're doing nothing illegal! I'm conducting scientific research, and . . .'

'Have no fear, doctor. Your work interests me greatly, and I would like to be present at this unwrapping.'

As the anatomist's dream was to dissect a mummy in front of as many spectators as possible, he agreed with enthusiasm.

Belzoni opened the door, lit the lamps and led his guests

149

to a small room. The previous evening he had laid the mummy on a rough wooden table.

'It's not in excellent condition,' he lamented.

'On the contrary,' exclaimed Pettigrew, 'I think it's magnificent! Well, gentlemen, we shall study this specimen and verify the theories of the ancients, in particular those of the Greek traveller Herodotus. Did you know that various classes of mummification existed? The poor were simply given a purgative to clean out the intestines and were then immersed in natron. The second-class treatment comprised the use of the same natron and an injection of cedar oil into the anus, followed by the insertion of a cork. The oil was allowed to act, then the cork was removed and the liquefied viscera ran out of the body. To tell the truth, only the first class really interests me. There, the embalmers experimented with techniques, enabling a deceased person to endure for centuries.'

The doctor took a large number of instruments out of his case.

'My task will not be easy,' he remarked. 'The wrappings have hardened, and there's a shell of resin and dried unguents around the body. I must break it.'

With the aid of a hammer and chisel, Pettigrew attacked the mummy. His energy seemed inexhaustible, and it took him an hour of hard work before he was able to free the remains from their shell.

The unwrapping could begin.

'Would you like me to help?' asked Belzoni.

'I wish to check everything myself,' decreed Pettigrew.

With the aid of scissors and knives, he managed to remove the linen bands protecting the head and revealed the face of an old woman, with her hair still intact.

Immediately, the doctor examined the nostrils and the top of the head.

'The first operation was the removal of the brain,' he explained. 'Bronze hooks, bent at the end, were used, following either the nasal or occipital route. The first demanded time and dexterity, for the brain matter had to be removed fragment by fragment, causing as little damage as possible. The length of the hooks proves that the embalmers knew the exact distance between the internal surface of a skull and the nostrils. Gentlemen, let us pay homage to the first anatomists! Thanks to them, Egyptian medicine succeeded in treating many illnesses, and its reputation in the ancient world was justified.'

Imitating the actions of an ancient specialist, Pettigrew used a long rod, explored the nostrils, reached the back of the skull and retrieved some blackish material.

'As I supposed, they filled it with a liquid, which has now solidified, and which was designed to dissolve the remainder of the brain. This mummy underwent a first-class mummification.'

'Was the brain always extracted?' asked Higgins.

'No, inspector. I've seen one case where it remained in situ, but it must have been an exception.'

Pettigrew removed the bandages from the torso.

'And there's my incision! Look at the left flank, gentlemen: with an obsidian or flint knife, the embalmer cut a four-inch-long opening. The wound runs from one of the last ribs to the iliac crest and, sometimes, along the fold of the groin. The hand was slipped inside to withdraw the intestines, the stomach, the liver and the spleen, rarely the kidneys and almost never the bladder. The embalmer also removed the lungs after sectioning the trachea and the oesophagus.'

'These viscera were themselves mummified, using aromatics and natron,' added Belzoni, 'and they were placed in vases.* In later periods, they were merely made into packets, which were placed near the mummy or even inside it.'

Pettigrew removed a small copper plate which hid the incision and, like the embalmer, explored the thorax.

'That's the case here,' he said. 'The abdomen and thoracic cage have been filled with bags containing aromatics and pieces of linen. The interior of the body was purified in this way, and the wound was sewn up again before proceeding to the natron bath. That's an improper term, in my opinion. It was really a matter of covering the body and salting it! Those natron crystals, a natural mixture of sodium chloride, carbonate and sodium sulphate, were extremely effective. Natron was abundant in the Wadi Natron, to the west of the Nile Delta. This salt oasis supplied the raw material essential to embalmers. Its contact dried out the tissues and rendered them immune

---

* They were protected by the four sons of Horus, symbols and guarantors of resurrection.

to decay. The process of decomposition was interrupted, and the mummy need not fear the wear and tear of time.'

'What about the heart?' asked Higgins.

'Most of the time, it was left inside. In the eyes of the ancient Egyptians, it seemed more important than the brain. Was this a symbolic concern or a religious prescription? Research is only in its early stages, inspector, and I shall have to examine hundreds of mummies before deriving definitive conclusions.'

Pettigrew finished the unwrapping. From the final pieces of linen he removed two faience amulets representing the throne of the goddess Isis and a magical knot. 'I shall leave these for you, Mr Belzoni.'

The old lady had been completely laid bare. She must have been very attractive in her youth, and there was no trace of anguish on her face.

'This is an excellent example of the specialists' work,' said the doctor. 'Successful dehydration, satisfactory internal filling and that delicious smell coming from the balms and unguents. I must tell you, a successful mummy smells good! And I would very much like to examine the mummy of a pharaoh, which has received special treatment. You don't have any in stock, do you, Belzoni?'

'Not at the moment.'

'What a pity! Bestir yourself, my friend, and you'll make a fortune, as long as you keep all your finds for me. This experiment has proved to be a positive one, and I'm convinced that our collaboration will be fruitful. I scour the auction rooms and cabinets of curiosities in order to obtain mummies, and your help would be welcome.'

'You shall have it,' promised Belzoni. 'Be wary of counterfeits.'

'There have been attempts to trick me,' conceded Pettigrew. 'But my experience enables me to avoid tricksters.'

Yards of bandages and two shrouds lay at the mummy's feet. Higgins picked one up and covered the old lady, whose nobility touched him.

'You are a gentleman, inspector,' observed the anatomist.

'What have you learned from this examination, Dr Pettigrew?'

'Many details and confirmations. Numerous questions remain unanswered, though, and my efforts aren't at an end!'

'Are you searching for the secret of preserving life?'

The doctor's expression froze. 'No . . . of course not! And I don't understand your question.'

'Don't feign innocence. Beyond the preservation of bodies, the Egyptians were attempting to produce a vessel for the immortality of the soul, were they not?'

'Such considerations are beyond me, Higgins! A mummy is a dried-out body, nothing more.'

'I doubt your sincerity.'

'And I don't permit you to doubt it!'

Irritated, the doctor thrust his instruments back into his leather case and left, looking most offended.

'You annoyed him,' observed Belzoni.

'He'll recover. And you, who knows Egypt: do you think that certain mummies have preserved a form of life?'

'That's absurd, inspector! Don't succumb to the attraction of false mysteries. Corpses are corpses, and they don't come back to life.'

Higgins walked round the old lady, torn from the land of her birth.

'What are you planning to do with this mummy, Mr Belzoni?'

'It will end up in the rubbish, like the others. Once the unwrapping process is over, these poor remains are of no interest to anybody.'

'If I'm not mistaken, they no longer belong to you, and Dr Pettigrew cares nothing for them. So it's possible for me to grant this body a burial place worthy of its rank.'

23

Built in 1812, the Theatre Royal, Drury Lane, stood close to the Royal Opera House and was devoted to the plays of William Shakespeare. These featured the famous actor Peter Bergeray, who created a delicious society scandal by appearing on stage in the form of a mummy, the symbol of death, punishment and the cursed hero. Although swathed in bandages, he managed to move and to speak in an other-worldly voice, terrifying those of a sensitive disposition.

A close friend of George Brummell, who was known as 'Beau' Brummell and prince of the dandies, Bergeray was distressed to witness the fall of this king of fashion following his falling-out with George IV. His valet still brought him his suits to 'clean off the vulgarity of the brand new', but Brummell[*] could no longer repay his gambling debts, and the actor was obliged to break off

[*] He died mad and ruined in 1840.

all contact with him. Displeasing the monarch was an unforgivable fault.

It was now the task of the brilliant Peter Bergeray to bear aloft the standard of the dandies and of London fashion, the reference point for all people of taste. One obligation was vital, because so much dust polluted the London air: changing one's shirt five times a day. Also, one must choose the best tailors, refuse to tolerate any hint of imperfection, demand zeal and competence on the part of one's servants, and always be at the forefront during important receptions and society events. Consequently, Peter Bergeray was constantly playing a part and never tired of the applause.

As usual, the performance had been a triumph. Although divided as regards the appearance of the mummy, the critics recognized Bergeray's incredible audacity and his supreme elegance. No one was better at declaiming Shakespeare, making even the boring passages attractive. The actor showered the hacks with gifts, invited them to dinner, provided them with false revelations about some rival or other and reaped the rewards of his strategy.

There was just one black spot on the horizon: women. A horde of young beauties and mature ladies continually pursued him. Escaping from them without vexing them and losing their admiration demanded exhausting efforts.

Someone knocked at the door of his dressing room.

'It's the director.'

'Come in.'

The young, brown-haired man was eager to guarantee

his hero's satisfaction. Before going to a dinner at which several important individuals would be present, the actor must make himself look beautiful again.

'Some admirers wish to congratulate you.'

'Not now.'

'They insist, and claim to have important information to give you.'

'How many are there?'

'A man and a woman.'

'Elegant?'

'Presentable.'

Bergeray let out a sigh. 'Pass me my indoor jacket, will you, and tell them that I shall grant them two minutes.'

Delighted to serve this theatrical genius, the director bowed to his every desire.

When the couple appeared, Peter Bergeray leaped to his feet in a state of panic. And this time he was not acting. 'Belzoni! Are you . . . are you well?'

'That is hardly Shakespeare,' commented Sarah, an aggressive glint in her eyes. 'Is that the best you could come up with?'

The size of the Titan of Padua and his Irish wife terrified the actor. With a single slap, that hag could knock him over. And how could he enchant his public with a swollen cheek?

'Let's sit down and enjoy a glass of port,' he suggested, his voice trembling.

'We've come to talk business,' stated Sarah. 'You play

a mummy admirably well, Bergeray, but you forget to pay your debts.'

'I don't know what you're talking about, dear lady.'

'You acquired the wrappings which covered the face of *my* mummy,' Belzoni reminded him, irritated. 'Pieces of linen of exceptional quality. You know the price, and I demand settlement.'

'You have the wrong buyer . . . I don't remember this transaction.'

'My husband can rally a dozen burly men,' Sarah reminded him with a smile. 'They'll enjoy dismembering a runt, a liar and a thief.'

'Don't touch me!' squeaked the actor, flattening himself against his dressing room wall.

'People of quality should be able to reach an understanding.'

'Very well, yes, I bought those bandages!'

'And you haven't paid for them,' the Irishwoman reminded him fiercely.

'Understood, understood!'

'We're making progress,' commented Belzoni, whose enraged bull expression would have put a Roman legion to flight.

'Listen, I'm a little short of funds at the moment.'

'You, short of funds?' Sarah was astonished.

'Don't trust appearances, dear lady! An actor of my stature has to lead an expensive lifestyle. You cannot imagine the extent of my expenses: clothes, dinners, receptions and goodness knows what else! I live from one day

159

to the next and fill my purse, which constantly empties itself.'

'Do you take us for imbeciles?' roared the Irish-woman.

'I can give you proof! An artiste's life is not like a tranquil lake. Success isn't always accompanied by wealth, and art is often a long way from money. As a lover of antiquities you should understand me, Mr Belzoni. You and I care only for artistic expression, do we not?'

'We shall give you time to pay,' decided Sarah. 'Shall we say . . . one month?'

Bergeray looked down. 'That's not long enough!'

The Titan of Padua cracked his fingers. 'What did you say?'

'A month – perfect!'

'Surviving or not surviving can sometimes depend on a detail,' said Sarah, 'so I would avoid breaking your promise, Mr Bergeray.'

'Have no fear.'

The actor lit a pipe engraved with hieroglyphs. Belzoni's eyes widened.

'Who sold you that?'

'A traveller returning from Egypt. According to him, it's a real treasure dating from ancient times.'

Belzoni burst out laughing. 'It's a coarse fake, manu-factured by the peasants! If you wish to avoid ridicule, break that pipe into a thousand pieces. And don't forget to keep your promise.'

Once the couple had left, the actor changed his shirt for the fifth time.

The mummy was stretched out on a granite bed, reminiscent of the one used by the embalmers. The rescuer covered it with natron crystals, to prevent any degradation due to the dampness of the crypt. For seventy days, the Osiran body would undergo a ritual period of regeneration during which time the star Orion was not visible in the southern sky. When it reappeared, it would once again regularize the movement of the decans, causing the annual Nile flood, which brought fertility, and the resurrection of Osiris.

This mummy was a masterpiece, triumphing over death. Its brain had not been destroyed, its heart remained intact and the vital humours continued to circulate. Firmly linked to the body, the head maintained the cohesion of the many aspects of its being.

'It will never be separated from you,' declared the rescuer, speaking an ancient ritual incantation. 'You will know a new life, and the parts of your body will not be scattered.'

The rescuer kissed the mummy's left ear to prevent death from entering it. The left shoulder and eye had to be similarly protected, as these were potential entrances for the thief of life, and incessant attacks must be repelled.

This task took up a great deal of the rescuer's time. By taking the mummy from the pathologist, the clergyman and the old aristocrat, the worst had been averted. But it was a fleeting, fragile success, for the Osiran body could not long resist the attacks of a world in which nothing was sacred. As soon as relative stability had been achieved, the saviour would set off in search of the protective elements without which the mummy would be condemned to destruction.

Willingly or by force, the profaners must give back what they had taken.

24

Dressed in a coarse jacket and serge trousers, with a workman's cap on his head, Inspector Higgins was unrecognizable. Leaving the prosperous West End and venturing into the industrial area of the East End meant that he must take certain precautions. If the Tsar of all the Russians had not spotted any poor people in London when he visited in 1814, it was only because the government had avoided showing him the capital's poverty-stricken districts.

Although it could not escape the fog, the West End enjoyed several advantages: green spaces, cleanliness and tranquillity. The East End was a noisy world, seething with humble folk, and the majority of the streets never saw a refuse collector or a policeman. Here, people worked hard, earned little, suffered pollution from the factories and breathed in the smells emanating from tanneries, vinegar works and match factories, where phosphorus was used.

The district of Whitechapel was one of the most

deprived of all. Made up of a labyrinth of narrow streets and courts which the sun never reached, it housed a labouring population battling with poverty, and was a hotbed of anti-establishment figures, anarchists and social-ists who wished to be rid of the government. The author-ities were unaware of the danger, convinced that the quest for food would be enough to occupy this rabble.

Sugar refineries and small clothing workshops employed the majority of the workers in Whitechapel, who were forced to live in hovels. Polish and Russian Jews manufactured garments and shoes and maintained a meat market supplied by their ritual abattoirs, not far from the hay market. Bullocks and horses pulled heavy carts, and pigs cleaned up the narrow streets by eating the rubbish.

Higgins walked past tailors' shops surmounted by brick dwellings. He stopped next to a costermonger, whose wares were spread out on a cart that he pulled himself. His fruit, vegetables, slices of coconut, herrings, dried cod, shellfish and game were not within reach of every purse. But the fellow knew how to make himself respected, and thieves dared not approach him for fear of being beaten up.

Higgins bought a herring and a piece of bread.

'You're perfect, inspector. I almost didn't recognize you.'

'Have you located Tasquinio?'

'That man is like an eel! He never stops moving, but I've found his lair, a tumbledown shack a short distance from here, at the end of a blind alley. Foul-smelling smoke emanates from it, and nobody knows what he's brewing up. There's an illegible sign above the door.'

'How does he make a living?'

'He delivers packages to all kinds of people, in the West End as well as the East End. Some colleagues followed him.'

As he did not trust uniformed police officers, who were too visible and corrupt, Higgins had set up his own network, spearheaded by the costermongers. They were all over London and knew how to observe and gather precious information.

'Does Tasquinio have a family?'

'Apparently not.'

'Any friends?'

'Just work contacts and comrades from the pub. In my opinion, he's a brutal and dangerous man. Don't cross swords with him, inspector.'

A gossip had no hesitation in interrupting the two men. Having decided to tell the trader all her troubles, she started reminiscing about her early childhood.

Higgins walked away and soon found the blind alley. A stray dog licked his hand. He gave it the fish and the bread.

The place seemed abandoned, with the doors and windows of the hovels bricked up. A sickening odour assailed his nostrils.

Why had Paul Tasquinio taken an interest in Belzoni's mummy, and why had he bought the expensive linen wrappings? The man's lifestyle hardly seemed that of a collector of antiquities.

Rain began to fall, and a tomcat with torn ears chased away a rival.

Higgins approached Tasquinio's lair. The door seemed flimsy, and it did not resist a vigorous push.

The inspector accustomed his eyes to the half-light.

He was standing in a large room, with a properly made bed, a table and two chairs, wardrobes, large vats, walls blackened by smoke, and a vast fireplace where the embers were dying down.

As Higgins headed towards a wardrobe, the point of a knife sank into his back.

'Are you looking for something, my lad?'

'No, somebody: Paul Tasquinio.'

'You'll wish you hadn't found him! When I catch thieves, I get rid of them.'

'What about police inspectors?'

The knife-tip edged away.

'Do you think you can save yourself just like that?'

'My name is Higgins, and I'm investigating three murders that you may have committed, since you were present at the unwrapping of Belzoni's mummy.'

'By all the gods of hell, who are you?'

'I've just told you: Inspector Higgins.'

'Then you are armed!'

'No.'

'Impossible! I must search you. If you move, I'll skewer you!'

Higgins remained motionless.

'An unarmed police officer in Whitechapel . . . that doesn't hold water! Turn round.'

With a swift, precise movement, Higgins struck Tasquinio's wrist with the edge of his right hand, forcing him to drop his weapon. With his left, the inspector caught the knife as it fell and used it to threaten the suspect.

'Calm down, friend.'

'How . . . how did you do that?'

'It's a matter of training. Why did you kill a clergyman, a nobleman and a pathologist?'

Paul Tasquinio's coarse face turned purple. 'You're talking nonsense, inspector!'

'Let's sit down and start at the beginning. Whatever you do, don't attempt to run away. The blow to the wrist was just an appetizer, and I assume you value your legs.'

Imagining his bones being broken terrified Tasquinio. He sat down opposite this calm-looking policeman who knew only too well how to fight. Ten more like him, and the troublemakers of Whitechapel would leave the district.

'Paul Tasquinio: is that your real name?'

'My mother was from Naples. She had a rather diverse clientele, so she didn't know the identity of my father.'

'What's your profession?'

'I deliver meat.'

'In Whitechapel?'

'Not only here . . . Sometimes I venture into other districts.'

'To the West End?'

'If the occasion presents itself.'

Higgins lit a large candle. It lit up Tasquinio's face. 'What are these vats for, Tasquinio?'

'For boiling quarters of beef and pork.'

'Who are your suppliers?'

The fellow looked embarrassed. 'It's a little . . . confidential.'

'No secrets between us! A lack of trust would upset me.'

'You know, inspector, life is very hard. Knowing how to get by sometimes leads one to leave the path of strict legality. Otherwise you're liable to die of hunger!'

'I'm only interested in murders.'

'I haven't committed any!'

'In that case, tell me about your little trade.'

Paul Tasquinio bowed his head. 'I get on well with the man who runs the abattoir. He sells me the second-choice meat at the price of the third, without declaring the transactions, and I sell the second choice at the price of the first. Do you follow me?'

'Everyone benefits, so it seems.'

'We get by . . . You're not going to denounce us, are you?'

'Did you steal and hide Belzoni's mummy?'

Paul Tasquinio choked. 'Are you joking?'

'Shall we open these cupboards?'

'They contain my stocks and . . .'

'Open them,' insisted the inspector.

They contained packages, carefully tied up with string. Labels indicated the names and addresses of the recipients. Higgins took his time checking: none of them had been spectators at the unwrapping.

'Drop of gin, inspector? I've got some good stuff.'

The two men sat down again, and Tasquinio filled two glasses.

'Your interest in mummies surprises me', admitted Higgins.

'Opportunity makes the thief! One of my customers gave me a ticket, as that kind of display terrified him. It amused me, though, and I had an idea: I could put up my prices by wrapping the luxury packages in Egyptian linen. Shrewd, eh?'

'So you've disposed of your acquisition, then?'

'Not yet. I shall use it for the end-of-year celebrations. My rich middle-class customers in the West End will be thrilled! You have to have imagination when you're in business. Tell me, did you mention a clergyman?'

'I did.'

'Well, there was one, when Belzoni and his doctor unwrapped the mummy. And that preacher was furious! He was brandishing a Bible, threatening them with demons, and he wanted to burn the old Egyptian's body. Belzoni manhandled him to the back of the room, threatening to break him in two if he didn't calm down.'

'Interesting,' commented the inspector, taking notes in his black book.

'And the confrontation was repeated at the end of the

spectacle! The clergyman tried to stab the mummy with a knife, but Belzoni caught him by the arm. It was obvious they hated each other. That mad clergyman was no match for the giant. One punch would have burst his head open!'

'This gin of yours is excellent.'

'Will you . . . will you allow me to stay at liberty?'

'I'm looking for a mummy and a murderer. Since you're neither of those things, I have no reason to arrest you. Ah! One last detail: have you met a man called Littlewood?'

Paul Tasquinio frowned. 'Never heard of him.'

'So much the better for you. Avoid crossing his path.'

There was no denying the success of the exhibition. The public continued to flood into the Egyptian Hall and enthuse about the drawings of the bas-reliefs from the tomb in the Valley of the Kings and the items brought back by Belzoni. The alabaster sarcophagus drew everyone's attention, and visitors wondered if the strange scenes adorning this funerary vessel concealed the secrets of resurrection and eternal life.

The price of tickets to the exhibition ensured that the Belzonis had sufficient to live on, and the regular income enabled Sarah to maintain her status by paying her servants properly. But the surprise effect would not last for ever, and they must prepare for the future by selling the treasures they had wrested from the sands of Egypt.

By dint of perseverance, the Italian had finally aroused the interest of one of the administrators of the British Museum, who was in charge of purchasing antiquities.

And he granted him the immense privilege of honouring his invitation to visit the exhibition after hours.

Professor John Smith, a Cambridge graduate, was small, portly and bad-tempered. An expert in Greek vases, he collected decorations and coveted a better post more commensurate with his skills, which were insufficiently recognized.

Sarah Belzoni had lit the room skilfully, making the most of the smallest piece and emphasizing the sarcophagus.

'Call me professor. We mustn't waste any time; I've had a tiring day and I'd like to return home as quickly as possible.'

Belzoni decided not to tell him all about his exploits.

'It seems you have an exceptional monument in your possession. Show it to me.'

The administrator ignored the drawings, the statuettes and the other remains. Irritably, he followed the Titan of Padua to the foot of the alabaster sarcophagus, which was lit from inside.

The spectacle was magical, as if the pharaoh's soul inhabited this place, so far from his native land. Belzoni could almost feel the atmosphere of the immense tomb in the Valley of the Kings whose entrance he had found. Suddenly, the centuries were wiped away and the past came back to life.

'Is that it?' asked John Smith.

'This is one of the masterpieces of ancient Egyptian art,' declared Belzoni. 'In removing it from the tomb, I had the idea of offering England a priceless treasure. Only the British Museum is worthy of housing it.'

'Housing what?'

'This . . . this marvel!'

'What marvel?'

'Are you not dazzled by this finely decorated sarcophagus?' demanded Sarah in astonishment.

'This large block of badly cut stone doesn't correspond to the canons of Greek art, which is the sole reference for beauty.'

'Look at it closely, I beg of you!' insisted Belzoni. 'This incomparable piece contained the mummy of a great pharaoh, and its inscriptions certainly conceal numerous secrets. As soon as Thomas Young has deciphered hieroglyphs, every scholar will rush to this sarcophagus, and visitors to the British Museum will admire it constantly.'

'A great institution such as ours can invest only in certainties. Burdening ourselves with exotic items would make us objects of ridicule.'

'You have before you a veritable prodigy of Egyptian art,' said Belzoni. 'I had a hard struggle bringing it back to London.'

'Your past does not interest me, dear sir, and you have no authority in art or archaeology.'

'By purchasing this masterpiece, you will honour the kingdom!'

'Do you venture to dictate my conduct? I'm an expert, and I know the value of antique items. Your showy exhibition doesn't move me, and there's nothing attractive about this enormous, extremely invasive alabaster object. What coarseness, in comparison with an elegant Greek vase!'

The specialist walked round Seti I's sarcophagus. 'How much do you want for it?'

The Italian whispered an amount.

For interminable seconds, time was suspended. In a state of shock, the British Museum's administrator had difficulty recovering his composure. 'I detest jokes, Belzoni. You may think yourself amusing, but you'll regret it! My report will be extremely negative, and the British Museum will never pay out a single penny to encumber itself with this horror. I'm sorry to have met you.'

Without bothering to acknowledge Sarah, Smith strode out of the Egyptian Hall.

Fists clenched, the giant almost went after him to teach him a lesson, but his wife held him back.

'Stupidity runs the world, Giovanni, and we cannot change that.'

'This sarcophagus must enter the British Museum, and nowhere else! My reputation is at stake.'

'We shall find someone else to approach,' promised Sarah.

The pub was smoky. Patrons drank pints of beer and gin, listened to songs, some of which exceeded the limits of decency, and on Saturday evening the workers of Whitechapel received their pay. Prostitutes and bandits of every kind frequented the establishment, where no representative of the forces of law and order would have dared show his face, on pain of being beaten up.

Here, Littlewood met the principal figures in the local underworld and recruited henchmen who were capable of training his troops. Wearing a perfectly fitting wig and a false beard, he looked like a lord of the slums and a feared and respected gang leader. Many of his employees did not know that they were preparing the way for revolution.

The coachman Littlewood wanted to see was sitting at a table with an enterprising brunette.

'The summer sun will burn the paving stones,' declared the bearded man.

The coachman looked up. 'And the horses won't run away,' he responded.

'Happy to meet you, friend! The young lady can wait for you in her room upstairs.'

The brunette smiled and left. The money paid to her in return for her favours would incline her to wait.

'So you're the one who wanted information about the royal carriages?'

'Here's your reward,' said Littlewood, slipping a sheaf of banknotes into the coachman's pocket. 'And you'll have more if you give me good information.'

The coachman described King George IV's horses and carriages.

'That's not much.'

'It's all I know.'

'You're married with two sons,' said Littlewood. 'You deceive your wife and you drink. She and I would both be upset to hear that your elder son had had an accident.'

The coachman paled. 'Are you threatening me?'

The bearded man was terrifyingly cold.

'What do you want to know?'

'Get me a timetable of George IV's movements.'

'Only the steward of the royal stables knows that!'

'Is he incorruptible?'

'That depends. He plays a little too much billiards, and often loses.'

'I'll obtain the necessary money for you, and you'll repay his debts in return for the information.'

'I'll try . . .'

'You'll succeed.'

The coachman's trembling knees knocked together. 'Yes, yes, I'll succeed!'

'You'll be watched, friend. If you were to have the stupid idea of selling me to the police, you'll be a dead man.'

'You can rely on my silence!'

'Our collaboration promises to be fruitful, and you'll not regret having met me.'

The coachman swallowed hard, emptied his tankard of beer and dared to ask the question that tormented him. 'Do you . . . do you intend to attack the king?'

'I? Not at all!'

'Then why do you demand this sort of information?'

'Because I'm a lover of horses. Our dear sovereign

possesses some magnificent specimens, and I intend to seize one during one of his stops. While the animals are resting, surveillance will be relaxed, and nobody would imagine such a plan.'

'You have a point there,' admitted the coachman.

26

Since the start of the nineteenth century, London, the country's principal port, had witnessed the construction of docks which had become vital for the development of trade and the security of goods. West India Docks, Surrey Commercial Docks, London Docks and East India Docks formed a string of warehouses through which all the world's riches passed. These tall brick buildings loomed over the line of quays.

Nearly a hundred thousand labourers and workmen toiled at the docks, loading and unloading boats from all four corners of the British Empire. An army of Customs officials examined the products and levied taxes before the tobacco, tea, wines, spices, furs and other luxuries were stored in warehouses separated by towers. Nobody paid any attention to the stink rising from the open-air sewer of the Thames, nor to the atmosphere filled with smells from tanneries and breweries, the odours of burning tobacco, chocolate, fish and other substances, some more easily identifiable than others.

Everyone talked loudly, the ships' hulls bumped against the quayside, carpenters and coopers made their tools sing, and London grew rich, thanks to the labour of these battalions of workers, whose kingdom was the docks.

Among the casual or permanent dock labourers were a number of unemployed workmen and ex-soldiers, and also servants who had been dismissed and even young middle-class men running away from their families. This ill-assorted population was sensitive to the speeches of agitators like Littlewood, though they dared not rebel openly against the authorities.

Donning the dress and manner of a trader, Higgins spoke to a blacksmith who was repairing a ship's chain. The man loved his job, and he was one of Higgins's best informants.

'Out hunting, inspector?'

'I'm looking for a woman called Kristin Sadly.'

'Ah, the plump, overexcitable woman! If you were to put her in the dark for a while, that might calm her down. Most of her employees don't last a week. She's an exploiter, a yelling tyrant, a fearsome shrew and the queen of liars! There must be some justice in the world, if she's about to have you on her back. Has she killed someone?'

'Possibly.'

'That wouldn't surprise me! Kristin Sadly can't stand anyone contradicting her, and she'll do anything to develop her paper mill. She's already eliminated several competitors and bought out some small businesses very cheaply, ruining their owners in the process. That predatory female has no morals and never keeps her word. Be wary of her, inspector. She's an expert in dirty tricks!'

'Where can I find her?'

'Walk along the West India Docks, follow the quayside, go past the spice warehouse and you'll be there. And . . . good luck!'

Higgins walked along at a brisk pace. Watchful and alert, he slipped between dock workers, bales, chests and assorted packages. The sound of a shrill voice told him that he had arrived.

A small, fat woman was insulting a workman whom she had accused of spoiling a ream of coarse paper. The unfortunate man was sacked on the spot and threatened with terrible punishments.

Her hair impeccably styled, and wearing earrings that resembled two pigeons' eggs, the owner then began berating two delivery men who were too slow for her taste.

Higgins approached. 'Mrs Sadly, I presume.'

Irritated, she wheeled round and glared at the intruder. 'And who may you be? Oh, I see! I see suppliers late in the afternoon. Try to offer me something good and inexpensive, or you may as well stay at home. I have no time to waste!'

'I've not come to offer you anything, only to ask you some questions.'

'Questions? How ill-mannered! And in what capacity?'

'The capacity of police inspector.'

Kristin Sadly's aggression dwindled. 'The police ... But everything is in order!'

'Could we converse somewhere quiet?'

The fat woman's murderous look did not bother Higgins. 'Is it urgent?'

'Rather.'

'Follow me. What's your name?'

'Inspector Higgins.'

Kristin Sadly led her guest through the vast paper mill, where tons of rags were stored. Around fifty workers were bustling around, and at the sight of the owner they all stopped talking. One word out of place, and they would be shown the door.

There was nothing attractive about Kristin Sadly's office; just piles of invoices and drawings on the walls, depicting the owner in triumph. She never tired of looking at herself. The owner of the paper mill sat down in a leather armchair and glared at Higgins.

'Let me guess, inspector. Was it that old crook Holmes who denounced me? Yes, it must have been him! He's on the verge of going out of business, and he's trying to bring me down by talking nonsense! But he's bound to fail, because my accounts are in order! And I would be happy to buy up what's left!'

'Forget about Holmes, madam.'

'Are you saying that crook is innocent?'

'I don't know him.'

Kristin Sadly clenched her fists. 'Then why are you bothering me?'

'Because you've stolen a mummy, have you not?'

The businesswoman's eyes widened. 'You're quite mad!'

'Did you not purchase the linen shroud from a magnificent mummy that Belzoni unwrapped in front of an invited audience?'

The mill owner threw him a disdainful look. 'Is that a crime?'

'Your interest in this strange relic intrigues me.'

'Each unto his own, inspector! The spectacle amused me, and I wanted to keep a souvenir of it. I've added the shroud to my collection of ancient objects, and I hope to acquire others. And now it's my turn to be surprised: what's the real reason for your visit?'

'Being present at the unwrapping of a mummy is no ordinary experience. Do you remember any notable incidents?'

Kristin Sadly thought at length. 'A priest shouted curses, and Belzoni threw him out . . . An old aristocrat tried to cause a disturbance, and some elegant ladies fainted. Nothing of any consequence! The rich have oversensitive hearts. That mummy is nothing but dried-out flesh.'

'Are you sure about that?'

'Do you mock me, inspector?'

'The doctor who assisted Belzoni, the aristocrat and the clergyman were all murdered.'

The plump woman started. 'Murdered . . . By whom?'

'I shall succeed in finding that out. Did you notice any suspects?'

'No, truly I did not! I was interested only in the mummy.'

'Did the price of the shroud strike you as excessive?'

'I approached Belzoni discreetly and didn't haggle. Such an opportunity doesn't arise every day! I whispered in his ear, "I shall pay for it and take it away with me" and the deal was done.'

'And you didn't know any of the three victims?'

'None! I don't move in such circles.'

'And Belzoni?'

'I had never met him before and I have no intention of seeing him again. I don't like the man.'

'What about Littlewood? Do you like him?'

'Who's that?'

'One of the enthusiasts who was present at the unwrapping of the mummy,' ventured Higgins.

'There were so many people there! Will that be all, inspector?'

'For the time being, yes.'

'Your horrible crimes don't concern me and I've nothing else to tell you. I do my job, and you do yours.'

'Good day, madam.'

As he walked through the mill, Higgins noticed a heap of brown rags. 'I didn't know those sorts of materials were used,' he said to a foreman.

'They're liable to produce a poor-quality, brownish

paper,' conceded the specialist. 'But all the same, we're going to try to obtain something decent.'

Watched in fury by Kristin Sadly, Higgins left the paper mill.

27

Giovanni Battista Belzoni was furious. Some despicable newspapers were continuing to attribute his discoveries and research to other travellers, and certain writers, notably the French, did not even mention his name! Faced with so much injustice and ingratitude, the giant felt shaken. His fabulous discoveries in Upper Egypt had demanded a great deal of effort and courage. And now, because of ignorant people or liars, his adventures were being reduced to nothing! Fortunately, his book, which was an undeniable success, proclaimed the truth. But how much longer was it going to take to establish it all over Europe and re-establish his reputation?

He regretted having written letters of protest to highly placed individuals, such as the Comte de Forbin. Instead of helping him, the French scholar had encouraged journalists to sully the Italian archaeologist's reputation and deny his merits.

He opened a chest containing terracotta and faience

figurines, small alabaster vases with lids in the form of a lion, a falcon, a monkey and a jackal, items of crockery, and gold leaf beaten wafer-thin. These little treasures came from Theban tombs which he had explored. Sarah sold them to rich aristocrats, who were delighted to acquire these marvels from a magical land. With great effort, the young woman managed to persuade those who were hesitant, and obtained sizeable sums of money, which were vital in order to maintain the Belzoni household.

There was still the masterpiece, the alabaster sarcophagus. To him alone, it was worth a fortune. Despite his first failure, the Italian persisted: such a monument must have pride of place in the British Museum, where it would ensure its discoverer's fame. Admittedly, it was a difficult task, but had the Titan of Padua not transported an obelisk and a colossal head, entered the pyramid of Khephren and dug through the mountain of sand blocking access to the temple of Abu Simbel? He refused to give in to pessimism and would continue to toil until he obtained satisfaction. All the curators and administrators of the British Museum could not be as stupid as that man John Smith!

The difficulty lay in forming solid relationships in the world of scholars who did not recognize the extent of the work Belzoni had achieved. But Sarah believed in her husband and his destiny and did not give up. No fortress was impregnable.

Dressed in magnificent orange livery, the servant James

Curtain ventured to disturb his employer. 'A man by the name of Carmick wishes to see you. The fellow is most unpleasant and extremely self-important.'

'Take him to the Egyptian drawing room. I shall be there in a moment.'

Disdainfully, the politician refused the port which Curtain brought him. He shrugged his shoulders irritably as he looked at the drawings hung on the wall, recalling the landscapes of the Theban region which had enchanted Belzoni.

'I detest waiting,' he raged when the Italian joined him. 'You cannot imagine how busy I am!'

'I too was extremely busy and had to interrupt what I was doing. We had not arranged a meeting, as I recall.'

Francis Carmick looked daggers at his host. 'Don't attempt to be haughty with me, Belzoni, or you'll regret it! I'm an important man, and you . . . you . . .'

'And I?'

'I warned you, and you've taken no account of my warnings!'

The giant sat down and lit his pipe. 'Doesn't a gentleman retain his composure in all circumstances, Mr Carmick?'

'You're not a gentleman, Belzoni, and I don't give you permission to lecture me! At least keep your promises.'

'In what respect?'

'I demand to know every detail of the process of mummification.'

'Why?'

187

'That doesn't concern you! You would be extremely unwise to ignore this request. I have numerous connections and I can destroy your career and your reputation.'

The Italian drew on his pipe. 'One good turn deserves another,' he declared, raising his eyes to the heavens.

'What does that mean?'

'I wish to meet a curator or an administrator from the British Museum who appreciates Egyptian art.'

'That's possible.'

'In exchange, I'll offer you the name of the leading specialist in mummies.'

Francis Carmick scrawled a name on a visiting card. 'Go and see this scholar and tell him I sent you. He'll treat you as a friend.'

'Dr Thomas Pettigrew, the distinguished anatomist, is dedicated to the study of mummification,' revealed Belzoni. 'He'll tell you what you wish to know.'

'A fine harvest!' announced Sarah, displaying a sheaf of banknotes. 'A duchess and two baronesses were very taken with my little faience figurines. At teatime they can tell their insanely jealous friends that they risked their lives entering Egyptian tombs filled with evil spirits, which might slide under a lady's skirts. When I described how you extracted these treasures from the chests of menacing mummies, they almost fainted! You are a hero, my Giovanni. Even hell and the dead cannot resist you.'

She set down the banknotes, and they embraced like two young lovers.

'I haven't been wasting my time,' he revealed. 'Thanks to a visit from Carmick, the doors of the British Museum are about to open.'

'Let's celebrate with champagne!'

They were finishing off the bottle when Curtain announced the arrival of a high-society lady.

'A new buyer?' hoped Belzoni's wife brightly.

The young woman was breathtakingly beautiful. Her pale rose-pink gown, created by a couturier on Regent Street, hinted at a perfect body.

Belzoni coughed.

'My darling, allow me to present Lady Suzanna. We met as I was coming out of the Travellers' Club.'

Sarah's gaiety evaporated. 'Were you not present when the mummy was unwrapped?'

'Indeed, Mrs Belzoni.'

'Do you wish to acquire Egyptian objects?'

'That's not the purpose of my visit.'

'Ah . . . So what do you want?'

'Your husband's help.'

The Irishwoman's expression grew strained. 'Kindly explain.'

'Inspector Higgins told us about a murder case and the disappearance of the magnificent mummy, which almost came back to life before our eyes. If I read his thoughts correctly, he believes it is guilty of the murders.'

'That's completely insane!'

'Perhaps, Mrs Belzoni, but I've decided to take an interest in this case and to conduct my own enquiries.'

'In what capacity?'

'I'm a barrister and fond of difficult cases. Either Inspector Higgins was mocking me and I shall laugh at my own naivety, or I shall defend this mummy. A human being, even one which is several hundred years old, must be protected from injustice.'

'Lady Suzanna, your actions seem hardly rational to me. And I wasn't aware that women were permitted to exercise such a profession.'

'I didn't study in England. Nevertheless, my skills have been recognized by the law courts in London. And I don't have to tell you, Mrs Belzoni, as a great traveller and a specialist in the East, that there are many bizarre and unexplained phenomena which elude the control of reason and science.'

The pretty brunette had scored a point.

'What do you expect of my husband?'

'The initial results of my investigation surprised me. I believe that I must pass them on to Inspector Higgins and I don't know how to contact him. Would Mr Belzoni be kind enough to inform me?'

'I'm sorry, Lady Suzanna, but I don't know the police officer's address.'

'If you ask the porter at the Travellers' Club, he'll tell you. He'll not respond to a woman.'

Sarah nodded.

'My carriage will take you to the club and bring you

back home,' proposed the lawyer. 'Forgive me for inconveniencing you in this way, but you would be doing me a great service.'

The giant looked at his wife, who nodded her approval. 'Lead on, Lady Suzanna.'

28

In the little gardens of Spitalfields, Huguenots had planted mulberry trees to enable them to raise silkworms, and the area was packed with weaving workshops and haberdashers; the silk trade was at its height. Ordinary folk lived a little better than those in Whitechapel, and the majority were respectably dressed. They went to second-hand clothes dealers and bought clothes that had belonged to aristocrats and were resold at good prices. The women-folk were happy to wear faded hats that society ladies no longer wanted.

Higgins waited until the seller of second- and third-hand coats had concluded a sale. The dimly lit shop was filled with old clothes. The purchaser left, delighted to be able to parade in a lord's threadbare, cast-off coat.

'Out hunting, inspector?' asked the dealer.

'Has the district been quiet lately?'

'People are restless and complain, and accuse the

government of putting up prices. The atmosphere is deteriorating.'

'Do you know a man called Henry Cranmer?'

'He owns a dozen or so workshops and as many shops. He's an important man in Spitalfields, a hard worker and a hard man in business.'

'Does he have any family?'

'He's divorced, without children. Prostitutes are sufficient for him.'

'Any problems with the authorities?'

'No, he's straight as a die, or at least he appears to be. Here, people respect him. He pays his employees well, and nobody complains about him. Personally, I can't stand him because he has a big mouth and is full of himself. That man has only one passion: money. I'm sure he must have sold his parents for a penny! As I see it, a good half of his business is conducted under the counter. He bribes the police and officials, and the district turns a blind eye. He lives in the two-storey house at the end of the street.'

Higgins thanked his informant and went to Cranmer's house. A manservant with brutish features greeted him. 'Can I help you, sir?'

'I would like to see your employer.'

'He's at lunch. And when he's eating his lunch, nobody disturbs him.'

'I'll wait until he's finished.'

'After lunch, he goes off to work. And when he's working, nobody disturbs him either.'

'So it's impossible to get near him?'

193

'My employer talks to men he knows. He keeps his distance from strangers.'

'Isn't this an opportunity to get to know one?'

The brute seized a club hanging from his belt. 'Do you want a taste of my stick?'

'I wouldn't start hostilities if I were you. I shall summon your employer to the police station, and if he doesn't arrive we'll come and fetch him. Goodbye.'

'Hey, wait a minute. Don't go . . . ! So, you're . . .'

'Inspector Higgins.'

'Don't move. I'll be back.'

The servant charged up a flight of stairs, four at a time, consulted his employer and hurtled back down.

'Mr Cranmer will see you in the drawing room. He'll join you for coffee.'

The house was a little museum, filled with pastels, seascapes and vaguely antique bronzes, some of which must be fakes. Despite the quality of his clothes, the businessman appeared poorly dressed, as if no garment could adapt to the shape of his body.

'I'm Henry Cranmer. You wished to see me?'

'I did.'

'I suppose someone has denounced me? My competitors cannot bear my success. They hope for large profits without doing any work, whereas I'm always on-site and I sleep for only four hours a night. The results are there for all to see, and I congratulate myself on them.'

'This is not a question of professional jealousy, Mr Cranmer.'

The industrialist shrugged. 'In that case, what's the reason for your visit?'

'A triple murder.'

Cranmer blinked. 'Are you serious?'

'Unfortunately I am.'

'I'm a cloth merchant, inspector, not a criminal!'

'I'm not accusing you, Mr Cranmer.'

The businessman let out a sigh of relief. 'Let's sit down and enjoy this excellent coffee. You won't drink any better in the whole of London.'

Higgins was lucky; he was allergic to tea. At least this beverage wouldn't make him sick.

'Exceptional flavour,' he agreed.

'The coffee merchant is a friend, and he spoils me. Three victims, you were saying?'

'An old aristocrat, a clergyman and a pathologist.'

The merchant with the Asian features tutted and plunged into his memories.

'How strange; you remind me of a curious event! I was recently present at an exceptional spectacle, the unwrapping of a mummy brought back from Egypt by Belzoni, the organizer of a highly successful exhibition. The advertisement intrigued me, and I procured a ticket. It was a fabulous moment, believe me! As that old Egyptian appeared, the audience thought they were witnessing a resurrection. The man revealed seemed alive! Admirers bought wrappings, and I took part in the game. Shouldn't a specialist in fabrics be interested in such remains? Despite the high price, I acquired some linen bandages covered in strange signs, which had wrapped the feet. They won't disgrace my collection of antiquities. Belzoni praised the skills of his assistant, a pathologist whose name I've forgotten. And two incidents occurred, disturbing this surprising ceremony: the intervention of a hysterical clergyman, and then a scene caused by a sarcastic old aristocrat. Those two detested the mummy and promised it a thousand misfortunes! Were they in any way connected with the murders?'

'They are the three victims,' confirmed Higgins. 'And your testimony is most interesting.'

'A strange affair! A unique entertainment, which ended in a frightful manner.'

'Any other memories, Mr Cranmer?'

The businessman reflected. 'No, nothing significant. To tell the truth, we were all uneasy. We'd expected to see a desiccated, repulsively ugly corpse, not that magnificent mummy, which was far more evocative of life than of death.'

'It's disappeared,' revealed Higgins. 'Do you have any idea where it might be?'

'Me? Indeed not!'

'So that superb collector's piece did not attract your attention?'

'Not to the point where I would think of stealing it, inspector. Would you like to search my house to check that the mummy isn't here?'

'That would be most kind of you.'

196

'Do you suspect this mummy of having perpetrated a sort of . . . curse?'

'At this point in my investigation, I'm not ruling anything out.'

'Follow me.'

Henry Cranmer seemed proud of showing Higgins the many rooms in his house, from the cellar to the attic. They were overloaded with furniture, pottery and paintings.

But there was no trace of the mummy.

Back in the drawing room, the owner of the house offered his guest some Scotch whisky, which he reserved for enlightened enthusiasts.

'This is a marvel,' commented Higgins. 'When you were at Belzoni's ceremony, did you encounter a man called Littlewood?'

'What does he look like?'

'I don't know. Was his name spoken in your presence?'

'I don't think so, inspector. In any event, he's not one of my suppliers or one of my major clients. Is he the principal suspect?'

'It's impossible for me to give you an answer, Mr Cranmer.'

'I understand, I understand!'

A look of intensity came into Cranmer's eyes.

'Listen, inspector. I'm not in the habit of acting as an informer, but this matter is both strange and serious, since men have died. Now . . . now, I may perhaps be in possession of a clue.'

Higgins remained perfectly calm.

Cranmer stood up and opened a mother-of-pearl box. He took out a ring and showed it to the inspector. 'Have you ever seen anything like this?'

'The decoration appears to depict a phoenix rising from the pyre which it lit in order to overcome death.'

'Correct, inspector. Examine the inside of the ring.'

There was a finely engraved inscription: *Brothers of Luxor*.

'This object came from a lot of jewellery which I purchased at an auction six months ago. I first studied the catalogue, but didn't come up with any specific details, and the auctioneer was unable to tell me anything. Doesn't the term "Brothers" suggest Freemasonry? One of my best customers confided to me that he belonged to that secret society, so I asked him if he knew of the existence of a lodge called the "Brothers of Luxor". And I obtained an answer: that lodge does indeed exist, but the Masonic authorities don't look favourably on it as it has escaped from their control and is conducting its own research, completely independently. You can imagine my surprise during the unwrapping of the mummy, when I spotted an identical ring on Belzoni's right middle finger!'

'Are you quite sure?'

'It was the same phoenix, I'm certain of that. On the other hand, I don't know if Belzoni's ring had the inscription "Brothers of Luxor" engraved inside. Legend has it that the Freemasons execute traitors and liars. Perhaps the three victims of whom you speak had committed

198

these offences, and the Italian was instructed to punish them?'

'Would you be kind enough to lend me this ring, Mr Cranmer? I shall be sure to supply you with an official receipt.'

'At your service, inspector. Sometimes one tiny detail is enough to lift the veil.'

29

Despite Belzoni's considerable weight, Lady Suzanna's barouche was pulled by two sturdy horses and it made swift progress. The lawyer's delicate perfume enchanted the Titan of Padua, though he felt very awkward sitting next to the young aristocrat.

'The unwrapping of the mummy was a great moment in the London season,' she commented. 'No one will forget it. Doesn't success like that fill you with joy?'

'Living in London is expensive, and I hope to give my wife a pleasant life. During our long stay in Egypt, we experienced some difficult times, but Sarah showed exemplary courage, and she deserves to enjoy the pleasures of wealth.'

'Your wife is a remarkable woman, Mr Belzoni, and you were very fortunate to meet her. Take great care of her.'

'You can be sure that I will!'

'Don't you miss the land of the pharaohs?'

'I spent wonderful times there, but my work was under threat, and I could no longer conduct my explorations as I wished. Now, the importance of my work must be recognized, but that battle is by no means a foregone conclusion!'

'Mediocrity is the worst of adversaries. It can rally entire legions of imbeciles and envious people. As you cannot pass unnoticed, you form a perfect target. And you suffer from a terrible drawback: you're not a member of the inner circle. I know how hard you've fought, and I wish you all the energy you need.'

The barouche halted in front of the entrance to the Travellers' Club.

Belzoni got out and addressed the porter. 'I had the honour of being Inspector Higgins's guest here,' the giant reminded him.

'I remember, sir.'

'I need to contact him quickly but I don't know where to find him. Could you give me an address?'

The porter assessed the situation and came up with an acceptable solution. 'The inspector frequently visits the Piccadilly police station.'

'Thank you so much.'

'Don't mention it, sir.'

The Italian passed the information on to the lawyer.

'I'm greatly obliged, Mr Belzoni.'

'I shall leave you, Lady Suzanna. You must be in a hurry to get to Piccadilly.'

'I promised to take you home.'

'The walk will do me good.'

The aristocrat's smile was enchanting. The door of the carriage closed, and the barouche hurried away.

The sergeant was going through a pile of documents, checking the signature of his senior officer, an alcoholic who often spent the night in a cell singing operatic arias. The police station walls ought to have been repainted, but there was insufficient money.

'I'm sorry to disturb you,' said a voice that was as cool as spring water.

The sergeant lifted his head and saw a creature from a dream. He tugged down his jacket and stood to attention. 'How can I help you, milady?'

'I should like to speak to Inspector Higgins.'

'Ah . . . He's not here at the moment. Are you . . . related?'

'I don't have that honour.'

'Ah . . . May I know your name?'

'Lady Suzanna. I've met the inspector before and I should like to see him as a matter of urgency.'

Inspector Higgins – what a charmer, thought the sergeant. How does he do it? 'Very well,' he said. 'I shall see to it.'

'I hope it won't be too long?'

'I'll contact a senior officer.'

The sergeant abandoned his paperwork and ran to the common room, where several police officers were playing cards and drinking tea spiked with rum. One of them was the contact for Higgins's informants, and at regular intervals he passed on the information gathered to the inspector.

The sergeant presented his request, listened to his superior's answer and ran back to the reception desk.

'Inspector Higgins will call at the station at noon tomorrow. We'll inform him that you'll be visiting, Lady Suzanna.'

'Well, then, I shall see you tomorrow.'

The sergeant's dull day was suddenly brighter. Sometimes the life of a policeman had its good points.

The strolling musician was entertaining passers-by on Tottenham Court Road by playing a hurdy-gurdy, a tambourine and a set of bagpipes. Higgins listened to him and gave him some money.

'I'm going to visit one of the district's leading citizens, Sir Richard Beaulieu. Does he have a good or bad reputation?'

'Execrable, inspector. He's an odious, contemptuous man, detested by his neighbours. His servants are for ever changing. The oddest thing is that he owns a cabinet-maker's workshop which is run by a former convict. It's behind his home, but little work seems to be done there.'

'Can you keep a close watch on it?'

'I have a good network of discreet lads. They'll report any incident, however small.'

Higgins headed for Professor Beaulieu's home. An emaciated woman in her sixties was washing down the doorstep.

'May I step over your work?'

'Go in if you want.'

In the lobby, the cook and the maid were coming to blows over a delivery of milk.

Higgins's appearance interrupted the sparring match.

'I should like to see Sir Richard.'

'First floor, first door on your right. I haven't got time to take you up there.'

The inspector climbed the staircase nimbly. The atmosphere in this residence did not seem at all good. The look of some of the steps and a window frame drew his attention. They were made of old wood, perhaps acacia, worked with remarkable skill.

Higgins knocked at a heavy oak door.

It opened slowly.

The professor looked his visitor up and down. 'I don't recall you having an appointment.'

'Inspector Higgins. Would you be kind enough to answer a few questions?'

'It's extremely inconvenient, but . . . I suppose you would only come back?'

'Indeed.'

'Then let us dispense with this formality. Be brief; my time is valuable.'

Sir Richard Beaulieu sat down at his desk, an impressive piece of furniture with numerous drawers. The room was austere, adorned with old wooden panelling of varying hues. One of the panels, above Beaulieu's head, was covered in strange signs, like hastily engraved hieroglyphs.

'I'm listening, inspector.'

'Were you present at the unwrapping of a mummy belonging to Belzoni, the organizer of the Egyptian exhibition?'

'I was.'

'Did you buy anything?'

'A carnelian amulet.'

'Do you still have it?'

'Who do you take me for? I'm not a shopkeeper!'

'So the item has special importance in your eyes.'

'Not at all, inspector. That bauble illustrates the credulity of the ancient Egyptians, and I've added it to a collection of documents designed to prove their stupidity.'

The professor donned a monocle.

'The purchase was perfectly legal, and I paid that man Belzoni, who is an adventurer utterly lacking in culture. The matter's been settled, it seems to me.'

'I still have to find a murderer who perpetrated three killings.'

'Killings? They have nothing to do with me.'

'Ah, but they do, since you knew the victims, who were all present at the spectacle whose centrepiece was the mummy. They were the pathologist, an elderly nobleman and an angry clergyman.'

The professor tapped his lips with his index finger.

'I do vaguely remember those people, especially the doctor who removed the wrappings. But they weren't members of my social circle, and I have nothing to tell you about them.'

'Was Littlewood a friend of yours?'

'Augustin Littlewood, the hundred-year-old Latin professor who died last year?'

'No, someone much younger.'

'I don't know any other Littlewood. Have you finished, inspector?'

'I suspect that the mummy played a decisive role in all three crimes. Unfortunately, it's disappeared, and you may be able to help me to discover the identity of the thief.'

Sir Richard got to his feet, fists clenched. 'You're going too far, inspector, and I shall certainly report this to your superiors! Get out of my office!'

'My proposition didn't strike me as insulting.'

'Well, it was! No one mocks an Oxford professor.'

Higgins looked round the office. 'Admirable wood panelling, Sir Richard. Where did it come from?'

'From various castles. This pointless interview is at an end!'

As he left, Higgins turned back. 'If you hear anything about that mummy, leave a note for me at the police station in Piccadilly. It will be passed on to me.'

30

The thick fog which hung over the sordid district of Whitechapel was Littlewood's closest ally. The conspirators' leader was a veritable chameleon, and he had taken on the appearance of a dejected, poverty-stricken workman. With a weary hand he rejected an offer from an ageing prostitute and headed for the agreed meeting place, a disused warehouse overrun with rats.

As planned, a corrupt police officer brought him the coachman who worked at the royal stables. Strangers who ventured into the narrow streets ran serious risks, and Littlewood wanted to keep his informant intact.

He emerged from the thick layer of evil-smelling mist and barred his guest's way. 'You've arrived, friend.'

The man started. 'You're not the man I've come to see!'

'Oh, yes, I am; it is I, Littlewood.'

Terrified, the coachman tried to run away. But the policeman caught him by the collar and flattened him against the damp wall of the warehouse.

'Calm yourself,' advised Littlewood. 'Come in here, where we can talk in peace. Don't you recognize my voice?'

'Possibly . . .'

The conspirator reminded the coachman of the terms of their first meeting. At last the coachman grew calmer. 'You really know how to disguise yourself!'

'It's a question of security. And it enables me to be everywhere. In other words, don't try to lie to me. What do you have to tell me?'

'The steward of the royal stables does indeed need money, because of his gambling debts. His wages and the money he's borrowed are no longer enough to pay them off. My proposition came at just the right time. On the other hand, he was furious about your plan. Stealing the king's horses, how shameful! I didn't budge: no information, no money. The discussion was long and tough, but I won him over. In exchange for the money, he gave me a list of the king's movements for the next month. If you want precise details about the times, the people who'll be there and the number of servants, he demands more money.'

'Your superior is a greedy man!'

'I didn't promise. Here's the list.'

A big black rat brushed past the coachman's foot, and he flinched backwards, bumping into a pile of crates. Littlewood didn't move a muscle.

'Credit granted, friend.'

The conspirator handed him a fine sum in banknotes.

'And . . . my share?'

'Take ten per cent. When will you have the information?'

'In two or three days.'

'This police officer will contact you and bring you to me.'

'Here?'

'You'll see. Don't ask questions, friend. Just carry out your mission correctly.'

The police officer and the coachman walked away. Littlewood's plan was taking shape, and the assassination of George IV would strike the kingdom like a thunderbolt. The conspirator was not some lowly revolutionary greedy for power and privileges. He wanted to establish the reign of evil, to unleash dark powers that would prevail for centuries. Doing so meant finding the mummy and making use of its capacity for destruction. Belzoni had not awakened an ordinary dead man, but a being endowed with terrifying power.

Being present at the unwrapping had made Littlewood aware of the powers of that apparent corpse. Was the person who had stolen the mummy planning to use those powers, or was he satisfied with possessing an archaeological treasure? In any event, he had had no hesitation in slaughtering a nobleman, a clergyman and a doctor.

The hunt was up. And Littlewood possessed a precious ally: one who, like him, had been present at the unwrapping of the mummy.

The sergeant at the police station in Piccadilly waited impatiently for Lady Suzanna to arrive. He was not on duty today, and ought to have been fishing on the banks of the Thames.

At one minute to twelve, she appeared.

She was clad in a red gown, with a silk cape and a delightful little spring bonnet. And her complexion was peach-perfect, so unlike the cold pallor of most society ladies.

'Good day, officer. Is Inspector Higgins here?'

The sergeant's eyes bulged.

'Officer . . . Do you feel quite well?'

'Oh, yes, yes! Ah, the inspector . . . I'll go and fetch him. Don't leave, whatever you do!'

Higgins was listening to the report from a subordinate, whose task was to gather information supplied by his network of informants. Some of the officers at the Piccadilly station were honest men, dedicated to respecting law and order. The only leader they recognized was Higgins, and they supported his plan to train a body of true professionals, capable of preventing London from descending into corruption and falling prey to gangs. The enterprise seemed doomed to failure, but the inspector's determination had raised the troops' morale, and more and more people were supporting his ideals.

One passage in the report had intrigued Higgins. He was about to ask for an explanation when the desk sergeant interrupted him.

'Lady Suzanna awaits you, inspector.'

'One moment.'

Wondering how he was going to repel a new threat, Higgins greeted the beautiful lawyer. 'Do you need my services, Lady Suzanna?'

'I've just acquired a new barouche. What would you say to a drive in Hyde Park?'

'As you wish.'

The magnificent black-lacquered carriage was comfortable, and the four horses which drew it were positively princely.

'I found myself in competition with the steward of the royal stables, but I offered a better price. An amusing victory, don't you think?'

'Clearly you possess an appreciable fortune.'

'An inheritance, and a few successful business deals.'

The barouche sped along, quickly covering the short distance between Piccadilly and Hyde Park.

Gentle sunlight bathed the hundred and fifty hectares of the royal park, which had opened to the public in 1600. All year long, people swam in the Serpentine, an artificial lake created in 1730, the favourite time being at Christmas. In 1814 a reconstruction of the victory at Trafalgar had been staged.

Chauffeur-driven carriages toured the park from five until seven in the evening. Between noon and two in the afternoon there were equestrian parades, where male and female riders displayed their talents.

Lady Suzanna and Higgins dismounted from the barouche and set off along a peaceful path lined with limes. Maple, ash and chestnut trees served as playgrounds for red squirrels, which had become accustomed to passers-by. A pair of northern lapwings, with black beaks and dark green feathers, soared above the walkers, while a tiny little wren warbled a powerful song.

'Forgive me for gleaning information about you, inspector, but I wanted to find out if you really were searching for the truth. Your reputation flatters you, and you're regarded as an exceptional police officer, without equal in the kingdom. Nevertheless, your independent spirit disturbs many important people, and the authorities aren't in favour of your grand plan.'

'Scotland Yard will see the light of day,' promised Higgins, 'for its creation is vital.'

'I share your opinion and I intend to help you. Many judges and barristers approve of this course of action, and I shall ensure that it receives the largest possible audience. Shifts in opinion will eventually persuade the government to yield to your demands.'

'Your encouragement warms my heart, Lady Suzanna. However, I should like to eliminate all traces of ambiguity.'

'You mean a sort of blackmail: my support in exchange for you abandoning your investigation? Have no fear; that's not my intention. I'm sincere, inspector, and I share your vision of the future.'

A blue tit fluttered round Higgins and, to the lawyer's astonishment, perched on his shoulder.

'Do you have a gift for taming birds?'

'It's the only way to safeguard them from my cat, Trafalgar. He's well fed and spends most of his time in front of the fire, but he's still a cat, and from time to time his hunter's instinct regains the upper hand. It's up to me to protect the birds that visit my property.'

'Before a new police force is born, you must find the murderer of a clergyman, a nobleman and a doctor.'

'And the mummy mixed up in these killings,' Higgins reminded her. 'So you've identified the three victims.'

'I've begun my own investigation,' revealed Lady Suzanna, 'and I shall use my own network in an attempt to get the better of you. The struggle promises to be a fierce one, inspector, and I hope to discover the truth before you.'

The blue tit flew off with a burst of song.

'I assume you're not the kind of woman who listens to advice.'

'On the contrary! It's important to listen carefully to practise my profession.'

'In that case, avoid running risks, Lady Suzanna. This case is both complicated and dangerous. There have already been three victims, and they are probably not the last.'

The young woman sat down on a wooden bench in the shade of a beech tree, and invited Higgins to sit down beside her.

'Why don't we become allies?' she suggested.

'I appreciate your taste for truth, but I fear that it may lead you too far.'

'I've discovered a suspect,' the lawyer declared solemnly. 'His name is Thomas Pettigrew. He's a doctor specializing in anatomy, and his hobby is the study of mummies.'

Higgins opened his black notebook and jotted down this information.

'This is my hypothesis,' he confided. 'The murderer was present at the unwrapping of the mummy and procured a souvenir by buying some part of the remains.'

'Do you have any proof?'

'I have some interesting clues.'

'And what about the person who stole the mummy?'

'He too is one of the buyers. I'm continuing my investigation step by step, bringing scattered details together.'

'Thank you for confiding in me, inspector.'

They stood up and walked back towards the barouche. The sun had vanished behind a cloud, and it was about to rain.

'A sort of demon named Littlewood is prowling in the shadows,' added Higgins. 'He aims to cause chaos and is probably no stranger to the case of the mummy. His involvement will make this investigation particularly dangerous.'

'And consequently you would like me to give up . . .'

'A vain hope, I assume?'

'I fear so, inspector. In the event of an emergency, may I continue to use the police station at Piccadilly?'

Higgins nodded. The first drops of rain began to fall.

31

The rescuer entered the crypt where the mummy lay. Little by little, life was returning to this former alchemical laboratory, which had been abandoned long ago. Several hiding places had been opened up, containing retorts, dishes, stone vases and treatises devoted to the creation of the philosopher's stone using the short way and the long way. This tradition had been inherited from the *Book of the Two Paths*, engraved on the sarcophagi of ancient Egypt's great initiates.

When the Arabs invaded during the seventh century AD, the voices of the sages were silenced. The temples were laid waste and the houses of eternity looted. Foreseeing the disaster and the annihilation of their civilization, a few priests had managed to flee and reach Europe, where the secrets had continued to be passed on. The heirs to the pharaohs had set up the first monastic communities and lodges of artisans, the creators of cathedrals, veritable books in stone which offered their teaching to those who had eyes to see. Alchemists and Freemasons had taken up the torch, but very few people possessed knowledge of hieroglyphs, 'the words of God'.*

The rescuer belonged to this minuscule brotherhood and would soon be its last survivor, for its master, Abbot Pacomas, would soon die. Would the gods decide to deprive humanity of the sacred language or would they permit a seeker such as Champollion to rediscover its keys?

The rescuer had one particularly vital task: to preserve this extraordinary mummy, bearer of the life of the ancients. This being with the radiant, peaceful expression was a masterpiece of the House of Gold, the place of supreme initiation. Seventy-five ritual stages had been necessary to activate the magic of embalming and fashion the *sâh*, the 'noble body'.

Only someone who was 'righteous of voice' could attain this dignity, which was capable of vanquishing the second death, the annihilation of the heart and of consciousness, and of attaining eternal life, a perpetual voyage across the universe.

The parts of the immortal body of Osiris had still to be reunited and protected. By stripping the mummy of its magical attributes, the profaners had placed it in great danger. The rescuer recited the words of transformation, wafted incense over the mummy and celebrated the ritual of the funeral vigil.

* *Medou Neter.*

It must be kept from the darkness.

At all costs.

Belzoni handed Francis Carmick's card to the curator at the British Museum, who agreed to see him. The scholar had an angular face, framed with side-whiskers, and occupied a cramped office crammed with shelves, which groaned under the weight of heavy bound volumes. His Elizabethan-style desk was covered in files, keeping visitors at a distance. Here, no one played games with science.

The Titan of Padua found it difficult to breathe. He was missing the vast spaces of Egypt and Nubia. The damp summer made his joints painful, and autumn would not improve the situation. Just for a moment, he thought of the gentle warmth of an October in Luxor.

'Are you the organizer of the exhibition which is taking place at the Egyptian Hall?' demanded the curator with pursed lips.

'I am. It is an immense success.'

'The common people often have poor taste, Mr Belzoni. In fact, it's their principal characteristic. They don't frequent our museum, God be praised. How could they appreciate great art?'

'Have you been to the Egyptian Hall?'

The curator's cold gaze became positively glacial. 'The weight of my responsibilities precludes such frivolities.'

'It's an extremely serious exhibition,' protested the Italian. 'I've assembled drawings of the most beautiful tomb in the Valley of the Kings, many ancient objects and an incomparable masterpiece, a great alabaster sarcophagus adorned with figurines and hieroglyphic texts.'

'The incomparable masterpieces are in the British Museum.'

'Precisely. And on the recommendation of Francis Carmick, I have a proposition to make.'

'Let me make this clear, Belzoni. I have encountered that politician only once, at a society event. His friends are not mine, and he plays no part in the administration of this museum.'

The Italian held in his anger. So Carmick had made a fool of him!

'So what is this proposition?'

'The sarcophagus is a unique piece. Bringing it back to England was quite a feat, and I'm convinced that it will be regarded as one of the most fabulous treasures of the British Museum.'

'My dear fellow, there's nothing scientific about your convictions. For, I have been told, you have no qualifications and no recognized competence in archaeology.'

'My book proves the extent of my discoveries!'

'It's not a work of reference, Belzoni, but the narrative of a treasure seeker, designed to entertain the idle reader.'

The Italian swallowed hard. 'The alabaster sarcophagus is neither an illusion nor a curiosity!'

'Supposing it merits that description, the art of ancient Egypt interests only a small minority of enthusiasts.'

'My exhibition demonstrates the contrary!'

'I was talking about informed enthusiasts,' objected the curator. 'Perhaps I and my colleagues could work out a donations procedure and admit your sarcophagus to the museum's reserves.'

Belzoni started. 'A . . . donations procedure?'

'It would be a favour. From my point of view, sarcophagi are minor objects.'

'This one is worth a fortune!'

'I assume you are joking?'

The giant rose to his feet. 'You are the one who is joking! And you have no right to reject such a marvel.'

'Does a foreign adventurer presume to teach a British Museum curator his job?'

'I shall do without you. The museum must buy the alabaster sarcophagus from me, and it will!'

Belzoni left the airless office, slamming the door behind him.

Higgins was growing accustomed to his City refuge, with its modern comforts. But he missed his dog Geb and his cat Trafalgar. Long walks, evenings in the drawing room, Mary's excellent cooking, the calm of the countryside . . . these were joys to which he hoped he would soon be able to return.

Alas, the immediate future did not look any brighter. Rereading his notes had proved interesting but had not as yet provided him with the keys to all these tangled enigmas. He was guided by a hunch: the three murders, the disappearance of the mummy and Littlewood were all inextricably linked. One or more suspects were concealing their identity, and all those he had questioned had something to hide, including Belzoni and his wife.

Higgins did not believe in chance or circumstantial crime. Carrying out such an act implied a state of being and a progression. It was up to him to discover the cause and to do so unerringly.

Following the old alchemists' method, he would accumulate materials and observations, without any preconceived notions, and allow the truth time to blossom. Wasn't the most important thing to ask the right questions?

After moistening his face with a hot towel, he covered it with shaving soap scented with rosewater. Stropped on a length of leather, the blade of his pearl-handled cutthroat razor guaranteed a perfect shave. All that remained was to smooth down the pepper-and-salt moustache, taming a few rebellious hairs. Respecting others and understanding began with taking care of one's own appearance.

As he dabbed on some old-fashioned Chèvrefeuille Tradition cologne, the inspector recalled the investigations he had conducted since the start of his career, putting many criminals behind bars. This time, the situation was unlike any other, and the experience he had gained would be of no use to him. Higgins was venturing into unknown territory, and no one could help him.

Dressed in a well-made suit, so as to resemble a City businessman, the inspector left his refuge and headed for a restaurant, where he would enjoy scrambled eggs, bacon and grilled fish.

A gentleman in a top hat fell into step beside him.

'Quiet night, sergeant?'

'Not as quiet as the preceding ones. When you came home, someone was following you.'

'Man or woman?'

'A hat, a long coat . . . Impossible to say. I decided to observe and not get too close. Whoever it was tried to find out where you were living, but failed and went round in circles. He'll try again, and I suggest doubling your protection.'

'Do the best you can, sergeant.'

'Are we to intercept him?'

'Only in an extreme emergency.'

'We wouldn't want to lose you, inspector.'

'I tend to agree with you there.'

The two men separated, and Higgins ate with an excellent appetite. His first kicks at the ants' nest were already producing results.

32

Bloomsbury was a sort of Georgian paradise, elegant and tranquil. Its squares, enclosing lawns, provided wealthy families with pleasant living conditions, away from the poverty of the East End, whose troubles did not reach Russell Square and Bedford Square. Bloomsbury was made up of small, peaceful streets and open spaces. Some aristocrats regretted the presence of newly rich businessmen, proud of living in the shadow of the British Museum, but had resigned themselves to this cohabitation.

Higgins approached the doorman of a superb private house adorned with Corinthian columns topped with capitals in the form of baskets of fruit.

The servant listened to the visitor's request, bowed and went off to inform his master, the famous actor Peter Bergeray, who had only just woken up.

The hallway was plastered with posters proclaiming the glory of Bergeray, a man who was capable of inter-

preting all the major roles in the Shakespearean reper-
toire.

The servant came back down and led the police officer
to the drawing room, overloaded with sofas, armchairs,
pouffes, low tables and mirrors, which were being polished
by a young maid who was asked to leave. The vast room
was lit by an oversized chandelier. As Higgins was gazing
at it, the actor appeared, his blond hair drab and his face
as pale as death. He wore a blue cape and Turkish slip-
pers, and his gaze was vague.

'Excuse me, inspector, I've just got out of my bathtub.
There's nothing more restful than a good bath! I take at
least three a day. This marvellous district never lacks for
water. I'm quite convinced that tomorrow all of London
will have baths! Technology is taking great strides forward,
and our good king encourages scientists. Soon, we shall
take our inspiration from the example of Pilâtre de Rozier,
and we shall fly! What a wonderful idea his dirigible
balloon was! Didn't Blanchard succeed in crossing the
Channel in 1785? He ought to have become more famous.
History can be unjust sometimes, don't you think? Ah,
chocolate and cakes!'

A butler placed a silver tray on a low table.

'My pastry chef is an artist, inspector. These macaroons hardly put any weight on me, and George IV himself
likes them. What a magnificent idea the new Buckingham
Palace is! When it's finished,[*] the British monarchy will

---

[*] It was not occupied until 1837.

have a fabulous stage, worthy of a theatre. We are living in an exciting era, inspector, and each day brings us new surprises. You like chocolate, I hope? I'm mad about it! Two cups, and all my energy comes back. And my art demands a great deal of it, believe me! Choose a good armchair, sit down and make yourself at home. I cannot stop buying sofas and armchairs; this house is becoming a showroom.'

As if he was returning to reality, the actor fixed his gaze on Higgins. 'You are from the police . . . Why did you want to see me?'

'Three murders have been committed.'

'Ah, yes . . . Anyone I knew?'

'They were present at the spectacle hosted by Belzoni.'

'The unwrapping of the mummy! Let me guess – I adore riddles. Let's see . . . First, the hysterical clergyman, determined to destroy the mummy. Obviously, it took its revenge! Next, the sarcastic, contemptuous old nobleman. The curse struck him too. Finally . . . I would bet on the doctor. A cold man, who showed the relic no respect. Do I win, inspector?'

'Remarkable, Mr Bergeray.'

'Don't look any further for the culprit: it's the mummy. And I shall prove it to you. Let's sit round this circular ebony table and allow our fingers to touch. Now, we must close our eyes.'

Higgins yielded to the actor's demands, but he continued to observe him out of the corner of his eye.

'I'm journeying,' murmured Peter Bergeray, 'I'm

ravelling back through time. Pyramids, temples, tombs
. . . A bronze door, a long corridor, torches, priests, a
sarcophagus bathed in golden light . . . The mummy is
there, it's breathing . . . Yes, it's breathing! Demons
emerge, slit the throats of the priests and approach the
sarcophagus. They want to destroy the mummy. It gets
to its feet, it curses them and it triumphs!'

The actor staggered away from the table and collapsed
into an armchair, soaked in sweat. He struggled to get
his breath back.

'Did you see the attackers' faces?' asked Higgins.

'Hideous masks, phantoms . . .'

'Did the mummy resemble Belzoni's?'

'It was the same one, I'm certain of it! I heard a word,
just one: *Magnoon*. That's him, the leader of the assassins.
Contrary to our own, the world of the dead does not lie.'

Higgins noted down the information.

Bergeray calmed down and drank a cup of chocolate.

'Do you often communicate with the afterlife?' asked
the inspector.

'Such voyages are exhausting, and I only embark on
them when absolutely necessary.'

'Many thanks for your help, Mr Bergeray.'

'If anyone tells you about a similar experience, be
suspicious of him. He's trying to steal my vision and is
one of those criminals who want to destroy the mummy.'

'It's disappeared,' revealed Higgins.

'Vexing, very vexing. I fear there may be new dramas.'

The actor devoured a dozen macaroons.

'You bought some wrappings,' the inspector reminded him.

'Long, broad linen bands which covered the face of that admirable mummy, indeed. I needed them to prepare for some new stage play which aroused the public's enthusiasm.'

'I was present at your show and was most impressed. Transformed into a mummy, you seemed to emerge from nothing, and moved round the stage animated by supernatural life.'

'I was rather pleased with that effect,' admitted the actor, lighting up a long mother-of-pearl pipe. 'This delicate object was given to me by the Smoking Club, when I was admitted. And to think that certain venomous tongues dare claim that it's a fake!'

Higgins noted the hieroglyphs coarsely carved on the stem. 'Would that venomous tongue belong to Belzoni?'

'You are an intuitive man, inspector!'

'Did you invite him here?'

Peter Bergeray looked embarrassed. 'After the unwrapping, we met again, in my dressing room at the theatre. And the encounter wasn't a very pleasant one.'

Nervously, he stuffed more tobacco into the bowl of his pipe.

'It's difficult to talk about, inspector. Since you are conducting a criminal investigation, I would rather not hide anything from you, although the event does not embellish my reputation. Do you promise me your discretion?'

226

Higgins nodded.

'The word of a gentleman is worth its weight in gold! When I saw the mummy, I felt a profound emotion. Other spectators were acquiring wrappings, and I tried my luck. The price Belzoni fixed was exorbitant, but I didn't pay attention to the amount. Fascination sometimes makes one do foolish things! In short, I took away the linen bands and forgot to pay for them. Devoting oneself to art makes one neglect the sordid, mercantile sides of life. But the Belzonis remember them! I, Peter Bergeray, was the victim of an assault.'

'Were you wounded?' asked Higgins anxiously.

'Only my pride, for I managed to extinguish their fury by promising to pay my debt swiftly. That monster of an Italian is an angry man, and his horrible wife is just as dangerous! They threatened me with the most terrible things if I didn't pay them. My close acquaintance with Shakespeare's words has given me a sense of grandeur and repartee. I met bestial violence with dignity.'

'And the matter was settled?'

'Almost! Because of a recent furniture purchase, I'm a little short at the moment. The forthcoming performances of *Hamlet* and the mummy scene will earn me substantial sums. The Belzonis will have their money, and I shall hear no more about them.'

'Do you believe them capable of committing murder?'

The actor puffed on his pipe. 'A difficult question . . . In my soul and my conscience, I believe so. Their violence is terrifying! I wouldn't risk attacking them, for fear of being crushed. In my opinion, anyone who opposes the Belzonis is in danger of his life.'

The inspector finished his delicious cup of chocolate. 'Thank you for enlightening me, Mr Bergeray.'

'You ought to watch the Belzonis,' advised the actor. 'It would be better to prevent them doing anything bad. That woman Sarah is a veritable demon!'

As he was leaving the drawing room, Higgins turned back. 'One last detail: have you heard of a man named Littlewood?' Peter Bergeray pondered. 'The name isn't familiar. In any event, there's no actor called Littlewood! Is he a prime suspect?'

'Have a good day. This evening, you will enchant an adoring public, and the mummy scene will be unforgettable.'

33

'That imbecile of a curator! I almost picked up his desk and hit him over the head with it!' Belzoni admitted to his wife. 'The administrators of that museum despise me and refuse to pay the slightest attention to the alabaster sarcophagus. If we don't get a good price for it, we shall not make our fortune.'

'There are still plenty of visitors to the exhibition, the publisher is reprinting your book and I'm carrying on a satisfactory trade in the statuettes and other small objects we brought back from Egypt. The situation isn't bad, Giovanni; we have enough to cover our expenses and lead a pleasant life.'

'The exhibition will close its doors, I don't feel capable of writing a new work and our stock is running out. If I could sell that sarcophagus to the British Museum, I would fill our coffers and earn myself a fine reputation!'

'How can we go over the heads of the curators?'

'We need the support of an influential politician. That

filth Francis Carmick lied to me and betrayed me! The hypocrite deserves to end up in Egyptian hell, devoured by a monster. But I haven't spoken my last word.'

The Italian showed his wife the ring adorned with a phoenix. 'Circumstances oblige me to use it.'

'Is that wise?'

'I shall not betray any secrets, and I have nothing to lose. I want to obtain an official mission, Sarah. It will enable me to force the British Museum to buy the sarcophagus and return to Egypt to carry out new excavations. There's still so much to discover!'

'Will the pasha Mehemet Ali and his henchman Drovetti allow you to act?'

'I'll be in charge of the mission, and I'll have them where I want them! I shall open tombs, remove treasures from the ground, bring statues back to London and write an account of the adventure. This time, the name of Belzoni will shine with an everlasting brilliance. Moreover, I shall bring back mummies for Dr Pettigrew.'

Sarah threw her arms round the giant's neck. She loved to see him dream, and adored the madness that led him on to improbable paths. He would never calm down and never become wealthy, living on unearned income.

The police officer in the pay of Littlewood led the coachman to a haberdasher's shop in the East End. A herd of pigs were running round the narrow street, housewives were yelling insults at each other and dirty urchins were playing with balls of rags.

'The boss is waiting for you in the room behind the shop,' said the police officer. 'I'll close the door and stand guard.'

A small candle feebly lit the room, which was cluttered with wooden chests and tools. The coachman could not make out Littlewood's face.

'Mission accomplished,' he declared, his voice quavering. 'Here's the complete list of George IV's official engagements for the coming month, the timetables and the number of people accompanying him. It won't be easy, I can assure you! The steward of the stables is a suspicious man, and he's demanding explanations.'

'What did you tell him?'

'I gave him the sum he asked for and advised him to hold his tongue, like me. The theft of a few horses doesn't concern us.'

'Excellent, my friend.'

Littlewood lit a second candle and examined the document. He swiftly noticed a curious visit to the north of London. A single carriage drawn by eight horses and only two soldiers! The reason for the journey was not stipulated.

'Do you know any more about this?'

'The entire palace is entertained by the king's latest fancy. She's a country girl with flaming eyes and milky skin. He thinks he's travelling to an inn in absolute discretion, forgetting that his personal valet is a complete gossip. George IV will quickly tire of this young girl once the shine has worn off, and return to his society mistresses.'

This was the opportunity he had been dreaming of! This depraved puppet king was living his last days. Littlewood was already dreaming up a plan of action, simple and swift. The tyrant would have no chance of escape.

'I would like to make a request of you,' whispered the coachman.

'I'm listening.'

'I've given you total satisfaction, haven't I? An additional bonus seems only right to me.'

'You're right,' agreed Littlewood, 'and I tend to recognize my collaborators' merits. Follow me. We shall leave the back way.'

They stepped into a narrow alley cluttered with rubbish.

Four dock workers stood there, armed with iron bars.

'Get rid of this for me,' Littlewood ordered, pointing to the coachman. 'And make sure his body isn't found.'

Belzoni was still hesitant.

A stone's throw from the bookshop, he almost retraced his steps. But why should he? At the last meeting of the Brothers of Luxor, the Venerable Master has wished him good luck and given him a name and address to use in the event of need.

The Italian preferred to get by on his own and owe nobody anything. But given the circumstances, it was impossible to maintain this approach.

A sudden downpour was the signal for umbrellas to open. A customer emerged from the bookshop on Oxford

Street, and Belzoni went in. It housed thousands of books, and three zealous salesmen were advising potential purchasers.

'Can I help you?' one of them asked.

'I should like to speak to Mr James.'

'I'm sorry, he's busy.'

'I'm in no hurry.'

'Would you be kind enough to give me a visiting card?'

Belzoni handed the salesman a copy of his book, dedicated to the owner of the bookshop. His signature was followed by three dots in the form of a triangle.

'Mr Belzoni! Delighted to meet you! Your book is a fine success; readers love it. What adventures you have had! I shall take you to my employer's office.'

The two men climbed a spiral staircase to the first floor.

'Please wait a moment.'

The wait was a brief one, and the salesman showed the giant into the bookshop owner's office. He was a man aged around fifty, with a high forehead and piercing eyes.

The door closed.

'Whence do you come?' asked James.

'From a hermetically sealed place where the light is born.'

'How old are you?'

'Seven and more.'

'Can you decipher the secret?'

'I cannot read or write, but we share the letters of the sacred language.'

'Be seated, brother. I am happy to welcome you.'

An old armchair creaked under the giant's weight.

'What is the name of your respectable lodge?' asked the bookshop owner.

'The Brothers of Luxor.'

The shop owner scratched the tip of his nose.

'So it really does exist ... I would have wagered that it didn't! In any event, it has no equivalent in London, and the Masonic authorities don't number it among the regularly affiliated lodges. Such independence is frowned on.'

'Am I to understand that you belong to the high spheres?'

'I have that honour.'

'My lodge works in the greatest secrecy. Surviving in Egypt is no easy task, and the pasha's police aren't fond of free spirits.'

'Have you attended a lodge since your arrival in London?'

'I haven't had the time,' confessed Belzoni. 'Making one's mark here isn't easy, and I've attempted to fly with my own wings. As the Venerable One gave me your name, I have dared to importune you.'

'Despite administrative strictures,' said James, 'I'm not hostile to certain forms of unorthodox research. Although many Freemasons are hostile to Egypt, I remain convinced that she is our spiritual mother. It's vital that the works of your lodge are passed on. Are you willing to speak about them to those brothers who are interested, under the seal of secrecy?'

'I am.'

'Your presence here is a call for help. What are you hoping for?'

'An official mission to Egypt and support to force the British Museum to buy an extraordinary alabaster sarcophagus from me.'

'That won't be easy, and I can't promise you success.'

'My future depends on it,' declared Belzoni.

'I shall do my best, brother. Unfortunately, you don't mix in influential circles, and I shall have to be extremely eloquent.'

'Doesn't my knowledge of the terrain speak in my favour?'

'Certainly. Come to the bookshop next Wednesday, at seven in the evening. I shall take you to my lodge.'

34

The private residence in Portman Square emphasized its owner's wealth and importance. Even the wrought-iron gate at the entrance to Francis Carmick's property was worth a fortune. The stucco rendering on the façade had been painted and cut to imitate stone, and there were finely wrought shutters at the high, large-paned windows. Two marble columns framed the entrance, which was surmounted by a triangle in the Greek style.

Thanks to his banker friend, Higgins had obtained some valuable information about Carmick. A born politician, corrupt and a corrupter, he bought those important electors who were vital in order to obtain a seat in Parliament. A formidable and charming individual, he had created an extensive network of contacts and now pulled a considerable number of strings. Many senior government officials ate out of his hand, and he would soon be entrusted with an important Ministry.

The inspector gave a series of vigorous knocks with the aid of the bronze door knocker.

The door opened, and the visitor handed the footman his hat.

'Kindly announce Inspector Higgins.'

'Mr Carmick did not inform me of your visit, and . . .'

'I'm conducting a criminal investigation. Anyone who attempts to hinder my progress will end up in prison.'

'If sir insists . . . Please wait in the office.'

The politician's dwelling corresponded to the status of the various people who inhabited it. The basement housed the kitchen, the wine cellar and the coal shed. Servants reached the space reserved for them via a service entrance. A massive staircase connected the three storeys, which were made up of relatively small rooms, while the staff used the narrow back stairs. The dining room and office were on the ground floor, the large reception room on the first floor, and the bedrooms, bathrooms and lavatories on the second and third floors. The domestic staff occupied small rooms under the eaves.

A valet took the place of the footman and led Higgins through the hall, whose décor was a hymn to ancient Egypt. Drawings, paintings, tapestries and sculptures conjured up – often naively – the world of the pharaohs.

On the office door was a depiction of the goddess Isis, dressed in a gown adorned with stars. The valet opened the door slowly, and the inspector stepped into a room decorated entirely in the Egyptian style.

Francis Carmick was standing with his hands clasped

behind his back, dressed in a perfectly cut frock coat. He glared at his guest. 'Your visit surprises me, inspector. May I know the reason for it?'

'Three murders and Belzoni's mummy.'

'By the devil! You certainly come here for good reasons!'

The valet left, closing the door behind him.

'Sit down, Inspector Higgins. Would you like some tea or coffee?'

'Coffee, please.'

'I have the best in London.'

Carmick rang a small bell and a maid appeared, dressed in a mobcap and an immaculate white apron. She hurried off to do her master's bidding.

'I was present when that mummy was unwrapped,' conceded the politician, 'and I purchased a superb linen shroud. An authentic shroud: could one wish for anything better? It was tied by a thread at the chest and ankles. There was something unreal about that spectacle – or should one say ceremony? We civilized citizens of a progressive century witnessed the resurrection of an Egyptian who had been dead for thousands of years! Resurrection is an excessive term, of course, but you understand what I mean. And the perfection of the mummy, its youthful features and the incredible state of preservation of the body created the illusion. In truth, it was a curious experience. And you mentioned ... three murders?'

'Were there any incidents during the unwrapping?'

Francis Carmick reflected as he took a mouthful of coffee.

'I remember an old madman brandishing his cane and roaring: "Meat for my dogs: that's how this corpse will end up!"'

'He was one of the victims,' revealed Higgins. 'An elderly, wealthy nobleman.'

'Ah ... Belzoni wasn't happy, and neither was the audience. The madman was expelled, and then another one appeared. This one was a clergyman, I think. And he hurled curses at the mummy!'

'The second victim.'

'Clearly,' observed Carmick, 'one should not have insulted that old Egyptian! One detail comes back to me, regarding the nobleman. I saw Belzoni and his wife at the home of John Soane, an art lover whose house has become a museum. Your first victim was there too! He promised to buy the pieces of the mummy from the pathologist Dr Bolson and throw them to his hounds. Belzoni was furious, and told his wife that he would smash his skull! Just idle words, probably.'

'The pathologist was the third victim,' stated Higgins.

'By the devil! Did the mummy exact its vengeance?'

'It's impossible to say until I've found it.'

Carmick appeared astonished. 'You mean it's ... run away?'

'Someone stole it when Bolson was about to carry out an autopsy on it.'

'What a fabulous story! You seem like a serious,

thoughtful man to me, inspector, and I'm obliged to believe you. Nevertheless, you must confess that these facts go beyond ordinary understanding! It's true that ancient Egypt is full of mysteries and still has many surprises in store for us.'

'Your passion for that civilization surprises me,' remarked Higgins. 'Does a politician of your stature have the leisure to take an interest in antiquity?'

'Ancient history is a source of teaching and reflection. Did the Egyptians not attempt to overcome death, an enemy which is both repulsive and fascinating?'

'It seems that you are particularly preoccupied with mummification.'

'Does it not illustrate the result obtained by Egyptian experts? If you had gazed on that mummy, you would not doubt their skills. But you're right; politics takes up almost all my time. Serving one's country is the most noble of ideals, is it not? A daily struggle, ferocious adversaries, countless traps to avoid . . . Fortunately, the kingdom has the benefit of a responsible government, which is aware of the problems and open to the future. The development of the capital is a spectacular success, and progress will eradicate poverty.'

'Have you heard of a man known as Littlewood?'

For an instant, Francis Carmick's smooth expression changed. Anxiety mixed with aggression replaced the façade of friendliness. Immediately, the politician regained his composure.

'Are you unaware that this is a sort of . . . state secret?'

'It's my task to arrest Littlewood.'

'Then do not delay, and ensure that that conspirator is in no condition to do harm!'

'What do you know about him?'

'Rumours were circulating, so I questioned Ministers, and the head of the government confided in me, requesting that I didn't say a word to anyone. Littlewood is the code name of a dangerous revolutionary who is fascinated by the French example and wishes to import it into England. Tracts which we have seized have told us of his intentions: to overthrow the monarchy, establish the rule of the people and distribute wealth to the labouring masses. The majority of politicians fall about laughing, but a few take the threat seriously.'

'Such as yourself, I presume?'

'Indeed, inspector. Agitators are inciting the folk of the East End to contest the government, and this man Littlewood is attempting to unify them. Underestimating such an adversary is liable to lead the country into chaos. Fortunately, the authorities have realized the gravity of the situation, and I wish you good luck. Identifying and arresting Littlewood are priorities.'

'You don't possess any information yourself which might help me?'

'Unfortunately not. Do you have the necessary manpower?'

'I have no cause for complaint.'

Francis Carmick stiffened. 'England is counting on you, inspector.'

'I shall attempt to prove worthy of her trust. On the subject of the missing mummy ... Can you recall the name of any suspect?'

'No, I don't think so.'

'Thank you for seeing me, Mr Carmick.'

'Cooperating with the police is a duty.'

Someone knocked at the door.

'Enter!' snapped the politician.

The valet opened the door and took one step into the office. 'Sir, Mr Andrew Young has arrived.'

'My meeting is over. Bring him up.'

Higgins consulted his notebook. 'As I recall, your visitor was also present at the unwrapping of the mummy.'

'Correct, inspector. We met on that occasion, where he warmly congratulated me on my political activities and requested a meeting. Because of his numerous contacts in London and the provinces, he hopes to develop a network of friendships: a considerable contribution on which I congratulate myself. I am delighted to have met you and, once again, I wish you good luck. Get rid of that scum Littlewood.'

Andrew Young appeared.

Higgins had rarely seen such a sinister-looking individual. Tall, stooping, with a limp appearance, he had an ugly, contemptuous face. At the sight of the police officer, he froze.

'If I am disturbing you, my dear Carmick ...'

'Allow me to introduce myself, Mr Young: Inspector Higgins. I had intended to contact you and I should like to take advantage of this opportunity to ask you a few questions. Of course, I shall wait until the end of your meeting, with Mr Carmick's consent.'

'My small drawing room is open to you, inspector. Ask my valet for whatever you like.'

Higgins used this pause to reread all his notes. Main themes were beginning to stand out, and some hypotheses were fading while others continued to hold water. He was careful not to favour one at the risk of overlooking the truth. There were still too many shadowy areas and major aspects which needed clarifying.

Perhaps Andrew Young would enable him to make progress.

35

When Andrew Young stepped into the small drawing room, he looked like an undertaker. The austere individual was suffering from several defects in taste: a mud-stain on his left shoe, a scarf and a grey hat.

'I'm sorry, inspector,' he said hoarsely, 'but I don't have the time to grant you an interview. I don't live in London, and my timetable is very tight. We shall meet another time.'

Calmly, Higgins rose to his feet. 'I'm equally sorry, Mr Young. I shall be waiting for you at six o'clock this evening, at the police station in Piccadilly. If you don't arrive, you'll be guilty of evading justice and will be strongly suspected of serious offences. I shall see you this evening.'

As Higgins was about to leave the room, Young barred his way.

'Understood, inspector. I shall answer your questions! Will you accompany me to Burlington Arcade?'

'An excellent idea.'

'My carriage will take us there.'

Young's carriage was not in the first flush of youth, and his coachman was covered in mud. The tired horses refused to quicken their pace. Fine rain refreshed them.

'Where do you live?' asked Higgins.

'I have a country estate, and I farm many acres. The population is constantly growing and must be fed. Whatever progress is made in technology, wheat will still be the basic foodstuff. I don't regret buying the estate from a crippled old landowner, who was attached to ancestral customs. Without me, the workers would have been reduced to poverty. They don't earn a great deal, but they eat their fill and lack for nothing. It's certainly a profitable investment. And my lands enable me to satisfy my taste for hunting, which is a healthy form of sport.'

'It seems this country existence doesn't prevent you taking an interest in politics.'

'Does it not govern our world? The future of the land is in the hands of those gentlemen in Parliament. In reading Francis Carmick's articles on agriculture, I discovered a competent official and decided to support his course of action. In my opinion, he will make an excellent Minister and defend the cause of landowners. That's the reason for my visit: a declaration of friendship and the formation of a support committee.'

'If I'm not mistaken, you have met Francis Carmick before.'

The landowner sniffed embarrassedly. 'The dampness

of the capital does not agree with me. The country air is healthier.'

'Does my question embarrass you?'

'To tell the truth, a little.'

The cab halted near Burlington Arcade, a street lined with shops and covered with a glass canopy, built in 1819 between Piccadilly and Burlington Gardens.

'I have purchases to make,' explained Young. 'One cannot find everything in the country.'

This new street was very popular with Londoners. Sheltered from bad weather, they strolled there for hours, searching for the latest fashionable bauble or the ideal Christmas present. The members of high society and the nouveau riche encountered each other there, and shop-keepers fought to secure premises.

Higgins could not imagine Young's large, flaccid body transformed into a lover of shopping. Indeed, he seemed ill at ease among the passers-by, apologizing as he avoided them. He halted before a shop window.

'I'm looking for pewter pots and copper basins to complete my kitchen equipment. Shall we go in?'

A salesman offered a vast choice, and left Young to think about it.

'Your question embarrasses me, inspector, because I was present at a bizarre and disturbing spectacle, the unwrapping of an Egyptian mummy. Curiosity drew me, and I regretted it. Belzoni was wrong to unwrap that corpse in public. On that occasion, I had the good fortune to meet Francis Carmick and tell him of my admiration.

He gave me an appointment, and today we have begun a collaboration which promises to be fruitful. Are you satisfied, and is that the end of the interrogation?'

'I haven't yet dealt with the important points.'

'Which are?'

'Certain incidents punctuated that strange spectacle, did they not?'

The landowner put down a pot-bellied vessel. 'Two individuals, a priest and an old man, protested vehemently and came out with words of madness. They were thrown out, and the unwrapping continued.'

'Did you know these troublemakers?'

'I'd never seen them before, inspector. Listening to them rant, one wondered if they had lost their reason. Threatening a mummy ... What could be more ridiculous?'

'Do you not believe it capable of doing harm?'

The landowner looked the inspector up and down. 'Is the police force lapsing into fantasy?'

'Yet the two troublemakers and the doctor who unwrapped the mummy have been murdered. And the mummy has disappeared.'

Andrew Young bought two small pots and left the shop, looking vexed. 'These sad events don't concern me, inspector, and I must make another purchase. Will you accompany me?'

'I should like additional clarification.'

'As you wish.'

With his slow, heavy tread, the landowner approached

a recently opened armourer's shop, which had a display of old weapons.

'I'm a collector,' explained Young, 'and I'm always looking for rarities. In manufacturing pistols, rifles and cannon, man's genius has proved his immense abilities, and this is my way of paying homage. What weapon do you use, inspector?'

'None.'

The landowner looked at the police officer as though he were some curious beast. 'Given your profession, is that not unwise?'

'Have no fear, I know how to defend myself.'

A British army musket attracted Young's attention.

'A small marvel . . . One placed it on a forked support and lit a wick. It's heavier than an arquebus but also more effective.'

'Do you know where the missing mummy is?' asked Higgins calmly.

'I? Certainly not! I don't collect corpses.'

'However, you did purchase a sort of relic during the unwrapping.'

'Indeed: a small vase which was placed along the mummy's left flank. A curiosity, you will agree.'

'Did it contain any substance?'

'I don't know; it was sealed.'

'Aren't you planning to open it?'

'It would lose its value, inspector. Yes, I really do like this musket. Just a moment, I must haggle over the price. These shopkeepers are all thieves.'

The discussion was long and tough, but eventually the buyer and seller came to an agreement.

'The musket will be delivered to me,' said Young, who seemed vaguely delighted. 'I've finished my errands and can now return to my estate. Do you require any further clarification?'

'Do you know a man called Littlewood?'

The landowner pondered. 'My footman is called Bramwood, and my cook Woodford . . . No, I don't know anyone called Littlewood. Is he a fourth victim of the fugitive mummy?'

Higgins wasn't thrown by Young's sarcasm.

'May I set you down somewhere, inspector?'

'That will not be necessary.'

'I feel sorry for you, having to live in London. The air is becoming more and more difficult to breathe. Industrial development is vital, and no one can deny that, but we must not forget agriculture! Since we shall not meet again, I wish you success in arresting the guilty party.'

Andrew Young settled himself in his carriage, and the tired horses continued on their way.

Higgins could not resist a perfumer's display, notably an eau de toilette which reminded him of the subtle aromas of the East. A long stay in Egypt had helped him to sense the immense scope of that civilization and its mysteries.

The case of the mummy had nothing to do with chance. A simple police officer would have lost his way completely, faced with the riddle of the hieroglyphs.

Higgins had met all the purchasers of the precious relics belonging to the mummy and had raised a small part of the veil. There was no lack of lies by omission, travesties of the truth and false trails.

There was also one important detail: someone was watching him. Someone particularly skilful, who had never entered his field of vision. Nevertheless, the inspector had sensed his presence, and the inspector's instinct never let him down.

The anthill was continuing to swarm.

36

Autumn was setting in, and the sun was deserting the London sky. Several months had passed since the unwrapping of Belzoni's mummy, and the rescuer was continuing to celebrate the ancient rites in the crypt where the Osiran body rested.

The alchemical laboratory was fully functioning and, thanks to the regular addition of vegetable gold, the flesh had retained a perfect consistency, equal to that obtained by initiates at the time of the pharaohs. The soul with the body of a bird and a human head, the *ba*, was travelling from earth to heaven and heaven to earth, each morning reanimating this man who was 'righteous of voice'. The creative power, the *ka*, was being exhausted little by little, despite the words of protection, but the rescuer, the heir to the sacred language of initiates, still had effective resources to fall back on.

The rescuer, who had been assumed to be a simple onlooker during the atrocious unwrapping spectacle, possessed a decisive weapon against the attacks of time: a heart scarab. The word 'scarab' in hieroglyphs was synonymous with 'to be born, to come into existence, to be transformed incessantly'. And such was the key to life in eternity, the incessant changes of the Osiran being which this mummy symbolized.

The heart had always been the subject of great attention. The embalmer left it in place and, if the cutting instruments damaged it, it was restored to its original appearance before being placed back inside the body. According to the ancient Egyptians, thoughts, intelligence and sensitivity did not come from the brain, but from an immaterial heart, whose presence was indicated by the beating of the material heart.

'Your head is reunited with your neck,' declared the rescuer, 'and your heart will not be cut out.'

On the mummy's solar plexus, the rescuer placed a scarab made of serpentine, a dark green stone. Engendering a new sun, which itself embodied the morning light, this scarab caused energy to flow within the mummy.

To bring it to life and make it effective, the rescuer spoke the ritual words:[*]

'O my heart of my mother, my heart which ensures my transformations, do not rise up against me, do not side against me before the trial of the afterlife, do not make the scales tip against me in the presence of the master of knowledge. You are my creative power inside

* *Book of the Dead*, Chapter 30.

my body, you protect me and you maintain the unity of my being, you fashion me by bringing my limbs to life. Keep my name intact among the gods, bring me to the place of accomplishment.'

The green stone attached itself to the mummy, and a soft glow proved that the operation had been a success.

This success must not hide the need to recover the wrappings and other original elements which had ensured the mummy's true protection. The rescuer was obliged to reassemble them one by one, and that task would be long and arduous. Identifying the owners would not be enough; their hiding places must be found, and action taken only when it was certain to bring success.

Striding down the London streets was no substitute for long walks in the woods, but Higgins liked to walk, and this means of travel helped him to think. The last letter from his housekeeper, Mary, had reassured him: Geb and Trafalgar were in fine form, although they did not approve of their master's long absence.

The City had emptied of businessmen and, at this late hour, several gas lamps had unfortunately gone out.

Higgins did not need to turn round to know that he was being followed.

Whoever was following him was a wary – and therefore dangerous – professional. Perhaps he would not be content merely to find out where the inspector was staying and wished to kill him. So Higgins adopted the plan he had devised in case of immediate danger: he altered his usual route and headed for the Bank of England.

If his men were alert, there was no reason to worry. If they were less than vigilant, he would have to defend himself alone.

So Littlewood's privileged collaborator had not lied! Contrary to what the leader of the revolutionaries had believed, Inspector Higgins was well and truly alive. Admittedly, his questioning would produce no results, since the conspirator's right-hand man had not provided him with any useful information. However, this over-curious police officer was in danger of discovering the beginnings of a lead.

That was why Littlewood must kill him.

Littlewood's ally had proved to be an excellent second in command, ordering one of his zealous henchmen to follow the inspector and keep him in view at all times. His leader planned to offer him a major role in the country's new government after the death of the tyrant George IV.

Despite his numerous contacts within the police, Littlewood had not succeeded in discovering Higgins's intentions; and Higgins had a reputation for stubborn incorruptibility. One thing was certain, though: he was asking questions about Littlewood and was not interested only in Belzoni's mummy and the three murdered men. The inspector was looking for him: the soul of the advancing revolution. A battle to the death had been joined between them.

The prey had become the hunter.

As he returned to his headquarters, Higgins thought he was safe and would lower his guard. That would be the ideal moment at which to kill him.

At last Littlewood reached a poorly lit area, with not a single passer-by in sight.

He would speed up, approach his prey, launch a surprise attack, slit his throat and walk calmly away.

Suddenly, Littlewood gripped his dagger very tightly, as if his hand was acting independently of him and signalling danger. The revolutionary never ignored this type of sign. A trap . . . That accursed policeman had laid a trap for him!

He heard the sounds of running feet, coming from both right and left! Forgetting Higgins, Littlewood attempted to run away.

The sergeant struggled to get his breath back.

'We lost him,' he told Inspector Higgins shamefacedly. 'The man's like an eel, I swear to you! There were three of us, and we thought we had him in a pincer movement, but he managed to get away by using his fists and his elbows. He's quite a fighter, and faster than a galloping horse. How did he manage to escape from us? Ah, I forgot one detail: the person following you was a woman.'

'A woman? Are you certain?'

'She was wearing a dark skirt and a sort of knitted garment with long sleeves. Poor people's clothes.'

'Did you see her face?'

'She had a shawl covering her head; we just saw the lower part of her face for a second. We couldn't recognize her. Given the speed at which she was moving, she's obviously a fit young woman. In my opinion, inspector, the area is becoming unhealthy. In Whitechapel, the gangs are accustomed to using a prostitute to obtain information on their future victim's habits. Someone has it in for you, that's for sure. You must change your place of residence.'

Higgins was forced to see reason. If the woman following him was in the pay of Littlewood, he was in real danger. And since they were persisting in trying to kill him, he must be on the right track.

'Very well, I will move house.'

'My colleagues and I will stay with you,' decided the sergeant. 'There may be miscreants waiting for you in your apartment.'

They checked, but this worry was unfounded. Higgins decided to move into the police station in Piccadilly, where he could discuss the situation with his principal informants. In the light of the information they had gathered, the inspector glimpsed an explanation for why he was being followed.

It was up to him to regain the upper hand.

Littlewood had got away scot-free.

Without his instinct and his ability to react swiftly, he would have fallen into the hands of the police, for if it had come to a brief, rough confrontation, he would not have succeeded in overcoming the three sturdy officers who had protected Higgins and set the trap.

Clearly that accursed inspector had assembled a team of loyal officers who were extremely difficult to corrupt. Attacking Higgins had become a perilous task, demanding forays into unknown territory. After this failed attempt, Higgins would take even greater precautions, and his men would be permanently at his shoulder.

In the first instance, it was better to get round the obstacle by allowing the inspector to believe that his shadowy adversary had given up trying to attack him. Meanwhile, Littlewood would search for a means of getting through his defences and attacking him without running any risks.

And besides, Higgins was only Higgins, a mere inspector, incapable of opposing the giant wave that would soon be unleashed on King George IV and his society of exploiters! Devoid of a leader and without any central command, incompetent and rotten to the core, His Majesty's police would put up only derisory resistance against the people's anger.

Basically, this investigator was destined for failure.

37

The police station at Piccadilly had become the operations centre for the reorganization of the capital's police forces. Many uniformed officers and plain-clothes inspectors could no longer bear the passivity of their corrupt, lax colleagues. Higgins's great project was doing the rounds, and his ideas were gaining ground. On the day Scotland Yard came into existence, insecurity would retreat and crimes would no longer go unpunished.

Higgins occupied rather pleasant official rooms in the police station's attics. They comprised a drawing room, an office, a bedroom, a bathroom, a lavatory and a small kitchen. The door was under permanent guard and the inspector's safety was assured.

He rose at dawn, washed and dressed in a classic frock coat made by the best tailor in Regent Street. An orderly brought him coffee, eggs and bacon, toast and Oxford marmalade. As he ate his breakfast, Higgins reflected on the night's events. There was nothing illogical about them, in truth.

Freezing rain and fog hindered traffic. The inspector walked to the Belzonis' residence and knocked on the door, which had recently been repainted green.

The servant James Curtain opened the door, looking barely awake.

'I should like to see Mr Belzoni.'

'Come in, inspector.'

The explorer's house did not resemble the traditional house of a gentleman. Chests were piled up in the hall and bore various inscriptions: STATUETTES, VASES, POTTERY and FRAGMENTS OF SCULPTURES. Normally reserved for visitors, the drawing room housed the pieces of a sarcophagus and the small mummy of an ibis.

Sarah Belzoni came to greet Higgins, wearing a purple dressing gown and with her hair hanging loose about her shoulders.

'Good day, inspector. My husband worked late, and he's still asleep. May I help you?'

'Unfortunately, I have specific questions which I must ask him personally.'

The tall Irishwoman looked worried. 'Is it serious?'

Higgins merely gave her a kindly smile.

'I shall go and wake him. James, ensure that our guest is made comfortable, and bring him some coffee.'

The inspector was shown into the Italian's office, a superb shambles of a room worthy of an Eastern bazaar. Belzoni had amassed heaps of files, boxes filled with drawings, naive paintings depicting Egyptian temples, mother-of-pearl pipes, vials of perfume, pairs of babouches and a few other souvenirs of his stay in Egypt.

The coffee was strong, with a remarkable flavour. It reminded Higgins of magical evenings in Rome, on the terrace of a palace, beneath a starry sky. Life had seemed light-hearted, the future bright. The young man he was then had had no idea of the fierce battle he would have to wage against crime.

Belzoni's heavy tread made the wooden floor creak. Hastily combed and unshaven, and clad in a striped woollen dressing gown, he looked weary, as if he had not slept.

'An emergency, inspector?'

'Indeed, Mr Belzoni.'

The giant chose a high-backed armchair and poured himself a cup of coffee. 'Have you found my mummy?'

'Unfortunately not.'

'Have there been any more murders?'

'Fortunately not.'

The Italian swallowed a bread roll.

'What is the significance of the word *Magnoon*, Mr Belzoni?'

The giant almost choked. 'I don't know.'

'Have you never heard it before?'

'Never.'

'It seems to have an Arabic resonance, but I haven't had time to check.'

'Is this word particularly important in your view?'

'The actor Peter Bergeray heard it in a dream, and it might designate the murderer of the clergyman, the nobleman and the pathologist.'

Belzoni looked astonished. 'Do you grant credence to the words of that dishonest fellow? He bought the wrappings from the mummy's face and forgot to pay the price even though he'd agreed to it! My wife and I tracked him down, and he promised to pay his debts swiftly. If he continues to behave like a thief, I shall break his bones!'

'I would advise against doing so.'

'Must I accept such behaviour? He may be an actor, but that man has no right to establish his own law!'

'If Bergeray does not keep his promise, use the services of a lawyer.'

'I have little faith in them, inspector. In the East, I learned how to get by on my own.'

'You're not wearing a ring this morning.'

Belzoni looked at his hands. 'My tastes vary.'

'Will you show me the ring with the phoenix emblem?'

The Italian put down his cup. This time, he was completely awake. 'Is that absolutely necessary, inspector?'

'I fear so.'

Belzoni stood up and opened a metal box which was balanced atop a pile of books. He took out the ring.

'Does it bear an inscription?' asked Higgins.

'You know it already, I assume? Check with your own eyes.'

The giant handed the object to the inspector. Inside

the ring, finely engraved letters made up three words: *Brothers of Luxor*.

'This is the ring I was given by Henry Cranmer, one of the purchasers present at the unwrapping,' said Higgins, displaying the item.

Belzoni examined it and did not hide his astonishment. 'How did Cranmer obtain it?'

'At an auction. Which you did not, I assume?'

The Italian hesitated. 'I cannot lie, inspector. This ring was given to me in Egypt, at Luxor.'

'On what occasion?'

'On that point, I must remain silent.'

Higgins looked Belzoni in the eye. 'When do the works of the Sovereign Court open?' he asked.

'At the hour of truth in action.'

'Do you know Hermes and Mithras?'

'I am a knight of the sun.'

Higgins shook the giant's hand in a very particular way.

'So, inspector, you are a brother!'

'Do not draw hasty conclusions, Mr Belzoni. I owed it to myself to study the symbols and signs of the Freemasons, whose role is far from negligible. But you belong to that brotherhood and were initiated into an original, independent lodge, the Brothers of Luxor.'

Belzoni nodded.

'According to my investigation, it doesn't feature on the administrative table of the Grand Lodge of England, and is therefore considered "wild". Nevertheless, will you consent to talk to me about its rites and works?'

'Initiation into the ancient mysteries was never completely lost, and a handful of sages carried on teaching an important lesson: the Egypt of the pharaohs was the earthly realization of the celestial plan of the Great Architect of the Universe. In Luxor I had the good fortune to encounter one of its initiates, and the door of the lodge was opened to me. It enabled me to experience certain ancient rites and to better understand their importance. The Brothers of Luxor made my task easier by helping me in difficult times.'

'Have you appealed to the Freemasons in London?'

'Given the situation and the obstinate attitude of those donkeys at the British Museum, I've been forced to do so.'

'Are they not displeased by the secrecy surrounding the Brothers of Luxor?'

'It's not an advantage, and I don't know if my course of action will prove successful.'

'Did your lodge tackle the mystery of mummification?'

'The great mysteries are those of Osiris, who was murdered, embalmed and brought back to life,' Belzoni recalled. 'Both spiritually and materially, mummification embodies them. I have perceived only a tiny part of them, but I know that our short existence is a simple parenthesis between the world beyond, from which we come, and the one towards which we are heading. Do our hearts remain inert and our consciousness dulled? Do we seek to lift a corner of the veil? It's up to each individual to decide. The phoenix creates its own funeral pyre, the sole means of burning perishable flesh and death, in order to be reborn with a new life.'

'One point troubles me,' said Higgins. 'Among Freemasons, the myth of Osiris has become that of Hiram, who was also betrayed and murdered. Now, the guilty parties – evil companions determined to obtain the masters' password by force – are three in number.'

'Are you thinking about ... the clergyman, the old nobleman and the doctor?'

'Did they belong to the lodge of the Brothers of Luxor, and did they betray their oath?'

'No, inspector! I met them for the first time at the unwrapping, and none of them approached me with the signs of recognition. In my opinion, they were not Freemasons.'

'Stealing a mummy is no ordinary act; you yourself regard it as a sort of revelation of the great mysteries. I find it difficult to imagine an outsider stealing such a relic.'

'Collectors will commit any madness in order to satisfy their passion,' objected Belzoni.

'Are you the only Brother of Luxor currently present in London?'

Belzoni did not flinch at the inspector's gaze. 'To my knowledge, yes.'

'Do you intend to travel?'

'Not in the immediate future.'

'Be careful, Mr Belzoni. This case is complex, and I

fear there may be other incidents. If you feel threatened or if you're seriously suspicious about a possible culprit, don't hesitate to come to Piccadilly police station and alert me.'

After Higgins had left, the giant felt a desire for a boiling-hot bath. Sarah had managed to obtain a large bathtub, and enjoyed rubbing the adventurer's back. He told her every detail of Higgins's interrogation.

'I have the impression that the inspector doesn't believe I'm totally innocent,' lamented the Titan of Padua.

'It's just a professional attitude, my darling.'

'Why would we be in danger?'

The hard-bristled brush stopped in mid-stroke.

'That mummy might blame you for exposing it to the eyes of outsiders,' mused Sarah. 'Have no fear. I shall protect you.'

38

It was a windy Sunday, and a lazy one. Some people were preparing to go to lunch, others to receive friends or relations, while some were planning a carriage ride in the park. But Higgins did not allow himself any rest. Given the proximity of grave events, he must speak to the official who, in theory, was his superior.

The address given by Peter Soulina corresponded to a house in John Adam Street, dating from the eighteenth century. Austere and stiff, the house was inspired by Greek architecture, and pilasters, columns and pediments made the front of the house look a little pompous. The first storey was adorned with wrought-iron balconies, and the solid-oak door seemed designed to repel visitors.

However, just as Higgins approached, it opened.

'Are you looking for someone?' asked a square-faced doorkeeper with the arms of a fairground strongman.

'Peter Soulina.'

'Who wants to see him?'

266

'Inspector Higgins.'

'Come in and don't move.'

Two other burly men appeared.

'We have to search you.'

'I'm not armed.'

'We have to check.'

Higgins consented and stood motionless. Once satisfied, the doorkeeper invited him to follow him. They climbed the stairs to the first floor.

On the landing stood Peter Soulina, hands clasped behind his back. His small, inquisitive eyes glittered with aggression.

'About time, Higgins! I've been waiting for a long time for your report. One week longer, and I would have made an official complaint about you.'

'Certain investigations take time, Mr Soulina. And this one has proved particularly arduous.'

'Hmm . . . I don't care for excuses. Come into my office.'

The room was icy-cold and almost empty, save for a small desk in burr walnut and two medieval-looking chairs.

The two men sat facing each other.

'Have you made any progress, Higgins?'

'I hope so.'

'Do you have a suspect?'

'Several.'

'Ah! So you have serious clues?'

'More . . . disturbing than serious. Multiple investigations will be necessary.'

'How long will they take?'

'I don't know.'

'Do you think I'll be content with that answer?'

'You'll have to be, Mr Soulina. Rushing would be catastrophic, and we would run the risk of overlooking the truth.'

'Very well . . . Give me your report.'

'I haven't written one.'

'What?'

'Such a document would be pointless and would harm the progress of the investigation if it fell into the wrong hands.'

'Do you not trust my department?'

'Indeed not.'

'You go too far, inspector!'

'Certainly not.'

Irritated, the government emissary stood up and paced the room. 'I've heard a great deal about you lately. You're striving to defend a plan for reorganizing the police, and certain important people support you.'

'I'm happy to hear it.'

'Don't imagine that success will come swiftly! The government is hesitant to alter the current situation and set out along a road which may lead nowhere.'

'It's the current situation that is a dead end.'

'The authorities have entrusted you with a mission, inspector, and politics is not your job. Let's concentrate on what matters: have you identified and located Littlewood?'

'Not yet.'

'Unacceptable!' snapped the senior official. 'You place more importance on your criminal investigation than on the arrest of that dangerous revolutionary.'

'Everything is linked.'

Intrigued, Peter Soulina stopped pacing. 'What do you mean?'

'The three murders, Littlewood, the disappearance of the mummy: everything is linked.'

'Is this a hypothesis or a certainty?'

'Intuition.'

'Misplaced intuition, in my opinion! Littlewood linked to a mummy . . . Can you imagine defending that absurd thesis in front of a Minister?'

'The truth is sometimes surprising, Mr Soulina. Has Colonel Borrington's team obtained any interesting results?'

The government emissary returned to sit down. 'Nothing decisive, unfortunately. Will you agree to work alongside him again?'

'The colonel observes military discipline and is not accustomed to conducting investigations. As for his team, it's rotten to the core, and I wouldn't be surprised if several of the police officers he commands are in the pay of Littlewood.'

'Do you have . . . names?'

'It would be a mistake to arrest the corrupt individuals. Better to leave them in place and let them believe they haven't been identified. Provide them with false information, which they will pass on to Littlewood. Littlewood will believe he's master of the game, and I shall continue to make progress in the shadows.'

'You demand a great deal, Higgins. And this strategy could prove as risky as it is ineffective.'

'I know personally each of the men who are helping me to combat crime, and I know that none of them will work for Littlewood. Moreover, they are working in the field, unlike bureaucrats.'

'Of course, it's pointless to ask you for a report concerning the conspirator and his group of revolutionaries.'

'That type of paperwork would ruin the work that has been accomplished.'

'Do you dare assume that senior officials are Littlewood's accomplices?'

'I do, Mr Soulina. By envisaging the worst, one manages to avert it.'

'I'm your direct superior, inspector. You must inform me in a detailed manner.'

'That would be pernickety. It's the results that are important.'

'I don't see any!'

'The classic methods have failed; Colonel Borrington and those like him have failed to identify Littlewood and prevent him doing harm. You've entrusted me with a mission, and I shall fulfil it, well aware that I shall come into conflict with many adversaries, not forgetting the mummy.'

Peter Soulina frowned. 'Now is not the time for jokes!'

'That was not a joke.'

'Are you losing your mind, inspector?'

'I repeat: everything is linked.'

'Forget about that mummy, and track down Littlewood!'

'I'm more preoccupied with doing so than you suppose.'

The firmness of Higgins's tone impressed the senior official. 'Shall we meet again next Sunday?'

'Probably, Mr Soulina.'

39

Despite the cold and damp, Higgins would willingly have returned to Hyde Park to walk in peace, away from the noisy, bustling city. But he still had important details to sort out along with a dozen police officers, and he had decided to use the information provided by Lady Suzanna.

So he headed for the entrance to the lecture theatre at Charing Cross Hospital, where lectures were given by leading experts.

A guard barred his way. 'Are you a doctor?'

'No, I'm sorry.'

'Today, only professionals are allowed in.'

'I'm Inspector Higgins. I'm interested in the theories of Dr Pettigrew.'

The guard bowed.

About a hundred doctors and students had taken their places in the stepped seats. Higgins sat down in the back row and observed Pettigrew's theatrical entrance, followed by two assistants carrying the body of an old man, which they laid on a low, rough wooden table.

Using abstruse language, the anatomist talked about his latest research, which he considered essential, and announced a series of publications questioning age-old ideas. According to him, the study of ancient medicine, particularly that of the Egyptians, would provide information useful to modern science. Filled with enthusiasm, Pettigrew talked at length about mummies, lamenting the lack of serious investigations. He was planning to fill this gap and discover the secrets of the embalmers.

Next, he turned to the corpse and called on the services of two students destined for the profession of pathologist. Following his instructions, they dissected the body and Pettigrew described its various component parts, from the brain to the ankles. Feeling nauseous, two spectators left the lecture theatre, watched angrily by the professor.

At the end of the lecture, the audience applauded. The master agreed to answer questions, then the remains of the dissected body were removed, and the anatomist exchanged a few brief words with some of his departing students.

Higgins was the last to introduce himself.

'I'm sorry. I have to go,' said the doctor.

'Will you permit me to accompany you?'

The doctor looked impatient. 'Why?'

'I need a consultation.'

'Are you ill?'

'Three corpses are causing me real worries.'

'How do they concern me?'

'They're linked to Belzoni's famous mummy.'

'I missed that one! According to admirers, it was exceptional. Finding fine specimens, that's the real problem. I frequent the salerooms and can obtain only second-rate remains. Your three cadavers . . . Are they ancient or modern?'

'Modern. A clergyman, a nobleman and a pathologist, Dr Bolson.'

This revelation left Dr Pettigrew unmoved.

'They were present at the unwrapping of the mummy,' added Higgins, 'and their only desire was to destroy it.'

'Was it saved?'

'It's disappeared.'

'You mean . . . It's been destroyed?'

'No, stolen.'

'A mummy thief! I should like to meet him. He must possess treasures vital to the progress of science.'

'You asked Belzoni to obtain mummies for you.'

Pettigrew looked at Higgins suspiciously. 'That does not concern you, inspector. Are you investigating my private life? I advise you not to do so. I have the good fortune to number highly placed individuals among my friends, and they will not tolerate the police persecuting me.'

'May I know the identity of the corpse you studied?'

'A tramp from Whitechapel, I believe. It was found in a filthy alley. Not a penny, no family. At least he will have served medicine. Alas, it's often the way. Those poor devils lead a miserable existence and die without a name. It's up to the government to resolve the problem.'

'Do you have any idea where Belzoni's mummy might be found?'

The anatomist stiffened. 'Do you dare suspect me of having stolen it?'

'Did I say so, Dr Pettigrew?'

'You think it, I'm certain, and you're not far off accusing me of a triple murder – I, a man of science and progress! It's monstrous, inspector, and I shall not forgive you. Your unacceptable behaviour will be punished.'

'Yours intrigues me.'

'Well, I care not a jot for your opinion! This conversation is at an end.'

Offended, the anatomist strode out of the lecture theatre.

Higgins succeeded in questioning the director of the hospital, his deputy and several doctors. They had no hesitation in talking about Dr Pettigrew, and their statements enabled Higgins to draw up a portrait of the man. A brilliant student who had become a renowned specialist, he seemed destined for a fine career despite an all-consuming passion for Egyptian mummies. He was willing to spend large amounts, even fritter away his personal fortune, if the opportunity arose to acquire well-preserved specimens. Hard-working, stubborn and irritable, the anatomist had no shortage of contacts and attracted the friendship of aristocrats who were amused by his research. He was not known to have any major vices.

Deep in thought, Higgins walked back to his head-quarters in Piccadilly.

At the entrance to the sordid alleyway stood an armed lookout. A workman approached, wearing a cap whose broad peak concealed his face.

'The sun isn't up,' he declared softly.

'The rich have stolen it.'

'I shall drown them in the Thames.'

From these words of recognition, the guard identified the leader of the revolutionaries.

'No prying eyes spotted, sir. Our friends are waiting for you.'

Littlewood walked swiftly to the end of the narrow street and knocked twice on a brick wall.

The wall swung open and pivoted round. Littlewood stepped inside the main weapons cache in Whitechapel, which was accessible only to his lieutenants. Pistols and rifles were accumulated there day after day, following thefts and burglaries. Although not yet adequate, stocks were beginning to be substantial.

A dozen men hailed their leader. Two oil lamps lit up the storeroom, which had an escape route in case of danger. But the police did not risk taking an interest in the most destitute corner of Whitechapel, and security measures would prevent any unpleasant surprises.

'Tomorrow is the great day,' he announced proudly. 'By this time tomorrow, the tyrant George IV will be dead, and a wind of freedom will blow across England.'

'Shouldn't we fear a violent reaction from the forces of order?' asked a conspirator worriedly.

'The police are disorganized, the various departments are at each other's throats and nobody is coordinating them. The government isn't expecting this kind of attack, and it will be completely at a loss. It may order random arrests, promising the imminent capture of the guilty parties. We shall allow the hue and cry to die down and then unleash the insurrection. Gentlemen, we must show that we are worthy of this historic moment! A wealthy and powerful empire is about to be offered to the people, whose guides we shall be. Have the district committees been mobilized?'

'We're ready,' replied the official. 'I've appointed leaders who are capable of stirring up the crowd.'

'We shall go over the details of the operation together,' said Littlewood. 'Each participant must carry out his task to perfection, without the slightest hesitation. I'm listening.'

The revolutionaries spoke in turns, each recalling the precise part he would be playing. Their determination delighted Littlewood. George IV would not escape from a raiding party like this one.

40

George IV's carriage left his residence at the appointed time. Eight fine horses drew it swiftly towards the Shepherdess Inn, where the monarch would spend a pleasant few hours with a deliciously beautiful country girl. Two experienced coachmen were driving the comfortable carriage, with two soldiers escorting it.

This liaison was extremely unpopular with the close advisers to the king, whose amorous exploits had caused him to be detested by the population. If news of the affair got out, it would only make the situation worse. As the seducer was already tiring of the country girl's charms, the government hoped that his next prey would be a member of the aristocracy and would not cause a scandal.

The revolutionaries were waiting for the king at the inn. They had bound and gagged the innkeeper, his staff and the stable lads, and taken their places.

Ordinarily, the tyrant arrived around eleven, took his mistress upstairs, had lunch in bed and then returned to

London. On the days he visited, the inn was cleared of customers by the innkeeper himself, who was delighted to receive a sizeable sum for his trouble.

In the name of discretion, there was no police presence. Littlewood, suspicious, had explored the old building from top to bottom, but he found nothing abnormal.

'He's late,' said one of the conspirators, glancing at the tavern clock.

'This wet weather and the bad road must prevent the horses moving at their normal speed,' said Littlewood.

'Or else that skirt-chaser has had an accident!'

The revolutionaries' leader took a pinch of snuff for good luck. He was thinking of the moment when George IV would descend from his carriage, in a state of high excitement. He would step inside the inn, not even glancing at the staff, and climb the stairs four at a time. The king would open the door of his mistress's bedroom, expecting to find her naked, ready to welcome him with open arms.

There was going to be one small alteration to this programme: the king would find himself facing the barrel of Littlewood's pistol, as the conspirator aimed at his heart. The puppet king would collapse, and so would his kingdom.

As the minutes went by, the conspirators became increasingly tense. Had the philanderer decided not to join his mistress because of the fog? It would not be easy to obtain new information and mount a similar operation.

Suddenly they heard the sound of galloping hooves.

His Majesty's carriage and its escort were approaching the inn.

'Is the girl out of the way?' Littlewood asked his second in command.

'She's locked in a cupboard. She can't move or cry out.'

'Are all the men at their posts?'

'We're ready, sir.'

'Long live the revolution, and long live the common people!'

Suddenly a cloudburst rained down from the heavens.

Taking care to avoid the puddles, the carriage slowed down and the horses trotted the last few yards which separated them from the stables.

The carriage halted. Umbrella in hand, Littlewood's second in command ran out of the inn to prevent the king getting wet.

The soldiers dismounted, an officer opened the carriage door and the despot stepped out.

With the umbrella in his left hand and his right gripping the pistol in his pocket, the conspirator threw the sovereign a look of utter hatred.

'Don't move an inch, Littlewood,' ordered Higgins, who had taken the king's place. 'Surrender. The inn is surrounded.'

'Death to the tyrant!'

The soldiers fired, and Littlewood's deputy fell to the ground, his chest oozing blood.

Twenty soldiers came rushing out of nearby woods and

ran towards the inn. The conspirators began returning fire, attempting to drive them back; but Higgins's men were disciplined and their attack well planned. Assisted by four elite soldiers, they eliminated the substitute stable lads, then fired at the windows.

Their precise marksmanship caused carnage. Abandoning his men, Littlewood ran down to the cellar, removed the grating from a small window, squeezed through into the open air behind the building and ran for all he was worth towards the willow-lined riverbank.

As he panted for breath, he wished he had not eaten, drunk and smoked so much. But no bullet put a stop to his escape.

One police officer was seriously wounded and two slightly, while ten conspirators had been killed and the hostages were all unharmed. The operation planned and executed by Higgins was a success. He comforted the young beauty as she was released from her cupboard.

'Will I see my king again?' she asked, sniffing back tears.

'Probably not, miss. Try to forget him.'

'We had such fun! Shall I tell you about it?'

'That will not be necessary. Go to the kitchen, and you'll be given a tot of something to raise your spirits.'

This success owed nothing to chance. Realizing how dangerous Littlewood was, Higgins had immediately worried about the king's safety. As he did not trust the sovereign's bodyguards, he had contacted members of the palace staff who occupied strategic posts, including the steward of the royal stables, who was a true servant of the state. Such men, who genuinely loved their jobs, were often worth more than courtiers and politicians. They had promised to tell Higgins, and only Higgins, if anything abnormal occurred.

One of the coachmen, an adulterous drunk with debts, had offered the steward a large sum of money in return for a list of the king's forthcoming movements. Once alerted, the inspector arranged for the suspect to be followed, but he had vanished in Whitechapel. In other words, he must have sold himself to Littlewood and was now helping him to plan some kind of attack.

The disappearance of the coachman had reinforced this belief. There was one major weak point in the list of royal movements: this inn, which provided the setting for his clandestine liaisons. During the king's official engagements, guards would be on hand to dissuade any possible aggressors; but here, the small and discreet escort would be swiftly exterminated, leaving the king at Littlewood's mercy.

By some kind of miracle, the palace had agreed to take note of Higgins's warnings. Heeding his anxious and persuasive advisers, the monarch had resolved to break off his country liaison, and Higgins had been authorized to take appalling risks in order to arrest the revolutionaries' leader.

The inspector checked that none of the inn's staff had been injured in any way. In a state of shock, the innkeeper had uncorked several bottles of wine and offered them to his saviours, along with sheets to cover up the conspirators' bodies.

Higgins examined them one by one, before exploring the inn in its entirety, accompanied by two armed police officers. One of the conspirators might have succeeded in hiding. When they were satisfied that this was not the case, the trio rejoined their colleagues. The innkeeper and his staff served up roast duck with potatoes, then cheese, which had been destined for the king's lunch.

'Enjoy it, gentlemen! Times like these teach us to make the most of life,' declared the innkeeper.

The tension relaxed, and the policemen and soldiers accepted the invitation. Only Higgins left the establishment, to take a second look at the faces of the dead conspirators.

As he was doing so, the officer in charge of the small cavalry squadron joined him. 'My congratulations, inspector. Everything went according to plan.'

'We were lucky, and our men conducted themselves admirably.'

'They deserve a medal, and my report will say as much. Thanks to your foresight, a dastardly conspiracy has been destroyed, and our king is now safe.'

'Nevertheless, you should advise him not to lower his guard.'

The officer frowned. 'What do you fear? The proof of victory is at our feet! No one will now dare to attack our sovereign.'

'I pray to heaven that it is so.'

'I have decided to bury these villains in this remote spot. The press will hear nothing of the incident, and the innkeeper will be firmly instructed to keep his mouth shut. Come inside and have some food, inspector. Then we shall return to London. You will be a hero, and rightly so.'

This prospect did not make Higgins feel any happier.

True, the worst had been averted. But this success was nothing but an illusion.

41

Ploughing through muddy thickets and along narrow paths, Littlewood put as much distance as possible between himself and the inn, and finally reached the road to London. Although soaked to the skin, exhausted and shocked by the disaster, he still burned with a furious desire for victory and revenge.

By the time he reached one of his lairs, in the middle of the night, he did not even feel like sleeping. He drank a large glass of gin, ate some slices of smoked ham and reviewed this unexpected defeat.

He had been betrayed.

It was that scum of a coachman, of course, playing the part of a double agent! Littlewood was glad he had killed him.

A high-ranking police officer, or perhaps a Minister, had arranged this expedition, designed to cut off the head of the revolution. The king had had the intelligence to listen to his advisers, and was now out of reach. In the future, he would have the benefit of close and permanent protection.

Higgins . . . Yes, that accursed inspector must be at the heart of this operation! Littlewood's informants would tell him the exact extent of Higgins's responsibility. Instinctively, he sensed that the inspector was the real brains behind it. After all, he was attempting to form an effective police corps, stripped of its corrupt elements and capable of fighting crime. If the government encouraged this course of action, the revolutionaries would be faced with a sizeable adversary.

This sombre prospect did not discourage Littlewood and, despite the deaths of his best lieutenants, he would not give in. He possessed one major advantage: the enemy believed he was dead! The corpses would be buried secretly, the press would not be informed about the assassination attempt on the royal person, and good society would continue to live happily, completely ignorant of the misery of London's poverty-stricken districts. Now that the leaders had been eliminated, the authorities would believe themselves invulnerable.

This feeling of security would serve the cause of the revolution. Forced to alter his strategy, Littlewood would rebuild a team of agitators drawn from among the most radical members of the competing groups. He would train them in underground action and kindle their zeal with his speeches, which were extremely popular with the common folk. Promising wonderful tomorrows, wealth for the poor and poverty for the rich always produced excellent results. When lying served the revolutionary ideal, it was a positive virtue.

Attacking George IV again would be impossible. On the other hand, he must be led to believe that he was still the main target. Consequently, the forces of order would be preoccupied with a decoy while, step by step, Littlewood prepared for a popular uprising. A monstrous wave would wash away this middle-class society, eaten away from the inside.

Evil and violence fascinated Littlewood. The guillotine, the heads of the nobility displayed on pikes, the wild, howling crowds attacking châteaux and private residences, summary executions and torture: all these things haunted his dreams. No better methods of governing existed, and his people's revolutionary republic would hone them to perfection. All-powerful torturers on the one hand, and on the other docile subjects who continued to believe in liberty, equality and brotherhood: that was his programme. Robespierre had failed because he was too soft, but he, Littlewood, would succeed.

During this struggle to the death, the use of occult forces would be far from negligible. That was why he must find Belzoni's mummy and utilize the black magic it contained. The power of this revenant would terrify large numbers of his adversaries as well as his supporters, convincing them that the leader of the revolution possessed supernatural powers. Simple souls were sensitive to this kind of argument, and so, sometimes, were senior officials.

The mummy . . . What a wonderful spearhead!

His hunger sated, Littlewood fell asleep. First thing tomorrow, he would set off once more on his crusade.

'Inspector . . . Lady Suzanna would like to see you!'

Fortunately, Higgins had finished dressing. The starry-eyed sergeant had been delighted to see the magnificent young woman again and exchange a few words with her before alerting the inspector, who had become a real hero in the police officers' eyes.

Embellished as it passed from one police station to the next, the story of his success was becoming positively epic, rivalling the conquests of Alexander the Great.

The barrister was wearing a most becoming long, beige cloak to ward off the cold. 'My congratulations, inspector. The whole of London talks of nothing but your exploits. By saving the king's life and destroying a formidable conspiracy, you have done the country a great service.'

'My merits have been exaggerated, Lady Suzanna.'

'One of the brigands fired at you, did he not?'

'He merely attempted to.'

'You might have been killed!'

'Those are the risks of the job.'

'Will you accompany me on a walk in Hyde Park?'

'Unfortunately, I have to lunch with a representative of the government, but I do have a couple of hours to spare.'

It was mid-morning, and the park's pathways were almost deserted. The cold did not favour leisurely walks, and only those who really loved the place came to put down grain and fat for the birds. The squirrels were stocking up on provisions, and mice were making themselves comfortable nests. Fat blackbirds were hopping about among the oak trees.

'I plead your cause every evening,' revealed the young woman. 'I select dinner invitations according to the guests who will be present, and I'm interested only in politicians, influential members of court and judges. Putting an end to divisions in the police and creating a large, effective police service doesn't find favour with all these gentlemen, and the battle is bound to be a hard one. But since I'm stubborn by nature, I shall continue to confront them. Your recent deeds speak in your favour and will persuade those who are undecided. You now have some fervent supporters at court.'

'The road will be long and filled with obstacles. The most important thing is that Scotland Yard comes into existence.'

'Have you looked into the case of Dr Pettigrew, inspector?'

'He is a curious individual, with a difficult personality.'

'Doesn't his passion for mummies intrigue you?'

'It is rather uncommon, I agree.'

'I'm convinced that he's somehow mixed up in the theft of Belzoni's mummy. He must have contacted his colleague, Dr Bolson, and stolen his treasure.'

'If so, Pettigrew became a murderer.'

'Preserving such a fine mummy was so vital to him that he lost his mind!'

'Our conversation didn't go well,' said Higgins. 'The brilliant anatomist threatened me with reprisals if I attempted to investigate him.'

'Do such threats frighten you?'

'Have no fear, I shall not lose sight of that strange practitioner.'

'You don't seem convinced of his guilt!'

'I must have solid evidence. And Dr Pettigrew wasn't present when the mummy was unwrapped.'

'Do you feel that point is decisive?'

'It is, Lady Suzanna.'

'Perhaps a search of his house in Spring Gardens would produce some interesting results?'

'In the event of failure, the doctor would cause a scandal which would compromise the rest of the investigation.'

'All the same, will you consider my suggestion?'

'Absolutely, Lady Suzanna.'

The young woman smiled. 'Since the conspirators have been eliminated, you can devote yourself entirely to the murderer of the aristocrat, the clergyman and the doctor, and to the search for the mummy. For my part, I'm continuing my investigations and will report back to you with my findings.'

'I must repeat: be very careful. This affair is exceptional, for malevolent forces are on the prowl and are continuing to spread. These are no ordinary crimes, and

I'm not certain that even the finest police force could succeed in solving the riddle.'

Crows cawed as they soared above Hyde Park, and a strong wind began to gust.

'Are you trying to frighten me, inspector?'

'If I succeeded in doing so it would please me greatly.'

'Fear must not prevent one from going forward. Now, I possess the list of people who bought relics at the unwrapping of the mummy, and I'm going to investigate them.'

'Please don't approach them. One of them is a sort of cold monster, who's resolved to kill anyone who stands in his way.'

'I promise you that I shall keep my distance and act with perfect discretion. At the slightest suspicious sign, I shall alert you.'

42

The Salmon and Partridge was a chic restaurant in the
City, catering only to a wealthy clientele composed of
industrialists and politicians. They came to the restaurant
to make business deals that would be advantageous to
both sides, deals that were frequently on the fringes of
legality. Wasn't morality just a matter of words?

Peter Soulina had reserved a private room decorated
with heavy beige draperies and paintings of fruit and
flowers. The rather claustrophobic atmosphere suited the
private discussion to which he had summoned Inspector
Higgins, who was rigorously punctual.

'To celebrate our triumph, we shall have champagne
with our lunch. The head waiter has put together a special
menu: foie gras, lobster, haunch of venison and exotic
sorbets. Will that be to your taste?'

'It sounds wonderful.'

Soulina's complexion was decidedly pasty.

'Are you unwell?' enquired Higgins worriedly.

'You are the cause, inspector.'

'In which case you have my apologies.'

'Don't feign innocence with me! You had the audacity to go over my head and approach the palace directly. May I remind you that I am your direct superior, appointed by the government, and that you ought to have described your intentions to me in detail. Mounting an operation of that kind was extremely perilous.'

'The danger concerned only a number of volunteers, who knew exactly what was involved. As for the king, he was safe.'

'That was for me to judge, Higgins, and it was up to me to give the orders! Are you trying to make me look ridiculous?'

'Absolutely not. My sole objectives were absolute secrecy and effectiveness.'

'Objectives which you attained. Congratulations!'

'Your gratitude means a great deal to me.'

Peter Soulina's gaze became openly aggressive. 'So you suspect me of involvement with the conspirators!'

Higgins took the time to savour a mouthful of champagne and a forkful of foie gras.' 'I wouldn't go that far. Given the circumstances, I had to use my own network, outside the official framework, to avoid leaks and obstacles. The fact that you didn't intervene proves your honesty.'

Soulina almost choked.

'Would you like me to pat you on the back?'

'No, thank you! Do you realize the gravity of your

suspicions? I, an ally of Littlewood!'

'Have similar collusions not occurred in the realm of politics?'

'You're going too far, Higgins!'

'The mist has now cleared, and His Majesty has been warned of the risks.'

Soulina scratched his throat. 'You are too modest, inspector! The conspirators have been eliminated, and all the glory for doing so has come to you. This time, your mad idea of forming a new police corps is gaining ground.'

'Are you opposed to it?'

The senior official at last began to eat. 'To tell the truth, no. I think you are right and that the creation of this Scotland Yard, as you wish to call it, would be an excellent solution. But I shall have my revenge, for I was able to defend my position, and the government continues to place its trust in me. I'm still your superior, and I'm in charge of matters relating to the reorganization of the forces of order. It is I, not you, who will receive all the glory. You will never head Scotland Yard, Higgins.'

'Excellent news.'

The rodent-like face took on an expression of astonishment. 'Wasn't that your main ambition?'

'I'm a man who works in the field, not in an office. And my only aspiration is to return to my retirement in the country. Make my idea reality, Mr Soulina, and derive as much benefit as you like, so long as you serve the people and combat crime.'

Somewhat at a loss, the government emissary drained

his glass. 'I don't understand you, Higgins.'

'Don't try. We're not made of the same stuff.'

The lobster, although excellent, did not make Peter Soulina look any happier. 'His Majesty intends to grant you a private audience, and there are rumours of a medal. But don't forget that I head all the security services. Now that Littlewood has been destroyed, you will devote yourself to searching for the triple murderer. I'm forced to raise you to the rank of chief inspector, but I demand weekly reports and results. The honour of the police is at stake.'

'And what about Colonel Borrington's team?'

'It's been dissolved, and the colonel will enjoy a pleasant retirement.'

'Do you believe that the conspiracy is at an end?'

The senior official choked, had a coughing fit and emptied another glass of champagne. 'I don't like your sense of humour, Higgins. You've exterminated Littlewood's evil band and you'll derive the benefits, understood! Don't add to it.'

'You persist in misunderstanding me. The battle at the inn didn't mark the end of the clandestine war.'

Soulina's appetite suddenly failed him. 'Explain yourself.'

'In my opinion, Littlewood is not dead.'

'Was he not less than a yard from you? Did he not threaten you with a pistol, and did the king's escort not kill him?'

'That was one of the conspirators, not their leader.'

'How can you be sure, Higgins?'

'I examined the corpses. Not one of them had bought relics from Belzoni's mummy. And Littlewood is hiding behind the identity of one of those individuals.'

'That's a hazy theory.'

'I should add that he fled via the cellar, by removing the grating from a basement window, which he replaced roughly.'

'Why would that be Littlewood and not one of his lieutenants?'

'I've just explained that. The man is both cunning and cautious. He will never show himself in the front line before he has triumphed. He has trained devoted, fanatical soldiers who are ready to make the supreme sacrifice.'

'It was Littlewood's task to open the door of the carriage and kill George IV! It would be impossible to abandon that task to a subordinate,' objected Soulina.

'Littlewood wouldn't run the risk of being killed,' declared Higgins. 'He feared resistance from the soldiers escorting the king. Once they and the coachmen were eliminated, he would have appeared in triumph.'

'I don't share your convictions, chief inspector. They rest on an inconsistent hypothesis, and you're mixing up cases with no relationship between them. It's clear that Littlewood is dead and his revolution has been decapitated.'

'With respect, I would still maintain strict protection measures around the king.'

'Indeed, they come under my responsibility, and I have every intention of doing so. Thanks to you, I admit, the Littlewood case is closed. Now apply yourself to the criminal investigation with which you have been entrusted.'

The haunch of venison, accompanied by fried potatoes and bilberry jelly, was close to perfection, but Soulina's stomach was in knots and he could hardly eat.

'One question deserves to be asked,' said Higgins. 'Why, despite multiple investigations, do we not have a description of Littlewood – not even an approximate one?'

'Because of an absence of precise reports and administrative deficiencies,' replied Soulina. 'The reorganization of the forces of order will enable us to avoid that kind of mistake.'

'Let's hope so, but another reason exists.'

'Would you be good enough to enlighten me, chief inspector?'

'Littlewood is a chameleon. He's constantly adapting, changing his appearance, his mannerisms, his clothes, even his habits. Those close to him have no knowledge of his real activities, and the revolutionary committees which have been set up in the various districts don't know the true identity of this leader with many faces.'

'My head is spinning, Higgins! Stop inventing nonsense to confirm your illusions. One last time, forget Littlewood and arrest the triple murderer. Are your lodgings in Piccadilly suitable?'

'I lack for nothing.'

'So much the better! In principle, our paths will no longer cross. My career is moving on to another level, and the weight of my responsibilities will prevent me from taking an interest in run-of-the-mill matters. Nevertheless, in the event of absolute necessity, you know where to contact me. The whole of the building on John Adam Street is under my control. Good luck, chief inspector.'

43

'Everything is right and perfect,' declared the Venerable Master, closing the works of the lodge at which Belzoni had been a guest, speaking about the research carried out by the Brothers of Luxor.

The temple was spacious, and the benches comfortable. To the east was a delta containing an eye, which the Italian had often noticed in Egyptian inscriptions.[*] The Freemasons left the premises in a procession and headed for the 'damp room', where they took their places around a well-laden table. Numerous toasts were drunk to the king, to England and to brothers all over the world, before the brothers sampled chicken with rice. The Titan of Padua was a noteworthy guest and had to answer numerous questions about Egypt and its mysteries.

Only one person remained silent. Old, sober and cold, he seemed bored. At the end of the festivities, when the

---

[*] The eye is a hieroglyph meaning 'create, do'.

brothers were dispersing, he approached Belzoni. 'I should like to see you in private.'

The Italian followed the austere individual, who led him to a small library and carefully closed the door behind them. The shelves were filled with works devoted to the history of Freemasonry.

'Be seated, brother.'

Belzoni and his host sat down on opposite sides of a solid-oak table.

'You have appealed to our brotherhood in order to resolve delicate problems,' recalled the austere man. 'And it's my task to deal with this issue, since I belong to the administrative council of the British Museum.'

Was this good or bad news? Not knowing how to react, Belzoni chose to remain silent.

'A minority among us ascribe relative credibility to your Luxor lodge. I do not. No one who does not obey the laws of the Great Lodge of England can claim any legitimacy. Our institution was born in 1717, and the references to Egypt and the cathedral builders have no pertinence. Our sole goal is humanism, not the study of mysteries and symbols. And membership to good society remains the principal criterion for admission.'

Belzoni clenched his fists and tried to remain outwardly calm. The austere man opened a bag at his feet and took out a file.

'Let's deal with the precise facts. When the Earl of Elgin offered the British Museum the marbles from the Parthenon, it had to pay the exorbitant sum of thirty-five thousand pounds, and this enormous expenditure unleashed a wave of indignation. Paying such a price for foreign antiquities rightly shocked people. When Consul Henry Salt sent us his collection of Egyptian objects, it didn't arouse enthusiasm and the price of eight thousand pounds appeared exorbitant to us.'

'Yet it was a derisory amount! My sarcophagus is worth at least twice that!'

An icy stare silenced Belzoni. 'We offered Salt two thousand pounds, and he accepted. As for your sarcophagus, it doesn't interest us. And that decision is final. The British Museum has other preoccupations.'

The Italian got to his feet.

'One moment, please. Now that this file is closed, let's deal with your second request, an official mission which would enable you to return to Egypt and direct excavations.'

Belzoni dared to hope again.

'Senior authorities have examined the situation seriously,' declared the austere individual. 'The skills of the eminent Henry Salt have not been questioned, and he will continue to select works destined for enthusiasts. Undertaking archaeological research with uncertain results would require a budget which nobody has any intention of making available. And we must be clear-headed: you are not a scientist, but a sort of treasure hunter, skilled in handling simple materials and poor workmen. The general opinion is that no more monuments and riches remain to be discovered in Egypt. So forget this ridiculous plan for an official mission and devote yourself to business activities. I am happy to have met you, brother. Good luck.'

As he walked through the blizzard like an automaton, Belzoni remembered.* In the middle of a sun-baked desert, his camels were so exhausted that they could barely move. Three had already succumbed, and a fourth was dying. All that could be seen, as far as the eye could see, was an immense expanse covered with sand and stones, sometimes interspersed with mountains, without shelter, vegetation or any trace of human habitation. A few rare trees braved the drought, but the blazing heat made them disintegrate to dust. It was often six to eight days between water sources, and some provided only brackish water, to the despair of the thirsty men. The worst thing was to dream of a well and then find that it had run dry. The last, desperate solution was to kill one's camel, open its belly and drink the remains of the water its stomach contained. And this horrible sacrifice was not always enough. During the death throes of a traveller who could not escape the desert's trap, his eyes would bulge, his tongue and lips swell, unbearable sounds made him deaf and the brain burned in the skull.

Belzoni tasted a little snow and returned his thoughts to London. Wouldn't that terrible, far-off death have been preferable to humiliation? Basically, that cruel brother

---

* According to a text by Belzoni.

had made him face up to reality. Originally, he had been an engineer, but he had not succeeded in establishing his hydraulic machine in Egypt. Yet the machine had been extremely useful, making peasants' work easier. But the pasha and his advisers did not want to make the Italian rich and had prevented the project from succeeding.

What about his discovery of the entrance to the pyramid of Khephren, on the Giza plateau, on 2 March 1818, a date the giant had written himself on the smoke-blackened wall of the chamber of resurrection? A deed which was barely recognized. And, unfortunately, the pyramid was empty, like the Nubian temple of Abu Simbel which Belzoni had been the first to explore. The difficult and dangerous journeys to the Red Sea, in 1818, and to the Bahariyah oasis, in 1819, had not produced spectacular results.

It was he, the Titan of Padua, who had brought the bust of Memnon to Europe, managing to transport it from the Ramesseum* to the British Museum, whose ingratitude passed understanding. Instead of establishing his own collection of antiquities, Belzoni had made the mistake of working for Henry Salt, who was amoral and cunning. The diplomat would have no hesitation in taking the shirt from his back and would be of no help to him.

Disenchanted, he hurried back to his London residence.

---

* The Ramesseum, on the west bank of Thebes, is the 'temple of millions of years' of Ramses II, known in the nineteenth century by the name of Memnon.

Sarah herself opened the door, as if she had sensed his distress. 'You look like a snowman! Come in and get warm.'

'They refuse to give me an official mission, and the British Museum will never buy the alabaster sarcophagus.'

'There's no point in catching an even worse cold.'

She undressed him, rubbed him with eau de cologne and led him to the fireplace in the large drawing room, where enormous logs were burning.

'Do you remember your own words, Giovanni? "Everyone can be happy, if they want to be; for happiness certainly depends on us. The man who is content with what fate gives him is happy, especially if he is really convinced that it is all that he can obtain."'

Wrapped in a woollen dressing gown, the giant tenderly embraced his wife. 'I'm tired, Sarah. The strength of youth is abandoning me. So many struggles, so many disappointments, so little success, an uncertain future . . .'

'Remember Egypt, my love, remember the land of the gods, and Lake Faiyum.' "The bank where we were going to spend the night offered traces of ancient greenery; one could see the leaves of palm and other trees, almost petrified; vines were abundant. In the moonlight the effect of this landscape was delightful. The solemn silence which reigned in this solitude, the vast carpet of water reflecting the silvery disc of the star of night, the ruins of an old Egyptian temple, our boatmen's strange appearance, all this mixture of objects acted in a gentle, agreeable way on my soul, and transported my imagination back to the times when this lake was one of the wonders of Egypt. Abandoning myself to my reveries, I walked along the water's edge, and found that I was happy in a solitude where desire, jealousy and all the hateful passions of men could not reach me. I almost forgot the entire world, and I wished I could spend my life on those enchanted banks.'"*

The Italian opened his eyes wide in astonishment. By heart and from the heart, Sarah had just recited a passage from his book, which he had quite forgotten. The fireplace and the drawing room faded away, and the flames conjured up an enchanting landscape, beneath a sky filled with thousands of stars, forming the soul of Osiris.

'Sarah . . .'

The Irishwoman's ardent lips silenced the giant, and the goddess of love imposed her gentle laws.

---

* Text extracted from Belzoni's book.

44

The Masonic temple was plunged into half-light. At this grade, the brothers wore a sort of ancient-style robe and an apron. Given the exceptional nature of Chief Inspector Higgins's request, the Venerable Master had agreed to receive him in the lodge.

Only the light of the East shone.

At the Venerable Master's command the Coverer, whose task was to look after the sacred place and keep it completely sealed, opened the door.

He brought the visitor to the centre of the shrine, facing a basin.

On the walls were a set square, compasses and a level. Higgins could not make out the faces of the small number of brothers present at this unusual ceremony.

'The sons of the darkness shall not sully this temple,' declared the Venerable Master. 'So that we can be sure that you do not belong to the cohort of destroyers, please plunge your hand to the bottom of this basin. It contains molten lead but, if your heart is pure, you have nothing to fear and you will not suffer any hurt.'

The necessities of the investigation forced Higgins to take the risk. Obtaining this interview was quite an achievement, and it would have been unimpressive to refuse this disturbing invitation.

So he plunged in his hand.

The sensation was not unpleasant. The 'molten lead' was, in fact, just quicksilver and it was not heated. The Coverer wiped Higgins's undamaged flesh and invited him to sit down.

'You were right to confide in us,' declared the Venerable Master. 'Our sole goal is to deliver ourselves from our impurities. May the Great Architect of the Universe engrave his eternal word within us and preserve us from malevolent beings. Let's devote our efforts to the construction of the temple, and let's bow our intelligence and our hearts before God, the unknown and mysterious power which human reason cannot define.'

The assembly meditated at length.

'You who come in peace, do you possess the sign?' asked the Venerable Master.

Higgins displayed a ring bearing the inscription *The Rule is the Master*.

'Now, you may express yourself in complete freedom. To serve the truth, we undertake to answer you frankly and precisely.'

The chief inspector knew the voice of the master of this lodge, whose membership included eminent members of His Majesty's government. He was a senior judge, who favoured the creation of Scotland Yard and had long been a Freemason. This place seemed to him the only framework appropriate for revelations under the seal of secrecy.

'Before coming here,' recalled Higgins, 'I sent you a dossier concerning the murders of a clergyman, a nobleman and a pathologist. Were they Freemasons?'

'None of them belonged to a lodge,' replied the Venerable Master.

'And what of the list of suspects?'

'The businessman Henry Cranmer was a member of a small London lodge eight years ago. He swiftly handed in his resignation.'

'For what reasons?'

'According to the secretary's report, this former brother's conduct was not exemplary and he confused his lodge with a business where everything can be bought and sold. An unremarkable kind of error, of which we see many.'

'Will you tell me about the Brothers of Luxor?'

'That lodge does not come under our jurisdiction and does not answer to our administrative criteria. Its research goes beyond the framework of our usual work, and the senior Masonic authorities do not approve of its independence.'

'Is Giovanni Battista Belzoni one of its members?'

'He does indeed belong to that brotherhood.'

'To your knowledge, are there any other Brothers of Luxor in London at the moment?'

'We don't think so.'

'There are many passwords in Freemasonry. Is *Magnoon* one of them?'

'No, inspector.'

'Has your internal investigation produced any information I should know?'

'As promised, we have hidden nothing from you.'

'Thank you very much, Venerable Master.'

The Coverer took the chief inspector out of the room.

Deep in thought, he left the building that housed the lodge. Snow was falling heavily, and the few passers-by were in a hurry to get home.

Although well aware that he could not completely trust anyone, Higgins attributed a certain weight to the words of the Venerable Master, who had never been found to be at fault in his duties. From what he had said, the Masonic trail was not the right one. But did London Freemasons, however high in rank, know the true identities of all the Brothers of Luxor? Certainly, given the difficulties Belzoni was encountering, they did not seem to possess effective support.

One fact had been established: the three victims were all outsiders. So the theory of a Masonic plot had fallen to pieces.

The mummy seemed to be dozing.

The rescuer walked slowly down the steps into the crypt, unrolled a papyrus covered in hieroglyphs and spoke the words of transformation into light.

The soul of Osiris continued on its journey. After being recharged with energy at the heart of the sun and the cosmic paradise, it returned to bring life to this apparently inert body.

Modern science claimed to explain everything. By rejecting the great mysteries, it made men infantile and turned them away from the true battle, victory over death. People forgot the Word in favour of idle chatter and became intoxicated with false certainties, which were swiftly replaced by others.

In this world where stupidity and greed had taken power, who could comprehend the importance of a mummy created according to the rites of the initiates of ancient Egypt?

While watching the unwrapping, the rescuer had suddenly relived the happy ancestral times. Temples were erected to the glory of the divinities who rendered the earth celestial, houses of eternity housed the bodies of light of those who were 'righteous of voice', and the words of power uttered during the rituals unleashed the forces of creation which linked the afterlife and the world here below.

The rescuer's task promised to be particularly difficult. It was not enough to have identified the profaners who were in possession of the wrappings and objects vital for the mummy's survival. Their hiding places must also be found, with the utmost delicacy so as not to alert the guilty parties. The smallest error would be catastrophic. If the rescuer did not reassemble all the scattered elements, the mummy would be condemned to death and the empire of darkness would grow.

Talking to the profaners and getting them to confide their secrets, studying their timetables and their habits, discreetly questioning their servants and searching their homes without their knowing ... this work demanded time, a great deal of time, and there was no certainty of success.

But the work must go on.

The rescuer still possessed some effective weapons, beginning with four alabaster vases,* which were kept in a sycamore-wood chest. Each stone stopper represented one of the sons of Horus, symbols of successful resurrection.

The rescuer took the first and placed it to the north. It bore the head of a baboon, and its task was to protect the mummy's lungs. The second, with the head of a jackal, was placed to the east, and was designed to protect the stomach and the spleen. The third, which bore the head of a falcon, protected the intestines, and was placed to the west. And the fourth, which was human-headed and protected the liver, was placed to the south.

---

* These are the four vases in the names of Hapy, Douamoutef, Kebehsenouf and Imsety. They are called 'canopic' because, in the Greek era in Canopus (now the port of Aboukir), people venerated a symbol of Osiris which took the form of a jar surmounted by a stone stopper representing the god of resurrection. When archaeologists found similar objects dedicated to the sons of Horus, which were in use from the Old Kingdom onwards, they designated them 'canopic vases'.

Arranged in this way, they formed a magic square, reflecting the community of never-changing stars. With their aid, the mummy would not suffer from hunger or thirst and would be nourished with the milk of the constellations.

Declaiming the thousand-year-old words of the embalming ritual, the rescuer brought them to life, crying: 'May the Osiran organs be regenerated by the lymph of the divine body.'

The four vases lit up, and the light radiating from the alabaster surrounded the mummy with a protective halo.

An unguent appeared on the stone lips of the baboon, the jackal, the falcon and the man. The rescuer scooped it up with a fingertip and smeared it on the mummy's forehead, throat, solar plexus and navel.

The four sons of Horus became flaming torches, dispelling the night and driving back the forces of darkness.

At peace now, the mummy smiled.

45

The area round Spring Gardens was slumbering under the snow. Higgins had taken care to send Dr Pettigrew an invitation to a society soirée, where some travellers returning from Egypt might be selling a mummy. These good friends from the Travellers' Club would keep the anatomist busy for several hours, giving the chief inspector a chance to explore the strange practitioner's house.

Decorated the previous day by King George IV, Higgins could not risk endangering his reputation and the creation of Scotland Yard. But he must continue his investigation and know for sure whether or not Pettigrew was guilty.

Of course, the chief inspector decided to act on the servants' day off. One of his informants acted as lookout and would whistle loudly in the event of danger.

Higgins used the skeleton key he had been given by the king of burglars when he retired. Perfected during long years of practice, this remarkable object could open any lock and left no mark.

The hallway was decorated with anatomical plates taken from treatises published since the sixteenth century. Some provided more of an artistic impression than a scientific study, but overall the display provoked a feeling of unease. The small drawing room contained a series of cut-away diagrams which hardly incited visitors to stay too long. Instead of a dining room, there was a medical surgery equipped with scalpels, saws and pots filled with acids and various solutions. As for the kitchen, it at least contained edible substances.

Upstairs, there were three sparsely furnished bedrooms resembling libraries, with shelves overloaded with books on surgery and medicine.

There was still one more door, resolutely closed by means of three first-class locks that proved quite reluctant to yield. This was clearly a good sign. Dr Pettigrew had something to hide.

The door creaked open.

Higgins stepped into a room with bare walls, painted green. In the centre was an enormous trunk, the size of a sarcophagus.

If Pettigrew had stolen the mummy, he was also the triple murderer. And the mask of an honourable anatomist probably concealed Littlewood, the leader of the revolutionaries.

Higgins carefully removed the padlock and lifted the lid, preparing himself to gaze on the face of an ancient Egyptian.

Instead he found children's clothes, little shoes, naive

drawings, wooden toys and a personal diary. Evidently, it was possible to be a doctor and still be nostalgic.

Lady Suzanna and Higgins took a boat to reach Royal Vauxhall Gardens, which had acquired their name following the recent visit of George IV to this place of pleasure. The gardens were situated on the south bank of the Thames, where good morals were not always de rigueur.

The winter granted Londoners a truce. A pale sun made the river waters shine. Many citizens were taking advantage of this moment's respite to stroll along the pathways, among impeccably maintained lawns and tall, protective trees. The gardens' special feature was their antique aspect, with false ruins, statues, artificial grottoes and waterfalls. Chinese pagodas and pavilions added a note of exoticism, which was highly prized by the aristocracy.

'I love to come here and think,' remarked the young woman. 'I feel as if I'm far from England, in an imaginary land. Isn't it delightful to dream of a wondrous past without crimes or violence?'

'My memory fails me,' confessed the chief inspector. 'How did you obtain a list of the buyers of the Egyptian relics?'

'I was at the unwrapping of the mummy, remember. I knew two of them, the actor Peter Bergeray and the politician Francis Carmick. I asked Giovanni Belzoni for the names of the others, since you're convinced that the person who committed the murders and stole the mummy

315

belonged to that small circle. It's a remarkable hypothesis, quite remarkable. Have I deciphered your thoughts correctly?'

In the shelter of a bandstand, an orchestra was playing a Mozart serenade. The graceful music enchanted passersby and the few attentive listeners. The police officer and the lawyer enjoyed one last melody before continuing their walk.

'The mummy isn't at Dr Pettigrew's house,' revealed Higgins, 'and I have no reason to believe that he's involved in this affair.'

'My own investigation has led to different conclusions,' countered the young woman. 'As I studied the land registers, I made a curious discovery. Francis Carmick owns a large estate, close to Greenwich. There is no house on the vast expanse of land, just a sort of mausoleum resembling an Egyptian tomb.'

'Have you visited it?'

'Duty and curiosity insisted that I did, inspector. And as the bronze door wasn't locked, my task wasn't difficult.'

'You were hoping to discover Belzoni's mummy?'

'I was almost certain that I would! But I was cruelly disappointed. I found a sepulchre that was icy-cold but not completely empty, for it contains a stone trough, clearly designed to receive the body – or should I say the mummy? – of Francis Carmick. And that's not all. Carmick constantly harassed Belzoni to give him more details about mummification. As he wasn't satisfied, he searched for those rare scholars who have dealt with this question. Whom did he unearth? Dr Pettigrew! They often lunch together and, according to witnesses, their discussions are very animated. Does this not disturb you, inspector?'

'You have obtained remarkable results, Lady Suzanna.'

'I was lucky. I've known Carmick's solicitor for a long time, and he confided in me. He considers his client's political plans dangerous, and sometimes wonders if his passion for mummies is driving him completely mad.'

'I should like to know your opinion of Mr Belzoni.'

'He's a fascinating individual, generous and a dreamer, a man incapable of keeping his feet on the ground. Fortunately, his wife, Sarah, brings him back to reality from time to time. She's an admirable woman, of unshakeable courage. Their adaptation to London society seems seriously compromised. Despite their efforts, they will not succeed in becoming respectable middle-class citizens. Their temperament as adventurers will regain the upper hand and they will set off again in search of new treasures. Belzoni's success and the general public's fervour have brought him a great many enemies, who are preventing him from obtaining the official recognition he so desires. Shall we have lunch together, inspector? I've ordered a simple meal at a quiet place.'

The Royal Vauxhall Gardens boasted restaurants, ballrooms, Chinese shadow-plays and acrobats, fireworks and concerts. The young woman had reserved a pavilion, sheltered from the wind and from curious eyes.

The chef came immediately to greet his guests and

served them salmon trout on a bed of leeks. The house wine was a light, fruity red.

'Have you seen Peter Bergeray's latest play, inspector?'

Higgins nodded.

'Surprising, is it not? Our great Shakespearean actor transformed into a mummy and terrorizing a whole auditorium! And that mummy moves, grimaces and menaces. You would swear it had returned from hell, determined to destroy the whole of humanity.'

'It's only theatre, Lady Suzanna.'

'Let's hope so!'

'Do you doubt it?'

'Bergeray claims to be a medium, and highly placed individuals consult him, led by Francis Carmick. I should love to know what he tells him!'

'How did you find this out?'

'Once again, with the aid of the solicitor. According to him, a politician besotted with the occult doesn't deserve to enter government. And our actor possesses other talents which he prefers to hide!'

'Also linked to mummies?'

'Quite so, inspector! During a boring evening at the home of a baronet who adores the theatre, I met Bergeray's most recent lover: a young dandy of a man, obliged to change his shirt five times a day and devote his afternoons to his tailors. An excess of champagne loosened his tongue, and he proved quite revealing. Bergeray's secret passion is painting, and not just any sort: exclusively portraits of mummies! When his last mistress saw the paintings, she was horrified and ran away, screaming. Since that episode, the actor has lost all interest in women, who are incapable of appreciating his genius, and he chooses dandies with a delicately decadent sensibility. Ah, I was forgetting: that philistine with an unpardonable lack of taste goes by the name of Kristin Sadly.'

'The same Kristin Sadly who was present at the unwrapping?'

'I wanted to be sure, so I attempted to locate her.'

'Successfully?'

'It wasn't easy, but my profession opens many doors. In reality, in her own domain, the woman is rather visible! She owns a paper mill and warehouses on the docks, where she exploits underpaid workers. She's a veritable dragon, utterly ruthless in business. The dandy Peter Bergeray was not man enough to stand up to her!'

'Have you met Kristin Sadly?'

'I merely observed her. She is indeed the same person who was present at the unwrapping. Is it mere coincidence, or the beginnings of a lead? I haven't yet gone deeper into the question.'

They finished off the delicious trout.

'Will you permit me to do so, Lady Suzanna?'

The young woman's smile would have seduced a regiment of ferocious warriors. 'I'm just a modest auxiliary of the police, inspector.'

'Too modest, in fact. Your findings represent a precious contribution to my investigation and I thank you for them. Don't forget, however, that a sort of monster, who is capable of killing without the slightest remorse, is still at large. And if the mummy is responsible for these murders, our miserable human condition will not interrupt its deadly work.'

'You have almost succeeded in frightening me, Mr Higgins! Would you like some apple tart and cream?'

'It's difficult to resist.'

'Allow me to recommend the coffee too. It's some of the best in London.'

Delighted not to be offered tea, the inspector followed the barrister's advice. The sun disappeared behind grey clouds, and the temperature plummeted.

'You haven't mentioned the other protagonists in this affair, Lady Suzanna.'

'I have no intention of ignoring them, and I shall attempt to obtain as much information as possible about them. At the moment, I have nothing very exciting. Andrew Young is a skilful self-made man, large-scale farmer and a cheap lord of the manor. Henry Cranmer is a wealthy fabric trader, Paul Tasquinio is an ambitious trader who is prospering in Whitechapel, and Sir Richard Beaulieu is a pompous, self-important university don.'

As she drank her coffee, the young woman grew sombre.

'On two occasions recently I have seen Beaulieu and Carmick talking privately in expensive restaurants. Carmick was behaving like a cat stalking its prey, and the professor appeared annoyed.'

'Did you hear what they were saying?'

'Unfortunately not.'

A flock of seagulls flew overhead, their cries sharp and unearthly in the cold air.

'Have I been of use to you, inspector? Sometimes I have the impression that you already know everything that I'm telling you!'

'That's not the case at all, Lady Suzanna.'

'Then I shall continue.'

46

Snow was falling steadily. As he sipped an infusion of thyme enlivened by a little rum, Higgins spent the evening consulting his notes, his informants' reports and the dossier set up by a friend who was a judge and an ardent supporter of the creation of Scotland Yard. Enjoying the comfort of his official apartments, the chief inspector read the pages devoted to Lady Suzanna with great interest.

The brilliant lawyer was a specialist in lost causes and aroused both jealousy and admiration. Unmarried, she enjoyed a large fortune, with a residence at Lincoln's Inn Fields, an estate north of London, agricultural lands in Gloucestershire and excellent investments on the Stock Exchange. Lady Suzanna invited the cream of society to her table, and the cream of society returned the favour. A woman of influence, she had countless contacts at the highest level. An intrepid voyager, she had travelled through Africa, Asia and Europe, and deserved to be a member of the Travellers' Club.

An orphan, she had been taken in by an extremely wealthy baron with a fondness for poetry and the fine arts. A supporter of the emancipation of women, he had encouraged her to study law in Germany, Italy and England. Brilliant, serious and competent, she had made a name for herself in a world of men who all made the same mistake of thinking that they could easily outwit her. Given the extent of her successes, people were beginning to fear her, and a growing number of experts were asking her for advice.

Higgins eased his aching neck with an earthenware hot-water bottle. Once he was back home, he would call on the expert hands of the local bone-setter, who knew how to treat humans as well as horses and cattle. Closing his eyes, he thought of the tranquil days he had experienced in the country, away from this octopus-like city whose violence gnawed away at the soul.

How many weeks or months would it take to solve this unusual enigma? Higgins knew that he was not in control of events, and that he must keep adapting to the unforeseeable. True, he had managed to impede Littlewood by preventing him from assassinating George IV, but the revolutionary would not give up his sinister plans. After rebuilding his forces, he would launch a new attack. This time, would the chief inspector find the right answers?

'Mr Bergeray has only just risen, inspector. His triumph at the theatre last night has exhausted him.'

'I shall wait,' Higgins told the manservant.

323

His pocket watch showed eleven in the morning. Low clouds filled the London skies.

When the actor finally appeared, without make-up, his lined face looked ten years older.

'Is this an emergency, inspector? I must confess that I'm quite worn out. Would you care for some hot chocolate with rum?'

It was served with apple pastries, which the actor devoured as he gazed vacantly ahead.

Suddenly, he stared at Higgins. 'It wasn't a dream . . . Are you really here, in front of me? Then something new has occurred! Ah, yes, that series of frightful murders . . . Have you identified the culprit?'

'I'm making slow progress.'

Peter Bergeray stretched out on the sofa and closed his eyes.

'Death is terrifying. Each night, at the theatre, I succeed in taming it. Far from the stage, it laughs at me and tears me apart. We artists learn to lie to ourselves and deceive it, for the space of a play. But afterwards reality stares us in the face. In reality . . . Does reality actually exist? I, the great Bergeray, transform it into theatre, and an audience of ghosts cheers me on! I am the voice of the darkness, I revive the dead, I give life to words. What a destiny! Without me, Shakespeare would remain dumb. Have you thought about that, inspector?'

'You have given me the opportunity to do so, Mr Bergeray.'

'By the way . . . Why are you here?'

'I wish to address the medium.'

'My visions don't come on demand. In the mornings, my mind is muddled.'

'I should like to talk about one of your clients, the politician Francis Carmick.'

The actor sat up suddenly. There was a kind of panic in his eyes. 'It's not true! I don't know him. He has never come here!'

'Let's avoid the path of falsehood,' advised Higgins quietly. 'You met him in the presence of Belzoni's mummy and he consults you.'

The actor threw in the towel. 'Very well. Is that a crime?'

'What questions does he ask you?'

'That's strictly private, inspector.'

'Your cooperation is vital to me.'

'Very well, I understand! Carmick asks me to travel into the past and to reach the lost world of the ancient Egyptians. He wants to be present at a mummification, to find out every detail of the embalmers' techniques and follow what they did, step by step.'

'Do you succeed?'

'Scraps of visions, that's all! And that annoys Carmick, and Carmick irritates me. They're all the same, these politicians! They think only of their careers and despise the whole world. That tyrant regards me as a machine; he demands results that are impossible to obtain. At our last meeting, the atmosphere became heated, and I ordered him to leave me in peace. His obsession disturbs me, and I will not submit to his whims.'

'Don't you fear reprisals?'

'A politician, attacking Peter Bergeray? It would result in complete failure!'

The actor stuffed exotic tobacco into his mother-of-pearl-stemmed pipe and lit it nervously.

'Carmick isn't the only person interested in mummies,' ventured Higgins.

'A fashionable, theatrical mystery! Belzoni gave the impetus, I agree, but my interpretation has unleashed the fervour of everyone in London. Even hostile critics admire my boldness and are won over. Peter Bergeray is no ordinary actor. He creates what touches him and gives it a new dimension.'

'Your artistic qualities aren't limited to the theatre, so it seems.'

Curls of heavy, scented smoke emerged from the pipe. 'What are you implying, inspector?'

'You're interested in art, are you not?'

Bergeray stiffened. 'Is that forbidden? I appreciate all the arts!'

'Do you have a favourite theme?'

'Who's been telling you about my paintings?'

Higgins smiled calmly. 'It's my job to discover what people try to hide.'

Peter Bergeray's gaze wilted. Cut to the quick, he got to his feet. 'Since you want to see my canvases, follow me!'

The two men climbed a spiral staircase leading to an attic. The actor opened a heavy oak door and lit an oil lamp.

The walls were lined with around thirty paintings devoted to a single theme: Egyptian mummies. Some were realistic, others almost nightmarish.

Higgins examined them at length. 'Impressive, Mr Bergeray. Do you intend to exhibit them?'

'Certainly not! These works would distract my public and make them believe I'm obsessive.'

'Is that not the case?'

The question caught the actor unawares, and he was unable to reply.

One of the canvases captured the chief inspector's attention. 'That woman's face reminds me of someone. Let's see . . . an active woman, who runs a business . . . Ah, yes, I remember her name: Kristin Sadly. She was at the unwrapping of the mummy and you seem to have used her as a model.'

Bergeray folded his arms. 'A bad memory, very bad.'

'Did she do you wrong?'

'I should never have become involved with that overexcited woman! She wore down my nerves and battered my ears with her business exploits. To listen to her, you'd think she'd built all the docks single-handed and developed the paper trade throughout the entire world. She was always right, knew everything about everything and listened only to herself. When I got rid of that fury, I understood the meaning of the word "freedom"! Beware of women, inspector. They are a malevolent crew whose only goal is to destroy men. I now regard them as a horde of praying mantises.'

'Did Kristin Sadly agree to act as your model?'

The actor turned the painting to the wall. 'To tell the truth, I was inspired by her face and only showed her the canvas when it was finished. That hysterical female started to scream! And yet she would only be bearable in the state of a mummy. Since the unfortunate creature is devoid of all artistic sense, she decided that she had been insulted and threatened to wreck my home. I bought my peace and quiet by swearing never to show this painting to anyone and to burn it at the earliest opportunity.'

'Has she left you in peace?'

'Fortunately, I haven't heard from her!'

Higgins contemplated the series of paintings anew. 'I don't see the face of Belzoni's mummy. Didn't you like it?'

'On the contrary, inspector, I felt it was too perfect! Mummies fix death, but that one preserved a form of life which is unknown to us. Let's not forget that the Egyptians passed through the doors of the other world, and I didn't want to risk offending their magic. We shall pay dearly for destroying mummies.'

'Are you opposed to scientific research?'

'When it profanes corpses, yes! It gives free rein to hostile forces, which the ancients knew how to imprison.'

'Couldn't your visions reveal to you where Belzoni's mummy has been hidden?'

Peter Bergcray put out the oil lamp. 'Probably not, inspector. In any case, is it not better to leave it to sleep in peace?'

'It may have committed three crimes. Will it not seek to avenge itself against all those who stripped it of its wrappings?'

'I have a play to rehearse; my time is short.'

The actor closed the door to the attic room and led Higgins back downstairs.

The sky was so low that day resembled night. The chief inspector turned up the collar of his overcoat and confronted the cold, thinking of Lady Suzanna. Her information was proving to be remarkably correct.

47

'Have you finished?' asked Belzoni anxiously.

'Almost,' replied Sarah.

'And what is the result?'

'This winter, we can maintain our standard of living. After then, it will depend on the number of visitors.'

'The exhibition's success will not continue for ever,' lamented the giant.

'Up to now, it's holding up. Why don't we put up the cost of tickets at the start of next year?'

'I'm afraid of driving the public away.'

The Italian opened a chest filled with terracotta figurines.

'These little sculptures aren't difficult to sell,' he reminded his wife, 'as long as we don't charge too much for them.'

'Are you forgetting our last treasures? We still have ten amulets, some prettily coloured mummy cartonnages and some fragments of papyrus. I shall take charge of selling them myself.'

'I was expecting so much of the alabaster sarcophagus!'

'What about a collector?'

'There's Sir John Soane, but . . .'

'And you, my darling, always think of the British Museum.'

The Titan of Padua lowered his gaze and put an arm around his wife's waist.

'It's its natural destination. I can imagine it resplendent in the middle of a vast hall, to be gazed at by thousands of admiring eyes. There would be a plaque, saying: "Masterpiece of Egyptian art discovered by Giovanni Battista Belzoni and brought to London."'

'Isn't John Soane's house a sort of museum? He'd be happy to exhibit this marvel.'

'I'm wary of him, for he's linked to Consul Henry Salt and I'm afraid he may play some devious trick on me.'

'It's up to us to drive a hard bargain! Soane loves to amass antiquities and to boast about his exceptional collection. If he wants an enormous royal sarcophagus, he'll put up the necessary money.'

Belzoni was beginning to waver. It would not be easy to forget the British Museum; he still needed a little time before resigning himself.

James Curtain interrupted his employer's thoughts. 'An ugly, dirty visitor is asking to see you.'

'In the small drawing room.'

'The décor and cleanliness leave a great deal to be desired.'

'Given the state of the visitor, he will be content with it.'

The landowner Andrew Young did not present a proud picture. His coat was filthy, his hat worn out and his boots coarsely made. His yellow rabbit teeth did not improve the overall effect.

'So, Belzoni,' he demanded hoarsely, 'where are we?'

'In what respect?'

'Have you forgotten my demands?'

'I'm afraid I have.'

Unfriendly by nature, Young now became openly aggressive. 'We didn't understand each other properly, Belzoni, and I must therefore be more specific. You sold me two sealed vases at an exorbitant price, and I paid in order to commence business relations. I must have other similar vases, perfectly sealed, from Egyptian tombs.'

'I'm sorry, but I have none in stock. On the other hand, I do have a scarab, a papyrus, a . . .'

'That's enough! I will not be mocked. You undertook to supply me with these items; now keep your promise.'

'That promise exists only in your imagination, Young.'

'Return to Egypt, discover some tombs and bring me back all the vases you can find!'

'I'm sorry, but my work keeps me in London.'

'You're wrong to speak to me like that, Belzoni. No one defies me with impunity.'

'Is that a threat?'

Young glared daggers at the Italian. 'Either you obey me or you will be destroyed.'

'Get out of my house and don't come back!'

The landowner turned on his heels and slammed the door behind him.

Higgins received Belzoni in his new office at Piccadilly police station, where the paint was barely dry. On the walls were watercolours of the English countryside. The furniture, of rustic light oak, comprised a rectangular desk with four drawers, a cupboard for files, an armchair and four chairs. The ensemble was more reminiscent of a researcher's office than an interrogation room.

Although agitated, Belzoni sat down. 'I was hesitant to come to see you, inspector, but my wife persuaded me to tell you the truth.'

As the giant was ill at ease, Higgins tried to help him. 'Is there a new press campaign against you?'

'It hasn't stopped! At the moment, it's rather calm. But as regards these threats . . .'

'Who made them?'

'I don't like playing the informant; I think I should leave.'

'As you choose, Mr Belzoni. But don't forget that three murders have been committed and you could be in danger.'

The giant cracked his knuckles. 'Andrew Young came to my home to bother me,' he admitted. 'He's haunted by an obsession: to acquire sealed vases from Egyptian tombs. They're quite rare and, ordinarily, most people

333

aren't interested in that kind of object. He ordered me to obtain some for him, and I rejected his ultimatum. So he threatens me with reprisals. Our first contact wasn't very pleasant, and the second was hateful! According to my wife, the man is more formidable than he appears, and his apparent flaccidity conceals a fierce wickedness. In Egypt we would have explained ourselves, man to man. But here I must keep my status.'

'A praiseworthy attitude, Mr Belzoni. Don't worry, I shall tell Andrew Young firmly to stop bothering you. If he does, inform me and I shall have him arrested. Tell me . . . What's inside these vases which so excites him?'

'The residues of perfumes, unguents, medications or dried cereals and seeds . . . Never gold or precious stones.'

'And you have none in your possession?'

'None, inspector. That man Young is a collector of antique weapons, but he may also handle more recent ones! In Luxor I found myself faced with pistols and rifles, ready to fire on the orders of Drovetti's looters, and I wouldn't like to relive that experience.'

'If you wish, I shall have your home discreetly watched, and Young will be intercepted before he crosses the threshold.'

'Thank you. My wife will be reassured.'

'What do you think of Dr Pettigrew, Mr Belzoni?'

The giant considered. 'He's a strange fellow . . . But he seems skilful and determined to study mummies in a serious way.'

'In your opinion, would he be capable of finding out the secrets of the embalmers?'

'Some are lost for ever. Mummification stopped after the Arab invasion of the seventh century AD, and the techniques faded away. Pettigrew is searching everywhere for fine specimens, and unfortunately I don't have a single one to sell him. Are you hoping to recover the superb mummy unwrapped by the unfortunate Dr Bolson?'

'I'm doing all I can.'

'If you succeed, will it be restored to me?'

'I cannot promise you that.'

'Bolson had bought it, I admit, but I doubt that his heirs will want it. Wouldn't it come back to me as of right?'

'We shall study the problem,' promised Higgins. 'I should like you to confirm one detail: did you put the politician Francis Carmick in contact with Dr Pettigrew?'

'Indeed I did, inspector. Since Carmick wished to know everything about the mummification process, he needed to talk to the foremost specialist. Thus I managed to get rid of him.'

'Your exhibition is an undeniable success, and the sales of your book are remarkable. What new surprises do you have in store for us?'

'I have no lack of plans!'

Belzoni stood up.

'Thank you for your help, inspector. And . . . will the triple murderer soon be under lock and key?'

'The case is not a simple one. Nevertheless, he will be identified.'

Higgins completed his notes. This brief conversation had provided a good deal of information.

48

Littlewood quickened his pace.

He had just encountered two new police officers, on the edges of Whitechapel, his ultimate sanctuary. The rumours were confirmed: under the aegis of Chief Inspector Higgins, who had recently been promoted and decorated, the police forces were being reorganized and beginning to patrol the capital.

Without a doubt, Higgins was the man principally responsible for the failure of the assassination attempt on George IV. That accursed inspector had prevented the conspiracy from succeeding and bringing the kingdom to its knees. He was now running the manhunt from his headquarters in Piccadilly. For Littlewood had not fallen for the illusion of security: Higgins believed that he was still alive and would not lower his guard. That adversary would never leave him in peace. The struggle to the death between them would continue.

The leader of the revolution must reassemble an inner

circle of loyal supporters, willing to give their lives for the cause. It would be a long and difficult task, demanding extreme caution. By exterminating his lieutenants, the chief inspector had dealt him a severe – but not fatal – blow. One by one, Littlewood was gaining recruits.

In Whitechapel some people accepted their miserable living conditions, but others were raising their heads and declaring that they were ready to fight. But they still needed to be given the means to do so, and that was Littlewood's job.

He was setting up small district committees, comprising only hardened revolutionaries who accepted the need for violence, and identifying the most fervent of them. His speeches filled their minds with ardour, and they could already imagine the royal residences and official buildings in flames. The king and his supporters would be beheaded, and – as in France – their heads would be exhibited on pikes around the capital.

Fortunately, the weapons caches were intact. Littlewood had appointed new guards and would soon resume deliveries. If any police officer, even in plain clothes, approached the entrance to these stores, which were hidden in sordid alleyways, he would be spotted and eliminated.

Littlewood had sent a letter to the palace, announcing that 'the tyrant George IV, oppressor of the people, will soon receive rightful punishment'. The authorities would strengthen the security around the sovereign, as the prime target, and forget the rumblings in the East End.

Someone was following him, not far behind.

Was it a routine check, or a deliberate tail?

If Higgins's men had spotted him, the future looked grim. First, he must save his skin! Littlewood took refuge in the recessed doorway of a hovel, facing an abandoned shop, and took out a knife.

The man following him got nearer ... and he was groaning! He must be an old imbecile; Littlewood could slit his throat like a pig.

And indeed it was a pig, on its usual rounds, searching for rubbish. It trotted past Littlewood and continued on its way.

Relieved, the head of the revolution turned back.

No one.

Whitechapel was still a protected area, where the conspirators were safe. Tonight, the district committee meeting would be particularly important. Littlewood was going to entrust one of his men with a vital mission: to attempt to discover Chief Inspector Higgins's plans.

The snow had stopped falling, and a strong wind had blown the clouds from the sky, drying out the roads. This was a godsend for Higgins, who had set out to find Andrew Young's estate. His agricultural lands extended as far as the eye could see, planted with wheat, barley and spelt.

The chief inspector spotted the main farm buildings, dominated by an imitation castle, one of those pretentious buildings where successful English social climbers liked to live. The proportions were all wrong, the building materials were second-rate and there was the inevitable turret, giving the owner a feeling of power. Of course, there was no Young in the Domesday Book of 1086, which listed possessions and persons of note.

Thanks to his banker friend, Higgins had obtained some interesting details regarding Andrew Young's recent wealth. It came from moneylending, skilfully concealed swindles and judicious investments. A friend of certain politicians whose consciences he had bought, he continued to acquire land and take advantage of the high price of cereal crops.

A bizarre sound disturbed the calm of the countryside. As he approached, the chief inspector spotted a metal monster equipped with a chimney, from which black smoke was pouring. Backfiring, it succeeded in advancing on its four wheels, tracing circles in the yard beside an ivy-covered porch.

The intruder was menaced by a farm labourer, armed with a pitchfork. 'Who are you, stranger?'

'Police. I want to talk to Mr Young.'

'Why? What's he done?'

'I'll talk to him about that. Lower that pitchfork, will you?'

The metal monster spat out a final column of black smoke and stopped. Out of it climbed the large, flaccid body of Andrew Young, dressed in leather overalls.

'Inspector Higgins! Were you prowling around here?'

'I was just realizing how immense your estates are.'

'This is only a start! People must be well fed. Given the extent of my lands, I need to move swiftly. That's why I've improved this model of a steam carriage, devised by Richard Trevithick in 1802. This little marvel transforms the horizontal movement of the pistons into a continuous rotary movement; it can travel at twelve miles per hour and transports eighteen passengers, six inside and twelve outside. Is that not fabulous? Soon, there will be hundreds of vehicles like this on the streets of London!'

Yet more pollution and noise, thought Higgins.

'And this fine beast weighs only two tons,' added the landowner. 'There's nothing more exhilarating than progress and mechanization! Come inside and have a drink.'

A liveried servant opened the door of the manor house.

'Take a seat in the drawing room, inspector. I must go and change.'

The impaled heads of stags and wild boar gave the endless corridor a sinister atmosphere. As for the vast drawing room, it was devoted to exhibiting a multitude of antique weapons, proving the human race's inexhaustible capacity for destruction. Pistols, arquebuses, muskets, blunderbusses and other guns formed a menacing cohort, apparently ready for use. Maintained to perfection, these relics contrasted with a tired sofa and rustic furniture.

'A superb collection, isn't it?' enthused Andrew Young as he stepped into the drawing room.

He had exchanged his leather overalls for the last word in country suits. A manservant with grubby gloves entered stiffly, carrying a pewter tray.

'Apple juice and liqueur from the estate,' announced the landowner. 'I can heartily recommend it. Do sit down, inspector!'

The local alcohol was hardly worth a detour, but at least it was not tea.

'You are a specialist in widely differing fields, Mr Young. What do ancient Egyptian vases have in common with ultra-modern machines?'

'My tastes as a collector don't prevent me from being at the forefront of progress.'

'I don't understand your passion for those Egyptian vases.'

'It's difficult to explain the meanders of the human soul! They are a simple distraction, which gives me respite from my cares as a farmer.'

'A distraction which leads you to regrettable excesses.'

The landowner's expression hardened. 'Is that an accusation?'

'The serious threats you directed at Giovanni Belzoni amount to a crime, Mr Young.'

'It was simply a rather lively discussion! I spoke without thinking.'

'The desire to obtain a number of sealed vases from tombs is causing you to lose your composure. I should like to know the precise motives for your research.'

'Collecting, solely collecting! Since that Italian doesn't want to sell me any more, I shall obtain a supply elsewhere. With that kind of foreigner, it's impossible to have good business relations for long. That adventurer isn't content to offer modest finds at exorbitant prices; he also dares to make accusations about me! It is he who insulted me, not the other way round, and I have no intention of seeing him again. If the police were doing their job, they would expel him.'

'Do you wish to lodge a complaint?'

'I'm above that! If he keeps on attacking and stealing from decent folk, that man Belzoni will end up being arrested and convicted.'

'Do you have any precise accusations to make against him?'

'My opinion doesn't have the status of proof, and I would rather forget that miscreant. Don't take your eyes off him, inspector. He's sure to flout the law.'

49

It was not easy to obtain an appointment. Francis Carmick was giving his all, and his public declarations sometimes caused a certain amount of disturbance, because of his support for progress. Taking care not to go beyond the bounds of decorum, he continued to acquire numerous supporters, and authoritative voices were promising him a ministerial post. His network of contacts was constantly growing, thanks to society dinners which brought together members of the government, journalism, the arts and letters and the theatre. Little by little, Carmick was making himself indispensable by promising the world and persuading everyone that he was their close personal friend.

The wrought-iron gate stood open, and servants were washing the windows of the house on Portman Square.

The doorman took the chief inspector's hat.

'Mr Carmick awaits you in his office.'

A valet led the visitor to his master's lair. Ancient

Egypt had taken possession of the vast dwelling, in the form of paintings, drawings, sculptures and tapestries adorned with scenes which were often naive.

Carmick remained seated and continued to work on dossiers.

'Good day, inspector. I can spare you only a few minutes, so be brief and precise. Congratulations on your success and your decoration. The death of the agitator Littlewood has removed a thorn from our flesh. What about your murderer?'

'He's still at large.'

'By the devil! You will catch him eventually, I'm sure. And I shall support your plan for coordinating the various police forces. Scotland Yard has a fine ring to it. Is that all?'

'I haven't begun, Mr Carmick.'

The politician looked up. 'What else?'

'You have built a mausoleum, near Greenwich.'

Francis Carmick's expression hardened. 'Have you the audacity to conduct an investigation into me?'

'That's my duty and my profession.'

The future Minister reined in his rising anger. 'That mausoleum does indeed belong to me.'

'Its Egyptian style corresponds to your tastes. Are you planning to be buried there?'

'My last wishes do not concern you, inspector, and I consider that question misplaced and indiscreet.'

'The complexity of the case forces me to make these kinds of digressions,' lamented the chief inspector, turning a page of his black leather-bound notebook. 'I would be most obliged if you could give me clear answers.'

Carmick fiddled with a paperknife. 'I have a long career ahead of me,' he declared, 'and I have no desire to think about my death. That mausoleum is an architectural fantasy, nothing more.'

'The anatomist Thomas Pettigrew has become one of your close friends, has he not?'

'I spend time with hundreds of important people, inspector, and that includes the medical sphere! These scientists contribute to progress and to our society's well-being.'

'There's something striking about this particular doctor.'

'Really? What?'

'Giovanni Belzoni revealed it, did he not, in advising you to consult Dr Pettigrew?'

'Belzoni is a clown and a buffoon! His word has no weight, and his skills are limited to organizing an exhibition, whereas Dr Pettigrew is an expert and will become one of the most brilliant university professors. His friendship honours me, and he may count on mine.'

'Do your conversations go beyond the framework of contemporary anatomy?'

'The health system seems to me to be of fundamental importance, inspector. Too many poor people are excluded from it, and this injustice is liable to cause serious social disturbances, orchestrated by a new Littlewood. A politician's honour consists of averting them by becoming aware of the danger and acting effectively. Dr Pettigrew will be one of the spearheads against poverty, and the future Ministry of Health will make medical treatment accessible to everyone.'

'A magnificent project,' agreed Higgins. 'This eminent specialist shares your taste for ancient Egypt, does he not?'

'We speak of it sometimes. But we are more preoccupied with the important idea I've just revealed to you. Very few people know about it, and I hope I may count on your discretion.'

'You may indeed, Mr Carmick. However, I would advise you to be wary of Dr Pettigrew.'

The politician frowned. 'Has he committed a crime?'

'His passion for mummies intrigues me.'

'That's not a crime, inspector!'

'Have you forgotten Belzoni's magnificent mummy? Its disappearance is still a mystery.'

'Don't stray from the matter in hand, my dear Higgins, and continue to apply the methods which enabled you to eliminate Littlewood and his henchmen! There's nothing reprehensible about Pettigrew's little foibles, believe me. I couldn't say the same about Belzoni.'

'Do you have any precise facts?'

Francis Carmick stood up, folded his hands behind his back and gazed through his office window at the falling snow.

'Precise facts? That would be saying a great deal. That excessively visible adventurer's actions have displeased the establishment. How did a former fairground strongman, and a foreigner at that, dare to demand an official post? Belzoni has lost his head, and his dreams of greatness will lead him to disaster.'

'Is that the opinion of your friend, Professor Richard Beaulieu?'

Carmick swung round, irritated. 'Why do you call him my "friend"?'

'You've often lunched together recently.'

'Have you given orders to have me watched, inspector?'

'Indeed not, Mr Carmick. Your notoriety prevents you from passing unnoticed.'

This explanation pleased the politician. He sat down again and used the syrupy tone of voice which charmed most people.

'It's not friendship, but strategy. Professor Beaulieu exerts considerable influence on the university world, and I need the support of the intellectuals. I'm attempting to persuade him that my views are right, so that he will propagate them. It's a delicate task, and success is uncertain. The first results are encouraging, and I shall persevere. That's how one conquers a territory, with conviction, step by step. Public health isn't my only preoccupation; education is also in need of profound reforms. Professor Beaulieu isn't opposed to this, and his support could prove decisive.'

Higgins consulted his notebook. 'Rumour is a veritable poison,' he said, 'and defending oneself against it isn't easy. I suppose a public individual of your importance must struggle against it every day.'

Carmick gestured wearily. 'One becomes accustomed to it, inspector! Wanting progress and social justice unleashes the venom of evil tongues. But experience enables one to develop armour.'

'Have you not been criticized for consulting the visions of the medium Peter Bergeray and submitting to occult powers?'

The politician gave a forced laugh. 'Those stupid words have reached my ears. Bergeray is the most famous of actors, and our cordial relations are also part of my strategy. He knows how attached I am to culture and the arts. Encouraging them seems vital to me, and I listen to the suggestions of this great actor, who is invited to the best tables. Health, education, beauty: do these things not touch on the fundamental demands of humanity? Many politicians tend to neglect these basic values; my primary mission is to remind them.'

Francis Carmick got to his feet, his expression haughty. 'You have had all the necessary explanations, inspector. Now, urgent files await my attention.'

'One small formality remains.'

'Which?'

'Given your position, I assumed that unofficial action would be preferable to an invasion of uniformed police officers, and I'm planning to act alone.'

'And . . . What are you intending to do?'

'Search your house.'

'What?'

'You show a great interest in ancient Egypt, Mr

Carmick, and I'm looking for a mummy, which is at the centre of a criminal case. Using healthy logic, I hope to discover clues here.'

'Have you gone mad, Higgins? That's out of the question!'

'In that case I shall come back tomorrow with a detachment of officers. Your house will be placed under surveillance, so don't attempt to remove any compromising items.'

'You'll never be in charge of Scotland Yard, Higgins.'

'I've already been told that. I shall see you tomorrow, Mr Carmick.'

'One moment, please! If you act alone, will you behave with delicacy?'

'You will scarcely notice I'm here.'

'My valet will accompany you. And be swift.'

Catlike, Higgins explored the vast dwelling, from the servants' rooms under the eaves to the dining room on the ground floor and the storage chests and cupboards. Nothing escaped his investigations.

'Is sir satisfied?' asked the valet, piqued.

'I still have to search the kitchen and the outbuildings.'

Offended, the servant took him there.

Higgins had to face facts: there were no signs of any mummy.

'Where does that door lead?'

'To the coal cellar. Does sir wish to search it?'

'Of course.'

With eyes in the back of his head, the chief inspector saw the valet shrug his shoulders.

The coal store was tidily arranged. Beside a heap of coal lay shovels, buckets and a stack of chests. The first three, which were made of wood, contained logs, while the fourth was made of metal and was locked.

The chief inspector's skeleton key made easy work of the obstacle. He raised the lid and found himself looking at a strange treasure.

'Kindly ask Mr Carmick to come here,' Higgins said to the valet.

'My master is busy, and I . . .'

'Be persuasive.'

The politician soon arrived.

The chief inspector had taken out a hook used to extract the brains from mummies. The chest also contained knives, needles, various types of spoon, pincers and carefully folded linen bands.

'What's going on, Higgins?'

'I've discovered this collection of objects.'

'At first sight they appear to be unimportant baubles. You shouldn't have disturbed me. Since your . . . your visit has produced no result, you may leave.'

'This result is rather interesting, Mr Carmick. Few enthusiasts, even knowledgeable ones, possess the equipment used for mummification.'

The politician bent over the chest. 'Mummification – are you certain?'

'Do you doubt it?'

'I hadn't noticed! If my memory is correct, I bought these miserable items at an auction. They were part of a lot comprising statuettes, fabrics and a stela covered in hieroglyphs. Doubtless I should have got rid of them. They were relegated to this cellar and have long since been forgotten.'

'Strange . . . There's no trace of dust, as if someone had recently used this hook and these cutting instruments.'

'There's a simple explanation, inspector: this chest is perfectly airtight. And it hasn't been opened for several years. My servants will confirm that this is so.'

The valet nodded.

Higgins lowered the lid and replaced the padlock. 'Police officers will come to remove this.'

Francis Carmick looked the chief inspector up and down. 'Would that not be a sort of theft?'

'It may be an important piece of evidence, which must be kept in a secure place.'

'Your investigations tire me, Higgins. Take whatever you want, then, above all, go away! This humiliation will not go unpunished, you can be quite sure of that.'

50

It was as cold as death in the crypt. But the rescuer did not lose hope, for the magic of the sons of Horus was proving remarkably effective and was keeping the mummy in perfect condition. Capturing the energy emanating from the four corners of the universe and restoring it to the Osiran body, the canopic jars drove back the forces of destruction and created an impenetrable field of protection.

So the tight thread linking the mummy to the life of the other world and to the light of eternity remained strong. The rescuer would have additional time in which to reassemble the wrappings and ritual items stolen by the profaners and make the mummy whole again.

Investigations were progressing slowly, and the rescuer still lacked vital information, which was proving difficult to obtain. Once all the details had been gathered, action would have to be swift if adversaries were to be outwitted.

Inspector Higgins's investigation seemed to be treading water. Was the formidable police officer taking his time in order to strike one, decisive blow?

Perhaps he was weaving a web in which he hoped to catch the triple murderer, Littlewood and the mummy. Would he understand the inestimable value of the mummy; would he be content merely to serve the law; would he choose the vandals' camp and become an enemy to be struck down?

The rescuer recited the words of resurrection, which would prolong the unity of the mummified being. In these times of idle chatter, thought was drowning in tides of useless words and losing the power of the Word. Egyptian rites, on the other hand, used it to the maximum, and each hieroglyph was the bearer of a vital force, which was enunciated by the 'servant of the *ka*', the initiate charged with establishing contact between the visible and the invisible.

This *ka* was immortal and was fixed to each living being for the time of his or her existence, without losing any of its universal reality. Many individuals were detached from it at their physical death and returned to the cycle of nature. A few were bonded with their *ka*, beyond the extinction of the body, and were transformed into Osiris, the vanquisher of nothingness.

By destroying mummies, the barbarians were depriving themselves of the witnesses of resurrection and celestial truth. Slaves of the material world and of appearance, they fed on naive, violent beliefs, systematically fashioning their own misfortune.

'Be at peace,' said the rescuer to the mummy. 'I shall not give up, and we shall win this battle.'

During his regency, the Prince of Wales and future George IV had been anxious to make his mark on London. He had chosen to do so by instructing his favourite architect, John Nash, a great stucco expert, to devise a vast town-planning project that would alter the face of the capital. The advent of peace and the country's economic prosperity had enabled these great works to be financed. They comprised the transformation of Regent's Park, formerly Henry VIII's hunting ground, into a sort of immense garden bordered by fine houses known as the Nash Terraces; and the development of Regent Street, a main thoroughfare linking Regent's Park to Carlton House, where the Prince Regent lived. Curved in shape, this street had become a favourite with well-heeled Londoners, who enjoyed its many busy shops.

Lady Suzanna and Higgins walked calmly along, taking advantage of a sunny spell. The young woman's manservant was carrying her shopping, and her carriage waited nearby.

'I'm making progress, inspector. It wasn't easy, but eventually I managed to obtain information about Henry Cranmer. I threatened the head of the weavers' guild with severe reprisals if he refused to answer my questions.'

'Is that quite legal, Lady Suzanna?'

Her smile disarmed all criticism. 'We lawyers are sometimes obliged to go beyond certain boundaries to bring out the truth. That man Cranmer is a veritable scoundrel, remarkably skilful, and no one has managed to slow down his rise to power. He originated from a modest background and spent a long time in accounting posts. An expert in falsifying accounts, he dethroned his employer, a manufacturer of furnishing fabrics, and launched himself into the industry by buying up small, struggling businesses at low prices. Each time, he stole from their owners.'

'No complaints against him?'

'Cranmer is excellent at legal procedure, and his contracts reduce his prey to helplessness. Today, he's a rich man and his fortune continues to grow through suspicious transactions. His workers are poorly paid, his factories unhealthy and his profits are rising. His sole aim seems to be to amass as much money as possible.'

'How does he use it?'

'He buys respectability and hopes to establish himself as a new member of the London establishment. Here, moreover, is his future conquest.'

The pair had just left Regent Street for Regent's Park and were looking at the remarkable view formed by the stucco façades of John Nash's sumptuous houses. They were still under construction and the overall effect was of one immense palace, whose frontage looked out on to trees and a lake.

'Henry Cranmer dreams of living here,' revealed the lawyer. 'If he could become the owner of one of these marvels, he would finally belong to the elite and could lay claim to be a supplier to the Crown.'

'Egypt and mummies don't seem to play any part in this far-from-illustrious career,' observed the chief inspector.

'Apart from the purchase of some ancient wrappings which intrigued him, as the owner of weaving work-shops,' the young woman reminded him. 'His active presence at the unwrapping led you to add him to the list of suspects.'

'And I haven't removed him,' said Higgins.

A crow hopped insolently towards the couple. From his trouser pocket, the chief inspector took a bread roll wrapped in a handkerchief and threw down pieces for the bird to peck at.

'The industrialists' madness will kill the birds,' he predicted. 'One day, the air of this city will no longer be breathable.'

Lady Suzanna and Higgins walked slowly round the lake, where mallards were paddling.

'I also took an interest in Andrew Young,' she went on. 'He's fanatical about industrializing agriculture. He's made numerous purchases of land in recent years and is in search of the maximum yield. Outwardly, there's nothing illicit about him. He's a keen hunter, and extremely avaricious. And we mustn't forget his passion for antique weapons, the only things that can make him open his wallet.'

'There's something else,' Higgins reminded her. 'Sealed

vases from Egyptian tombs. I had to intervene to stop him pestering Belzoni about them.'

'That man Young is detested by everyone,' said Lady Suzanna, 'but he is among the country's principal cereal producers and boasts of his political supporters. He often goes to London, and it's said that he has secret ambitions.'

'To be Minister of Agriculture in a Carmick government, for example?'

'I don't know any more than I've told you, inspector. Have you looked down that avenue?'

The lawyer and the policeman sat down on a bench, facing the lake. A breeze rippled the surface of the water, and ducks chased each other playfully.

'Our last meeting ended stormily,' admitted Higgins. 'Francis Carmick intends to destroy me and he has the means to do so.'

Lady Suzanna's delicate face wore an expression of concern. 'What happened?'

'During my search of his home, I found a chest containing mummification equipment. His explanations were rather muddled, and our politician didn't tolerate this attack on his private life.'

'Have you found . . . the murderer?'

'We mustn't rely on individual clues. The behaviour of the actor Peter Bergeray and his morbid taste for mummies are also suspect. The quality of your information was most useful to me, Lady Suzanna.'

The young woman blushed slightly.

'I shall now look into the case of Kristin Sadly,' announced Higgins, 'and I should like you to look at Paul Tasquinio's business activities.'

'Are you entrusting me with . . . a mission?'

'On one condition: don't approach Tasquinio. He prospers in Whitechapel, a dangerous area where people can easily disappear. Confine yourself to an administrative investigation and don't run any risks. Do you promise?'

The pretty brunette acquired an air of seriousness. 'You have my word as a barrister!'

A red squirrel scampered along a pathway, drank from the lake, scampered back past the couple as they sat absolutely motionless, then climbed up a tree.

'Life can be magnificent,' commented Higgins. 'Don't play games with death; it's always one step ahead.'

51

'Could sir remind me of his name?' asked Sir John Soane's private secretary.

'Giovanni Battista Belzoni.'

'One moment, I shall check . . . Yes, indeed. You have an appointment at five o'clock. Please follow me.'

The archaeology enthusiast's museum-like house was impressive. The Titan of Padua crossed the lobby, whose walls were painted to look like porphyry, and was shown into the arched library, where mirrors reflected the sheen of hundreds of rare works of art.

Soane was examining an antique bronze which was to join the funerary urns, castings and fragments of sculptures exhibited in the Dome, the main part of the house, which was lit by a rotunda set with red, blue and yellow glass.

'Mr Belzoni! Delighted to see you again. Your exhibition continues to draw in Londoners, and your book is being reprinted. You must be very pleased.'

'Certainly, Sir John.'

'Do you need my opinion?'

'Indeed so.'

'Well, let's sit down and drink some port. This vintage is excellent.'

A servant brought over the drink and two crystal glasses, then left.

Thanks to Sarah's efficiency, the sale of the small objects from Egypt was bringing in good sums, and the Belzonis could maintain their lifestyle. But the chests were emptying at an alarming rate, and the Italian had no mummies to offer Dr Pettigrew.

'What do you think of this nectar, Mr Belzoni?'

'It's a marvel.'

'When one appreciates the arts, one must search for excellence in all things. Is a wine of this quality not a sort of masterpiece? Now, let's talk of the reason for your visit.'

The words were hard to say. 'I brought a unique piece back here, the alabaster sarcophagus of one of the greatest pharaohs of Egypt, and I intended it for the British Museum. Alas, the curators cannot see its worth.'

'I've heard about your problems, Belzoni. The administrators of our museums are not brilliantly intelligent. The majority are petty accountants devoid of artistic sensibility and scientific knowledge. From their lofty authority and the height of their stupidity, they behave like tyrants and make many stupid decisions. Remember: I was the first to praise the beauty of your sarcophagus and its unique character.'

'I know, Sir John, and ask you to understand my course of action. In my eyes, the British Museum symbolized England, and I wanted to pay homage to my adopted country.'

'A noble aspiration, dear fellow! Today, you can see that this institution is in the hands of bureaucrats with a limited vision.'

The Titan of Padua hung his head.

'I've given up trying to convince the British Museum and I should like to offer you a chance to buy this unique monument, which will become the beacon of your museum.'

John Soane remained silent for a long time. The Italian feared that his reaction would be negative and the failure resounding.

'I'm very happy indeed, Belzoni! That marvel will have pride of place at the heart of my collections. We still need to reach an agreement about the price. Despite my wealth, I don't have a budget comparable to that of the Crown! Would you accept . . . fifteen hundred pounds?'

'Sir John . . .'

'Let's say two thousand, and that's my final word!'

The architect's tone of voice forbade any argument.

'Understood,' conceded Belzoni.

'Then we have a deal, and you have my word on that. However, we must be cautious and patient. Those gentlemen at the British Museum will not be pleased to see your sarcophagus arrive at my home, and I have no desire to fall out with certain administrative authorities.

Consequently, the delivery will not take place for several months.'

'The payment, on the other hand . . .'

'Have no fear, Belzoni. You will receive it with all speed. Dear friend, you've made the right decision. I shall entrust you to my secretary, who will sort out the paperwork.'

The cut on the elderly workman's hand was deep, and he had to bite his lips to stop himself crying out.

'We should send for a doctor,' said the foreman.

'I shall deal with it myself,' decided Kristin Sadly. 'Go and fetch my first-aid box.'

Not content with having built half the docks single-handed, controlling almost the entire paper industry and planning for England's future, the agitated little woman could also treat all kinds of illnesses and handle the labouring masses.

She cleaned the wound, bandaged it and sent the man back to work. Here, there were no good-for-nothings and no half measures. Workers did not count their hours, and their employer dictated the pace.

The owner of the business examined some invoices, admonished her accountant, checked a delivery, ran to one of her workshops and lectured a technician who was too slow, before receiving a supplier whom she reproached for setting exorbitant prices.

It was then that she noticed a stranger, dressed in an elegant overcoat. He was standing motionless and seemed entirely useless.

'Who are you, and what are you doing on my premises?'

'I'm Chief Inspector Higgins. Could you spare me a few moments?'

'Ah, yes! We've already met. I see so many people, I'd forgotten your face. Accompany me to my main warehouse; I wish to evaluate my stock.'

Thick fog covered the docks. Tense and fidgety, Kristin Sadly walked through it.

'Has your investigation made any progress? If I were in charge, the murderer would long since be in prison! The police don't give themselves the means to act, and there are ruffians everywhere. When will this city finally be safe again?'

'I share your indignation, Mrs Sadly, and I hope for better times.'

The vast warehouse contained tons of paper of various qualities. Labels specified their origins and destinations.

One of them sent Kristin Sadly into a rage. 'Illegible and incomplete! Whoever wrote this will have to find himself a job elsewhere. This kind of error loses me precious time. And what about you; what do you want?'

'I would like you to confirm something.'

'Concerning?'

'The actor Peter Bergeray.'

Anger flared in the little woman's eyes. 'That man is mentally ill, and an obsessive. I don't wish to discuss him any further.'

'I'm sorry to insist, but were you his mistress?'

'Without me, that weakling would have been no more than a third-rate ham! He owes everything to me; I fashioned his career and built his success. And what's my reward? To see myself portrayed as a mummy! That was too much. I slapped him a hundred times, until he was half-dead, and my only regret is that he's still alive. His gifts as a clairvoyant are one vast joke! He's acted in so many plays that he believes his own lies! Send him to the asylum and rid us of that lunatic. Otherwise he will do something terrible.'

'What if he's already done so?' ventured Higgins.

Kristin Sadly stared at him for a few seconds. 'Then that's your problem!'

'Can you imagine Peter Bergeray as a murderer?'

'That's also your problem. Any more questions?'

'No, I've finished.'

'A good thing too; I have work to do! I'm not a member of the police force. Don't linger on my premises, or my guards may take you for a thief and deal with you most unpleasantly. Farewell, inspector.'

The little woman marched out of the warehouse and back into the fog.

Higgins walked slowly away from the paper mill. He had seen what he wanted to see.

52

All along the docks, numerous cargo vessels were at anchor. As soon as dawn broke, stevedores would load and unload cargoes of coal, bricks, cement, barrels of wine, bales of cotton and many other goods. But at two o'clock in the morning the only people around were drunks and paupers.

Dressed in a patched jacket and threadbare trousers, with a workman's cap on his head, Higgins blessed the presence of the thick fog, which enabled him to approach Kristin Sadly's warehouse without being spotted by the nightwatchman. At the back of the main building, he found a small delivery entrance which quickly yielded to a little persuasion.

Armed with a miner's lamp, the chief inspector set off along the central aisle, which was lined with heaps of rags and reams of paper. As he was examining a pile of old, brown-linen sheets, he was alerted by a growl.

A guard dog was glowering at the intruder, ready to

spring. Judging from its size, it must weigh as much as a man.

Higgins put down his lamp, faced the monster and managed to capture its gaze. One moment's inattention, and the wild beast would spring. Slowly, the chief inspector calmed it, persuading it that he meant it no harm.

He took a step in the dog's direction, and it did not move. Then he took a second, and a third . . . Higgins stretched out his hand and touched the dog's muzzle. Warily, it drew back. But its new master continued to advance and succeeded in stroking it. Relaxed now, the dog licked his wrist.

'Now, we're going to work together,' Higgins told the dog. 'If anyone comes in, you'll warn me.'

The new police recruit lay down across the little doorway. Higgins turned back to the old sheets, which had intrigued him since his first visit to Kristin Sadly's domain. He took a dozen or so, well aware that he was breaking the law by doing so. But his conscience was clear.

Giovanni and Sarah embraced for a long time.

'I succeeded,' he announced. 'The alabaster sarcophagus has been sold!'

'For how much?'

'Two thousand pounds. It's disappointing, I know, but John Soane didn't offer me any more, and I wouldn't have found another buyer. As he doesn't want immediate delivery, so as not to annoy the authorities at the British

367

Museum, the marvel will remain at the Egyptian Hall until the end of the exhibition.'

'Has he signed any kind of contract?'

'Don't worry. I sorted everything out with his secretary. John Soane will only become the owner of the sarcophagus after he's paid the agreed sum to its legitimate finder. Perfect guarantees, my love! Doesn't this success warrant some good wine?'

Belzoni opened a bottle of champagne.

'While I was searching through our last chests of antiquities,' revealed Sarah, 'I made two interesting discoveries. First of all, I found a few terracotta figurines, varnished and painted blue.* I shall sell them one at a time, to obtain the best price. The second discovery is this fine papyrus which, according to a note in your handwriting, accompanied the mummy.'

Belzoni unrolled it.

There were around fifty lines, groups of incomprehensible hieroglyphs, and a drawing of a bird with a human head, in front of a flame.

'I shall offer it to Dr Pettigrew.'

'You're sure to fail,' said Sarah. 'He's only interested in the anatomy of mummies.'

'Then John Soane . . .'

'Wouldn't the ideal client be Inspector Higgins?' suggested the Irishwoman. 'He's very anxious to find our mummy, it seems. This papyrus might help him.'

---

* Answerers (*ushabtis*) from the tomb of Seti I.

'Nobody can read this writing!'

'Aren't you always talking about Thomas Young's astounding progress?'

Belzoni nodded.

'Higgins will be grateful to us,' predicted Sarah, 'and that will help your application to join the Travellers' Club.'

'I fear he may not be very excited by this old parchment.'

'I'm convinced of the contrary!'

Gazing at her admiringly, he handed her a glass of champagne.

Dressed in a black hat, a long, thick overcoat and boots, armed with a baton and brandishing a lantern, the Charlie[*] patrolled a narrow street on the fringes of Whitechapel. This police patrol, which took place every night at the same time, did not hinder offenders, and the representative of public order had no desire to encounter any.

'Halt, Charlie,' ordered an imperious voice.

'Is it . . . you?'

'Have you forgotten the password?'

The police officer's throat tightened. If he did not remember it, he would not leave this alleyway alive. A thousand words jostled for position inside his head; he felt sick and then suddenly he remembered and blurted out: 'Death to poverty!'

---

[*] So called because King Charles I had attempted to reorganize the police.

'And the people shall be saved,' replied Littlewood. 'Don't turn round, friend. Did you succeed?'

'More or less. The majority of the officers at the station in Piccadilly are devoted to Higgins, and I had to walk on eggshells. The chief inspector is a suspicious man, who confides in no one and never leaves papers lying around. Only the desk sergeant who registers complaints was able to give me any information. That drunkard is happy to talk, and congratulates himself on his powers of observation.'

'Results?'

'Higgins holds a meeting with his informants once a week, but his investigation is treading water and no arrests are in sight. Rumour has it that he thinks the crimes were committed by a mummy which has disappeared and which nobody can find! His enemies claim he's losing his mind and will soon be forced to retire permanently. According to the official circulars, he's not in charge of protecting the king or searching for revolutionaries in the East End, and is confined to his criminal investigation. And protests are beginning to be made. Lords, clergymen and doctors are complaining that Higgins isn't doing anything and that unbearable attacks have been made on their dignity. At the police station, the atmosphere is rather sombre. Everyone thought that the hero who saved George IV would do something dazzling and cover the forces of order in glory. Now, people are becoming disenchanted and lamenting the chief inspector's lack of strategy. He's running round all over the place and not achieving anything.'

'What do his assistants think?'

'He has none, for he works alone. Sooner or later he'll have to account for his actions, and people are predicting a severe punishment.'

'No sizeable operations are planned in Whitechapel?'

'None at all! People are talking a great deal about a recent threatening letter sent to George IV, and security measures have been strengthened around the royal person. A crank is boasting that he's Littlewood, and the investigation has become localized in Scotland. The monarch will soon go there to re-establish his authority. Tomorrow's newspapers will announce this official visit, under high surveillance. There, I've told you everything.'

Littlewood handed a sheaf of banknotes to his informant.

'Continue to keep your ears open, friend, and walk your beat. If you have any new information to tell me, swing your lantern up and down a dozen times, and I'll contact you.'

The Charlie walked off, but Littlewood remained hidden for some time. No one had followed the corrupt police officer, whose words might perhaps contain a grain of truth. Higgins, devoid of a strategy? Unlikely. On the other hand, a hidebound, jealous hierarchy might constrain him to isolation and ineffectiveness.

The missing mummy intrigued the leader of the revolutionaries. Investigations in museums, hospitals, asylums and mortuaries had produced nothing. Someone was hiding the ancient body because it was the bearer of a malevolent power, and Littlewood hoped to find it before Higgins did.

This evening, he was addressing a district committee made up of young rebels, ready to fight the authorities and convinced of the need for violent action. A delivery of weapons had just arrived, and this good news would stoke up their ardour. The passivity of the common people was unfathomable, and it took a horde of intrepid and determined leaders to wake up this inert mass of humanity. Once it was moving, it would be like an unstoppable tidal wave. Humble housewives would be transformed into furies, submissive workmen into savage hordes. There would be no miracle, but a long and skilful preparation of minds, which Littlewood would instil with an incontestable truth. Manipulating these puppets gave him immense pleasure.

The failed assassination attempt on George IV had taught him an excellent lesson. Instead of hurrying, Littlewood would make sure that he did not make the same mistake twice. He would now trust no one and would control every detail. His supporters would be organized into unconnected cells, so as not to compromise the success of the movement if one of the recruits faltered.

And to think that the government thought him dead! He had covered his tracks with his last threatening letter, posted in Scotland and signed with the name Wallace, an old nightmare to the English. The king's reaction was most satisfactory. The monarch's advisers were blind, with no conception of the anger in the East End or the earthquake that would destroy the British monarchy.

53

The police officers charged with keeping watch on the Belzonis' residence had not reported any incidents. Visitors did not include any of the suspects who were present at the unwrapping of the mummy. The chief inspector's drawings were sufficiently precise for his men to recognize a face. So, bearing in mind his warning, Andrew Young had stopped bothering the Titan of Padua.

As Higgins had supposed, there was nothing ordinary about the old, brownish rags he had collected from Kristin Sadly's warehouse. The two chemists' findings had been quite definite: they were extremely ancient linen wrappings, impregnated with resin.

James Curtain opened the door, looking as impeccable as ever.

'Is Mr Belzoni available?' asked Higgins.

'One moment, please.'

Sarah appeared. 'Inspector, what a lovely surprise!

Giovanni is just putting our papers in order while we drink some chocolate. Do come in and join us.'

The tall Irishwoman was like a ray of sunshine, cheerful and warm.

The little drawing room was almost impossible to get into, cluttered as it was with documents and files.

'Don't worry about stepping on them,' advised Sarah. 'We shall be getting rid of most of this paperwork.'

The giant stood up and turned round. 'Ah, inspector! Thank you for getting rid of that miserable-looking landowner for me. Have you found my mummy?'

'Unfortunately not, but I have good news for you: I've lodged your application to join the Travellers' Club. Don't be impatient; the procedure will be long and complicated. But it will not be blocked, for I shall follow it closely.'

Sarah smiled broadly.

Higgins handed the Italian one of Kristin Sadly's linen wrappings. 'What do you think of this?'

Belzoni felt it. 'It's a mummy wrapping of mediocre quality. The Bedouins strip bodies and sell hundreds like this to enthusiasts. Although they have no value, they demand prohibitive prices for them.'

'I've been unable to discover the significance of the word *Magnoon*,' confessed the chief inspector. 'Have you thought about it?'

Belzoni picked up a sheaf of invoices. 'I haven't the faintest idea.'

Sarah handed her guest a cup of chocolate. The god

of investigators was protecting Higgins, enabling him once again to avoid drinking tea.

'Since my husband was talking about our famous mummy, while we were tidying up we made an interesting find: a small papyrus specifically linked to that mummy. Here it is.'

The hieroglyphs had been traced by a skilled hand, and the human-headed bird was the work of a true artist.

'This document must surely reveal the name and genealogy of the mummy,' added Belzoni. 'When this writing is deciphered, you'll obtain vital information. It seems that Thomas Young is making great strides forward.'

'Would you like to buy this key piece of evidence?' asked Sarah. 'We will sell it to you at a special price, as you are a friend.'

Higgins examined the mysterious signs for a long time. Belzoni expected an unfavourable response. At best, the chief inspector would requisition the parchment.

'Very well, madam. These lines may contain the key to the enigma, and I'd be wrong to ignore them. As for a price, you name it.'

Sarah suggested a reasonable price. Higgins paid immediately and rolled up the papyrus.

'Dare I ask a favour?'

'I'm listening, inspector.'

'I'd love a second cup of this excellent chocolate.'

The Titan of Padua congratulated himself on having

married an exceptional woman, who constantly surprised him.

To the west of London, on the south bank of the Thames, stood Kew Gardens, the enchanting Royal Botanic Gardens which covered several acres. Created in 1759, their ambition was to bring together one specimen of every known plant. Explorers and botanists enriched it from year to year, as they made discoveries. George III and Queen Charlotte had established their summer residence there, a modest red-brick dwelling known then as the Dutch House, where the couple led an austere existence.

Lady Suzanna showed Higgins round the admirably maintained greenhouses. Now, on the eve of Christmas, the sight of a palm tree drove winter away. And the surprising ten-storey Chinese pagoda, a major attraction of the gardens, inspired thoughts of the distant East.

'I've done my best to fulfil my mission, inspector, and I believe that the results will interest you.'

As she stood among various colourful species of orchid, the young woman rivalled them in beauty.

'Paul Tasquinio isn't an easy man to track down!' she continued. 'I had to call on numerous connections in order to find out the true nature of his business activities. He began his career twenty years ago, by buying a tailor's workshop in Whitechapel; then he exchanged it for a warehouse. He has acquired horses and carts, and delivers meat to the famous local market. Tasquinio is a bachelor, spends a lot of time in pubs, is violent and aggressive, bets a great deal of money on billiards, and spends at least three nights a week with prostitutes. Officially, the head-quarters of his activities is still the old Whitechapel ware-house, but in my opinion that's only a façade. He certainly possesses other premises, which are undeclared.'

'Remarkable,' said Higgins, admiring a rose of Isfahan.

'Those premises are close to Kristin Sadly's business, and recently the paper mill bought a collection of old rags from Paul Tasquinio. The amount invoiced was quite considerable, and this transaction differed from our meat merchant's usual occupations. An idea came into my head: what if they were ancient textiles, or even . . . mummy wrappings? I consulted some auctioneers and discovered the key to the riddle. During an auction in October, Tasquinio indeed purchased a large quantity of "used linen from Egypt", according to the deed of sale.'

A ray of sunlight lit up Kew Gardens. The lawyer and the inspector emerged from the greenhouses and walked towards the Chinese pagoda.

'You seem to have a gift for brightening the London sky, Lady Suzanna. Relieve me of one doubt: I hope that you followed my advice to be cautious and didn't yield to the temptation to explore Paul Tasquinio's domain.'

'I know how to behave rationally, inspector, and that indi-vidual's pedigree frightened me a little! Nevertheless . . .'

Perched on the corner of the pagoda's lowest roof, an owl was observing the couple. Did its strange eyes not see into souls, in search of the truth?

'Nevertheless,' continued Lady Suzanna, 'my curiosity

was aroused, and I wanted to know more. So I asked my butler to summon Paul Tasquinio.'

Higgins trembled. 'He may be a murderer!'

'I didn't run any risks, have no fear, and I didn't ask him any dangerous questions. I expected him to procure excellent meat for me, as he does for other important individuals, such as . . . Francis Carmick and Professor Beaulieu. I threw in these names at random and I wasn't disappointed! "Beaulieu, you're mistaken," Tasquinio replied, "but Carmick is a good customer. And I keep special packaging for him: old wrappings whose magic makes the meat tasty. Obviously, this increases the price." I gave my consent and asked Tasquinio to make arrangements with my butler. He delivered pork and beef of acceptable quality, and here's the famous packaging.'

The linen bands were similar to those Higgins had found in Kristin Sadly's warehouse.

'Don't receive that individual again,' demanded Higgins. 'Your butler will tell him that he doesn't like his products and isn't going to retain him as a supplier.'

'I could have . . .'

'Don't tempt the devil, Lady Suzanna. If one gets too close to him, he kills.'

'So Paul Tasquinio is the murderer and the person who stole the mummy?'

Higgins did not reply.

The ray of sunlight vanished, and mist rose up from the Thames, covering Kew Gardens. But in the shelter of the glasshouses, the flowers survived.

54

Blanketed in snow, London was preparing for a traditional Christmas. Even the poor districts forgot their poverty and uncertain futures, and people stuffed themselves with rich foods and pudding.

Exiled for long months, Higgins had decided to return home and share this festive time with his dog Geb and his cat Trafalgar. Mary's delicious goose would delight the household.

The police officers on duty accepted their fate. On the insistence of the chief inspector, they were to be paid a bonus, and were permitted to sleep late. As Higgins was wishing them goodnight before climbing into his carriage, one of his informants – an almanac-seller – approached him.

'A strange business, inspector!'

Higgins drew him to one side. 'Tell me.'

'Some clandestine boxing bouts were held in a soap works, close to the docks. Around a hundred people turned up to place bets, and most of them had been drinking. The fighting was bare-knuckle. As usual, there were some serious injuries and at least one death; but there was one unusual incident. A hysterical woman threw herself on one of the losers, who was bleeding profusely from the head, and tried to put out his eyes because he hadn't won and had lost her a lot of money. In preventing her from doing so, some spectators pulled off her hat and bodice – revealing that "she" was actually a man! Everyone laughed and tried to get rid of the troublemaker. He was making so much noise that a police patrol was alerted and took him away to Dough Street police station. All the way there, the man kept promising that he would have his revenge, on his word as Peter Bergeray, the most famous actor in the kingdom. He was thrown into a cell, but I thought I recognized him and felt I ought to inform you.'

'Many thanks, and a merry Christmas to you.'

Higgins got into his carriage. 'Change of plan,' he told the coachman. 'Forget about the country; we're going to the East End.'

'But the fee we agreed . . .'

'You shall have it.'

The coachman's smile returned, and the carriage sped away.

The police station on Dough Street was in serious need of renovation. Poorly lit, with a leprous façade and peeling paintwork, it presented a sorry picture. According to recent information, the officers' morale was low and they had lost their taste for work.

That evening, a slightly tipsy sergeant was on the desk. 'What do you want?'

'Chief Inspector Higgins.'

'Oh, it's you . . . What are you doing here this evening?'

'I'd like to see a prisoner who claims he is called Peter Bergeray.'

'The one disguised as a girl? He's finally calmed down! Would you mind if I give you the keys? We're short of staff at the moment. Cell number two.'

Cell number one was occupied by cases of gin drunk by the police officers. Dressed in a torn jacket and a brown skirt, the actor looked positively grotesque. When he saw Higgins, he gripped the bars.

'Get me out of this hell, inspector!'

'I should like a few explanations, Mr Bergeray.'

'I love bare-knuckle boxing and I couldn't miss that meeting! Ordinarily, I always choose the winner, and I bet an enormous amount. At the first decent punch, that coward collapsed and gave up the fight! Putting his eyes out would have been a small punishment. That wretch has almost ruined me!'

'Why disguise yourself as a woman?'

'My public wouldn't look kindly on this shameful passion, and would criticize my attachment to the seedy side of life. Keep the affair quiet, I beg of you, and get me out of here! You'll be acting in the interests of dramatic art, and I'll be eternally grateful to you.'

'Do you often frequent the East End, the docks and Whitechapel while in disguise?'

'Of course not! I confine myself to the places where clandestine boxing matches are being held. That outpouring of violence fascinates me. The blood, the roars of the spectators, the rage to win . . . Superb! I never tire of it.'

'While at these events, have you encountered any well-known individuals?'

His head pounding, Bergeray attempted to marshal his thoughts.

'No, no . . . It's not the kind of place those people frequent. Please free me, I beg of you!'

Higgins opened the cell door. 'I shall implore the world beyond to protect you, inspector!' promised the actor.

'Goodnight, Mr Bergeray.'

The sergeant watched the ex-prisoner walk past. 'What am I going to do with the police report?' he asked Higgins.

'Give it to me.'

One less dossier to file, thought the officer, happy to be rid of it. 'Would you care for a glass of gin, inspector?' he asked.

'No, thank you. But merry Christmas anyway.'

Higgins's cab set off back to Piccadilly. The night was cold and clear, the stars twinkling.

At the entrance, another informant was waiting for him.

'A result at last, inspector! My lads and I had been watching for an eternity, and I was beginning to despair. But tonight, things have just moved!'

382

'Come into my office.'

The orderly served them some piping-hot grog, made with excellent rum, and the informant was happy to warm himself.

'Late in the afternoon,' he revealed, 'an important delivery was made to the carpenter's shop owned by Sir Richard Beaulieu. A small, very excitable woman directed operations and yelled at everyone.'

Higgins opened his notebook and pointed to the drawing of Kristin Sadly.

'Yes, that's her! You don't forget a woman like that in a hurry.'

'What was the nature of the delivery?'

'A series of large and small planks, protected by sheets. The woman ordered the delivery men to be careful. Nothing was broken, they left and the manager of the workshop padlocked the door. This trade intrigued me, so I stayed close by, selling matches and candles. I was just deciding to leave when Beaulieu turned up! He was driving a cart himself, and he opened up the carpenter's shop and loaded up the planks. What a sight! Then he set off in the direction of the East End, and I managed to follow him. The old horse was moving at walking pace, and Beaulieu made slow progress. He's a terrible driver! He halted outside a superb residence on Portman Square. The area was almost deserted, and I took care not to be seen. A thickset man came out to meet Beaulieu, and they had a discussion.'

'Did you see his face?' asked Higgins.

'Distinctly, thanks to the light from a gas lamp.'

The chief inspector showed him the portrait of Francis Carmick.

'That's him! You draw very well, I must say.'

'The job demands it.'

'The discussion was swift,' went on the informant. 'The thickset man and Beaulieu unloaded the planks. The professor knocked one against the gate of the house, and his friend treated him like an imbecile! Those pieces of wood must be very valuable. Is there any grog left?'

Higgins asked the orderly to prepare another round. The informant's face was regaining some of its colour.

'Once his work was done,' he continued, 'Beaulieu went back home. The lights went out, and I ran to inform you, hoping I'd find you here.'

'Excellent work. You and your team will receive some fine gifts.'

Smiling broadly, the informant emptied his glass and thought of the pleasures he would enjoy that night. A wild-eyed Welsh cousin had prepared him a fine roast dinner.

As for Higgins, he returned to his official rooms.

In recent days the investigation had made significant progress, and this solitary Christmas marked the birth of a glimmer of hope.

Stretched out on his bed, propped up on pillows, the chief inspector read through his notes. Firm hypotheses were taking shape, now that some facts had been clearly established. So he allowed himself a couple of biscuits and a tot of Scotch before planning a new strategy.

It was time to launch the offensive.

55

Christmas night had been quiet, with no murders or spectacular thefts, only a few cases of drunkenness on the public highway and two carriage accidents. The police station at Piccadilly was slowly returning to work, and the officers on duty were glad of the cakes Higgins had provided.

Two gentlemen in top hats approached the desk sergeant. One had a pointed nose, the other a red beard.

'We wish to see Chief Inspector Higgins,' snapped the man with the pointed nose.

'He's working.'

'It's urgent. Very urgent.'

'I've been ordered not to disturb him. Come back tomorrow.'

'You don't understand, sergeant,' cut in red beard in his guttural voice. 'We also have orders, which take precedence over yours. If you wish to keep your job, go and fetch Higgins.'

Intimidated and cautious, the officer left his post and headed for the chief inspector's office. After a moment's hesitation, he knocked and entered.

'Two official-looking types are asking for you,' he announced.

Higgins was studying some plans, drawing lines, sticking down words and drawing circles round certain names. 'I'm busy.'

'It looks serious to me,' persisted the sergeant. 'Ministry types, do you see?'

Intrigued, Higgins put away the documents, left the office and found the two men waiting for him, looking cold and disdainful.

'Kindly follow us, inspector,' said the man with the pointed nose.

'May I know your identities, gentlemen?'

'I'm sorry, but our mission is confidential.'

'Why should I follow two strangers?'

'On the orders of the official in charge of security.'

'Ah, that dear fellow Soulina! How is he?'

The two envoys said nothing.

'Where are we going?'

'Sorry,' replied red beard. 'That's confidential.'

'One moment. I'll get my coat and hat. Sergeant, you'll accompany us.'

'Out of the question!' protested pointed nose. 'Our business is—'

'Confidential, I know. Nevertheless, I feel I have a right to take certain precautions. When one is dealing with a complex criminal case, stupid accidents may interrupt it.'

'You can't imagine that—'

'The sergeant is coming with me, gentlemen.'

The two men looked at each other.

'Very well,' said the man with the pointed nose.

A comfortable carriage took the four men to John Adam Street. Higgins recognized the building from its façade.

The two men accompanied the chief inspector and the sergeant to the door, which opened as they approached.

An armed doorman emerged.

'You can wait for me here,' Higgins said to the sergeant before stepping inside.

The interior of this state residence had changed a great deal. Paintings of politicians, bouquets of dried flowers and bronze statuettes of Roman emperors gave the place a dignified air.

The chief inspector went up to the first floor. The door of Peter Soulina's office was open. Here too the décor had changed. The walnut desk had not moved, but tapestries, velvet curtains and ebony furniture made the room look rather theatrical.

Soulina was soberly dressed, facing a window, and stood as stiff as a statue. 'Come in, inspector, and close the door.'

Peter Soulina turned round.

'I had hoped not to see you again, Higgins, but unfortunately circumstances demand it.'

'I'm sorry to have disturbed your holiday.'

'A good servant of the kingdom doesn't take days off. Sit down.'

Hands spread out flat on his desk, Soulina could barely contain his irritation. 'Are you proud of the results of your investigation, inspector?'

'Do I have to answer you?'

'Let's be honest: it's a total fiasco! No arrests, no firm charges, no serious suspects. Following your exploits, you've let things slide. Your lack of seriousness causes me consternation, and I consider it unacceptable. You've committed a grave error in scandalously importuning an extremely important dignitary.'

'Are you talking about Francis Carmick?'

'That insane course of action dishonours our police force and highlights your incompetence. Francis Carmick had the courage to complain to the Prime Minister, who alerted me. What got into you, inspector? You lost all common sense in attacking one of His Majesty's future Ministers. And don't attempt to apologize! Such a mistake is unforgivable. This time, Higgins, you've gone too far. Given your reputation and your recent dazzling exploits, I cannot unfortunately impose the punishment you deserve. Consequently, I've decided to send you into retirement and I advise you to accept. Your honour will be intact, and we shall avoid further faux pas.'

'And what about the investigation?'

'It no longer concerns you.'

Higgins rose to his feet. 'Have you forgotten Littlewood?'

'He's dead, inspector!'

'It's you who are making a grave mistake, Mr Soulina.'

'Your opinion is of no importance. The king's security has been entrusted to proper professionals, who are aware of their responsibilities. And we shall break the miserable troublemakers of the East End without requiring your derisory advice.'

'You're exposing yourself to great dangers. Littlewood is indeed alive and is drawing up a new battle plan.'

'Your nonsense doesn't interest me, inspector. It's my task to reorganize our police forces and, if any revolutionaries were insane enough to attack the monarchy, they would swiftly be crushed. Your Scotland Yard will come into existence, but you'll not even be a part of it.'

Picking up a paperknife, Peter Soulina dealt with his post.

'The slowness of my investigation was deliberate,' said Higgins. 'Assembling the pieces of the puzzle and forcing a formidable wild beast to emerge from its lair demanded patience and method. I was on the point of obtaining results, and I'd like to finish my work.'

'Refused. You're excluded once and for all from any investigation, and you'll no longer leave your country residence. The air is very healthy there, and the activities varied. You're a man of the past; our world is too much for you. Enjoy a quiet retirement and don't concern yourself with criminals you cannot identify.'

'Please pass on my notes and conclusions to my

successor. They'll enable him to appreciate the extent of the case and to take the necessary action.'

Higgins offered Soulina three small black notebooks. The senior official consented to look up.

'Keep them. My new team of inspectors will have no time to lose. Consign these inept notes to your attic or, better still, burn them.'

'They contain facts, not hypotheses.'

Soulina also rose to his feet. 'Your persistence annoys me, Higgins. And annoying me means annoying the Prime Minister. By humiliating me and not following the hierarchical path, you have offended His Majesty's government. Above all, don't give in to your legendary stubbornness and attempt to continue your investigation. If you do so, I promise you serious trouble. Your career is at an end, and you will leave immediately for retirement.'

Higgins replaced the three notebooks in his coat pocket.

The look he threw Peter Soulina made the senior official feel uneasy.

'We shall not withdraw your decoration,' he stated, 'and we shall not comment on your failure. Rejoice in our leniency and appreciate your good fortune.'

'It's bizarre,' commented the former chief inspector, observing Soulina as if he were some unusual phenomenon.

'What do you consider bizarre?'

'I shall reconsider some of my conclusions. Have you perhaps entered the service of crime?'

Peter Soulina turned purple in the face. 'Get out, Higgins! And never darken my door again!'

391

56

The year 1822 began well. Sitting by the fire, with his cat on his knees and his dog at his feet, former Chief Inspector Higgins reread *A Midsummer Night's Dream* as he recovered from the enormous New Year's dinner Mary had prepared. A lesser constitution would not have survived it.

While the housekeeper was cooking sausages and braised beef, Higgins would go and feed the birds in the forest with Geb, who delighted in rolling in the snow. It took quite a while to wipe his paws afterwards, for Mary was house-proud in the extreme and would not tolerate the slightest trace of mud.

After lunch, he would go for a walk and gaze at the tall, frost-covered trees. Geb would unearth one or two wild boar, with which the former chief inspector enjoyed excellent relations. Once back in his hermitage, he would file some records and rearrange his black leather-bound notebooks, but he could not forget his principal failure: he had not found the mummy, the real key to this surprising case.

The bell on the front gate rang, and the dog barked.

Mary appeared. 'Are you expecting anyone?'

'I don't think so.'

'Go and see. If I leave my kitchen, my recipe will be spoiled.'

The former chief inspector put on a sort of cape and headed along the sandy path. The sun was attempting to light up this ice-cold day.

At the gate he found Lady Suzanna, dressed in riding clothes. In her left hand she was holding the reins of an impressively strong grey horse.

'Could you grant me hospitality, Mr Higgins?'

'Gladly. First, let's take your mount to the stables.'

Geb showed the way, watching the horse out of the corner of his eye.

The barrister herself attended to her horse, which was thirsty and famished. 'This place is paradise,' she said, 'and your house is a real marvel.'

'Every day I thank my ancestors.'

'Illustrious individuals, who appear in the Domesday Book, as does your property.'

'Have you studied my genealogy, Lady Suzanna?'

The pretty brunette smiled. 'Lawyers are curious by nature. And you've certainly studied mine.'

'Come in and warm yourself.'

Mary was standing on the doorstep, hands on hips, proud of her immaculately white apron. She looked the unexpected visitor up and down.

'Allow me to introduce Lady Suzanna, a brilliant barrister,' said Higgins, who was slightly anxious.

'Barrister! Do you get the better of all those idiots in wigs?'

'I do my best.'

'I hope you're hungry? I can't bear people who nibble at their food and take nothing but water. We sit down to lunch at noon sharp. The inspector will serve you an aperitif in the drawing room.'

'I'm famished,' the young woman whispered in Higgins's ear.

The drawing room on the ground floor was adorned with souvenirs from the East: an eighteenth-century screen, a lacquered cabinet from Cathay, a meditating Buddha and an ebony armchair with arms carved in the form of Chinese characters meaning 'the Way and the Virtue'.

Higgins poured some champagne for his visitor, who was happy to sit on the soft sofa.

'I have an excellent saddle, but the journey was tiring,' she confessed. 'When I learned of your dismissal, I didn't remain idle. You have many admirers, inspector, no doubt more than you imagine. Unfortunately, your principal enemy, Peter Soulina, has the ear of the Prime Minister. Like a rat, he's dug tunnels in the direction of power and manipulated as many weak minds as possible. His obsession is to prevent the creation of Scotland Yard and to eliminate you. If he claims the contrary, Soulina is lying.'

'Does he have the support of Francis Carmick?'

'They've become the best friends in the world! When

Carmick is a minister, Soulina will run his office. Perhaps he's unaware that our lover of mummies has promised that post to a dozen other people.'

'Soulina has certainly planned fallback positions.'

'Don't doubt it! His job as a security official is just a means to an end. Now that your case has been sorted out, he spends his time establishing fruitful contacts. For my part, I'm leading the resistance!'

'Peter Soulina's decision is final, Lady Suzanna, and I don't take his threats lightly. He promised me severe reprisals if I came out of retirement.'

'Are you planning to abandon the investigation?'

Higgins placed another log on the fire. Geb and Trafalgar appeared and cautiously approached the lawyer, the dog protecting the cat. Satisfied, the cat curled up in the Chinese armchair and the dog lay down at his master's feet.

'Abandoning it would betray my ancestors, Lady Suzanna. And betraying one's ancestors amounts to denying oneself. That would be an inexcusable lack of elegance, is that not true?'

The young woman's anxiety was dispelled. 'I can confirm that Soulina is a venomous snake. Nevertheless, I've always believed in your determination and I've not been disappointed.'

'Resistance, you said?'

'First, the creation of Scotland Yard is gaining more and more support among politicians and lawyers. At each dinner I attend in London, I encounter more supporters of the plan. Next, I denounce Soulina's double game and his excessive ambitions. Finally, I emphasize your seriousness, your skills and your dedication, adding that you're the only person who can bring this investigation to its conclusion.'

'A little more champagne?'

'It's so excellent that I cannot resist.'

'Your attitude surprises me, Lady Suzanna. Why are you so eager to help me?'

Raising her glass to drink, the pretty brunette seemed suddenly lost in thought. A hint of nostalgia joined with her natural charm. 'Very few people prioritize the search for truth, whatever the circumstances. And your perseverance demands admiration. The case looks bad, I concede that, but I believe you're capable of succeeding.'

'Your trust honours me, and I shall attempt to prove worthy of it. Unfortunately, I was interrupted just at the moment when I was about to take decisive initiatives. Because of Soulina's hostility, it's impossible to approach the suspects and use the police force. So I must take a different path.'

'Don't you find Francis Carmick's behaviour revealing? By preventing you from acting, he places himself out of reach!'

'He's not the only one to benefit from the situation, and there may be manipulators in the shadows.'

The hands of the clock were approaching noon. Mary was very strict about mealtimes, so Higgins took the lawyer to the dining room. The smell of warm bread wafted from the oven.

Higgins talked of the pleasures of life in the country and questioned his guest about her recent cases, which she had won after a hard struggle. At the end of the meal, Lady Suzanna went to thank the cook. She was going to stay the night in one of her properties before returning to the capital.

'I shall continue to gather information,' she promised. 'If I obtain any interesting results, I'll write to you.'

'Once again, I advise you to be cautious.'

'You will come back to London and you will take action, inspector. I'm sure of it.'

Reinvigorated, the lawyer's horse galloped off into the distance.

'That little one has a good appetite,' commented Mary, 'and she appreciates good wine. Her beauty would charm any old curmudgeon, as long as he wasn't just interested in sordid crimes. Your dog needs a walk.'

Geb stood on his hind legs and placed his paws on his master's shoulders.

'Don't stay out there for too long,' warned the housekeeper, 'or you'll catch cold and I'll have to use the cupping glasses on you. When you come back, I'll give you some piping-hot vegetable broth. And put on your warmest coat. At least try to forget that business about the mummy. Good Lord! How can anyone take an interest in such horrors?'

57

During his patrol the previous evening, the Charlie had swung his lantern up and down ten times to tell Littlewood that he had important information for him. Tonight, he was hoping to make contact and receive the sum due in exchange for his good and faithful services. With fear in his belly, he walked slowly along the deserted, rubbish-strewn street. Rumour had it that Littlewood killed those informers who did not give total satisfaction. But he needed the Charlie, whose long service and friendly personality had enabled him to infiltrate the very heart of the London police force. The corrupt officer knew how to extract confidences without attracting attention.

Shivering with cold despite his heavy cape, the Charlie walked hesitantly on, hoping to encounter Littlewood. The area was not safe, and it was better not to linger.

'Keep walking, friend, and don't turn round.'

It was Littlewood's voice, coming from behind him!

The revolutionaries' leader appeared and disappeared like a ghost.

'I have excellent news.'

'That's for me to judge.'

'First of all, the plan to create a unified police force called Scotland Yard has been abandoned once and for all. The new head of security, Peter Soulina, doesn't want to change the current situation. And he has the ear of the Prime Minister. In other words, no one will come and bother you in Whitechapel, and the police stations will continue to work with a complete lack of coordination. Their only preoccupation will be to guarantee the safety of the aristocrats and middle classes in the West End.'

'Interesting,' conceded Littlewood. 'What else?'

'Chief Inspector Higgins's absence from Piccadilly intrigued me. Was he taking a few days' rest, or did he have health problems? The truth is much more heartening: he's been compulsorily retired! Your principal adversary's attitude displeased people in high places, who criticized his methods and his lack of results. On the orders of the government, he's been discharged from all duties and will spend the rest of his days in the country.'

'Very interesting, friend. Tonight you deserve a fine reward.'

Littlewood's tone worried the Charlie. It was both soft and menacing. And if . . .

A bundle of banknotes was slipped into the pocket of his cape.

'I'll continue to glean information,' he promised, 'and I'll inform you in the same way.'

Two rats scampered across the toes of his boots.

Despite the gusts of icy wind, the Charlie waited for a long time before looking round. Littlewood had vanished.

The days passed, and the two thousand pounds Sir John Soane had promised in payment for the great alabaster sarcophagus did not arrive. At the end of his tether, Belzoni decided to ask the illustrious collector's secretary for a meeting.

The start of February 1822 was marked by intense cold, but it did not slow down the bustling capital. Although satisfied with the numbers of visitors to his exhibition during the Christmas and New Year period, the Italian feared the inevitable decline in public interest; for the public were always greedy for something new. If he could keep going until the summer it would be quite a feat. And what would he do then to fill his purse?

The news from Egypt was not good. Drovetti and Salt, his sworn enemies, had a firm grip on the antiquities trade and would not permit him to make himself a place in the sun. It was impossible to buy mummies and undertake new excavations and be certain of being able to bring valuable items back to Europe. Unless he operated in a clandestine manner and used networks the consuls did not know about . . . This was just a fantasy according to Sarah, who was opposed to that kind of expedition.

A valet took Belzoni to John Soane's secretary, whose

small office was poorly lit and filled with impeccably shelved files. The man was thin and hollow-cheeked, with dull eyes and a distinct aversion to smiling.

'When will Sir John see me?'

'He's away on business.'

'When will he return?'

'I don't know, Mr Belzoni.'

'You must have some idea!'

'It is for Sir John, and him alone, to decide how he spends his time. I merely carry out his instructions.'

'Did he leave any regarding me?'

'Could you be more precise?'

'It's very simple! Here's the contract which commits Sir John to paying me two thousand pounds.'

'Show me the document, if you please.'

The secretary read it line by line. 'The contract is genuine,' he announced.

'Did you doubt it?'

'And I must add that its clauses have been respected.'

'No they haven't!' thundered the Titan of Padua. 'I haven't received the promised money!'

'Let me see . . . I shall consult the accounts ledger.'

The secretary unlocked the drawer of a cherry-wood writing desk and took out a ledger with a brown cover. He leafed through it.

'Here we are . . . The sum of two thousand pounds was indeed paid by Sir John to the legitimate owner of an alabaster sarcophagus removed from a tomb in the Valley of the Kings.'

'That's completely untrue!'

'Is your name Belzoni?'

The Italian froze. 'Of course it is! Giovanni Battista Belzoni.'

'Then that explains everything. The money was not destined for you.'

'What do you mean?'

'You're not the legitimate owner.'

'Then who is?'

'Consul Henry Salt, your employer. Your role was confined to opening the tomb, extracting the sarcophagus and transporting it to London. Officially and legally, it doesn't belong to you and you cannot therefore derive personal profit from it. In reality, you negotiated in the name of the Honourable Henry Salt, who received the agreed price.'

'That's . . . theft!'

'I advise you to moderate your language, Mr Belzoni. Such a grave accusation would shock Sir John. I can confirm that this transaction was perfectly legal. When your exhibition closes, the sarcophagus will be delivered to its new owner.'

'That's out of the question. I demand my two thousand pounds! Otherwise I shall keep the item.'

'I would advise against that, Belzoni, for such stupid behaviour would land you in prison. Sir John detests dishonest businessmen.'

'I, dishonest?'

'The matter is closed,' concluded the secretary, getting to his feet.

'You've deceived me, robbed me, you . . .'

'Don't talk nonsense, dear sir. I repeat: the matter is closed. Now kindly leave.'

Stunned, Belzoni left John Soane's home and museum.*

Too dazed to feel the torrential rain, the Italian rubbed his eyes. It was a nightmare . . . It must be a nightmare! He searched his pockets for the collector's two thousand pounds, the sum owing to him, the sum that was so vital.

Empty pockets, a useless contract, and a hypocritical collector who was in league with Henry Salt . . . The trap had been well set! How was he to escape from it?

He had no money, and no sarcophagus.

For the first time since he had been battling adversity, the Titan's back bowed. The weight of his ordeals and disappointments had become too much to bear. What was the good of carrying on the fight, since every door was closed to him?

Instinctively, the giant headed for the Thames, a river so different from the Nile, which was edged with dazzlingly green fields, palm groves and villages with white houses bathed in sunlight. And yet, on this winter night, mightn't this dark river, belonging to a city of countless factories, represent a haven of peace, a route to eternal oblivion?

---

* Seti I's alabaster sarcophagus, unfortunately seriously damaged by the dampness of the room in which it was exhibited, is still in Sir John Soane's Museum.

Belzoni strode along a deserted quayside. The sound of lapping water intoxicated him.

Alone, desperately alone . . . No, he must not think like this! In the worst moments, Sarah had always been there. To abandon her would be unforgivably cowardly.

Turning his back on the Thames, the giant drew himself up straight and headed back towards his home, choosing the path of hope.

58

Former Chief Inspector Higgins was a member of the Royal Historical Society, and he regularly received publications relating archaeological discoveries. After dinner, he read about the latest finds as he sipped an infusion of thyme.

This evening, as the full moon lit up his home, he was intrigued by a long article devoted to a small obelisk around twenty feet in height, from the island of Philae in the far south of Egypt. Dedicated to Cleopatra, the monument had been transported to Dorset, to the residence of William Bankes.* This archaeology enthusiast was a friend of Young and an adversary of Champollion, who had, however, obtained a lithograph of the obelisk bearing one inscription in hieroglyphs and a second in Greek. If the text was the same, would it not provide precious data to the scholars who were searching for the key to Egyptian writing?

* This obelisk is still in the gardens of Kingston Lacy House, Dorset.

And the man responsible for transporting the obelisk was none other than ... Belzoni! Higgins reread the passage in his book which related his misadventures and achievement. Insecurely lashed down, the obelisk had slid down a slope and sunk into the Nile. Stunned, the Titan of Padua thought that this 'fine antique piece [was] lost for ever'. Mobilizing his Arab workmen, who were already yielding to fatalism, the giant had managed to bring the monolith back to the surface, without the help of any machine.

'This is how I prepared for the operation,' wrote Belzoni. 'I had a large quantity of stones brought to the riverbank, and I sent several workmen down into the water, in order to form a sufficiently solid bed at the river's edge for the levers to gain purchase. After that, I raised up the obelisk with the aid of these long levers, and divers were instructed to place stones underneath as the mass was lifted up. I had also attached two ropes to the obelisk, one of which was tied to date palms on the riverbank, while some workmen pulled on the other during the operation, so as to bring the monument closer to the bank. By this means, we succeeded in turning it round and bringing it closer sideways-on; by rolling it in this way, we managed in the space of two days to raise it completely out of the water. I then loaded the obelisk on board using a kind of bridge which I extended from the bank to the middle of the boat, and along which the monument was rolled until it was on board the vessel.'

All night long, the former chief inspector dreamed about this achievement. By dawn, his decision was made.

'I have to return to London,' he announced to Mary.'my stay will be a brief one.'

'It's not about that mummy again?'

'I may have a decisive clue.'

'Hasn't the government forced you to retire?'

'Don't worry. I won't be conducting any police operations; this will just be a simple courtesy visit.'

The housekeeper shrugged. Higgins never let a case drop until he had resolved it, and his obstinacy had caused him a great many problems.

'Your suitcase is packed,' she told him. 'Try not to catch your death in that draughty city.'

The cat and dog sat and watched Higgins leave. Given the circumstances, they could expect an extra treat tonight.

At the age of forty-nine, the incredibly gifted Thomas Young was one of the kingdom's most brilliant minds. A member of the Royal Society and the Royal College of Physicians, he was an ophthalmologist at St Bartholomew's Hospital by the age of twenty, inventing optical instruments and learning languages with disconcerting ease. Fluent in Hebrew, Arabic, Greek, Latin, Syrian, Chaldean, French, Italian and Spanish, he conducted experiments into the relationship between sound and light, and introduced the use of gas to London while at the same time involving himself in naval construction. Honours and successes were heaped on him, and he

became wealthy and much admired. He stopped practising medicine in 1814. As well as running an insurance
company, playing the flute and attending society soirées,
Thomas Young had dedicated himself to a new passion:
deciphering hieroglyphs.

The arrival of the Rosetta Stone at the British Museum
had filled him with enthusiasm. In Egypt the stone had
been taken from Napoleon's defeated soldiers as they fled;
and this monument, which dated from a late period,* was
known for a particular feature: it bore the same inscription in three different kinds of writing, that is to say hieroglyphic and demotic† scripts, which had not yet been
deciphered, and Greek.

In 1818 an article appeared in the *Encyclopaedia
Britannica* entitled 'Egypt' and signed by Thomas Young,
summing up current scientific knowledge. Now the unchal-
lenged authority on the subject, in 1819 the English scholar
drew up a table of hieroglyphic signs, as a prelude to
imminent decipherment.

Unfortunately, this fabulous prediction failed to become
reality. Would the texts on the obelisk from Philae supply
the final piece of the puzzle?

Higgins and Thomas Young met at the Royal Historical
Society. Next to the library was a drawing room furnished

---

* The block of black basalt, one metre twenty by ninety centimetres and
approximately thirty centimetres thick, was discovered at Rosetta by
Lieutenant Bouchard in July 1799 and 'captured by the British army in
1801'. It bears a decree of Ptolemy V.
† A late form of hieroglyphic writing which lost the original signs.

in dark red velvet, a place where learned men could exchange opinions over tea. Fortunately for Higgins, the illustrious scholar preferred a pre-dinner aperitif, and appreciated good whisky.

Young was a man of contradictions: a society gentleman who was also happy in his own company, at once haughty and generous, sure of himself and open to other people's ideas. He seemed to have no desire to resolve these contradictions.

Sitting like a Roman emperor, with his forearms resting on the arms of his chair, he looked Higgins up and down. 'One of the members of our honourable society claims that you are a police inspector, Mr Higgins. Is that true?'

'Yes, it's true.'

'Do you suspect me of some crime?'

'On the contrary, I have great need of your help.'

'Medicine, insurance, ophthalmology or Egyptology?'

'Hieroglyphs.'

'You've come to the right place! That's my current speciality. Thanks to the Rosetta Stone, decipherment has made spectacular progress. I can now read two hundred and twenty words, notably the name of King Ptolemy.'

'Have you perfected a reading method?'

Thomas Young frowned. 'Method would be an exaggeration. One should rather talk of flashes of light in the darkness.'

'I would like to show you a papyrus and ask you if you can understand certain phrases. Your knowledge could enable me to identify a murderer.'

Young's eyes shone. 'How exciting! Let me see.'

From a metal tube lined with fabric, Higgins removed the precious document he had bought from Belzoni, and unrolled it.

The scholar took his time. Little by little, his face fell. 'I'm sorry, inspector; I can see nothing really readable. A letter here and there, but no names. Don't despair; I shall succeed in solving the final mysteries of the Egyptians, and your papyrus will become an excellent piece of evidence. I shall succeed by the end of this year.'

Showing not the slightest sign of disappointment, Higgins rolled up the old parchment. 'I don't wish to offend you, but isn't there a sort of competition between several scholars who are all searching for the secret of hieroglyphs?'

'Correct, inspector. The whole of Europe is excited by this new science, which I predict will enjoy a fine future! Without boasting, I'm enormously far ahead of my competitors.'

'Hasn't a young Frenchman, Jean-François Champollion, put forward some interesting hypotheses?'

Thomas Young's expression hardened. 'We have corresponded. In my opinion, Champollion is a fantasist who is pointlessly exploring false trails. As soon as I announce my definitive discovery, he'll throw in the towel and we'll hear no more of him. Dozens of amateurs are striving to study these enigmatic signs and are coming up with hazy theories, because they lack linguistic training.'

'I'll have to be patient, then. One last question: do you know the meaning of the word *Magnoon*?'

'It's Arabic from Upper Egypt,' he declared, 'and the word means "the madman". Your pronunciation is faulty, inspector, but I'm quite certain. To tell the truth, I owe my knowledge in part to Consul Henry Salt, a specialist in Egyptian antiquities. "The madman" is the nickname the Arabs give to one of his collaborators.'

'Did he give you the man's name?'

'It belongs to Belzoni, a treasure hunter.'

59

Sarah Belzoni was wearing a white bodice and a black skirt. She was doing her utmost to emulate a perfect, haughty English middle-class lady, but a wild gleam in her eyes doomed her efforts to failure. Wealthy or not, she would remain a fierce and dauntless adventuress.

James Curtain informed her of the unexpected arrival of Inspector Higgins. As he was shown into the drawing room, Higgins noted that the number of chests containing Egyptian items had considerably diminished.

'Good evening, inspector. Do you wish to see my husband?'

'Indeed, Mrs Belzoni.'

'Unfortunately, that's impossible. Giovanni has just left.'

'I shall come back tomorrow.'

'I fear that his absence will be a long one.'

'Is he travelling abroad?'

'He's travelling on business. Sir John Soane tricked

us in a scandalous manner by paying the two thousand pounds for the alabaster sarcophagus to its "legitimate owner", that is to say Henry Salt. We have no recourse against such a powerful man.'

'Couldn't a lawyer help you?'

'The transaction was completely legal, and we're no match for Soane. Given the lukewarm welcome we've received in London, apart from the exhibition, which cannot last for ever, Giovanni has been forced to go and seek his fortune elsewhere.'

'Would you be kind enough to tell me exactly where, Mrs Belzoni?'

'Is that a disguised command?'

Sarah patted a rebellious strand of hair back into place.

'Basically, there's nothing secret about his journey,' she said.'my husband has left for Russia, where he hopes to meet Tsar Alexander I and interest him in his research.'

'Are you planning on joining him?'

'No, inspector. Whatever the results of this course of action, Giovanni will return to London and we shall discuss the situation. Why did you wish to speak to him?'

'On a serious matter. I must dispel a misunderstanding, and he alone can help me. We shall meet again soon, Mrs Belzoni.'

The police were no longer watching the Italian's residence. And as he was unable to give official orders, Higgins found himself deaf and blind.

So *Magnoon*, "the madman", had suspected that the truth would eventually come out, and he had decided to flee. Sarah would soon join him. Heavy suspicions weighed on them, but had they committed the three murders and hidden the mummy, intending to sell it to a wealthy enthusiast? There were still too many burning questions left unanswered.

He must dream up a new strategy.

The magic of Horus's four sons was continuing to operate. Deriving energy from the four cardinal points, they maintained the mummy's vital organs in good condition. Donning the jackal-headed mask of Anubis, the first embalmer and the inventor of mummification, the rescuer regularly celebrated the ritual of the 'righteous of voice', thus ensuring that energy circulated inside the Osiran body. The soul was travelling the paths of the afterlife and seeing paradise without being cut off from its earthly anchorage.

However, it would not be possible to open the mummy's mouth, eyes and ears until the shrouds, wrappings and original symbolic items had been returned to the mummy. Despite strenuous efforts, the rescuer had not succeeded in locating all of them.

The sidelining of Chief Inspector Higgins was a catastrophe. In searching for the mummy and the killer of the three demons who had sought to destroy it, Higgins had obtained precious clues which he alone could gather. The rescuer's possible courses of action were more limited than it appeared, and over the last two months the obstacles had become insurmountable.

After the outrages it had suffered, the mummy's capacity for survival had been gravely damaged. Admittedly, the magic of the Word and the power of the four sons of Horus would prolong its existence to the maximum, but the future was looking darker.

With Higgins bound hand and foot, how were they to escape from this impasse? Sudden, hazardous action was liable to end in disaster.

Would the gods consent to provide the rescuer with another solution?

Thick fog had inundated the narrow streets of Whitechapel. The smoke pouring from factories and workshops rendered the air unbreathable. The price of bread had gone up, and many inhabitants of the East End hung round markets as they were packing up to collect damaged or rotten fruit and vegetables.

Discontent was mounting, much to Littlewood's delight. At the latest district committee meetings, violence had seemed to be the only solution, since the government refused to listen to the voices of the poor. Urged on by the revolutionary orator, moderates had been swept away, and hardliners were seething with impatience.

Littlewood congratulated himself on his patience. He now had a small army at his disposal, trained by determined instructors. There were no traitors and no infiltrators, they had an appreciable stock of weapons and the police were fragmented and disorganized . . . The picture was almost ideal!

But he still did not have the mummy! The country's future master had not, however, despaired of finding it and turning it into a symbol of the death of the past, of royalty and the aristocracy. Who had seized these disturbing remains and hidden them with such care?

As he entered the back room of the smoky pub where his general staff were meeting, Littlewood put this question to the back of his mind.

Wearing a workman's cap, whose peak masked the upper part of his face, he also sported a thick moustache and side-whiskers, which rendered him unrecognizable.

A young man barred his way, brandishing a knife. 'This is private.'

'Not for Littlewood!'

The guard stepped aside. He had recognized the great leader, the soul of the revolution, from his voice.

The door was carefully shut, and a dozen men assembled round a rough table on which pints of brown ale stood.

'I bring excellent news,' announced Littlewood. 'We've just bought ten police officers in the East End who feel they are poorly paid and disregarded. Convinced of the justice of our cause, they are supplying us with first-hand information and will provoke disturbances within their own departments. They hope to become instructors of the security forces in the new regime.'

'I refuse to obey those filth!' protested a bearded man.

'Have no fear, friend. We shall kill them as soon as we take power. In the meantime, they will help us to

416

triumph. Our weapons caches in Whitechapel contain some fine equipment, and the authorities continue to doze. The tyrant and his advisers believe that the people are incapable of rebellion.'

'I suggest we attack the royal palace,' ventured the man with the beard. 'Let's charge in and massacre the lot of them!'

'We all want to do that,' conceded Littlewood, 'but an offensive like that would very likely be cut short, and I don't want to strike until we're certain of victory. Our priority is to sow panic among our adversaries and make them lose their footing. Confronted with the anger of the poor, the government will not dare react with too much brutality. We shall widen the breach, and thousands of malcontents will rally to our crusade. Tomorrow, my friends, we shall achieve our first victory.'

The conspirators listened attentively to Littlewood's explanations. Seduced by him, they emptied their pints of beer and then refilled them, toasting their leader.

Lady Suzanna's cab approached Hyde Park. As she waited for news of the utmost importance, the young woman felt the need to walk along the pathways of this green space, where the air of the capital was more breathable.

She spotted two uniformed police officers running away. In their hurry, they jostled indignant passers-by.

Suddenly, she heard shouts. 'Bread for the starving', 'Work for the poor', 'A future for our children', 'Shame to the exploiters'. Unfurling like a giant wave, a roaring crowd mounted an assault on Hyde Park.

The leaders threw stones at the carriages of the well-to-do. Hit on the temple, a coachman fell and was trampled underfoot. Women and children pounded the coaches with their fists and attempted to drag the occupants out.

'Leave, quickly!' ordered Lady Suzanna.

Two stocky men blocked the horses' way and grabbed the coachman's boots. The lawyer opened the door, jumped to the ground, hitched up her skirts and ran like the wind.

A stone grazed her forehead, and blood began to trickle down her face. Her hat flew off, and the rain whipped her face. She dared not turn round, afraid that she would see her pursuers gaining on her. At the end of her strength, she thought she could hear their breathing. No, she must not give up her will to survive. One more step, a second, a third . . .

'This way, miss!'

A group of young army officers rescued Lady Suzanna. At the sight of their sabres, the pursuers drew back.

On the edges of Hyde Park, carriages were burning.

60

Geb the dog laid his left paw on his master's shoulder as Higgins struggled to concentrate, and Trafalgar the cat lay on his desk, preventing him from reading his notes. Since his return, Higgins had been searching in vain for a new strategy. If he did not do something, one or more suspects would succeed in placing themselves out of reach, and the truth would become inaccessible.

There was only one solution: to act independently, at the risk of coming into conflict with the authorities and being halted in his tracks. At least then the former chief inspector would have tried everything.

Preceded by his two famished companions, he walked down to the dining room with a heavy heart. Winter was drawing to an end and, to judge by the behaviour of the wild boar in the nearby forest, spring would arrive early this year.

Mary had prepared duck pâté and salmon trout, accompanied by chicory and chard.

'Don't tell me you're ill,' she scolded, pouring him a glass of wine. 'Drink that; it'll make you feel better. Upon my word, this business with the mummy is eating you up inside! Oh, yes, a messenger has just brought a letter from London.'

Higgins broke the seal.

The message was as brief as it was imperious:

Dear inspector, Kindly come to the police station at Piccadilly on Monday next at five o'clock in the afternoon. Your presence is vital.
Yours.

'And it's signed *Lady Suzanna*,' observed Mary, reading over Higgins's shoulder. 'That gives me two days to pack your bags.'

'It may only be a day's visit.'

'Surely not! That little one is a serious woman. There'll be news, just you wait and see.'

As Higgins pushed open the door of Piccadilly police station, applause rang out.

'On behalf of all my colleagues,' declared the desk sergeant, 'I'd like to congratulate you and say how pleased we are to see you again. Here's to your very good health!'

Everyone drank a toast in beer, and the sergeant invited his superior to admire his old office, which had been entirely repainted. Bunches of dried flowers and small

vases of coloured Venetian glass made the place much
more attractive.

Lady Suzanna was there, looking radiant in an elegant
pale green gown.

'Are you pleased with the redecoration, inspector?'

'I am indeed, but . . . Could you please explain?'

The sergeant closed the office door discreetly behind
him.

'Take a seat in your new armchair, chief inspector.
You're in charge of this police station once again and, in
my opinion, your duties will not be limited to that task.
We shall know more this evening at dinner, where you
will be the guest of honour.'

'Has Peter Soulina changed his mind?'

'That sad individual has handed in his resignation and
no longer belongs to the upper levels of government. You
can forget him.'

'What's happened, Lady Suzanna?'

'Politics, Mr Higgins, politics! It often turns our lives
upside down. As it happens, Castlereagh's reign has come
to an end and that of his successor, Canning, is beginning. Castlereagh will never recover from this.* Canning
is a learned man, an excellent orator and a good sailor.
He's opposed to any reform of Parliament, but he favours
each nation's independence and Catholic emancipation,
and he's already firmly in charge. Because of the gravity
of the situation, I succeeded in obtaining an appointment

---

* Indeed, he later committed suicide.

for you as a matter of urgency. George Canning is impatient to hear what you have to say, inspector. I've told him that you're the only man capable of facing up to these events.'

'Events . . . ?'

'The newspapers have been ordered not to mention them, and they have obeyed so as not to aggravate the situation. A band of rioters has been hurling stones and other missiles at cabs and carriages close to Hyde Park. As well as angry workers, the mob contained women and children, who were just as carried away. Unfortunately, a large number of people were injured.'

'Have the ringleaders been arrested?'

'I myself saw police officers running away, just before the disturbances broke out.'

'That little scar on your left temple . . . Were you threatened?'

'I got away, inspector. If I hadn't run fast and been assisted by some brave soldiers, I would have been trampled underfoot or stoned. Calm seems to have returned, but Canning – unlike Castlereagh – regards it as an illusion. So he persuaded the king to implement a change of Prime Minister in order to avert a terrible civil war.'

'So Littlewood is launching his great offensive,' remarked Higgins. 'This was indeed just a first step, and we must expect other crowd disturbances. The police are ineffectual and corrupt and will be incapable of containing them. The worst solution would be to send in the army and order them to fire. The majority of the population would rally to the insurgents' cause, and the entire kingdom would be in danger of collapse.'

'I share your point of view, inspector. That's why I've asked Canning to hear what you have to say.'

At fifty-two, the new leader of the British government was a determined and thoughtful man. Although well aware of the difficulty of his task and the danger facing government institutions, he did not yield to fatalism and planned to fight back strongly. He was extremely worried following the recent disturbances, and very displeased with the attitude of the police; and he was anxious to know the full extent of the threat.

Higgins expressed himself with complete frankness, making no attempt to reassure him. Contrary to the official opinion, Littlewood was not dead and, taking advantage of the authorities' naivety, he was continuing to foment his conspiracy against the monarchy. The poor districts of the East End would soon rise up, and a great tidal wave of violence would sweep away all obstacles.

Suddenly losing his appetite, George Canning put countless questions to the chief inspector before allocating him specific tasks: reorganizing the forces of order, preparing for the creation of Scotland Yard, arresting Littlewood without provoking the common people, and driving back the spectre of civil war.

Lady Suzanna feared that Higgins might refuse, that he might be more attached to his country retirement than to this battle with an uncertain outcome. He sipped his wine and took his time answering, as if he had no interest in the conversation.

Calmly, he set out his demands: to continue the search for the triple murderer, to find the missing mummy, whose role he considered vital, to eliminate corrupt police officers and pursue Littlewood in his own way. True, he could not avert all disturbances, for the revolutionaries were considerably ahead, owing to the blindness of a government nourished by its own illusions. The absolute priority was to prevent the capital of the Empire going up in flames.

None of these conditions was negotiable. Despite her talents as a barrister, Lady Suzanna was careful not to intervene. It was up to destiny – and the Prime Minister – to choose.

Canning also lingered over his wine. Did his position authorize him to satisfy the demands of a mere investigator? But after a long silence, he resolved to recognize the validity of the chief inspector's arguments.

Higgins was given carte blanche.

So he found himself in residence at the building on John Adam Street formerly occupied by Soulina. The furniture, curtains, wall hangings and carpets had been replaced, and the atmosphere was now warmer and more elegant. Higgins was to occupy rooms on the top floor and enjoy the services of a cook and a valet. Given the difficulty of his mission, which would not be mentioned in official documents, Canning had granted him every facility. And Higgins would report back solely to the Prime Minister.

The chief inspector convened a meeting of his team of informants and put the Belzonis' house under permanent surveillance. Higgins wanted to know as soon as the Titan of Padua returned home. And if Sarah attempted to leave the country and join her husband, she would be arrested and brought back. Giovanni would not abandon her and would return to England.

Next, Higgins attended to a delicate task: gathering together the officers in charge of the capital's police stations. He saw them first individually, taking copious notes, and then hosted a plenary meeting where he revealed his objectives: to reorganize the police, make sure that they served the people, identify and dismiss corrupt officers, combat crime and guarantee the safety of people and property.

This speech filled some officers with enthusiasm, while it worried others. In the days that followed, around ten inspectors and sergeants requested an interview and confessed what they had done wrong. Higgins proved to be a good confessor, and gave them a second and final chance. On the other hand, he proved merciless towards those ruffians who continued to use their status to enrich themselves and who neglected their duties. Eradicating the corruption that was undermining the police force would be long and difficult, but Higgins would continue to hunt down the profiteers.

A spring breeze chased away the harsh winds of winter, and rain showers helped nature to grow lush and green again.

'You have excellent lodgings,' commented Lady Suzanna, as Higgins showed her around the house.

'George Canning is a generous man.'

'His success depends to a large extent on yours, inspector. To be honest, I feared you would turn him down and I would have understood if you had. Defeating Littlewood and his underground army demands a great deal of courage and skill.'

'Littlewood, the mummy, the three murders ... Everything is linked. That belief has haunted me since the start of the investigation, and each new piece of information strengthens it.'

'I admire your tenacity, Mr Higgins. In your place, most men would have given up.'

'I owe you the opportunity to bring the truth to light, Lady Suzanna. Your approach to Canning was decisive.'

'He's surrounded by so many courtiers, flatterers, second-rate people and liars that your openness won him over.'

'I hid nothing from him: riots and murders are being planned. Even if I work day and night, I shall not succeed in destroying Littlewood before I have a police force worthy of the name.'

'Have you considered your own safety?'

'Time is short, and I shall not attack the adversary head on. Littlewood is a sort of octopus, whose tentacles must be cut off in the hope of reaching the head. That man lies, dissembles, destroys his own supporters if need be and cares only about taking power, establishing a reign of violence and injustice.'

'Anyone would think you were talking about the devil!'

'Who knows, Lady Suzanna?'

61

The official in charge of security at Hyde Park was a small, poorly dressed man with short hair and thick, greying eyebrows. He was also grouchy and aggressive.

'I didn't have to respond to your summons,' he snapped at Higgins, 'and I have nothing to tell you.'

'Relax, good sir, and let us analyse the situation calmly.'

'What situation? I do my job properly and deserve nothing but praise.'

'Were you not caught unawares by the recent riot?'

'I was in no way responsible. Nobody could control the movement of a whole crowd.'

'Nobody, except the police.'

'My men obeyed my orders and did nothing wrong.'

Higgins stood up and paced the floor of his office in the John Adam Street house.

'Correct, sir, since they weren't there.'

'What do you mean, not there?'

'A reliable eyewitness saw them running away before

the first troublemakers arrived. What do you make of that?'

The official fidgeted. 'I? Nothing, absolutely nothing.'

'I was hoping for more. Think harder.'

'That witness must be mistaken.'

'Having conducted a swift search, I actually have around thirty statements, all of which agree. All the police officers patrolling the perimeter of Hyde Park ran away at the same time. The conclusion is clear: they were obeying an order. An order given by their superior: you, good sir.'

'That doesn't hold water!'

'The police officers have been questioned and confirm that it's true.'

The accused faced Higgins. 'Those wretches are lying!'

'Why did you give that order?'

The official scowled. 'It's a necessity of the job. My officers were going to be relieved.'

'Incorrect. I've checked. Isn't it time to tell the truth?'

The surly fellow squared up to him. 'I'm an honest man, and I won't accept any criticism.'

'You knew the exact time when that violent demonstration would begin,' declared Higgins, 'and you'd promised your real employer that you would give him free rein by removing all your men. Several charges will be made: corruption, complicity in a crime, abuse of authority, active participation in a conspiracy against the state. In my opinion, the sentence will be a severe one.'

'Is this . . . a joke?'

'The evidence appears conclusive to me, and I must arrest you.'

'You wouldn't dare!'

'I'm obliged to do so.'

The official leaped back. 'You're not going to throw me in prison! They're full of ferocious animals which will devour me, and you'll be responsible for my death.'

'Don't your offences merit an exemplary punishment? If you wish to avoid the worst, talk.'

Higgins sat down in his armchair and gazed sternly at the official, whose thick eyebrows were quivering.

'I'm a perfectly honest man, inspector, and my career bears the seal of integrity.'

'When did you meet Littlewood?'

The official stared at him open-mouthed. 'How do you know that I've met him?'

'I'm listening.'

The official lowered his gaze. 'I have needs. My salary is miserable; I deserve better. I have needs, do you understand?'

'It costs a great deal to frequent prostitutes regularly, does it not? Littlewood offered you a fine sum to remove your men during the riot. In your eyes, it was a small offence, devoid of importance.'

'It doesn't seem all that serious to me. Didn't I prevent a bloody confrontation?'

'Did you meet Littlewood himself or just one of his henchmen?'

The official crossed his fingers, took a deep breath and

blurted out his confession. A series of names featured; Higgins noted them down.

Littlewood's first network within the police force was about to be dismantled, and the first dead branch lopped off.

The Charlie wrapped himself in his cape and checked his lantern, which he swung up and down ten times to alert Littlewood. The news he had just learned would not delight the leader of the revolutionaries: Higgins was back, and he was taking all kinds of measures aimed at reorganizing the police and making them effective. It was probably pure fantasy, but the inspector was an obstinate man and this time he had the support of the government.

The Charlie deplored the rioters' violence and would have preferred a gentler approach, without confrontations or injuries. But it was too late to step back. He must forget his remorse and continue to inform the future master of England in return for large amounts of money, with which he would buy comfortable accommodation. If he had been better paid, he might not have betrayed his force. It was a legitimate defence, in a way.

Given the importance of his role, didn't he deserve promotion? He would ask Littlewood for a post as a senior officer and would amuse himself by making his former superiors crawl and carry out lowly duties, from night patrols to cleaning out the privies.

Cold, fine rain was falling. On the edge of Whitechapel, the Charlie swung his lantern.

He detested this stinking street and never got used to this disturbing area. He was preparing to retrace his steps when a voice froze him in his tracks.

'Stay there, friend, and don't turn round.'

Littlewood . . . No, someone else! A thief determined to rob him, or a revolutionary who wanted to kill a policeman? The Charlie gripped his club.

'Drop your weapon. Or you'll regret it.'

The Charlie was not accustomed to fighting. And what if his attacker was not alone? Attempting to defend himself would make the situation only worse.

'I only have sixpence.'

'Keep your money, friend, and drop your stick. Just answer my questions, and no harm will come to you.'

Regaining hope, the Charlie obeyed.

'You had a meeting with Littlewood?'

So, thought the policeman, he's a messenger from the chief! 'No,' he said. 'I was alerting him. I have important information for him. During my patrol tomorrow night, he will contact me.'

'What does Littlewood look like?'

'I've never seen him; I only know his voice.'

'We're going to save time, friend. You will give me the information, and I shall pass it on to Littlewood.'

'That's not the usual procedure!'

'Name your price.'

It was a tempting proposition. The Charlie doubled the amount and provided a few minor pieces of information.

'I'm saving the rest for Littlewood himself,' he announced.

'We shall continue this conversation somewhere more pleasant – the police station in Piccadilly. Once we're there, you'll tell me everything.'

'Who . . . who are you?'

'Chief Inspector Higgins.'

The Charlie attempted to pick up his club. A foot crushed his hand, and he let out a cry of pain. Then Higgins's forearm gripped his neck, almost strangling him.

'Don't do anything stupid. Follow me quietly, and I'll try to be lenient.'

'I don't want to go to prison! The convicts will kill me!'

Higgins loosened his grip. 'Two conditions for avoiding that sad fate: revealing the names of your accomplices and making no changes to your routine. Tomorrow evening, you will walk your usual beat. And Littlewood will contact you.'

62

Setting the trap was not easy. A detachment of police officers on the fringes of Whitechapel, even in plain clothes, would have alerted Littlewood's lookouts. So Higgins made do with a small contingent, comprising himself and two men who were aware of the dangers they were facing in order to take the conspirators' leader alive.

One hour before the Charlie's patrol, thick fog invaded the capital. Because of this handicap, it was impossible to follow the policeman with the lantern at a distance. And if they got closer, the chief inspector and his men risked being spotted.

According to the corrupt officer's confession, Littlewood always contacted him the day after the signal and talked to him without showing himself. He listened, paid and vanished. The Charlie had never seen any accomplices and swiftly left the area.

The officer emerged from a deserted street and entered a run-down alley. As he passed, windows and doors banged shut. An urchin threw pebbles at him and ran away.

And then there was silence.

A silence as thick as the fog.

The Charlie continued on his way, brandishing his lantern. Higgins and his two colleagues attempted to keep him in view.

Suddenly, the chief inspector knew that he was being followed. He ran to the Charlie and grabbed him by the scruff of the neck. 'Did you tell anyone about our little expedition?'

'Tonight, at the station, the officer who said he'd shadow me. He's . . . he's a friend!'

'An officer who's sold himself to Littlewood, like you! And you thought he was going to rescue you? Your stupidity has endangered our lives. Swing your lantern and yell "police!" at the top of your voice!'

Higgins ordered his men to use their whistles. The din might disperse the attackers.

'Stay together and let's try to get back to the street.'

Shots rang out, and a bullet grazed the chief inspector.

'The reinforcements are arriving,' he shouted in his powerful voice. 'We shall head left!'

He led the little group to the right. Not far away, disturbing shapes were moving through the fog.

At last, the street. A cart carrying sacks of flour; a stray dog; a handful of passers-by.

They had escaped from Littlewood's territory.

*   *   *

435

All night long, Littlewood had dreamed of the mummy. It stood up, stared at him with its other-worldly eyes and slowly, very slowly, squeezed his throat. He tried in vain to escape, lost his breath and caught fire!

He awoke with a start, soaked in sweat, and managed to get back to sleep. And the mummy returned to haunt his dreams. It was gigantic now, its head touching the sky, and it was trampling on him. One by one, his bones cracked.

Awake once more, Littlewood drank some whisky, shaved, disguised himself as a poor man and went to one of his weapons caches in Whitechapel, which were permanently guarded. He bought some hot potatoes from one of the stalls, which were erected before dawn. Workmen made do with this meagre breakfast and then left for work.

According to a code which he altered frequently, Littlewood knocked at the door of a disused workshop. The correct response came back from inside.

The door opened a little way, and he slipped inside; then the door closed again.

Two armed guards were drinking ale and chewing pieces of brownish-grey bread.

'It was a bad night, sir,' declared the doorman. 'The Charlie betrayed us. He was accompanied by a squad of policemen who dared to cross into our territory. We almost surrounded them, but they called for reinforcements. We fired, and they retreated.'

Littlewood's nightmare was continuing. So the

mummy's appearance had been a salutary warning. The authorities were reacting timidly to the riot in Hyde Park. The cautious leader of the revolutionaries would immediately put his troops on alert. If the next few days passed without any further police attempts to enter Whitechapel, he would move on to the second stage of his plan.

The initial results obtained by Higgins were relatively spectacular: twenty-five corrupt police officers had been identified, four of them senior officers. Some repented, while others tried to justify their behaviour. The majority were members of a 'Littlewood network', charged with providing information to their secret employer. Unfortunately, not one of them knew what he really looked like. These double agents did not belong to the leader's inner circle, and they did not know anything about his battle plan, the real number of his men or their hiding places in Whitechapel.

Consequently, there was nothing decisive about this small victory. It would not prevent Littlewood from continuing to cause trouble by launching a new attack. There would be violent action, bloody confrontations, injuries, perhaps deaths . . . Higgins was not making sufficiently swift progress to prevent this catastrophe. With Canning's agreement, he had doubled the number of uniformed and plain-clothes officers close to official buildings.

As he planned a glorious feat, Littlewood was hoping for a devastating reaction from the government which would cause a popular uprising. By persuading Canning not to resort to the army, the chief inspector could avert civil war. But would his position be tenable? As long as Littlewood held sway, chaos would threaten the country. Would he succeed in finding the weak spot, enabling him to reach the octopus's head?

A report was handed to him concerning the watch kept on the Belzonis' residence. Sarah was attending to her usual duties, and her husband had not returned from his journey. The third member of the household, in whom Higgins had been wrong not to take an interest, had just thrown off a tail while out shopping: James Curtain, the Belzonis' faithful and utterly discreet manservant.

'Mr Belzoni is away, inspector, and Mrs Belzoni has gone to a soirée.'

'It's you I wanted to see, James,' said Higgins in a fatherly manner. 'Can you spare me a moment?'

'I'm at your disposal. Ah . . .'

'Is there a problem?'

'While my employers are absent, I cannot really take their place and receive you in the small drawing room, which is reserved for visitors.'

'Shall we walk? The weather's not too bad.'

James Curtain pondered. No emotion showed on his stony face. 'Very well. But I must lock up the house carefully.'

The Belzonis' manservant walked along slowly and precisely, ignoring the rain. The two men fell into step. The street was quiet, the sky lowering.

'Have you known the Belzonis for long, Mr Curtain?'

'For as long as I can remember.'

'Does your work give you satisfaction?'

'Full and entire satisfaction, sir.'

'And yet Giovanni Belzoni is not a tranquil man. Sometimes, is his behaviour not a little . . . excessive?'

'I haven't noticed, inspector. And it's not for me to judge. He's my employer, and I must serve him correctly.'

'Has he ever given you orders which . . . displeased you?'

'Never.'

'Do you know why he's left for Russia?'

'I don't have to know his reasons.'

'You don't seem very curious, Mr Curtain.'

'A good servant hears nothing, sees nothing and says nothing.'

'I assume the disappearance of Mr Belzoni's mummy left you indifferent?'

'I don't bother myself with archaeology, inspector.'

'During your long stay in Egypt, did you not take an interest in antiquities?'

'My only concern was to serve my employers as best I could in conditions which were often difficult. The rest didn't concern me.'

'Does the sale of ancient objects form part of your usual duties?'

'Not at all.'

'Does Mr Belzoni's future not appear compromised to you?'

'He knows how to take misfortunes and triumph over them.'

'In your opinion, will he come back to London?'

'Why would he not come back?'

'Because he's run away.'

'Giovanni Belzoni, run away? Impossible, inspector.'

·'Shouldn't he have taken you with him?'

'He asked me to take care of Mrs Belzoni and their residence. I'm carrying out his orders.'

'Does Sarah Belzoni seem worried?'

'It's not for me to concern myself with my employer's sentiments but to serve her as best I can.'

'One detail intrigues me, Mr Curtain. Why, as you were returning from the market, did you throw off the police officer in charge of . . . protecting you?'

The servant remained impassive. 'Do I require protection?'

'The current disappearance of Giovanni Belzoni obliges me to take certain precautions.'

'I hadn't noticed the presence of that police officer,' declared Curtain calmly, 'and I didn't attempt to throw him off my track. He must have lost sight of me because of the movement of the crowd.'

'What did you buy?'

'Leeks, turnips, potatoes and courgettes. Without wishing to boast, I do make an excellent soup.'

'So you were merely out shopping and then returned to your employers' house to do the cooking. You didn't have any unpleasant encounters during this little escapade, or any exceptional meetings?'

'Neither one nor the other.'

James Curtain was a perfect servant, and perfect he would remain.

63

Working like an ant was beginning to produce excellent results. Benefiting from regular contacts with a government emissary,* Higgins saw his grand plan for reorganizing the police taking shape. His action was well received among the forces of order, corrupt officers no longer felt safe and many of them abandoned their dubious practices. It was better to get back into line before being harshly punished. This time, the authorities had decided to deal with the Littlewood problem in depth and not merely launch some brilliant feat with no future. His networks were coming apart one by one, and he would soon lack information and be forced into isolation.

Preferring persuasion to rigid control, Higgins spent a considerable amount of time persuading officers of all grades to get behind his plans. True unity demanded it.

With Belzoni still travelling, Sarah led a quiet existence,

* Sir Robert Peel, who was the official founder of Scotland Yard in 1829.

attending a few society events out of a sense of duty and selling the last items from Egypt. James Curtain was not taking part in any unusual activities.

The mummy still could not be found, but Higgins had not forgotten either the three murders or the list of suspects. Although obliged to delay certain initiatives, he remained just as determined to pursue the investigation to its conclusion. For Littlewood and the mummy were linked.

On reflection, one individual merited more attention. That is why Higgins was meeting Sir John Soane, who was delighted to show him round his museum. Begun in 1790, his collection of antiquities continued to grow, and the three floors of three houses, knocked into one, held an impressive number of marbles, elements of Roman architecture, bronzes, funerary monuments, mouldings, manuscripts, engravings and books. The guided visit ended at the Monk's Parlour, a strange room adorned with grimacing figures in the medieval style. In the centre was a table supporting a bronze skull.

'Thank you for your valuable explanations, Sir John.'

'Do be seated, inspector.'

The red armchairs seemed threatening. The architect and collector, a haughty man with a long face and shifty eyes, seemed tired.

'This is a disguised search, is it not?'

Higgins's placid smile did not satisfy Soane.

'What are you looking for, inspector?'

'A mummy.'

'I have a horror of that type of object!'

443

'And yet you're interested in funerary art, and you've acquired the alabaster sarcophagus exhibited by Belzoni.'

'Ancient sculpture excites me, not the atrocious remains of old Egyptians.'

'Belzoni complains that he was defrauded, Sir John.'

'I paid the agreed sum to the legitimate owner of the sarcophagus. That Italian was merely an intermediary, and he's obtained large amounts of money by exhibiting that monumental piece, which will soon have pride of place in my museum.'

'Belzoni believes he's the victim of a sort of conspiracy orchestrated by some highly placed mastermind, capable of conducting a press campaign and closing the doors which lead to respectability and official posts.'

'And you suspect me, John Soane! The truth is far simpler: that adventurer has a habit of embroidering the truth, and he believes he's at the centre of the world, whereas, in fact, nobody is interested in his second-rate exploits.'

'The pyramid of Khephren, the temple at Abu Simbel, an immense and superb tomb in the Valley of the Kings . . . His discoveries aren't inconsiderable.'

'Let's not fantasize, inspector! Belzoni's past doesn't plead in his favour, and his book is just a bad collection of anecdotes. He will never be regarded as a scientist. When he settled in London, he was deluding himself. The harsh law of reality imposes itself, and no one can escape it. Let that giant set off again to conquer his chimeras and forget his irrational ambitions. No one is orchestrating a conspiracy against him, for Belzoni discredits himself. No other explanation exists, inspector. Don't waste your energy trying to find one.'

Higgins turned a page of his notebook.

'Do you ever go to Whitechapel, Sir John?'

The collector looked down on him from a great height. 'Who do you take me for? A man of my station doesn't frequent that kind of district. I'm opposed to the mixing of different classes, inspector. It could lead only to disorder. My role is to bring together works of art, and Whitechapel is hardly a hunting ground for me!'

The wooden devils in the Monk's Parlour stared evilly at Higgins.

'Thank you for your help, Sir John.'

'Is your investigation progressing?'

'At its own pace.'

'Few criminals have been arrested in London recently.'

'Times are about to change.'

The mummy's *ka* remained fixed, its soul-bird flew between the heavens and the earth, the gods' energy continued to bring life to its heart and the noble being still served as a vessel for Osiris. The process of decomposition had been halted, and the body was regularly purified, so death was kept at a distance. The gates of paradise remained open, but the maw of nothingness had not closed.

People who destroyed mummies were killers of the worst kind. Not only did they profane tombs, but they also destroyed the vessels of resurrection, the fruits of long and difficult work carried out by ritual priests and seers, who were capable of travelling the beautiful pathways of the other world. And the mummy was the embodiment of the great voyage. Like a boat, it crossed the frontier separating the mortal and immortal worlds.

By dismembering mummies, burning them and eating them, Egypt's invaders and explorers from so-called civilized nations had proven their barbarity and humanity's decadence.

The rescuer spoke the words of transformation into light and carried out the purification ritual. With the aid of the four sons of Horus, these maintained the unity of the spiritual and material elements making up the mummy. The rescuer was a filter for the light of Ra, which human eyes could not gaze upon.

The rescuer lit two torches, placing the first at the head of the Osiran body and the second at its feet. Two long flames rose towards the ceiling of the crypt, curving over and forming a protective vault. Formidable deadlines were approaching, and precautions must be strengthened. After a sombre period during which the rescuer had almost lost hope, the future at last looked brighter.

Inspector Higgins had been reinstated and was making progress, step by step. His vigilance and perseverance would lead him to the truth, and the rescuer would retrieve the relics necessary for the mummy's survival.

Littlewood awoke with a start.

Once again, the mummy had disturbed his slumber.

Hideous and gigantic, it had trampled on him! His head burned, his bones cracked and he cried out in vain.

Soaked in sweat, he gulped down a tot of whisky. And the painful reality of these last few months immediately hit him. There had been one failure and disappointment after another. One by one, his informers within the police had withdrawn, and his last network had fallen apart. Deaf and blind, he now knew nothing of the authorities' plans.

Higgins . . . That accursed man Higgins was responsible for an underground strategy that Littlewood had been unable to halt. Three riots had come to nothing, despite being well organized. The police had not retreated, and reinforcements had arrived swiftly, enabling them to re-establish order.

Official buildings were well protected and remained inaccessible. The previous day, two rebel leaders had been intercepted and arrested as they were attempting to incite the crowd to rise up. Only Whitechapel remained a sanctuary that Higgins's troops dared not enter.

In the district committees, people were beginning to lose hope and even criticize Littlewood's strategy. He had been forced to re-establish his authority and promise action on a grand scale. This bad spell would reunite the ranks of the revolutionaries, whose future promised to be bright.

He must face facts: it was impossible to carry out his initial plan. As a priority, he must maintain the hatred of the poor for the rich and continue to make them believe that they would soon take their rightful place; next, he must fall back and persuade Higgins that he had won.

As time passed, the chief inspector would lower his guard.

Littlewood's surprise attack would strike at a weak point, stunning the authorities and polite society. Higgins would be accused of negligence, and the revolution would once again have a clear run.

64

Chief Inspector Higgins's working days encompassed more tasks than there were hours, but the results of his efforts pleased him. The season had passed without any serious incidents, and London's high society had celebrated its usual festivities in peace. The threat of Littlewood seemed to be past.

To Higgins's eyes this was a cunning ruse, and as the days went by he allocated more men to surveillance and hunted down the revolutionary's allies who had infiltrated the government and the police. Enforced resignations and dismissals continued apace. Little by little, the noose was tightening around Whitechapel. Would it pull tight before Littlewood launched a new – and undoubtedly formidable – assault? The wounded beast would play his last card, attempting to regain lost ground, and he might win a decisive battle.

From time to time Higgins managed to spend part of the weekend in the country, along with his cat and dog.

Long walks and Mary's cooking provided him with the energy he needed to continue his mission. As usual rainy and cool, the summer was drawing to an end, to be succeeded by a cool, rainy autumn, tinting the leaves on the trees with gold.

That Friday night, the chief inspector had to honour a dinner invitation from Lady Suzanna. During the season, she had been one of the most glittering personalities, attracting glances from aristocrats, politicians and famous artists. Although evil tongues wagged constantly, they were unable to attribute any torrid liaisons or embarrassing faults to her. Beautiful and intelligent, with a gift for witty repartee, the young barrister outshone her rivals and was establishing herself as one of the rising stars of the Empire's capital.

Lady Suzanna owned a house in Lincoln's Inn Fields, the area where the judiciary were based, not far from Sir John Soane's home and museum. The barrister's residence, stone-built, had a Gothic air. A liveried butler greeted Higgins and showed him into a dining room adorned with hangings of dusky-pink velvet. English and Italian still lifes from the sixteenth century celebrated fruit, while marble statues of Greek goddesses provided a charming sight for guests.

'Delighted to see you again, inspector,' said the mistress of the house, who was wearing a taffeta evening gown whose colours changed according to the intensity of the light. 'It's a long time since we've had the leisure to talk about our respective investigations. I've been caught up in social obligations, but I haven't given up my quest to discover the truth. And I'm certain that you've not done so either.'

Higgins merely nodded.

'My chef has promised to surpass himself. Would you care for champagne with dinner?'

'That would be delightful.'

The menu was a delicious one, with caviar, salmi of black grouse, lobster with fines herbes, hare with mushrooms, an assortment of goats' cheeses, blackcurrant sorbet and a lemon soufflé.

'The new Prime Minister is delighted with your work, inspector. No disturbances spoiled the season, and the disorder in the East End has been reduced to a minimum. Your methods are remarkably effective.'

'Patience and precision guide me, Lady Suzanna, and one cannot go without the other. Unfortunately, the volcano's anger has not been extinguished, and I cannot rule out another eruption.'

'In other words, Littlewood is still at large.'

'He hopes that the appearance of calm will cause me to lower my guard, believing that after a series of failures he has renounced violence.'

'And what if that is the case?'

'I'm convinced that the opposite is true. Littlewood cares nothing for people's happiness and thinks only of being in power. By taking advantage of our society's weaknesses and injustices, he wants to provoke a civil war and set himself up as the saviour.'

'An insane plan!'

'By stirring up hatred, he might succeed. France during the Terror was no mirage, and the worst atrocities were committed there in the name of a supposed ideal. Believing that we are safe from such a disaster would be culpable vanity.'

'Are you hoping to find the trail leading to Littlewood?'

'The man has a multitude of faces and has surrounded himself with several protective circles. I've destroyed the outer ones and am getting closer to my goal. He will sense that this is the case and will react brutally. In all honesty, I'm not certain that I can bring him down.'

'A sombre prospect, inspector!'

'Littlewood will never give up his murderous crusade. It's his sole reason for existing.'

The food was exquisite, the champagne verging on perfection.

'Despite the balls, concerts and horse races,' declared the pretty brunette, 'I've continued to compile dossiers on our suspects. A fine collection of crooks! Kristin Sadly, the overexcited paper mill owner, should have been convicted of forgery and the use of forgeries, but she corrupted a magistrate who refused to recognize it officially. The accounting documents and real activities of Paul Tasquinio, the man who delivers meat, remain indecipherable. Henry Cranmer, the owner of textile mills, is a specialist in fixed contracts and rigged sales. He catches many unwary people in his nets and grows wealthy with apparent legality. Sir Richard Beaulieu sees his bank account grow sporadically, and the origins of large deposits remain unknown. The politician Francis Carmick manipulates at least ten financiers, creates companies in which he doesn't feature and derives substantial profits from them. Andrew Young took advantage of a really stupid accident suffered by a landowner to acquire his estate, with the aid of a solicitor who ought to be in prison. I shall put the precise information at your disposal, inspector.'

'Thank you for your help, Lady Suzanna. You didn't mention the actor Peter Bergeray.'

'Ruined in January, rich in February, in desperate straits in March, flourishing in April . . . A disjointed life, and finances to match.'

Glass of champagne in hand, the beautiful lawyer looked at the chief inspector. 'And one of these disreputable individuals is Littlewood, is that not the case?'

'Assuredly.'

'One . . . or several? Or all of them together?'

Higgins dabbed at the corner of his mouth with a linen napkin. 'You ask an excellent question, Lady Suzanna.'

'One person with many faces, or several faces forming a single person . . . Would the latter hypothesis not explain why Littlewood is indescribable?'

'It cannot be ruled out.'

'Would you confide your personal belief to me, inspector?'

'I don't even confide it to myself; it might lead me astray.'

Lady Suzanna smiled. 'You would make a formidable barrister!'

'Each unto his own.'

'When you were dismissed, you were preparing to launch an offensive. Given the extent of your powers now, why put it off any longer?'

'That incident was beneficial and enabled me to think more clearly. The missing mummy is at the centre of the mystery, and I have no clues leading to it in a direct way. So first I would like to put Littlewood out of action, and I was hoping that he would make a mistake.'

'A hope that has been disappointed?'

'Alas so. My adversary is an excellent chess player, who adapts to my strategy and pursues his own. And also an unforeseen event disturbed me: the disappearance of Belzoni.'

The lemon soufflé was both light and creamy. The young woman's chef had indeed surpassed himself.

'Belzoni,' she murmured. 'Do you consider him . . . a suspect?'

'Simply a journey, or an attempt to escape?'

'Belzoni, a triple murderer, and the thief of his own mummy . . . It's unimaginable!'

'The actions of killers often exceed our understanding, Lady Suzanna. And I need to clarify this case before continuing my investigations.'

As the barrister and her guest were leaving the dining room to take coffee in the drawing room, the butler intervened. 'Lady Suzanna, an individual claiming to be a police officer is asking to see Mr Higgins.'

'My men must be able to contact me at all times, and I was obliged to give them your address,' explained the chief inspector. 'Excuse me for a moment.'

The conversation was brief.

'Good news?' enquired Lady Suzanna when Higgins returned.

'Belzoni has just returned home.'

65

The vigorous sound of the door knocker told James Curtain that the visitor was an important one, and he hurried to open the door to the Belzoni residence.

'I should like to see your employer,' said Higgins.

'He's not yet awake.'

'What about Mrs Belzoni?'

The tall Irishwoman appeared, clad in a bright red dressing gown.

'Inspector! A courtesy visit, I presume? My husband returned late last night, and we talked a great deal. Would you like some coffee?'

'Thank you, I would.'

'James will make you some, and I shall wake Giovanni.'

For a moment Higgins wondered if Sarah was going to help the Titan of Padua to escape. But she knew that her home was being watched and that any such attempt was doomed to failure. So he waited in the small drawing room, which had formerly held so many Egyptian objects and which was now almost empty.

Half an hour elapsed, and then the giant's footsteps made the staircase creak. Despite his proud bearing, his face was tired. 'I have only just arrived, inspector, and you are here already!'

'Your long absence surprised me, Mr Belzoni.'

'My journey was essential.'

'Would you be so kind as to give me the details?'

The giant collapsed into an armchair, and James brought him an enormous cup of coffee.

'I went to Russia, where I met Tsar Alexander I, who was eager to hear about my discoveries. Egypt interests him, and he gave me an amethyst ring. Then I returned, by way of Finland, Sweden and Denmark.'

'Did you obtain an official mission, or funding to resume your excavations?'

Belzoni's face fell. 'Total failure. As usual, Sarah and I must fend for ourselves. We've decided to auction off our last antiquities and organize a new exhibition in Paris. The one in London is running out of steam, and we shall go and seek our fortune elsewhere.'

'Before you do so, I would like to clarify certain points.'

'What am I being accused of now? Have you at least found my mummy? I could sell it for a good price to the highest bidder.'

'I'm still searching for it.'

'A vain promise! It's certainly been destroyed.'

'What if you were using it to spread death?'

Belzoni knocked over his cup of coffee. 'You . . . you're talking nonsense!'

'Are you not the target of a conspiracy aimed at destroying your reputation?'

'Without a doubt!'

'Convinced that the person responsible was in London, you devised a plan to kill him. But you discovered numerous accomplices, beginning with an old nobleman, a clergyman and a pathologist, who were threatening your mummy. Did you not threaten to smash the nobleman's skull and snap the clergyman in two?'

'They were behaving like vandals, and I'm a hot-blooded man!'

'Once these three were eliminated, you had to deal with their leader: the politician Francis Carmick or Professor Richard Beaulieu?'

'I have no idea!'

'They mocked you, Mr Belzoni, and put spokes in your wheels. The university man, a specialist in the history of religions and a great enemy of Egypt, occupies an ideal position and closes all doors to you. You have returned to wreak your revenge, with the aid of the mummy.'

'That is false, completely false!'

'I think I've brought your intentions to light, *Magnoon*.'

The Titan of Padua leaped to his feet and slammed the drawing room door shut. If he charged at Higgins, the inspector would find it difficult to escape from his fists.

'You . . . you said . . .'

'*Magnoon*, "the madman". Is that not the nickname given to you in Egypt?'

Head bowed, Belzoni sat down again. 'Indeed, inspector.'

'Why did you lie to me?'

'That nickname isn't a very complimentary one, as you'll agree, and I detest it. But it doesn't make me a criminal! The conspirators have succeeded, inspector. I shall never make my mark in London, and the road to Egypt is barred to me. After the exhibition in Paris, I shall sell my finest treasure: the life-size colour drawings of the chambers of *my* tomb in the Valley of the Kings.* In France I hope to find an enthusiastic public and obtain substantial takings. I shall then set off aimlessly with Sarah and my servant. Unless . . . unless you forbid me to leave London! You would be sentencing me to death, inspector. The exhibition in Paris will be my only means of existing.'

Anxiously, the Italian awaited the verdict.

'You are free to go, Mr Belzoni. And I wish you good luck.'

Sarah's grateful smile had strengthened Higgins's opinion: the Belzonis were not mixed up in the triple murder and did not know where the mummy was hidden. The giant, however, had omitted to tell him about his journey to

---

* It took two artists, Ricci and Beechey, almost two years' work to reproduce the bas-reliefs from the tomb of Seti I.

Russia and had hidden his true plans for the future. So the chief inspector had only limited trust in him. Would he indeed go to Paris?

As he read a bulletin from the Royal Historical Society, Higgins learned that the battle to decipher hieroglyphs was raging fiercely. Thomas Young had declared victory, but the Frenchman Champollion had met this declaration with emphatic denials. He, and he alone, was on the right track.

Young had been incapable of reading the document presented to him by the chief inspector. Could Champollion? Champollion lived in Paris, the destination of Belzoni, who might be joined there by an accomplice, far from the British police.

Consequently, there were several good reasons to leave England and venture into hostile territory. There, the chief inspector would be merely a foreigner, devoid of any power. Before his departure, he must strengthen his security measures and put all his informants on a state of alert. The only other thing he could do was pray to heaven, hoping that Littlewood did not take advantage of Higgins's brief absence to launch his offensive.

66

On the morning of 14 September 1822 Jean-François Champollion resumed work. He had no great fondness for his attic office, on the third floor of no. 28 Rue Mazarine, near the Institute, but it was his only refuge, in the heart of Paris, 'that dirty capital of France', as he described it.

The thirty-two-year-old scholar, who had fine black hair and dark brown eyes, could not bear the arrogance and ridiculous pretensions of his English rival, Thomas Young. To be able to read hieroglyphs ... That was his whole life's dream, to which he had devoted taxing but tireless research. And that scholar from across the Channel was not going to reach the goal first!

The autumn rain made Paris even sadder and did not even succeed in washing it clean. Champollion looked at the hieroglyphic texts in his possession, assessed the progress he had made and attempted to organize his hypotheses.

Suddenly, the ancient Egyptian signs began to talk. Was it phonetic or symbolic writing? That was the wrong question to ask. In reality, it was figurative, phonetic *and* symbolic, on three levels of reading. It had an alphabet, but also signs equivalent to two or even three sounds, and others which were sometimes read, sometimes not, and which designated the category to which the word belonged, for example the category of abstract ideas or foodstuffs. Integrating these parameters as a whole and understanding the rules of their game seemed to exceed the capacities of a human brain.

Then a voice began to speak: the voice of Thoth, the god of scribes. And on the morning of 14 September 1822 Jean-François Champollion became a seer. In an instant the scattered materials were assembled, and the great book of ancient Egypt, which had been tightly closed for so many centuries, was open. And Champollion read the first names of illustrious rulers, bringing them back to life: Tuthmosis, Ramses . . .

Panting, his mind in a whirl, the scholar just had the strength to get to the office occupied by his elder brother, Jacques-Joseph.

'What's happened, Jean-François? You look so shaken!'

'I . . . I've done it!'

'You mean you've found the key to hieroglyphs?'

Jean-François Champollion fell to the floor, unconscious. If he did not reawaken, he would take his secret with him to the tomb.

*　　*　　*

On 27 September Belzoni's barges, laden with the materials for his forthcoming exhibition on the Boulevard des Italiens, near the Chinese baths, passed beneath the windows of the Institute where Jean-François Champollion, now fully recovered, was announcing to the academic world that he could now read hieroglyphs. During an official declaration, he described his method and brought back to light three thousand years of civilization, which had produced a formidable quantity of texts. The inscriptions on tombs and temples could finally be read, and papyri had ceased to be obscure grimoires. Titanic labours lay ahead for Champollion: he must translate thousands of signs, compile a grammar and a dictionary, and reveal to the world the thoughts of the ancient Egyptians.

Reassured regarding Belzoni's sincerity, Higgins listened attentively to the founder of Egyptology. Given the complexity of his discovery and the profundity of his vision, there could be no doubt that he was inspired by the gods.

Excitedly, Jean-François Champollion learned of the drawings reproducing the extraordinary paintings from the tomb of Seti I. Belzoni's exhibition was certainly not lacking in interest.

'Of course, they are no match for the originals,' commented a visitor, 'but you must see them.'

'That's my dearest wish!' confessed the Egyptologist.

'Allow me to introduce myself: I'm Chief Inspector Higgins, of the British police.'

'Are you travelling for pleasure or on business?'

'A little of both. I had the privilege of attending your lecture at the Institute. You're one of those exceptional men whose discoveries change the face of humanity. Thanks to you, Egypt has been reborn. And this miracle is certain to alter the way we see things.'

'Are you interested in ancient history, inspector?'

'Are we not Egypt's heirs?'

'You're right; she is a generous and radiant mother who has given us so much! As we read the hieroglyphs, we discover one surprise after another.'

'Have you had an opportunity to study mummies, M. Champollion?'

'Just one, in Grenoble. It was a man from the era of the Ptolemies, the successors to Alexander the Great. The body was in perfect condition, with gold sheaths protecting the fingers and toes. It was a disturbing testament to the past, most disturbing . . . My brother Jacques-Joseph and I re-bandaged that mummy and published the results of our observations in 1814. I had the strange feeling that I was gazing at an unknown form of life, not an archaeological object. If I had the power, I would forbid the destruction of mummies! We sometimes behave like barbarians, Mr Higgins.'

'To my mind it's an incurable defect in the human race.'

'Why did you mention mummies?' asked Champollion.

'An extraordinary specimen has disappeared in London, and I must find it in order to solve a murder case with many ramifications.'

'A murder case . . . Are you attributing malevolent power to this mummy?'

'Here's the papyrus that accompanied it. Would you be kind enough to translate the text?'

Champollion examined the document purchased from Belzoni.

'The human-headed bird symbolizes the soul emerging from the mummified body, which is assimilated into Osiris,' he explained. 'It flies up to the sun, feeds on its light and returns to bring life to the slumbering being. The flame facing it maintains the energy needed for survival. Now, grant me sufficient time in which to decipher this.'

As he concentrated on the text, Champollion appeared suddenly possessed by a supernatural energy. His eyes shone with a strange light, and his fevered voice dictated the translation, which Higgins wrote down in his black notebook:

Living ones, who pass by my house of eternity, make a libation on my behalf, for I am master of the secret. My head is fixed to my neck, my limbs are put back together and my bones knitted, and my body will not decay. I was asleep and I have awakened. The great god will judge profaners. Anyone who assaults a mummy, anyone who attacks it, will not be welcomed into the Western goddess's bosom. Criminals will suffer the second death, and the Soul-Eater will destroy them.

'This mummy does not appear very friendly, inspector. In your place, I would avoid approaching it. The magic of the Egyptians was a real science, and certain sages may have succeeded in crossing the frontiers of death.'

'Do you know a good restaurant?'

'Indeed I do, but . . .'

'On the one hand, I should like to invite you to dinner; on the other, I should like to ask a favour: teach me the rudiments of deciphering hieroglyphs.'

That evening the two men enjoyed dinner and an excellent wine, then Champollion gave a lesson to his first pupil.

67

The magic of the four sons of Horus was beginning to be exhausted. Soon, the mummy would start to decay, and the vital organs would die, one by one. The rescuer had already worked a kind of miracle, by going far beyond the ritual year and prolonging the existence of an Osiran body which had been stripped of its protection.

However, all hope was not lost. The information the rescuer had patiently gathered made it possible to launch a final expedition in search of the relics, though the chances of success were infinitesimally small. As there was no longer any choice, a last purification rite must be carried out. The rescuer donned a mask of Anubis, way-opener of the other world and possessor of the secrets of mummification, and opened the eyes, mouth and ears with the aid of an adze, a kind of carpenter's chisel.

This endowed the mummy with the ability to take on any form it wished, to use its senses and to move around. But outside the force field created by the correct wrappings, failure would result, and the noble body would be reduced to a cadaver.

The rescuer left the crypt, wondering if it was already too late.

With its blackened walls, sawdust-covered floor and rough wooden tables, there was nothing smart about Ye Olde Cheshire Cheese, a pub on Fleet Street where everyone enjoyed beer and tasty pork pies.

Seated by the fireplace, facing each other, Higgins and Lady Suzanna looked like regulars.

'I needed to see you urgently, inspector, and I chose this place to avoid indiscreet ears.'

'Is someone spying on you?'

'My investigations may have disturbed some big game. For several days now I've had the feeling that I'm being followed. And my butler recently spotted a man acting suspiciously near my home, although he was unable to provide a precise description.'

'Would you like police protection?'

'If my impressions are correct, I would not say no.'

'What have you discovered lately, Lady Suzanna?'

'The judge who was protecting Kristin Sadly has had a crisis of conscience. Yesterday evening, at the end of dinner, he told me that he was resigning in exchange for immunity from prosecution and produced evidence proving the woman's many frauds. She has constantly lied, stolen and corrupted people. Her considerable fortune has enabled her to control a sort of gang.'

'Are you thinking of a Littlewood in skirts?'

'Can you exclude the possibility?'

'Kristin Sadly interests me greatly, Lady Suzanna.'

The beautiful barrister took a sip of ale. 'Then there's a second set of evidence, which is both remarkable and disturbing,' she went on. 'This one concerns Andrew Young.'

'Disturbing?'

'He threatened to kill his banker, one of my business contacts, if he dared tell the government about the latest payment he had received, a considerable sum of money.'

'In connection with what?'

'My banker friend made the mistake of asking him that very question. He was terrified and asked for my assistance. I promised to help him.'

'Rely on me, Lady Suzanna. I shall deal swiftly with Young.'

'Is this . . . your great offensive?'

'The time has indeed come.'

'Was your decision influenced by any specific event?'

'My meeting with Champollion, in Paris. That young scholar has found the key to reading hieroglyphs, and his discovery has clarified my investigation.'

'Can he read every inscription?'

'Almost as though it were a newspaper.'

'Then Egypt has been brought back to life! Tomorrow we'll know its secrets and we'll be able to communicate with the dead or with those we believe to be dead.'

'Are you referring to mummies, Lady Suzanna?'

'Before, Egypt was a closed book, filled with mysteries, and now it's open! Can you not foresee extraordinary revelations?'

'I share your hopes,' agreed Higgins.

'Do you still believe that the missing mummy has a major part to play in this case?'

'Indeed. According to a papyrus which Champollion deciphered, it possesses considerable powers to defend itself from attackers.'

The pretty brunette appeared sceptical. 'Are we not being led astray by our enthusiasm for this prodigious civilization?'

'Have no fear, Lady Suzanna, I shall stick closely to the facts. And the disappearance of that mummy is a fact.'

Darts players were enjoying a furiously competitive game, concentrating so hard that they seemed ready to kill one another. Around them, spectators were drinking pints of ale. One of them glared briefly at the young woman, paid his bill and left the pub.

The incident had not escaped Higgins. 'Do you know that man?' he asked.

'No, inspector.'

'You've helped me greatly, Lady Suzanna, but I fear that you've taken too many risks. Our enemy is neither an amateur nor a joker. If he regards you as an obstacle, he won't hesitate to kill you.'

'Are you trying to frighten me again?'

'I would like to make you see reason. Whatever happens, Littlewood will never admit defeat. When someone gets close to his lair, he'll react like a wounded animal, and he'll tear you apart with one swipe of his claws.'

'You've succeeded, inspector. I *am* afraid.'

'Then I'm delighted, Lady Suzanna. Will you consent to halt your investigations and devote yourself to safer activities until the killer is arrested?'

Her charming smile expressed disappointment. 'May I at least be the first person you tell?'

'I shall do my best.'

'And you too will be careful?'

'I have a mission to carry out, Lady Suzanna.'

'Good luck, Mr Higgins.'

68

Andrew Young could not stop thinking about the anonymous letter he had received, warning him of imminent danger. It was a clear message, which had obliged him to take urgent measures, beginning with his own safety. Chief Inspector Higgins was getting close to the truth, and Young needed to get away with all haste.

At nightfall he entered his office, took a key from his pocket and unlocked a small cabinet adorned with grimacing devils. Inside lay the precious phial he had purchased from Belzoni. Its contents were worth a fortune.

'That object does not belong to you,' declared the voice of the rescuer.

Young swung round, eyes wide, open-mouthed.

'What . . . what are you doing in my house?'

'If you wish to avoid terrible torments, give me that vase.'

'Out of the question! I paid for it and it belongs to me.'

'Unfortunately for you.'

Fine, cool rain was falling on Andrew Young's estate. Accompanied by two crack marksmen, Higgins approached the door of the house. His colleagues were ready to open fire.

In the absence of any response, the chief inspector pushed open the door. The heavy building was dark and silent. Moving cautiously, the three police officers searched the rooms one by one. Everything appeared normal, with the exception of one horrible little cabinet, whose doors were standing wide open. The treasure it housed had disappeared, but Higgins knew what it was: the sealed vase which had lain along the mummy's left flank.

A vase whose contents Young must have examined before resealing and hiding it, for it preserved an extraordinary substance: seeds dating from the days of the pharaohs, seeds that were ready to live again! Belzoni's information had enabled Higgins to work out Young's intentions. He was planning to grow these ancient cereal crops and sell them at extortionate prices. But a single phial was not enough, and he was searching for others in order to obtain an adequate supply of seeds. If he succeeded, his fortune would be assured. As a plan it was insane, just like its inventor.

It was clear that all the servants had left the house and its outbuildings. Doubtless Young himself had fled.

However, Higgins continued his investigations, in search of a second treasure, somewhat less peaceful than the mummy's wheat.

He had to force open the door to a shed. Inside he found ten chests, which the chief inspector's two colleagues had to strain to open. They contained pistols, rifles and munitions.

So Young was not merely a collector of antique weapons, but also a trafficker in modern ones. A small label indicated the destination of this arsenal: *Whit. Litt.*, in other words 'Whitechapel, Littlewood'.

'Superb work, sir! We've just unearthed a stash that was obviously intended for the rebels.'

One detail bothered Higgins. Why had Young left before this delivery had been made? If he feared that the police were about to arrive, he ought to have either hurried to deliver the weapons to Whitechapel or defended himself. The probable answer was that he was still hiding here somewhere.

They searched the house again, but in vain. There was no one in the barns, the stables or the buildings occupied by the farm labourers.

On the other hand, the first grain silo had a surprise in store for them.

The head of Andrew Young – as ugly as ever – was sticking out of a large heap of grain. His eyes were open and glassy, his mouth hanging slackly open.

The officers dragged him out.

'He's alive,' said one of them, 'but he's hardly breathing.'

'Can you speak, Young?' demanded Higgins.

The landowner remained inert.

'It's as if he's frozen,' remarked the other officer.

'We'll take him back to London,' decided the chief inspector.

Several doctors had arrived at the same conclusion: they simply could not understand the case of Andrew Young, who seemed to be suffering from some kind of living death. Although his vital functions did not seem damaged, none of them were behaving normally. He was incapable of speaking, moving or eating. His survival was a scientific riddle, and eminent specialists would soon be brought in to examine him.

Higgins would have liked to question Young, but he felt that he knew the main facts. The landowner had two irons in the fire at the same time: producing exceptional cereal crops from ancient seeds and providing the revolutionaries with weapons. The chief inspector was certain of one thing: Andrew Young was not Littlewood. By choosing a supplier who was situated away from the capital, Littlewood had revealed himself to be a fine strategist. But the arrest of his accomplice would interrupt the deliveries of weapons and interfere with Littlewood's plans, unless he had a sufficiently large stockpile to launch his grand offensive.

This initial success did not intoxicate Higgins. It might have come too late.

Just as his carriage halted outside the house on John Adam Street, one of his assistants ran towards him.

475

'An emergency, inspector! One of your informants has some vital information.'

The almanac-seller had a friendly face. People would tell him anything, and no one ever suspected his secret role.

'That scoundrel Tasquinio has been making life difficult for me,' he admitted to Higgins. 'I've been trying to locate his real lair for months. This time, I've succeeded. And it seems suspicious to me, very suspicious.'

'What district?'

'Whitechapel, a blind alley. It's difficult to approach.'

Higgins kept the two marksmen with him and asked eight other police officers, in plain clothes, to accompany him.

Tasquinio was liable to react violently.

69

Paul Tasquinio examined the latest delivery from Alexandria, via Kristin Sadly's paper mill. A Portuguese ship had brought pieces of mummy and mummy wrappings, purchased from Arab traders who were constantly raising their prices. Tasquinio was one of the last experts in manufacturing *mummia*, a medicinal paste which was greatly prized by connoisseurs. He boiled up these remains of ancient corpses, broke open the skulls, which were full of resin and unguents, and extracted an oil that he reserved for wealthy enthusiasts, who were convinced that this elixir of long life could cure any illness.

The problem was the lack of raw material. So the trader had been forced to manage by procuring fake mummies. The customers didn't notice anything, and the profits were higher. Blackened walls, heaps of ashes, unpleasant debris . . . The secret workshop seemed rather sinister, but Tasquinio was fond of this lair where he was building his fortune.

With a smile on his lips, he contemplated the pretty chest wrapping he had bought from Belzoni. In comparison, the others seemed second-rate. After countless hesitations, Tasquinio had decided to use it to wrap a woman's feet in the correct manner.

He heard two short, sharp knocks on the oak door, then three more, spaced out this time, and then a final one.

It was the agreed code.

Nevertheless, Tasquinio peered out through a crack. There was no sign of danger.

He opened the door, and the purchaser entered.

'Here's your package. Pay and leave.'

Tasquinio had omitted to supply a precise detail: no one must know the location of his lair. So once he had the money in his hand, he would slit the throat of this unwary enthusiast and make good use of his remains.

'Your thoughts are impure, Tasquinio.'

The coarse face tensed. 'My thoughts . . . What are you talking about?'

'You're a profaner and a profiteer.'

'That's enough of that! Are you going to pay?'

'It's your turn to pay.'

Furious, Paul Tasquinio snatched up a butcher's knife. But his arm was blocked, and a surge of intense pain forced him to drop his weapon. Suddenly dizzy, he collapsed to the floor.

With great veneration, the rescuer picked up the chest band.

* * *

At any moment Whitechapel rioters might attack the little group of police officers who, using the directions provided by the almanac-seller, were approaching Paul Tasquinio's lair. Higgins never carried a weapon. He preferred to trust his instinct and use his intuition to sense any danger. In this uncontrolled district a single spark could set light to the powder keg. Tonight, the fog was a valuable ally.

The blind alley.

Two cats clawed at each other one last time and disappeared. Silence fell.

Higgins walked slowly towards the smoke-blackened oak door, which bore traces of peeling paint. To his astonishment, it stood ajar.

He ventured inside a sinister workshop filled with vats, piles of brownish rags and large candles. Fragments of mummies lay on a bench.

The chief inspector was not surprised. He had suspected Paul Tasquinio of manufacturing *mummia*, a bogus remedy based on mummy flesh, and selling it to wealthy enthusiasts who believed in the healing power of embalmed bodies. His trade in boiled meat concealed this horrible traffic.

At the back of the premises was a metal door.

Using his skeleton key, Higgins opened it. And what was revealed by the candlelight left him open-mouthed.

At first sight it was an ordinary butcher's cold room with carcasses hanging on hooks. In reality they were the remains of men and women, some naked, others still modestly dressed. The corpses of poor people from

Whitechapel, corpses which nobody would claim. These were Tasquinio's false mummies, his inexhaustible raw material; for the mummies he obtained from Egypt had become rare and were insufficient.

He had followed the example of his counterparts in Alexandria and Cairo, who sold slaves' bodies they claimed to have removed from ancient tombs. Men, women, children, old, young or sick: it did not matter. Their brains and viscera were removed, then they were filled with bitumen, wrapped in bandages blackened with pitch, dried out in the sun and became presentable mummies.

In the middle of the second row hung Paul Tasquinio, suspended by the collar of his serge jacket. He was in a stupor, but alive.

'Inspector, someone's coming!' warned one of his men in terror.

As he saw the abominable sight, the officer froze to the spot.

'Help me to get him down.'

A piece of paper was sticking out of Tasquinio's pocket. Higgins unfolded it. It was some sort of invoice, accounting for consignments of brown rags destined for KS. A fine sum which Kristin Sadly would have to pay in exchange for this delivery.

'Inspector, there's a mob outside barring our way out.'

'Get behind me, and don't use your weapons.'

Around twenty workmen were advancing, brandishing sticks, pickaxes and spades.

'We've just identified a criminal and we're taking him away,' announced Higgins.

A square-faced man with a beard stepped forward. 'He's bound to be one of ours! He's not leaving Whitechapel, and neither are you.'

'Paul Tasquinio steals corpses.'

'You're talking rubbish!'

'See for yourselves.'

Higgins signalled to his men to step aside. Flanked by several of his companions, the bearded man entered the sinister workshop.

A few seconds later, the sound of screaming echoed through the building. The bearded man reappeared, looking shaken.

'People we know . . . It's not right to treat them like that! It's up to us to bury them.'

'Understood, as long as you let us take away Tasquinio.'

The workman hesitated. 'Will you hang him?'

'Faced with such an abomination, the courts are unlikely to be lenient. And the man has already lost his mind.'

'Take him!'

As Tasquinio was carried past by two officers, the locals hurled insults at him.

Ten eminent practitioners examined Paul Tasquinio at length. Scratching his forehead, their spokesman summed up their strange findings. 'We don't understand it at all, inspector. Given his condition, this patient ought to be dead. But he's alive, in violation of all scientific principles!

His organs aren't functioning, and we don't know how he's breathing. It's an exceptional case, truly exceptional.'

'Comparable to that of Andrew Young, I presume?'

'Almost identical! If we succeed in solving this riddle, medicine will make remarkable progress.'

It was three o'clock in the morning, and the fog was growing thicker. Utterly exhausted, Higgins allowed himself a brief rest. He now knew something else for certain: Tasquinio was not Littlewood. Whitechapel had merely served him as a hiding place for his ignoble activities, not as a revolutionary command post.

70

The red-haired youth hammered on the door of Kristin Sadly's office. She had been up since five o'clock, and was going over her accounts. The recent drop in her profits had enraged her, and this situation could not endure for long.

Irritably, she opened the door. 'What do you want?'

'Your friend is in danger.'

'My friend . . . What's his name?'

'Paul Tasquinio. The police almost caught him and are heading for your place. Get away quickly, he said.'

The youth held out a hand.

Kristin Sadly handed him a shilling.

'I was hoping for more!'

'Get out of my sight, filthy urchin!'

Running away into the fog, the youth bumped into his accomplice, who wasn't so stingy and gave him a fine reward.

'The old bitch swallowed it. See you!'

At this time of the morning Kristin Sadly was alone. The rescuer tiptoed forward and saw her open a wooden box and take out a linen veil, the mummy's first shroud, which had covered it to the top of its head. According to the ancient texts, this 'battle garment' protected the Osiran body from its enemies.

Kristin Sadly owned two treasures: her book of secret accounts and this shroud, the model for her forthcoming mummy paper, which she was attempting to perfect using the rags impregnated with resin supplied by Tasquinio. The latest attempts had not pleased her, producing only a mediocre, brownish product which she had sold as packaging to grocers and butchers. Certain customers had complained of various ailments, but blamed them on meat or vegetables not being fresh. She needed finest-quality linen, the kind which embalmers used to wrap the mummies of nobles, to create a top-of-the-range paper which aristocrats would clamour to buy. The key to success was to reach both the elite and the lower classes.

'Give me that shroud.'

Kristin Sadly started and swung round. 'You! You certainly have a fine talent for acting!'

'Please give it to me.'

'Certainly not. It belongs to me.'

'That shroud does not belong to you, Kristin.'

'I bought it, and it's mine. Get out of here! I have work to do.'

'You *must* give it back to me.'

484

Fury glittered in the woman's eyes, and she seized a hammer.

'Get out, or I'll break your skull!'

Calmly, the rescuer came forward. 'All violence is futile. Be intelligent enough to obey.'

'Never!'

Delayed by a false alarm at the Bank of England, where officials had reported seeing a suspicious group of individuals, Higgins did not arrive at Kristin Sadly's paper mill until ten o'clock. Employees were wandering about on the quayside, smoking their pipes or chewing smoked fish.

The chief inspector approached a foreman, who was in charge of guarding the mill. 'Problems?'

'The boss isn't here, and my team hasn't received any instructions. This is the first time in ten years of work. She never leaves anything to chance. I don't understand. She should have warned me.'

'Have you been inside her office?'

'I knocked at least a hundred times, and then I dared to look inside. Empty. It's not normal, I'm telling you. The boss is never away.'

'I'll try to find her.'

Higgins walked into the mill, which was bordered by warehouses. He had long since fathomed Kristin Sadly's intentions, and her use for the brown rags. The former mistress of Peter Bergeray, in business with Professor Beaulieu and the trader Paul Tasquinio, she saw the mummy's shroud as a source of profit. She used cloths and bandages impregnated with resin to produce paste for manufacturing paper, despite the dangers of such a process.* And she was undoubtedly planning other, equally morbid, new techniques.

The chief inspector located the warehouse containing the suspicious fabrics. Just beside them he found a sort of large parcel, bearing an inscription: FOR THE ATTENTION OF SIR RICHARD BEAULIEU. Inside lay the body of Kristin Sadly.

'It's incomprehensible,' confessed the spokesman for the group of doctors who had just examined the patient. 'She's alive, but not according to the usual mechanisms! Don't hold out any hope of questioning her, inspector. She's incapable of expressing herself and is highly unlikely to recover her powers of speech. A coma which is not a coma . . . Inexplicable! This is a veritable epidemic! Let's hope that it stops here.'

'I'm not certain that it will,' lamented Higgins.

As he left the hospital, the chief inspector discarded the theory that Littlewood might be a woman. Despite her pretensions, Kristin Sadly did not have sufficient stature for the role. The list of suspects was shrinking, and Higgins wondered if his initial intuition had been incorrect. Allowing people to believe that he had become

---

* The American Auguste Stanwood used this procedure, causing an epidemic of cholera, which forced him to abandon it.

the plaything of events and had lost the initiative: ought he to review his strategy?

The mummy was controlling the game and had made this investigation unlike any other. Higgins must remember this if he was to stand any chance of getting at the truth.

71

All Professor Beaulieu's servants had assembled in the hallway of his house on Tottenham Court Road. They were hesitating about what to do when Higgins arrived.

'The police, thank goodness!' declared the cook, a robust woman in her sixties. 'Now they'll have to do something.'

'What's happened?'

'Sir Richard has disappeared.'

'Don't exaggerate,' protested Sir Richard's valet.

'Be quiet! I know that he's disappeared. I cooked one of his favourite dishes for him – herrings with garlic potatoes – and he always has his lunch at a quarter past twelve.'

'Have you searched the entire house from top to bottom?'

'Of course, inspector!'

'Did Sir Richard sleep here?'

'He rose at seven, as usual,' replied the valet.

'No incidents of note?'

'No . . . Wait a minute, yes! The postman brought an urgent letter. After reading it, Sir Richard dressed in a hurry and left, saying, "I'll be back for lunch".'

'Ah, you see!' exclaimed the cook. 'He's not a man to forget about my herrings.'

'I'd like to see his office,' demanded Higgins.

He was impressed by the large amount of old wooden panelling. Now Higgins was in no doubt: even the staircase was made out of fragments of Egyptian sarcophagi. Beaulieu had transformed his office into a sort of ancient coffin, made from remains stolen from Egypt, delivered to the docks controlled by Kristin Sadly and sold to the historian, who had developed an insane passion for these funerary items.

To the left of the main window a panel stood half-open.

A carefully hidden chest contained financial documents, bundles of banknotes and two gold ingots, but not the carnelian amulet bought from Belzoni. The professor was so perturbed on reading the urgent letter that he had forgotten to slide the panel shut again. Higgins left the room as it was, for the scholar would no longer have an opportunity to take advantage of his ill-gotten wealth, and his servants deserved some additional pay.

'Did you discover anything?' asked the cook.

'Your employer will not be returning,' declared the chief inspector. 'Before the various authorities arrive, put his office in order. May I count on you to ensure equal shares?'

'Equal shares . . . ?'

'You will understand. And share out the herrings too.'

Higgins believed that he knew where to find the strange professor. So he headed for his clandestine carpentry workshop, near his home.

It seemed locked. He hammered on the frosted-glass door. A curtain twitched aside, a dark eye peered at the intruder and a hand waved at him to go away.

'Police. Open up.'

After a long wait the door opened a little way. A hostile, hirsute face appeared. 'What do you want?'

'To come in.'

'There's nothing here. It's not been used for years.'

'In certain circumstances perjury can lead to imprisonment.'

'Hey! I haven't done anything wrong!'

'I wish I could be sure of that.'

'All right, come in.'

The workshop was perfectly maintained, providing storage for dozens of planks of different sizes taken from sarcophagi.

'Do you work for Sir Richard Beaulieu?'

The fellow looked disconcerted. 'Oh . . . you know.'

'What work does he give you to do?'

'I look after the workshop, restore these old planks, varnish them and store them. These ancient woods are fragile and robust at the same time. I'm a good carpenter, and I handle them well.'

'Do you receive frequent deliveries?'

'Sometimes; it depends. I work at my own speed, and Sir Richard is happy. If my work wasn't up to standard, he would dismiss me. And he expects miracles from me! It takes time to transform these old pieces of wood into stairs, library panelling or door frames.'

'What time did you arrive today?'

'About twenty minutes ago. I had errands to run.'

'Is there a room behind the workshop?'

'A storeroom, back there. I keep tools in it.'

Higgins drew back a curtain. In the middle of the room he found a sarcophagus, roughly knocked together.

'Good grief!' exclaimed the carpenter. 'That's not my work! But who . . .'

The chief inspector lifted the lid.

Inside lay Sir Richard Beaulieu, with glazed eyes and gaping mouth, just like Paul Tasquinio, Kristin Sadly and Andrew Young.

Buyer of fragments of fake mummy from Paul Tasquinio and destined for Peter Bergeray, and supplier of ancient planks from sarcophagi to Francis Carmick, Professor Richard Beaulieu did not have the stature of a man like Littlewood. He was too timorous, too second-rate, incapable of taking initiatives and risks. His own peace of mind and derisory acts of baseness were enough for him. He had made just one fatal mistake: crossing the mummy's path.

The Royal College of Physicians would now have a fourth specimen presenting incomprehensible characteristics. He would provide fuel for interminable debates and brilliant controversies.

Three suspects remained: industrialist Henry Cranmer, politician Francis Carmick and the actor Peter Bergeray. This time the mysterious individual who was retrieving the objects and wrappings stolen from the mummy, one by one, had not left any clues, as it was up to Higgins to find his own direction and, above all, to make sure that it was the right one.

A gentle autumn sun lit up the capital. As he turned over the various clues in his mind, Higgins walked to his headquarters on John Adam Street.

When he arrived, he found it in a state of uproar. One of his subordinates ran out to meet him. 'At last, inspector! We've been looking for you everywhere!'

'Trouble?'

'Hordes of rioters have invaded the West End. It's the revolution!'

72

Obeying Higgins's instructions, the few police officers whose task it was to protect the residential districts of the West End allowed the demonstrators to spread out and drew back without retaliating. The chief inspector had strictly forbidden the use of firearms, convinced that if a single civilian were to be shot, London would go up in flames.

Surprised to encounter no resistance, Littlewood's hordes felt the intoxication of victory. So the leader of the revolution had not lied to the poor of Whitechapel! All they had to do was express their anger and state their demands, and the authorities would withdraw.

Terrified, house owners slammed their doors shut and, cowering behind their windows, watched a howling mob invade the streets and gardens.

'Throw the stones!' ordered Littlewood in fury.

Men, women and children did so with joy in their hearts. They succeeded in shattering many windows, and their excitement mounted. Determined to sacrifice this first wave before bringing in his armed militia, Littlewood was pleased with this unexpected triumph. British royalty was nothing but a house of cards, and Higgins an illusionist! The lower middle classes would soon join the popular masses, and together they would trample on the aristocracy and the government.

The rioters began to sing as they continued throwing stones.

Break into the houses of the wealthy, violate the women, cut the throats of the well-to-do . . . It was clear what they had to do.

Wearing a woollen bonnet and coarse, worn-out clothes, and unrecognizable beneath his false red beard, the man who had inspired the revolution remained at the rear. Consequently, he was one of the last to see a barrage made up of hansom cabs, carriages, carts, horses and mules. Police officers stood in serried ranks, brandishing leather shields and clubs. Then cavalrymen came galloping out of an avenue, sabres in hand.

'Retreat,' roared one of the leaders, 'they'll slaughter us!'

Higgins's first trap had worked. The demonstrators fled in disarray, fearing that the forces of order would intervene brutally. His second trap presented greater difficulties. The finest police officers had infiltrated Whitechapel and taken on the identities of costermongers, labourers, artisans, coachmen and even tramps. Their mission was to isolate the groups of revolutionaries who were determined to use rifles and pistols, to bar access to the weapons caches, to close pubs temporarily and to intercept hotheads. The army had occupied Whitechapel Road, the major thoroughfare leading to the agricultural estates of Essex, and were watching the main routes that might allow the insurgents to leave the district. True, the labyrinth of narrow streets and little courtyards would provide hiding places for the revolutionaries, but the important thing was to avert bloodshed and to quell the insurrection.

The forces of order were swiftly and effectively mobilized, following long weeks of preparation. As soon as he became aware of the disaster, Littlewood abandoned his troops and slunk along walls in the direction of Whitechapel, where he would gather together the most stubborn revolutionaries. When they killed a few policemen, the officers' colleagues would be obliged to retaliate, and the uprising would be reborn from its ashes with even greater intensity.

'Don't throw yourself into the lion's mouth,' advised the rescuer. 'Inspector Higgins has found all your hiding places, and he's waiting to reel you in. But I can offer you a safe haven.'

'You . . . How did you identify me?'

'The art of disguise and months of discreetly following you. I know everything about you.'

Stunned, Littlewood consented to listen to this individual, who seemed to be his equal.

'I shall give you the key to the premises, where you'll

find food and can wait until calm returns. After that, we shall see. You'll probably have to leave England.'

'How much do you want?'

'A piece from your collection.'

'I own many!'

'The one you bought from Belzoni.'

Littlewood smiled. 'You're lucky. I always have it on my person because of certain nightmares.'

The rescuer pushed the revolutionaries' leader against a carriage entrance. Horses galloped past in search of the last rebels, only just missing them.

'It's over, Littlewood. Your little army has been annihilated; all that remains is to save your skin and make your fortune again elsewhere.'

'Why are you helping me?'

'I have no fondness for the world of today, and I shall fight it in my way, not yours.'

'We could become allies . . .'

'Who knows? Here's the key.'

'At heart, you support my cause but you dare not admit it to yourself yet.'

The rescuer's silence was eloquent. Assured of the favours of destiny, Littlewood had lost only one battle. He listened to the directions to his temporary refuge and left, dreaming of future exploits.

By the time night fell, the West End had regained its calm. Thousands of gas lamps were lit, and in his office on John Adam Street Higgins received detailed reports from the various districts of the capital. There had been no deaths, only minor injuries and damage to property. But the Littlewood case had still to be resolved.

At last the coordinator of operations arrived, wearing a workman's cap.

'Total success, sir! We had to rough up certain ringleaders a little, so that they didn't use their weapons, and the prisons are full to bursting. There are plenty of bumps, bruises and cuts, but no corpses. Thanks to your precise information, we were able to nip the violence in the bud. Tonight, the pubs will reopen under close surveillance, and women of easy virtue will be able to meet up with their clients. Whitechapel has received a bloody nose and will think twice before fomenting another revolution. Less poverty, and people would be calmer.'

'I shall tell the Prime Minister as much,' promised Higgins. 'Have you captured Littlewood?'

'Unfortunately not. His principal accomplices would have willingly betrayed him, but they haven't seen him since the first wave of demonstrators in the heart of the West End. It seems clear that the man has fled, and his cowardice has sickened his most fervent supporters. By acting in this way, he's done us a great service.'

'A special bonus will be paid to all men who took part in this operation,' announced the chief inspector. 'Go and enjoy a well-earned rest.'

'I won't say no, sir! We didn't have it easy. Ah, one detail ... One of my lads says he saw the actor Peter Bergeray near a weapons cache we had emptied. He was exhorting a group of youths to fight by declaiming Shakespeare.'

'Did you intercept him?'

'Realizing he was under threat, he ran off like a rabbit. Goodnight, sir.'

The slippery Littlewood, with his hundred faces and countless disguises; the many-faceted actor Peter Bergeray, who had recently been arrested in Whitechapel dressed as a woman . . . Reassured as regards the outcome of this difficult day, Higgins headed for the actor's residence.

If it was Littlewood who opened the door to him, he would have to act very swiftly indeed.

73

'Mr Bergeray doesn't wish to be disturbed,' declared his valet haughtily. 'He's resting.'

'I'm afraid I must insist,' said Higgins calmly.

'His orders were quite specific, and . . .'

'Kindly take me to his room. Otherwise I shall be forced to arrest you for obstructing a criminal investigation and as an accomplice to murder.'

This elegant, level-headed inspector did not appear to be joking, so the valet decided to comply. He would have to suffer one of Bergeray's famous theatrical tantrums, but at least he would remain at liberty.

Former lover of Kristin Sadly, with links to the sinister Paul Tasquinio, Richard Beaulieu and Francis Carmick, the actor, medium and painter of mummies seemed to be a regular in Whitechapel, where his gifts for disguise could enable him to assume the identity of Littlewood.

If that were the case, was this servant an accomplice?

Keeping his distance, Higgins watched him knock

worriedly at the bedroom door. 'Sir,' he whispered, 'it's the police.'

Getting no response, he knocked and spoke more loudly. But still no one replied.

'Open it,' ordered Higgins.

'It's delicate, I . . .'

'Open it.'

The bed was unmade. At its foot was a portrait of a mummy, inspired by Kristin Sadly's angry face. In the middle of the room stood an armchair, from which emerged the back of Peter Bergeray's head. Curls of perfumed smoke surrounded it.

'Sir,' repeated the valet, who dared not enter, 'it's the police.'

Higgins walked round to the front of the armchair.

Enveloped in a dressing gown, the actor seemed to be smoking the pipe identified by Belzoni as a fake. His eyes glassy, his mouth hanging open, he floated between life and death, barely breathing. The doctors would have the benefit of yet another case, just as inexplicable as the previous ones.

On Bergeray's lap lay a note scrawled in a nervous hand: *We must meet without further ado*. It was signed by Francis Carmick.

In Portman Square glaziers were already replacing the windows, which had been broken by the rioters, and the gardens were being tidied up. Before the end of the week, no trace would remain of these deplorable events.

The chief inspector's carriage had made swift progress, thanks to the scant traffic. The trauma of the riots had not yet been erased. Higgins was returning to his number-one suspect, for a long time inaccessible because of his social position. Liar, manipulator and a man ambitious to the point of committing crime, Francis Carmick was pursuing two objectives.

The first was to have himself mummified like the ancient Egyptians. His body, embalmed by specialist Dr Pettigrew, would be placed in the sarcophagus constructed with the aid of Professor Beaulieu. Paul Tasquinio and Kristin Sadly had provided the politician with large numbers of the vital wrappings as well as the large shroud, and Peter Bergeray's visions had furnished interesting details.

The second objective was to overthrow the government and the monarchy by provoking a revolution, of which he would be the principal beneficiary. The mastermind behind the conspiracy, which aimed to destroy Belzoni, and guilty of not helping him, Carmick had become the elusive Littlewood, possessing sufficient money to buy both souls and weapons.

A crowd had gathered outside the Egyptian house in Portman Square. Servants were gossiping with neighbours and passers-by.

Higgins emerged from his cab, and the butler came to meet him.

'Inspector, it's frightful! Mr Carmick is afflicted with some kind of sickness. I don't know if he's alive or dead. He's been under great stress, working all night and . . .'

'Have you called for a doctor?'

'We're waiting for him to arrive.'

'Take me to him.'

The butler took Higgins to Francis Carmick's office.

Seated, with his head tilted slightly back, his eyes glassy and his mouth hanging open, he was scarcely breathing.

It was pointless to look for the mummy's second shroud.

'Because of the rioters,' revealed the butler, 'Mr Carmick had a terrible time! We trembled with fear, especially him. He cursed the police, called for help and shut himself in here for the duration of that terrifying demonstration.'

Clearly, this was not the behaviour of Littlewood.

As he approached the man who was neither living nor dead, Higgins spotted a curious object lying on his knees. It was a magic wand made of hippopotamus ivory, curved in shape and decorated with a snake spitting destructive fire and spirits brandishing knives.

'Did your employer receive any visitors, today or yesterday?'

'Oh, no, inspector!'

'Are you certain, or didn't you notice anything?'

The butler hung his head. 'There is a separate entrance at the rear of the house. Sometimes Mr Carmick wanted absolute secrecy.'

Higgins turned over the magic wand.

A text was written on it in beautiful hieroglyphs, the

first three in red ink,* the others in black. Not trusting his memory, the chief inspector consulted his notebook and reread the copious notes he had taken during his conversation with Jean-François Champollion.

They enabled him to decipher a surprising message.

You will find me in the crypt at Paradise Street, opposite the statue of Osiris.

'Is the patient here?' asked a syrupy voice.

Higgins turned and saw a portly doctor, unshaven and struggling to carry a battered old bag of black leather. He was smoking a very pungent cigar.

'Do you have a speciality, doctor?'

'I usually carry out post-mortems on corpses. But in emergencies I take care of the living.'

'Then the case of Francis Carmick will be an exciting one for you.'

'Gracious me! Is he in between the two?'

'Somewhat.'

The doctor rubbed his hands, took a bottle of whisky from his bag, drank a swig and eyed the politician greedily.

As for Higgins, he headed for Paradise Street.

---

* The *rubric*, i.e. the start or title of a text. Red (*ruber*) is the colour of power and intensity.

74

Littlewood's rescuer had not exaggerated when he talked of a safe haven. The district was deserted and the street abandoned, with no sign of inhabitants or passers-by. The former leader of the revolution opened the heavy door without difficulty and entered a crypt, lit by flaming torches. He closed the inner door carefully behind him and drew a bolt.

The funereal aspect of the place made him shiver. The low vaulted roof dated from Roman times. Impressed, Littlewood advanced slowly until he reached a sort of shrine, where a body was lying.

As he got closer he recognized it: it was Belzoni's mummy!

Its face was calm, almost radiant. What was more, it had reacquired its wrappings and its symbols, and it seemed safe from all human harm.

'This is the last stage,' announced a strange voice.

Littlewood turned round.

No one.

He realized that the light in the shrine was coming from the mummy's body, enveloping it in a protective halo.

'The time has come to give back what you stole from me.'

No, it was impossible; mummies could not talk!

Once again, Littlewood fled.

Who had written the message? Littlewood, the mummy or a third person? The ancient, narrow street on the northern edge of the East End was made up of derelict houses, most of which were due for demolition. As Higgins approached, a rat scuttled away.

In the middle of the street was a niche containing a bronze statuette resembling Osiris, the god of the 'righteous of voice', who was recognized as such by the court of the afterlife. Opposite was a stone-built house covered in moss, with bricked-up windows. A staircase led from the pavement down into a cellar.

The lock on the solid-oak door resisted the skeleton key. Perceiving the nature of the obstacle, Higgins transformed the tool into a screwdriver and managed to unscrew the fixings on the inner bolt. Finally, it yielded.

At the entrance to the corridor, someone had placed a safety lamp, of the kind created by the ingenious Sir Humphry Davy, who wanted to save miners' lives from the threat of firedamp. Its light was fairly weak, but it did not cause explosions.

Higgins picked it up and found himself inside a Roman crypt worthy of the masterpieces of that period. And then he bumped into a body.

It was Henry Cranmer, the industrialist.

The cause of death was obvious. His throat had been cut with a knife whose hilt was decorated with an Anubis couchant, and whose bronze blade was razor-sharp. The murder weapon was sticking out of Cranmer's heart.

Higgins searched the dead man and discovered a revealing notebook. In it, Littlewood related his sinister exploits, proclaimed the revolution and gave the names of his principal accomplices.

So Littlewood was Henry Cranmer.

Since the door had been closed from inside, the killer must still be on the premises.

Caution and good sense suggested that Higgins should leave the crypt, but if he did so would he ever discover the truth?

Brandishing his lamp, he moved forward.

At the end of this forgotten lair he found a mummy. An admirable mummy, bandaged to perfection.

That which was scattered had been brought back together: the first linen shroud, sold to Kristin Sadly; the second to Francis Carmick; the chest band to Paul Tasquinio; the heart-shaped carnelian amulet to Professor Beaulieu; the oblong vase to Andrew Young; the face bandages to Peter Bergeray; and the foot bandages to Henry Cranmer, alias Littlewood.

These foot bandages bore hieroglyphs, which Higgins deciphered: *Do not disturb my peace in the afterlife. Or I shall unleash the fury of the lion, the snake and the scorpion.*

The chief inspector stood there for a long time, deep in thought. The mummy had been saved.

The head waiter served a fine wine, which emphasized the excellence of the lobster with macédoine of vegetables. Lady Suzanna, looking delightful, seemed enchanted to see Higgins again.

'I've come to keep my promise to you and reveal the truth,' he declared.

'Have you arrested Littlewood?'

'He's dead.'

'During the riots, I presume?'

'No, Lady Suzanna. He had his throat cut in a crypt.'

'Do you mean the crypt of a church?'

'Probably an ancient holy place, but disused now.'

'Before continuing, inspector, will you tell me Littlewood's true identity?'

'Henry Cranmer.'

The barrister searched her memory.

'The industrialist?'

'A very wealthy man who lived a double life and was skilled in disguising himself. At his home we found dozens of books about the French Revolution, tracts announcing that the masses were about to seize power and plans for attacking official buildings.'

'Congratulations, inspector. You've eliminated a serious threat, and the case is closed.'

'I think not.'

'I was forgetting ... You must find the person who slit his throat.'

'I know who that was. It was Belzoni's mummy.'

Lady Suzanna's fork hung in mid-air. 'Are you ... joking?'

'I'm keeping strictly to the facts. Having examined the scene of the crime, it's clear that only the mummy could have killed Henry Cranmer, alias Littlewood.'

'That's completely insane!'

'I have specific clues, and I intend to make that mummy appear before a court so that it may be charged and sentenced.'

'Are you serious?'

'Did we not discuss such an eventuality?'

The young woman stared at the chief inspector. 'Indeed! I thought it was mere speculation, but I was mistaken. As I promised, if you dare to charge that mummy, I shall defend it.'

75

Despite his reservations, Judge Abercrombie-Fernymore had yielded to Chief Inspector Higgins's extravagant request, although he had stipulated certain conditions: the judgement of the mummy would take place behind closed doors, with experienced magistrates acting as the jury, and the police officer himself as prosecutor.

Two of Higgins's colleagues had placed the mummy, covered in a large white sheet, in the middle of the small chamber at the Law Courts, reserved for sensitive cases. And to crown it all, the defending counsel was a woman, wearing a wig and black robes.

The judge was a difficult man, but he possessed qualities that Higgins appreciated: he was incorruptible, held no political opinions and conducted real debates, without any preconceived notions, whatever the condition of the accused.

As he entered, the participants rose to their feet. Once the ritual of opening the session was over, the judge addressed Higgins.

'Inspector, it is because of your reputation for serious-ness that I agreed to hold this unusual trial. I hope that I shall not have to charge you with contempt of court. Will you reiterate what you said in private, in my chambers?'

'Yes, Your Honour. I accuse this mummy of commit-ting four murders and reducing six people to a state of living death.'

Some jurors shrugged their shoulders, while others appeared irritated. Higgins was known as the 'saviour' of London, and clearly that success had cost him his mind.

'And I, Your Honour,' cut in Lady Suzanna, 'will destroy the prosecution's arguments.'

That won't be difficult, thought the judge. Even a trainee barrister could manage it. 'We're listening, inspector,' he said.

'Permit me first of all to show you the guilty party.'

Irritated, the judge nodded.

Higgins removed the large white sheet.

The superb mummy appeared, looking as if it had just emerged from the embalmers' workshop, where they had created a true masterpiece, re-creating the 'noble body' of Osiris.

Even hardened cynics were stunned by it, grudgingly admiring its perfection.

'A pathologist, an elderly aristocrat and a clergyman were all murdered with embalming hooks,' recalled the chief inspector, 'because they threatened the accused with destruction. I found one of these objects.'

Higgins showed the court the bronze hook with the curved end, just over a foot long, which had been used to kill Dr Bolson.

'In expert hands, this embalmer's tool becomes a dangerous weapon.'

'Agreed,' conceded the judge.

'The three victims wanted to destroy the mummy,' continued Higgins, 'thus condemning it to a second death and to the final dispersal of the being's elements, which were brought together at the time of embalming. One might plead self-defence, but it's not up to me to plead it.'

Several jurors raised their eyes to the heavens. Lady Suzanna remained calm.

'The misfortunes of this mummy do not stop there, since it was profaned and deprived of its magical protection during an unwrapping session. Because its survival was at stake, the mummy tracked down the purchasers and retrieved its wrappings and its amulets. Here it is, intact and regenerated. From its own point of view, it was a sort of legitimate crusade; from ours, a series of criminal, blameworthy acts.'

'I've had the pleasure of meeting Chief Inspector Higgins,' said Lady Suzanna, 'and I appreciate his professionalism and thoroughness. That's why his incredible allegations disconcert me. As defence counsel, I've heard only a vague theory, devoid of proof.'

The judge appreciated the young woman's moderation and the distinction of her words.

'Let's be done with this, inspector,' demanded Abercrombie-Fernymore. 'We all know that a mummy is an inert thing, devoid of life, and incapable of committing these crimes!'

'Permit me to express a contrary opinion, Your Honour.'

'Where is your proof?' demanded Lady Suzanna, at once gentle and ironic.

The chief inspector contemplated the mummy.

'In September 1822 a young genius, Jean-François Champollion, succeeded in deciphering hieroglyphs. This extraordinary discovery altered the course of my investigation by giving me access to vital documents that were passed to me by the founder of Egyptology. They greatly astonished me, Your Honour, but they oblige us to consider Egyptian science in general and this mummy in particular in a different light.'

Higgins opened a file containing a number of sheets of paper. The atmosphere in the courtroom had just changed.

What if the saviour of the capital had real evidence? The judge, Lady Suzanna and the jurors hung on his every word.

'According to the text placed in tombs,* these were the real powers of a mummy. Let us begin with the reanimation of the apparently inert body: "The gods open my

* The famous *Book of the Dead*, whose exact title is the 'Book of Going Out into the Light'. Extracts are quoted here from Chapters 26, 180, 68, 2, 64, 15, 18, 24, 10, 11 and 58. The French translations are those of the great Egyptologist Paul Barguet, who taught me to read hieroglyphs.

eyes which were closed, stretch out my legs which were bent, strengthen my knees so that I can stand up. I have consciousness once again thanks to my heart; I have the use of my arms; I have the use of my legs." And it is specified: "To give him walking and the freedom of movement." This autonomy is not limited to the empire of the dead, Your Honour. "He who knows this book," it is written, "he may go forth by day and walk upon the earth among the living; he goes forth by day to do everything he may desire among the living; he can do everything that a man on the earth can do." And the appearance of the mummy, you will ask me? The answer is clear: "It will go forth by day in all the transformations it may desire; it will take on all the forms it wishes, will escape all flame. No evil will harm it; it is faster than the hare, swifter than light." And its movements have a goal: "I travelled the earth in all directions against my enemies; I searched for my enemy; he was given to me; he will not be taken from me again." The final touch: once his work is done, the mummy returns to the other side of the mirror: "He who knows the incantation, he may return to the empire of the dead after emerging from it." Your Honour, gentlemen of the jury, I have traced the criminal career of this mummy for you. It used all the characteristics with which it was endowed at the embalming ritual and has not yet returned to the afterlife, where it is inaccessible to human justice. We therefore have a chance and a duty to sentence it, after demonstrating that its apparent slumber is not that of death.'

The listeners were in a state of shock.

'How will you do that?' demanded the judge, stunned.

'Its heart functions, and energy brings life to its being. I propose to unwrap it, take away its protection and check if it is sensitive to pain.'

'I object!' roared Lady Suzanna.

Although accustomed to outbursts during trials, the judge started. 'Kindly retain your composure. The inspector's request seems to me to be justified.'

'I object most severely, Your Honour.'

'Objection denied! Please carry out the checks.'

Lady Suzanna leaped forward and placed herself in front of the mummy. She stared fixedly at Higgins.

'I have a proposition for you. You will swear to preserve this mummy and to keep it safe from all profaners, and I will tell you the truth.'

'If it pleases the court . . .'

'It does,' snapped the judge.

'You have my word, Lady Suzanna,' swore Higgins.

The young woman's exaltation ebbed away, and she removed her wig and sat down on the bench occupied by the accused.

'It was I who killed the clergyman, the aristocrat and the pathologist, because they were preparing to destroy the mummy.'

'Give us the details,' ordered the judge suspiciously.

The barrister described her three crimes coldly and precisely. 'I hid the mummy in a crypt that belongs to me,' she continued, 'and I carried out the rites necessary for its survival. But I had to retrieve the amulets and wrappings that the profaners had stolen from it. It was a long and difficult task, even an impossible one because of Littlewood. To find him and know where he had hidden the linen wrappings from the feet, I was able to set a trap for Littlewood, alias Henry Cranmer, get rid of him and return the mummy to its initial state.'

'Will the six other profaners survive?' demanded Higgins.

'I merely administered an Egyptian drug, whose effects will dissipate. At least those miserable wretches will have suffered some atrocious nightmares.'

'Four murders,' the chief inspector reminded her. 'Why did you care so much about saving this mummy?'

A strange light appeared in the pretty brunette's eyes. Suddenly, her mind had left the trial. 'You cannot understand . . . A long time ago, so very long ago, we loved each other. I thought I had lost him for ever, and he returned, mummified, living a form of life about which our era of science and progress knows nothing. When you have hanged me, I shall find him again. But stop destroying these mummies, burning them and eating them! Otherwise – and if it's not already too late – they will have their revenge, and the doors of eternity will close for ever.'

Pale, Lady Suzanna collapsed to the floor.

'Incarcerate her immediately,' decreed the judge. 'That woman is completely mad!'

EPILOGUE

Christmas 1823 promised to be a good one. Mary had prepared a fat goose which Geb and Trafalgar had been coveting ever since it went into the oven. Higgins would make sure that his two companions received a generous share and uncork a bottle of champagne from his cellar, a sort of crypt resembling the one where he had discovered the mummy.

Lady Suzanna was being cared for in an asylum. She had retreated into silence but had given one last smile as she heard the chief inspector repeat his oath to preserve the mummy from all danger. It was now in a safe place and no scholars, slaves of curiosity, would be allowed to examine it. Higgins had moreover set up a committee of defenders of mummies, individuals determined to protect these Osiran bodies, the remarkable witnesses to the spirituality of the ancient Egyptians.

Remembering Peter Bergeray's warning, he had become aware of Lady Suzanna's exact role when she revealed herself by mentioning possible communication with the dead or with those who were considered to be dead. Modern society condemned such madness.

The barrister had not lied: the six profaners had emerged from their lethargy. Sentenced for his traffic in corpses, Paul Tasquinio was languishing in prison, as was Andrew Young, convicted of arms dealing. Abandoning the stage, Peter Bergeray had devoted himself to clairvoyance. Kristin Sadly was running a fish shop, Sir Richard Beaulieu had just been appointed honorary professor and Francis Carmick was continuing in politics.

Higgins opened his mail. The letter from the Travellers' Club informed him that, after long deliberations, Giovanni Battista Belzoni's application to become a member had been accepted. True, this was only modest recognition, but it would make him view London more kindly.

As he leafed through *The Times* by the fireside, he noticed a piece of sad news, erasing his previous satisfaction. On 3 December 1823 the Titan of Padua had died of dysentery in Benin, having returned to Africa to search for the sources of the Niger.

Mary served the port. As usual, she had read the newspaper before its rightful recipient. 'I liked him a lot, that man Belzoni,' she declared. 'He changed us from cowards and cretins who were leading the world to disaster. We could do with a great many more adventurers like him! Go and change. It's a special dinner tonight. And tell your two pets to behave properly.'

After dressing for dinner, Higgins filed the black

leather-bound notebooks devoted to the judgement of the mummy. One disturbing detail kept coming back to him: the door of the crypt had seemed bolted *from the inside*. And there was no one there but Littlewood's body and the mummy.

But on reflection the chief inspector was no doubt mistaken. When his dog stood on its hind legs and placed its enormous paws on his shoulders, he decided to turn the page and devote himself to celebrating the rebirth of the light.

AUTHOR'S NOTE
THE MYSTERY OF MUMMIES

What is a mummy, and what was its purpose? It is essential to answer these two questions in order to understand the world of Egyptian mummies, which continues to fascinate us. Let us begin by discarding some oft-repeated fallacies: ancient Egyptians were not all mummified – far from it – and a mummy is not just a human corpse designed to endure for centuries to make an individual believe that his soul's human form will not perish.

A mummy is the 'noble body' (*sâh*) of Osiris and symbolizes the reconstitution of the scattered elements of his being after his murder by the god Set. Creating a mummy is a fundamental and necessary work of art, and this creation process follows a precise ritual, designed to avert not the inevitable physical death, but the 'second death': annihilation and the inability to travel in the other world. By becoming an Osiris, with the reborn god's 'noble body' taking the place of their mortal body, a mummified man, woman or animal can relive Osiris's adventure, confront and overcome the ordeals of death and pass through the gates of the after-life. But it is not enough to die physically in order to become an Osiris and benefit from the rites of mummi-fication. Everything depends on the way in which a person has behaved on earth and to what degree he or she knows the 'words of transformation into light'. And the journey that leads to rebirth in Osiris begins with a twofold judgement.

The first is the judgement of the deceased by other humans. Initiates into the mysteries of the temple, rela-tives and friends – all deliver their verdict. Is the deceased worthy of attaining the afterlife? Have his actions, his way of life and his thoughts rendered him fit for this great journey? If so, the rites will be celebrated. If not, he will have only a simple burial place. The second judgement is the judgement of Osiris. The deceased is led into the Hall of Truth, where, in the presence of forty-two divine judges, he faces the goddess Ma'at, the Rule and unity of the universe. The person's heart, i.e. his consciousness and capacity for knowledge, is weighed. It must be as light as Ma'at's feather – in other words not weighed down by acts of disharmony such as murder, theft, broken promises, falsehood, slander, causing damage to a tomb or a statue . . .

In the event of failure, a monster composed of several different animals will devour the heart and condemn the individual to a state of nothingness. If the person passes the test, Thoth (the ibis-headed god) announces the result of the judgement, confirming that this pure, righteous heart is deserving of immortality, and the transfiguration ritual can begin.

As the myth of Osiris's dismemberment and reconstitution was fundamental to ancient Egyptian civilization, mummification was practised as early as the Old Kingdom.

We should remember that every pyramid represents the reborn Osiris, in the form of a monument built from everlasting stones.

Embalmers were both ritual priests and highly skilled technicians, trained for a very complex discipline. Francis Janot writes: 'Because of all the implements and the steady hand it required, embalming was much more refined than one might imagine.'*

In the tomb of Ankh-Hor, archaeologists discovered a

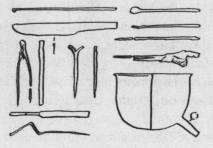

* See *Les instruments d'embaumement de l'Egypte ancienne*, Cairo, 2000.

series of instruments used by embalmers: knives, hooks, needles, pincers, spreaders, spatulas, wooden and iron chisels, filters and pots. These materials, known as 'the secret things', were placed in a mysterious casket, reserved for specialists who knew anatomy and who were capable of transforming mortal remains into an Osiran body.

These sketches[*] help us to understand the principal stages of mummification.

First, an incision is made in the corpse's left flank to extract the viscera, then the brain is removed and the body is dried out using natron. Next, the body must be protected with a series of linen wrappings. A shroud gives

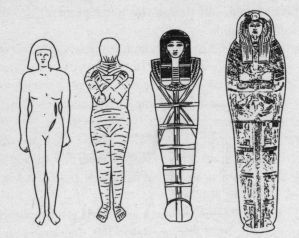

[*] From C. El-Mahdy, *Mummies*, Published 1990.

it a new face, the face of Osiris, no attempt being made to reproduce the deceased's own physical appearance.

Finally, a sarcophagus adorned with symbolic and ritual scenes contains the mummy and teaches those who see it.

One wall in the tomb of Tchay (nineteenth dynasty) shows embalmers at work, under the direction of a ritual priest who holds the text relating the operations which are to be carried out.

We witness the last phases of mummification, after which the prepared corpse was washed and oiled. The thorax and abdomen were filled with linen, lichen, sawdust, onions and even Nile silt.

Above left, two embalmers are bandaging a mummy, a long and delicate operation. Below left, they are brushing on an unguent prepared in a cauldron which can be seen underneath the mummy. Composed of beeswax, cinnamon, cedar oil, gum and tar, it will give the Osiran body a pleasant smell.

Five ritual priests are finishing the sarcophagus. One of them is wielding a hammer and chisel. Below right, a last task, doubtless of a magical nature, is being carried out.

Following the positive judgement that opens the gates of the other world, the *ba*, or soul-bird, must stay in contact with the dead person. A bird with a human head, the *ba* leaves the motionless corpse and flies up to the sun to regenerate. Nourished by the sun's radiant energy, it returns to the mummy to pass on this energy to it. The relationship between the mummy, the soul-bird and the sun's energy is merely a stage. At the end of the ritual, the regenerated person becomes an *akh*, a 'radiant one', symbolized by an ibis. This, in turn, is transformed into a source of light by those men and women who, in their turn, confront the ordeal of death.

It was jackal-headed Anubis who invented mummification. Capable, in the words of the *Pyramid Texts*, of 'making death die', he guides the souls of the righteous along the paths of the other world after transforming them into Osiris, reuniting their limbs and their bones, and thus creating a vessel able to fly towards the light.

Anubis fills the mummy's skull with consecrated oils and 'the seeds of the gods'. The chief embalmer, who bears the name of 'superior of the mysteries', dons an Anubis mask, for only this god can accomplish the transmutation. He is assisted by ritual priests who know the vital incantations, notably the 'official with the seal of the god's secret', whose task it is to perfume the mummy, oil its head and bandage its legs.

Anubis 'treats' the mummy, heals it of the sickness of death and turns it into the instrument for journeying to another life. The embalming couch is the body of a lion which, in Egyptian symbolism, is the guardian of the temple that no outsider may enter, and the supreme watchman whose eyes never close. Dead to the world of men, the mummy awakens in the world of the gods. During his work as an embalmer, Anubis is assisted by the four sons of Horus, who guarantee the integrity of the four canopic vases. They contain the carefully embalmed internal organs, that is to say the liver, lungs, stomach and intestines. Reborn as an Osiris, the person 'of righteous voice' becomes a Horus who, assisted by his four sons, will celebrate the rites for a new Osiris.

At the head of the ritual bed, Isis-Hathor watches over the mummy. Anubis makes a decisive gesture by bringing it a new heart, the heart of resurrection.

Often, the skill of the embalmer enabled him to leave the heart of flesh in place; if it was removed, it was replaced by a 'heart' scarab, bearing Chapter 30B of the *Book of the Dead*, an invocation to the 'heart of the Mother', begging it not to bear witness against the person at the moment of divine judgement. It is notable that in hieroglyphs, the words 'mother' (*mut*) and 'death' (*mut*) are homonyms. The celestial Mother, the sky-goddess Nut, leads the person with a new heart through the

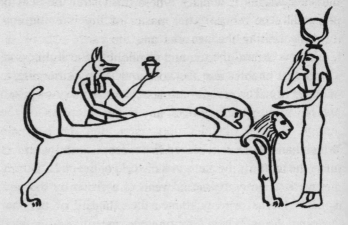

ordeal of death and brings him or her to rebirth in the universe of the gods. Now unchanging, the stone heart of the Osiran body lives according to the rhythm of the cosmos.

Inside the wrappings, a variable number of protective amulets were placed, depicting divinities, tools (set square, level) and protective symbols (the complete eye, the sun rising over the horizon, the knot of Isis, etc.), then the mummy was laid inside a wooden sarcophagus.

The Greek term currently used, 'sarcophagus', is a misinterpretation, since it means 'eater of dead flesh' and corresponds to our modern coffins, which are mere boxes for corpses, devoid of spiritual and symbolic significance. The Egyptian term is 'provider of life'. In reality, the sarcophagus is a place where the Osiran body will perpetually be reborn. This master of life is at once a dwelling uniting the heavens and the earth, a book of teachings containing texts and symbolic illustrations, and a boat that enables the soul to travel. Many sarcophagi, of exceptional symbolic richness, slumber in museums and have not been studied in any depth.

When the mummy was placed in a sarcophagus, it entered into contact with the universe of the gods. Here, we see a complex figure of Osiris, wearing a crown composed of ram's horns surmounted by a sun, flanked by two tall feathers, the whole magnifying the radiant power of a reborn life.

The god holds his two characteristic sceptres, the shepherd's crook *heka*, which enables the scattered to be brought together, and the *nekhakha* with its three thongs, evoking the threefold birth on earth, in the heavens and in the stellar matrix. The body of Osiris is made up of the pillar *djed*, whose name means both 'stability' and 'say, utter, formulate', for in the Egyptian mind only an utterance that is constantly renewed and anchored in the rites can be stable and durable. This pillar is marked with four horizontal bars, symbolizing the four sons of Horus, guarantors of resurrection. The mummy's vertebral column becomes this pillar which, when it is ritually raised up, represents the resurrection of Osiris.

Finally, the foot of the pillar rests on a sign which reads 'gold'. Here we see the origins of alchemy, which views the rebirth of Osiris as the transmutation of barley into gold, which constitutes the unchanging flesh of the gods.

Quite frequently, the interior or lids of sarcophagi carry a depiction of the sky-goddess, Nut, who contains the *nu*, or primordial energy, the key to all life.

Here, surrounded by eight worshipping baboons, the embodiment of the Odgoad, or collective forces of creation, she stands on the mound of earth that appeared at the beginning of time. At each new dawn this is reactivated, raising up the reborn sun, into which the soul of Osiris is assimilated, in order to travel through cosmic space. Along the goddess's legs, two lotus flowers symbolize the god Nefertum, 'he who accomplishes Atum', in other words the great work carried out according to the creator's instructions.

Other depictions show Nut surrounded by signs of the zodiac. By uniting itself with its sky-mother, the Osiran soul becomes integrated with the thousands of stars that make up her body and becomes a light, which guides humans who are searching for eternal life. Born of the stars and fleetingly on earth, the knowledgeable person thus rediscovers his origins and his true homeland.

Why does it take seventy days of mummification to complete this ritual? Because Sothis (the star Sirius) disappears for seventy days behind the sun. When it reappears, the annual Nile inundation is unleashed, abundance is reborn and the new year's festivals are celebrated (around 20 July). This is to say that the mummy, far from being a slave of death, announces the emergence of a renewed life.

Before reaching the 'Beautiful West', the calming goddess who will offer the 'righteous of voice' all they need to travel the roads of the other world, the mummy goes on a boat journey to Abydos, the holy city of Osiris, under the protection of the two sisters, Isis and Nephtys, who celebrated the funerary vigil and who prepare the wrappings. Thanks to the words of knowledge which they spoke, the mummy has become a travelling being, escaping the immobility of death. 'When you departed you were alive, not dead,' declare the first words of the *Pyramid Texts*. For the ancient Egyptians, physical death is a sickness from which one can recover if one knows the words of transformation into light. It is then no longer a cessation and definitive boundary, but becomes the point of departure for the great journey, that of incessant changes.

This scene from the temple at Dendera, dedicated to Hathor-Isis, takes us to the heart of the great mysteries

inside the sarcophagus where the mummy lies, shown here with a falcon's head. The sarcophagus is above a mound on which an acacia is growing. To the left is Isis, wearing on her head the throne which causes pharaohs to be born; to the right is Nephtys, on whose head is the hieroglyph symbolizing the temple, surmounted by a basket. The whole reads: 'The mistress of the temple.' Thus, throne and temple watch over the mysterious work which is carried out in secrecy, i.e. the transformation of the Osiran body into gold.

Another scene from the temple at Dendera shows us the victory of renewed life over the apparent death of the mummy, which lies on the lion-shaped ritual bed. Underneath stands a baboon (one of the forms of Thoth), two cobras

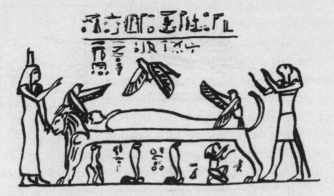

charged with driving back the forces harmful to ibis-headed Thoth, who is reciting incantations. To the left, Isis is making a gesture of magical protection; to the right, Heket, the frog-goddess, embodies the transformations offered to the reborn being. Three birds of prey, female kites, fly above the mummy. These are three expressions of Isis, who brought back together the scattered parts of Osiris's body and left her human form to take on her celestial appearance. Two of the birds are protecting the mummy's head and feet. The third is about to perch on the regenerated mummy's phallus so that it may be fecund and bring forth Horus, the falcon who protects Pharaoh, charged with safe-guarding the cult of his father Osiris. From this super-natural begetting, royal power is born, capable of maintaining the world's harmony.

This modest drawing comes from the tomb of Queen Nasa, who lived in the kingdom of Kush (modern-day Sudan). It reveals the process of illuminating the mummy in the darkness of the cave. The sun shines in the heart of the darkness, and its rays light up the lion's head serving as a support  for the Osiran body and the face of the mummy. This vital moment is also depicted in temples, such as Dendera.

Although seemingly inanimate, the mummy is in reality nourished by a secret light. In the eyes of the ancient Egyptians, overcoming death was precisely that: entering the light and uniting with it in its incessant metamorphoses, notably depicted in the tomb of Tuthmosis III.

The temple at Philae, consecrated to the goddess Isis, was the final Egyptian shrine to celebrate the great Osiran  mysteries. Here, we witness the awakening of Osiris, who emerges from death by rising up, protected by Isis's wings, whose beating has restored his vital breath. Facing the reborn Osiris, a ritual priest presents him with the looped cross whose meaning is 'life'. The texts specify that this mummified and regenerated Osiris has become gold.

POCKET
BOOKS

CHRISTIAN JACQ

Tutankhamun: The Last Secret

At the invitation of an anonymous letter,
American lawyer Mark Wilder arrives in the land
of the pharaohs in search of his true identity.

In Cairo's Christian quarter, he meets a mysterious monk
whose revelations will tear his life apart. Abbot Pacomas,
the last descendant of the High Priests of Amon, entrusts
Mark with a deadly mission: to uncover Tutankhamun's last
secret, a treasure carefully concealed by the pharaoh himself.

Ever since the tomb was opened, everyone has been
searching for this lost treasure in vain. It has become a
legend, just like the curse which pursues all those who
disturb the pharaoh's eternal sleep.

Aided by Ateya, a young Coptic woman, Mark enters the
whirlwind of an Egypt where the pharaoh's benevolent
magic is at risk of disappearing, leaving modern times alone
and helpless against the ascendancy of Evil.

ISBN: 978-1-84739-392-0
PRICE £6.99

**POCKET
BOOKS**

CHRISTIAN JACQ

The Queen of Freedom Trilogy

**In this superb value three-in-one edition, Christian Jacq
tells the enthralling true story of the Ancient Egyptian
warrior-heroine Queen Ahhotep.**

17th century BC. An army of barbarians has swept through
Egypt, destroying everything in its path. Known as the
Hyksos, the 'leaders from foreign lands', the invaders have
reduced the land of the pharaohs to slavery.

Only one woman resists. Fierce, beautiful and courageous,
the daughter of the last pharaoh refuses to accept defeat. Not
far from Thebes, the only city which retains its independence, she establishes a secret military base, training the
soldiers who will one day set her country free.

Heading an increasingly powerful army, Ahhotep prepares
the Egyptians for the final, fateful confrontation. After a
hundred years of occupation and thousands of violent deaths,
at last the Egyptian empire looks set to rise again from the
ashes - all thanks to the courage and determination of
a woman.

'A melange of history, romance and adventure by an author
who artfully combines story with truth' *Good Book Guide*

**ISBN 978-1-84739-367-8
PRICE £9.99**

POCKET
BOOKS

CHRISTIAN JACQ

The Judge of Egypt Trilogy

In this fantastic value three-in-one edition, Christian Jacq combines historical fact with a potent imagination to create a compelling murder mystery.

Summoned to investigate the mysterious deaths of five guards standing watch over the great tomb of Kheops, a young novice judge finds himself embroiled in a hotbed of greed and corruption. For Judge Pazair's refusal to sign a document he doesn't understand has led him to uncover a monstrous plot to assassinate the pharaoh, Ramses the Great.

With the aid of Neferet, the woman he loves, and the former scribe, Suti, Pazair sets out to solve a series of brutal murders, expose the conspirators and thwart a brazen attempt to overthrow the State. But can he stay alive in the process . . . ?

'Jacq weaves together an intelligent murder mystery and injects life into every page of this truly authentic tale' *Good Book Guide*

ISBN 978-1-84739-366-1
PRICE £9.99

**POCKET
BOOKS**

This book and other **Pocket Books** titles are
available from your local bookshop or can be
ordered direct from the publisher.

| 978-1-84739-392-0 | Tutankhamun: The Last Secret | £6.99 |

| 978-1-84739-367-8 | The Queen of Freedom Trilogy | £9.99 |

(includes *The Empire of Darkness*,
The War of Crowns and *The Flaming Sword*)

| 978-1-84739-366-1 | The Judge of Egypt | £9.99 |

(includes *Beneath the Pyramid*,
Secrets of the Desert and *Shadow of the Sphinx*)

Free post and packing within the UK

Overseas customers please add £2 per paperback
Telephone Simon & Schuster Cash Sales at Bookpost
on 01624 677237 with your credit or debit card number
or send a cheque payable to
Simon & Schuster Cash Sales to
PO Box 29, Douglas Isle of Man, IM99 1BQ
Fax: 01624 670923
E-mail: bookshop@enterprise.net
www.bookpost.co.uk

Please allow 14 days for delivery.

Prices and availability are subject to change
without notice.